THE BLOOD OF TYRANTS

PETER S. FISCHER

THE GROVE POINT PRESS
Pacific Grove, California

ISBN 978-0-615-32455-5

DEDICATED to the men and women of America who, throughout its history, made the ultimate sacrifice in the defense of liberty and freedom.

FOR WELL OVER TWO HUNDRED YEARS, the United States has stood proudly among the community of nations as a singular exemplar of hope, proof that Man, if he has courage, can create for himself a world free of tyranny and despotism where he and he alone decides the nature of his existence and the course of his future. In 1776 a handful of privileged men pledged their lives and their fortunes to realize that dream. Many paid a severe price, others survived to bring forth a nation where people of every faith and social stratum were guaranteed the freedom to live as they chose. Twice in its history, this country has endured terrible wars where brother fought brother, neighbor fought neighbor. Wise men have known that the destructive carnage of the Revolution and the Civil War must never be repeated.

And yet....

And yet there may come a time where the enemies of this nation, those who would usurp power and abolish personal liberties for the so-called "greater good" must be dealt with. And when the power of the ballot box has been neutered by the privileged few, then war must be waged. Not a war of bayonets and musketballs, but war all the same, a war that suffers not hundreds of thousands of casualties but a handful. Those who would deny our liberty should not and cannot be allowed to prevail. Not now. Not ever.

"The tree of liberty must be
refreshed from time to time with
the blood of patriots and tyrants"

—Thomas Jefferson

CHAPTER ONE

It should have been a great day. It WOULD have been a great day if not for that four o'clock call from Harry Bomford. Grim humorless Harry, everybody's favorite sack of melancholy. How he ever got to be Speaker of the House only God knows, though that is open to debate since no one ever accused Harry of being on speaking terms with the Almighty. Jerry, this is critical, says Harry. You've got to meet with this guy. He's got a lock on ten or fifteen thousand union guys which he can deliver this November. All he needs is a little schmoozing, you get the picture? Just butter him up a little and if he starts getting into HR 2365, tell him we're with him. Okay, so we're not with him but in November we'll hand him some bullshit line about terrorists or the Canadians or the Japanese whalers and he'll come away happy. Trust me, I know this guy. All he wants is a place at the table. So you'll meet him, a couple of drinks at Barbieries, that's all. Thanks. I owe you. Click.

Jerome C. Tolliver, four term incumbent from the once-great state of California, carefully fashioned the knot in his tie. A nudge left, a little tighter. Perfect. He took a moment to evaluate his reflection in the mirror. Hairline receding somewhat but still acceptable with a little extra combover. A trace of elegant grey over the ears. A few lines on the face, bespeaking character, not age. He smiled showing pluperfect teeth. Not pretty boy handsome, but attractive enough, considering the clout he had to go along with it. At least that was the effect he'd had on Alice Vecchio.

Alice. Now there was a babe he could relate to. Blonde, well stacked, just pushing forty but trim and tidy. Her only problem, something upstairs. Smart as hell, law degree, summa cum laude, and there she was wasting all those assets in a hole in the wall office in slumtown, fighting the good fight for the poor, the downtrodden, the neglected. Never winning much, of course, but still in there pitching, day in and day out. With equipment like hers she could have been taking down seven figures with any of a dozen lobbyists, but Alice preferred her own drumbeat. She wanted to matter. She didn't. She never would. That's how it worked in this town. He hoped she'd never catch wise to that. She made a nice punchboard for Jerome C. Tolliver and others of his standing. He recalled last night at the out of the way motel in Alexandria. Now that was a night. Yes, it would have been a great day except for that phone call from Harry Bomford.

One last check in the mirror. Grey striped tie, navy double breasted suit, properly positioned grey handkerchief, hair in place. He snatched up the car keys from the hall table and left his Watergate apartment and took the elevator to the basement garage. His vintage powder blue Jaguar XJ12 was glistening, recently washed and polished. Once in a while he thought about trading it in for a new model but he never got past the 'just looking' stage. Nostalgia, maybe, or the envious looks he got from his compatriots who couldn't, or wouldn't, emulate him. Some married with kids (impractical) others too cheap to make the investment, others just plain drab. He got in, revved her up and pulled out of the garage into the warm Washington sun.

Tolliver exited the elevator and started down the long corridor toward his office on the third floor of the Rayburn Building. He had a corner suite, thanks to his seniority and the correct party affiliation. The Democrats had been in total control now for a year and a half and showed no signs of loosening their grip on the House or the Senate and certainly not the White House where the new incumbent had two and a half years left to solidify his many groundbreaking programs and enhance his own personal popularity. It wouldn't be hard. The Republicans were wandering in the wilderness, trying to decide who and what they were. Conservatives? Moderates? Democrat Lites? (Anything you can do, we can do better). Rudderless and foundering, their prospects for the fall elections were abysmal. Perhaps not that good. Yes, it certainly was a good time to be a Democrat from an ultra-safe California district, a time when money flowed in from every direction and all you had to do was vote your conscience. Well, perhaps not always, but when the funds were available, the conscience was able to step outside for a smoke. He pushed open the door into his outer office. Katie flashed him a welcoming smile. "Good morning, sir," she said.

"Good morning, Katie," he flashed back, always happy to see her happy face which was mostly happy no matter what was going on. Katie Moran had been with him seventeen years now, starting in the early days at the California law office. Then she'd been his secretary. She was still his secretary but you couldn't call her that any more. Not without the ACLU hauling you back to the woodshed for a good whomping. She was an office aide, personal assistant, confidential file clerk, something like that. He couldn't remember. Whatever it was, it paid a helluva lot better than California.

"Anything going on?" he asked

"Four calls. Nothing important. They're on your desk. The Speaker called to say thanks. No need to call back." He nodded, went into his office, eyed the pink message slips on his desk, She was right as usual. Nothing urgent He looked out the window. The sky was silky blue, the temperature ideal. Was there anything vital on his plate this afternoon? Maybe Hailey was available. Hailey's 33 handicap was depressing, but he hated playing alone or with members he didn't know well. Get into a bad foursome and you spend the afternoon being wheedled and cajoled about legislation when all you wanted to do was try to stay out of lakes and bunkers.

The phone rang. He sat down at his desk, started to finger the messages. Beth, his ex-wife. That was never important. She called to whine about kitchen leaks and ingrown toenails. Why the hell didn't she find herself some guy or maybe she'd tried and there was no guy out there who wanted any part of her. Very possibly the case. There was a call from the County Supervisor back home. With Memorial Day right around the corner he knew what that was about. Grand Marshal of this or that parade, maybe a speech in front of the VFW. Strike that one. He had little use for those war mongering bastards. And no call from Alice Vecchio, of course. There wouldn't be. Alice knew the rules. For a moment he thought about sending her flowers, then reconsidered. That was another rule. Don't confuse fucking with anything like business.

The intercom buzzed.

"Yes?"

"There's a gentleman on the phone. No name that I recognize but he insisted that I let you know he was calling."

"Name?"

"Leonard Philby."

"Never heard of him," Tolliver said.

"He said to mention Naked Day at Santa Cruz your freshman year. You tripped on a log and fell into a mud puddle. He had to carry you back to the dorm."

"Jesus Christ," he said.

"No, Leonard Philby," Katie chuckled. "Are you in or out?"

"Put him through."

He lifted the receiver. "Lenny?"

"Jerry?" the man's voice said. "I wasn' t sure you'd remember."

Tolliver laughed. "Are you kidding? Someone mentioned Santa Cruz to me a couple of weeks ago and the first thing I thought of was you and that stupid Naked Day. Hey, buddy, just how dumb were we?"

Grogan's wasn't busy, not really, not compared to the dozen or so power places Tolliver could have suggested but didn't. Old friend or not, he wasn't quite sure what he was getting into and being seen with the wrong person by either a colleague or one of the movers and shakers or, God forbid, the Press, well, that wouldn't do. Tolliver was nothing if not careful. He still wasn't sure this was a good idea. After all twenty-some years had passed but when Philby hinted at a sizeable campaign contribution, Tolliver suggested a quick lunch. After checking with his AA, of course, who checked on Philby-Styles Inc. on Google and reported back that, yes indeed, the Congressman's old friend was a man of substance. Funny how things work out, Tolliver thought. Philby was always a little uptight, more than a little private, a budding professor maybe, or a researcher. Not a businessman. Not with his personality. But then it takes all kinds. He thought of Jobs and Gates. Maybe this truly was the Age of the Nerds. More power to them if they could handle the freight. The freight. That was Tolliver's corner of the world. This could turn into a very interesting lunch.

At first he didn't recognize him. Then he spotted him at the end of the bar. Tall and thin, thinner than he remembered. Once there'd been a shaggy mane of blonde hair on that smooth pate, now just a few wisps around the sides and in the back. Still shaggy but now nearly white. He was sipping what looked like a vodka tonic, slightly hunched over, eyes a little rheumy. Underneath an open Burberry raincoat, he was wearing an expensive worsted suit, a forest green silk tie and Italian loafers shined to a glossy brilliance. A well thought out power outfit but the man wearing it didn't seem to fit.

Tolliver slipped in next to him, squeezed his elbow. "I'll have one of those."

Philby looked up, a labored smile crossed his face. He raised his glass. "You don't want any part of this, old friend. Straight soda water."

"On the wagon?"

"Doctor's orders. It's either my stomach or my liver or, well, who knows, maybe my appendix. The Doc is very vague on specifics but he sure knows how to order me around."

They took a booth in the rear next to some plastic potted ferns and a gaudy print of the Bridge of Sighs in Venice. Out of the way or not, Tolliver was still not sure he wanted to be seen chatting with this guy who he remembered was not quite this strange. "You sure you don't want to hang up your coat?" Tolliver asked.

Philby wrapped himself deeper into its folds. "No, I'm fine. Just a little chilly, that's all."

At that moment Charlie Grogan bellied up to their table, his usual effusive self, making sure that the Congressman's guest knew that he was dining with one of the country's staunchest patriots. a true celebrity on the local and national scene, and, of course, by inference, Charlie himself was part and parcel of the Congressman's aura. Could he favor them with some wine, something fine, not the house junk? Perhaps a special appetizer. Nothing was too much trouble for his good friend. Tolliver allowed as how a vintage cabernet might be welcome. Charlie smiled and sidled off. They ordered. Lamb chops for Tolliver, Linguini Alfredo for Philby who reached ito his pocket and took out an old fashioned cigarette holder, the kind FDR used to sport with that jaunty smile of his. Philby placed it between his teeth and smiled apologetically.

"It took me seven months to quit. I'm still not all the way there yet." he said.

Tolliver nodded. "Yeah, those things'll kill you."

"So I've been told." Philby looked across the room at the open kitchen, at the cheeses and salamis hanging from the ceiling, the cooks in their toques moving quickly back and forth to keep up with the crowd which was starting to swell. If Philby had something to say, and Tolliver was sure he did, he wasn't quite ready to say it.

"So, Lenny, what have you been up to the past twenty five years, aside from your company? You married?"

"Was."

"Well, I've been down that road," Tolliver chuckled

Philby looked at him sharply. "Really? She died."

Tolliver squirmed a little. "Sorry. Didn't know."

"Sure. How could you? It was childbirth. Our fourth. All boys."

"Wow, that must have been rough."

"Not really," Philby said. "They're good kids and my sister pitched in." He paused. "I read about your divorce. Pretty messy. They shouldn't spread that stuff around. I mean, whose business is it anyway? All the goddamned trouble we're having today, I mean real trouble, and all they talk about is sex scandals, divorce, who screwed who in the john at the Sheraton. Jesus, Jerry, I remember when being a journalist actually meant something."

Tolliver nodded. "Well, for sure. The bastards certainly have no sense of decency."

Their food came and Tolliver dug in. Philby fiddled with the pasta, ate some bread, drank a little water and passed on the cabernet. Haltingly they chatted about old times, but Tolliver was having a hard time remembering just what those old times were, except for the misadventure on Naked Day. He glanced at his watch. Time to get to the point. "So, Len, you mentioned something about needing a little help. What can I do for you?"

Philby put down his fork. "HR 2365. It's a bad bill, Jerry. If it passes, it'll probably put me out of business."

Tolliver waved him off impatiently. "Come on, Len, I've heard that kind of stuff—"

Philby interrupted him sharply. "Don't shine me on. I'm dead serious. It'll put thirty-five hundred people out of work and cripple the town we live in. And for what? So the government can get still another piece of the pie? Haven't they got enough already?"

"You're reading this all wrong. If you knew what was really in the bill—"

"I know. I've read it. Six times. Have you?"

Tolliver shrugged. "My staff people tell me—"

"Your staff people." Philby said in disgust. He stared hard at Tolliver, something akin to hatred in his eyes. Then he shook his head sadly. "What's happened to you, Jerry? Back then you were the Man. Mister Go Get 'Em. Remember how we went out day after day punching doorbells for Reagan, up at all hours, manning the phones, making a difference and all those liberal weenies laughing at us. Mondale was going to whip our ass. They couldn't wait. Reagan the dunce. No way he gets a second term. Those were great times. I felt like I meant something. So did you."

Tolliver was becoming annoyed. "Those were different times. Things change. This country has changed."

"And you've changed, Jerry, and not for the better."

Tolliver squirmed in his seat. What the hell is with this guy? I didn't come here to be lectured by some nonentity.

"Len, you mentioned something about a campaign contribution. All right, I'll seriously consider your position on HR 2365. No promises, of course."

"But that's what I want, Jerry. Your promise to kill it. You're the Committee Chairman. You pull the strings. I can get you about $40,000 through the company and some key employees but I need your guarantee. You mustn't let this pass."

Tolliver slowly shook his head. Forty thousand. And he wants guarantees. Why have I been wasting my time with this schmuck? He put down his napkin. "Len, it's been nice seeing you but I really do have to get back to the office."

Philby's face contorted in sadness. "Please, Jerry. Take this time to make things right. You've got it in you. I know you do."

Tolliver leaned forward. There was no smile on his face, no humor in his tone. "Look, my friend, you want to play with the big boys, you'd better learn how the game is played. First of all, forty thousand won't even buy you a seat on the back of the bus and as for guarantees, here's one for you. If you call my office again, I guarantee I won't be there to take your call."

Philby hesitated, then nodded sadly. "I'm sorry I wasted your time, Jerry. And mine. I felt I had to give it a chance." He rose and reached into the pocket of his raincoat. A snub-nosed .38 caliber pistol appeared in his hand. Tolliver's eyes had just started to widen when the blast from the pistol reverberated in the restaurant and a gaudy red hole the size of a dime appeared on Tolliver's forehead. He slumped forward, face first, into the remains of his lamb chops.

CHAPTER TWO

The toast was cold, the eggs runny, the coffee was little better than brown water. As breakfast it was bad, as a sort of brunch it was even worse. How long until dinner? He tried to think. Did he have a date tonight? If so he wouldn't be eating until at least 8:30. And why this sudden preoccupation with food? Maybe because he'd given up his preoccupation with booze.

He stared out the window of the small cafe at the entrance to the apartment house across the street. The doorman was new, a big black guy, maybe a one time NFL linebacker. Phil must have gotten the boot. He should have, a long time ago. He was an obsequeous little guy who gave sniveling a bad name. Give him twenty for a little inside skinny and next time he was looking for fifty. Maybe the black guy'd be easier to get along with. Then again, maybe the black guy wouldn't play. That'd be too bad. A lot of interesting stuff went on inside the Trafalgar.

He checked his watch. Still no sign of Her Ladyship, a sobriquet that few used to her face. Almost noon. She should be up and about by now if only to make her daily deposit at the bank.

With a sigh he pushed at the eggs with his fork, thought better of it.

"Castle, right?"

He looked up. A skinny kid with moussed blonde hair and a bad case of acne was standing at his booth, peering at him suspiciously.

"Whatshisname Castle. The guy on TV. That's you, right?"

"Not whatshisname. Paul. Paul Castle," he said.

"Whatever."

Paul snorted. Whatever. Generation X Pluses' answer to everything, like so what, who cares, I don't give a crap, and who asked to be born into this world, anyway?

"I said it was you. My buddy, he didn't believe me." He head nodded behind him. "That's him over there." Paul looked. Another teenage misfit had been staring at him, then quickly looked away. Paul looked back at the blonde kid.

"Is there something I can do for you?"

"I don't know. Maybe an autograph or something. Is it worth anything?"

Paul shook his head. "Get lost."

"What?"

"You heard me."

"Yeah, well, fuck you, Charlie. That show you got, it ain't that good."

"Thanks for the encouragement."

Blondie looked blank. "What?"

"Take a hike, sonny, before I put you over my knee and spank you," Paul said.

"Yeah, well, fuck you."

"And I admire your eloquent use of language."

"Yeah. Well, fuck that too." The kid flipped the bird and turned on his heel, satisfied that he had told this television asshole where he could shove his stupid show.

Paul smiled wryly. Another chance meeting with a member of his adoring public. He wondered, is this who I reach every night? Snot nosed kids with beanbags for brains. Too depressing to contemplate. Ah, but then there was his six-figure salary, by far more than he had ever made when he was, as his mother loved to remind him, a real reporter.

He glanced across the street and just in time. She was just exiting the building, clutching her over-stuffed handbag packed with greenbacks which didn't include the likes of Washington, Lincoln or Alexander Hamilton. The ever present Theo at her side. Quickly Paul got up, tossed a twenty onto the table and hurried out of the cafe. Dodging traffic he reached the other sidewalk and jogged after them.

"Vivian!" he called out. They turned. A scowl crossed Vivian Blum's face. Theo took a step forward, blocking Paul's access to her. "I just need a minute, that's all."

"I'm in a hurry," she said, turning on her heel and continuing on.

"One lousy minute. C'mon, you see any cameras? Off the record, just you and me."

Theo grabbed his arm and squeezed. Pain shot up to Paul's neck. He'd always suspected Theo was a cyborg. Now he was sure of it.

"Mrs. Blum does not wish to be bothered. Move along."

Paul tried to ignore him, shouting after her. "Okay, next time I bring the camera and we'll talk about Spencer Davis and his 16 year old kid from Cornell."

Vivian turned toward him sharply, hooded eyes awash with venom. She looked around the street, checked a couple of nearby buildings. "No cameras," Paul said. "Hand to God. I just need a little help with something."

Vivian hesitated, then. "Russian Tea Room. Twenty minutes. Don't screw with me, Mr. Castle."

Paul got there first and took a booth in the rear, secluded, darkened. It wasn't that he minded being seen with New York's most notorious madame (after all, of such flamboyance a career was made), but he was quite sure that she would prefer not to be seen with him.

In a profession where discretion was prized beyond rubies and pearls, being seen chatting with a tall, dark haired, dashing, handsome if somewhat scurrilous muckraking reporter could have a depressing effect on business.

His phone rang. It was Murray.

"Murray, why are you calling me? Why aren't you out producing somewhere?"

Murray sort of laughed. Murray never really laugh-laughed, he just gave a raspy imitation of one. It passed for his feeble acknowledgmen of humor, even where there was none.

"Funny. Where are you ?"

"Having lunch."

"An hour ago, you told me you were having breakfast."

"A working lunch. Never mind with who. It'll be on my expense voucher."

"It better be good," Murray said, "what I see for tonight is pretty thin."

"I got Freida Bernard?"

"You got Frieda Bernard?"

"I got Freida Bernard."

"It isn't written down."

"Murray, then write it down. She's good for at least ten minutes."

"Okay, that'll help. What about that woman in the green dress you're so hopped up about. You got anything on that?"

"I'm working on it."

"Yeah, well, It's not that big a deal. Guy dies in the saddle. Babe runs away. So what?"

Paul rolled his eyes. Murray didn't get it. Guys like Murray never got it. "It wasn't just some guy in the sack, Murray, it was a United States Congressman."

"From East Noplace, New Jersey, not even married. So where's the scandal, huh? You never heard of consenting adults?"

"Murray, if you live to be a hundred—" He broke off.

"What?"

"Never mind. My date just arrived. Talk to you later."

Vivian Blum had just entered. When she saw Paul, she whispered to Theo and then started toward the booth. Theo took up a position by the doorway.

She slid into booth. "I don't like being threatened, Paulie."

"I'll try to remember."

"Try hard."

Paul smiled his grade A infallible most charming smile. "Viv, c'mon. Lighten up. I don't give a rat's ass what some Wall Street fat-head does to initiate his kid into the world's carnal delights. By the time my old man thought about doing it for me, he was three years too late, but that's a whole other story."

She laughed. "That figures. You know you could try using the phone instead of accosting a person on a city street."

"You could try telling your girls on the phone to put me through once in a while. Like maybe one out of thirteen."

She laughed again. "Maybe if you hadn't given them your real name. Some of them actually watch TV."

"Impossible! I'm not on the Cartoon Network," Paul grinned.

The waiter came by. She ordered a gimlet. He settled for ginger ale.

"Still dry?"

"Still trying."

"You know, you're a lot better than that show," she said.

"I could same the same about you, Viv, but we play the hands we were dealt."

"To coin a phrase."

He laughed. "And I'm supposed to be a writer."

Vivian shrugged. "All right, enough of this idle chit chat. What can I do for you?"

"The woman in the green dress," he said.

Vivian frowned, uncomprehnding.

"The New Jersey Congressman, Johansson. Died in the saddle at the Westin two nights ago. Body discovered the next morning. Security cameras have four different angles of this woman in the green dress who was seen going into his room around midnight. None of the camera angles are definitive. A guy I know in his district says he had no steady girlfriend or even unsteady for that matter. I began thinking pro. She looks much too classy for a street babe so I figure maybe a service. If a service, I start at the top. That's you."

"I'm flattered."

"And?"

"I can't help you."

"Can't? Won't?"

"First of all, I dont know her."

"You've seen the tapes?"

"I've seen the tapes."

Paul grinned. "Vivian, you've been watching my show. God bless you."

A wry smile. "Everybody needs a hobby."

"But she's not one of yours."

"Not ever, and certainly not now, I don't send my girls out any more. Too many lawbreakers out there. I like to keep my little brood of chicks safe and sound." She hesitated. "Anyway I doubt she's a pro."

"Why's that?"

"The way she carries herself. Edgy, moves a little too quickly, too furtive. In trying to blend in, she draws attention to herself. And I don't know, maybe the wardrobe, maybe that stupid floppy hat. Call it instinct. She's no working girl."

Paul sighed. "Then who?"

Vivian smiled. "There's your mystery. Maybe you've got a better story than you think you do."

Great, he thought. And just exactly how was he supposed to keep the story alive on tonight's broadcast? What exactly was he supposed to tell Murray? It came to him easily. Of course, he could do three hard-hitting minutes exposing just exactly who the Woman in Green was NOT. "Sources close to the investigation informed me that—"

Yada, yada, yada.

When he walked through his apartment door, he found the place empty. He expected it. Tina had walked out six weeks ago. At first he was sure she'd be back, hopefully with a touch of humility tinged with regret. It didn't happen. He knew now it wouldn't. There was something about a Barnard girl, especially a graduate student, a self-appreciatve mindset that allowed them to float above the inequities of the real world. She had no respect for his profession although it was the thing that drew her to him initially. But as they say, familiarity breeds contempt and with Tina it bred like a pandemic. She had once thought of him as a journalist, then came to realize that his relationship to journalism was no more accurate than Spielberg's kinship to skin flicks or Michael Moore's affinity for the truth. She hated the program, the sleazy revelations about the private lives of entertainers, the scandals involving perverted sex, the half-whispered rumors about drug use among the icons of American youth whose capacity for titilation knew no bounds. He wasn't particularly proud of what he did, but if he didn't spread the scandalous news, someone else would, and he was getting paid well for the effort. Damned well, in fact. And wasn't that what it was all about? When the chips were being counted, who had the bucks? Who had the power? It was a far cry from his life of only a few years back, when he was scrabbling to make a living at tiny stations in the Mountain states. He wasn't going back to that, not ever, and if self-rightious post-teens like Tina couldn't deal with it, it wasn't his problem. He'd felt lonliness before. He could deal with it now. Truth be told, he'd really been lonely most of his life, even with Tina and women like her who had shared his bed. His bed. Not his psyche.

On the heels of such depressing thoughts, he decided he needed a shower. With the water running full tilt, he never heard the phone and it was only when he went into the kitchen and saw the blinking red light that he knew he'd been called. He punched the play button.

"Paulie, it's Teresa. Call me when you get this message." There was a sound of urgency to her voice. He dialed her number. She picked up right away.

"Sis, its me. What's the matter?"

"Matter? Nothing's the matter." she said.

"You sounded funny. I got worried."

"Maybe I sounded funny because I've been waiting a week to hear from you. Did you forget? Yeah, sure. You forgot. So what else should I expect?"

"Forgot? Kid, I don't—"

"Pop's birthday. I called you the end of last week."

Chagrined, he remembered. "Shit. It's tonight."

"Correctamento, Sherlock. May 8th. VE Day. Its usually the only one you get right."

"Terry, I'm sorry," he said. "I really did forget."

"Don't apologize. Just show up."

"At the house?"

"No, at St. Nick's Arena," she said sarcastically.

"The show doesn't break until seven. It'll be eight o'clock. Maybe a little later."

"Just show, Paulie. No excuses this time."

"I'll be there. Promise."

He hung up, computed his father's age in his head. Born on VE Day in 1945, named Vittorio Emmanuel in honor of the victory over Nazi Germany, not the old long forgotten king. He'd be 65 today. A big one. Pop and Mama, he hadn't seen them in months even though they were only a thirty minute drive away. He'd make up for it tonight. A couple of bottles of good wine, roses for Mama. It would be a good night. He'd make sure of it. He checked his watch. He was late for the studio.

Paul exited the elevator on the third floor, the executive offices, one floor below the studios. It was quiet. The day people had left or were on their way. The nighties were just filtering in. He moved left down the corridor, passed the raised metal lettering that spelled out NATIONAL HEARTBEAT, and below it, in smaller letters, AMERICA'S CHANNEL. Wonder how CNN felt about that. Probably didn't much care. CNN, when it wasn't tanking in awed reverence at the feet of the administration, actually covered real news stories while America's Channel, of which Castle was an integral part, swilled around in the muck of sob stories, sex scandals, alien sightings over Idaho and other titillating stories which even The National Enquirer would be too embarrassed to handle.

He saw her sitting in an overstuffed chair across from the reception desk. Perhaps sensing him, she looked up, then rose and hurried toward him.

"We were worried. Your producer, he's been trying to find you for an hour."

"Guess he was looking in all the wrong places. Are you okay, Mrs. Bernard?"

"Freida, please, we agreed on that, and yes, I am all right. A little nervous, yes. I don't like being scrutinized. Especially in front of millions of people." There was fear in her eyes, like a wounded animal that didn't know which way to run. She'd been hurting for a long time.

"Just relax," Paul assured her. "I'll make it easy for you. And I know it's important to you."

"Yes, anything to prevent that beast from getting custody. The things he did to her."

"I know, I know." He took her in his arms, comforting, holding her close.

"Nine years old. My God, what kind of man is he? How could I have not known? All those years."

"Shhh. Shhh."

"He's the one that defiled her, Paul. Then why is it I feel so dirty?" She looked up into his eyes. "What kind of a mother am I?"

"Freida, don't punish yourself. This is your chance tonight, to tell the world."

She nodded. "Yes, but not everything. Not the details. I couldn't do that to Lucy. But not the details. I couldn't shame her in that way. You promised me that. None of the details."

"You have my word," Paul said. "Our audience is smart, they'll fill in the blanks. This is your chance, Freida. Make the most of it."

She inhaled deeply. "Yes, yes. It must be done."

He glanced at his watch. "We have to get upstairs."

They took the elevator to the fourth floor. In contrast to the executive floor, the studio floor was a beehive of actiivity. The far wall was banked with dozens of TV monitors, displaying feeds from all over the country. Paul's "Playback" set was off in the far corner, already lit, cameras and teleprompters in place. Murray was sitting on the edge of the desk issuing orders to one of the PA's. An unlit cigar jutted from his mouth. It was a semi-permanent appendage to his face, removed only for sleeping, Murray claimed. Paul once asked him how sex fitted into that equation. Murray just smiled.

Murray spotted him, waved him over. "Seventeen minutes. Try cutting it closer next time. My cardiologist needs the business."

"Have I ever failed you, Lord and Master?" Paul jibed.

"Often, but I don't have an hour to spare counting the ways. Where's Bernard?"

"In the green room, ready to go."

"No problems?"

"None. Where's the lineup?"

Murray handed him a clipboard. "You lead with the missing kid in Puerto Rico. It's on the prompter. We've got three minutes from Romano in San Juan and some so-so footage. Bottom line, the cops are still nowhere but they're still going with possible child abuse and kidnapping. I think we can milk this for a couple more days. Maybe something'll break. Then commercial, then you do your ten minutes with Bernard. I assume you got it worked out."

Paul tapped his head. "Up here." He scanned the clipboard. "Where's the woman in green slot?"

"No room," Murray said, then looked away.

"What do you mean, no room?"

"I mean, no room."

Paul shook his head. "Bullshit. I'm making room."

Murray looked at him grimly. "Don't do it, Paulie. This isn't coming from me."

"Who then? Finley?" Gregory Finley, the hated, pennypinching, humorless general manager.

"Higher," Murray said.

Paul looked at him in disbelief. "The old man?"

Murray nodded.

No, that wasn't possible. Not the Old Man. The Old Man had never stepped on his toes, not once in eighteen months. Your show, kid, he'd said. You run it. Anybody gives you trouble, come see me. Now, suddenly, over a piddling little story that wasn't going anywhere, the Old Man sticks his nose in. No, it was wrong. Wrong, no matter how you looked at it.

He tapped the clipboard. "This last segment, what does this say? Crazed veteran shoots—I can't read this."

"Some wacko ex-Special Forces. Blows away this California Congressman in the middle of lunch hour in a crowded restaurant in Washington D.C. We've got sixty seconds from a local guy an hour ago. Not much solid. We're still digging for answers."

"Shitcan it. I'll wing something on the mystery woman for the wrap up."

"Paulie, don't do it. You're trying to make something out of nothing."

Paul shook his head. "Look, you want to cut me off to protect your ass, go ahead. And then I'll pick up the phone and tell the Old Man where he can shove this program. He told me on Day One, it's my show. I run it. I take crap from nobody, including him."

Murray shrugged helplessly. "Do what you want. Who needs this job anyway?"

Paul watched as he walked away, shoulders hunched.

One of the PAs tapped him on the shoulder. "Five minutes, Mr. Castle."

The first eight minutes of the program went without a hitch. The Kansas City girl in Puerto Rico was still missing, the cops were still baffled and the hardhitting report was just as empty as a politician's promise. He followed with four minutes with Freida Bernard, then took the first commercial break. Immediately, the phone on the desk rang. Paul picked it up. It was the Old Man.

"What's the matter with you?"

"Sir?"

"Don't sir me, Paul. You're playing footsies with the Bernard woman. I'm not paying you to act like Larry King. Get down and dirty."

"I'm doing the best I can—"

"Bullshit."

"Look, sir, I promised her—"

"I don't give a crap what you promised. Have you looked at your ratings lately? You've flattened out, Paul. CNN's climbing up your ass. Maybe you're getting soft around the edges. Whatever it is, I don't like it and neither do your viewers. Now start talking about just what this son of a bitch of a husband did to his kid. That's why people tune in. Deliver."

"Sir, I—"

"I said, deliver. This is not a topic for debate." There was a pause. "Murray says you've still got a bug up your ass over this woman in green thing."

"It's a story, yes. I think it's a good one. My gut tells me it's bigger than it seems."

There was silence for a moment. "Okay, your gut's always been pretty good. Keep after it, but Paul, the Bernard woman. I want it all. The whole dirty business. Do you understand me?"

Paul looked across the desk at the trusting face of Freida Bernard.

"Yes, sir. I understand."

He hung up, suddenly feeling very unwashed.

CHAPTER THREE

"Hey, Paulie!"

The big man launched himself from his overstuffed easy chair and charged his son, arms wide, a delighted grin on his leathery face. He encircled him with his log-like arms, pounded his back with ham-like hands. It was a familiar and welcome greeting, accompanied by the faint aroma of cheap cigar smoke, garlic, and gardenia scented hair pomade which Vittorio Emanuel Castelli had been using ever since sixth grade when he first learned of (and learned to appreciate) those of the other sex. Emphasis on sex because at thirteen Vic Castelli was a fast learner.

The old man backed away and regarded his son at arm's length. "You made it. Sure, I knew you'd come, Mister Big Shot."

"Pop, come on. Your birthday? Gimee a break."

Vic shouted toward the kitchen. "Hey, Dee! Look what just walked in!"

Deanna Castelli peered into the living room, a damp dishrag in her hand. She scowled. She liked to scowl at her son, even when she didn't mean it. "Very nice. I thought maybe you forgot the address."

Paul grinned as he disentangled himself from his father, moved to kiss his mother. She turned her cheek.

"Mom—"

"My oldest son. I know the drive is hard. Did we put you out, Paulie? Did we inconvenience you? Six minutes past ten. Already past your father's bedtime, but no, he wants to stay up. Paulie, he'll be here. Don't you worry."

"Mom, please. Look, I am here. I just got stuck after the broadcast, you know, stuff I gotta do. It's important for the job."

"Sure, I know. Herb and Ethel were here. Joe and Margaret. Leo and Sylvia. They all asked about you, but you know, they gotta sleep too. Your brother Ernesto called first thing this morning from Atlanta."

"Okay, okay. I'm sorry. Mom, believe me—"

"Hey, I believe you. I'll say no more about it." Paul knew that was a lie but grinned and gave his mother a huge hug. "That's my girl."

She stepped back and looked him over top to bottom. "You look skinny. You're not eating."

"Really, I'm fine."

"Go wash up. I saved you a plate."

She turned on her heel and went back into the kitchen. Beyond her Paul could see his sister Teresa smiling at him as she dried a dish. She mouthed a thank you. Paul just shook his head.

A few minutes later he was digging into a plate of eggplant parmesan with asparagus on the side, a tossed salad and several steaming hot pieces of garlic bread, not to mention a huge glass of chianti to wash it all down with. This was his mother's idea of saving him a plate.

"Mom, this is great!"

His father, sitting across from him at the dining room table, puffing on a small dark foul smelling cigar, smiled broadly. "Your favorite. She never forgets."

Paul's eyes wandered around the room. Nineteen years had passed since he'd packed up and headed to Baltimore for his first year at Johns Hopkins, but it was as if time had taken that moment to freeze everything. The sounds, the smells, everything in place as it had always been. The little shrine to St Anthony in the foyer, the array of photos crowding the walls. Himself in a Pop Warner Yankees uniform, holding a bat almost as tall as we was. Paulie Castelli, no hit, bad field, but they had to play him. It was the rule. And there was Ernie in his 8th Grade graduation gown holding some sort of diploma which Ernie had certainly earned with his straight A's. And Terry, baby Teresa, learning to ride a two-wheeler while Pop helped guide her and Mom prayed to St. Anthony. And of course, there was Mom and Pop on their wedding day just a month before he reported for duty at Fort Dix, two years before he came home from Nam with half of his left foot shot off, three years before his father bought this little house in Rego Park and went into the taxicab business with his high school buddy Herb Weller. Three years before Paolo Lorenzo Castelli came into the world, the first son of a first son of a first son and christened weeks later in the names of two beaming grandfathers who rarely got along but who celebrated a joyous peace on this festive day.

"So how's it going, Pop. The business and all?" Paul asked him

His father shrugged, unsmiling. "Some days good, some days bad. You know how it is."

"Yeah, things are a little tight."

Vic regarded him with faint amusement. "A little tight, is that what you call it? Yeah, well, I guess. Big TV honcho, big paycheck. Why should things bother you too much?"

"Come on, that's not fair"

"Fair? What's fair these days, Paulie?. He puffed on his cigar, took it from his mouth an contemplated it. "You see this cheroot? You know what it cost me two years ago? Seventy cents in a box of fifty. You know what it costs me now?"

Paul shrugged. "No idea."

"Take a guess."

"I don't know. A buck maybe."

"I wish. A buck sixty-five, and it keeps creeping up every couple of months or so."

"Wow. Somebody ought to talk to those Eye-talian bandits."

Vic shook his head. "You really don't know, do you? Sure, I guess not. You got a nice salary, you probably eat out on an expense account. If something seems a little high, well, the station can afford it. You know how much a loaf of bread costs?"

"Pop, you win. You're right. I don't shop."

"Seven, maybe eight dollars for a lousy loaf of white bread. Two years ago, maybe two-fifty. I'm not talking when I was a kid, Paulie. I'm talking about two stinkin' years ago. You know what I gotta charge for cab rides these days. Double, maybe triple what it used to be. You wonder why I'm not retiring, why Herb's still working even with that bad ticker of his. I can't afford to quit. So, sell the business, your mother says. Sure, but who's gonna buy? These bastards in Washington, they keep spending and spending, kicking up our taxes every time we turn around. They got regulations on my business, my crumby little taxi business, that are choking the life outta me. We got colored sections—excuse me, I mean black sections of Jamaica they say I gotta service 'cause if I don't they can lift my license. Jesus, Paulie, I've been driving into those areas for over twenty years, never a problem, never gave it a thought. Now they're telling me what I can do, what I can't do. Pretty soon they'll be telling me how much I can make and where I can spend it."

"Pop, I know things have gotten a little different the past couple of years—"

"Different. Yeah. Different. A lot different and it's not gonna get any better, Paulie. Trust me. These guys in Congress have got themselves dug in so deep you couldn't get 'em outta there with a steam shovel."

Paul looked at his father with concern. Vic Castelli had a blue ribbon temper. When he was angry, you knew about it. But this was something different. He was angry, spitting angry, you could see it in his eyes, but his voice was soft, icy cold, tinged with fear, as if he were up against an enemy he knew he had to beat and he knew he couldn't.

"Listen, if you're hurting for money, no problem. Whatever you need, it's yours," Paul said.

"And have you got a few bucks for Herb, and maybe your brother Ernie? The government just took over the company he works for. They're cutting his salary by 30%."

"They can't do that."

"They just did it, Paulie. Last Monday. He says to me, hey, Papa it could be worse. At least I still got a job." The old man shook his head and pulled an errant shred of tobacco from between his teeth. "You like the way these Congress guys do business. They keep spending and spending until the dollar isn't worth a half-chewed wad of bubble gum and then they cut salaries to make up for it."

Paul heard the phone ring in the kitchen. It reminded him he had calls to make before he went to bed. He glanced at his watch. Just past eleven.

Teresa called out from the kitchen. "Pop. it's for you."

Vic lumbered to his feet. "For a smart guy, Paulie, about some things you can be pretty dumb. You might want to check it out, maybe for your program, instead putting that nice lady through hell just because she's trying to save her kid from that pervert husband of hers."

Paul flushed in embarassment and looked away. He pushed his plate to one side, took a deep swig of the chianti and leaned back in his chair. His gaze fell again on the photo of his kid brother Ernie in cap and gown, grinning broadly over his newly earned diploma.

There was another one in the upstairs hallway from Syracuse. Summa cum laude. Not bad for the son of a Queens County working stiff, but work, hard work, was the stuff that Ernie was made of. Kindergarten or graduate school, it made no difference, the kid always gave it everything he had. And for this, the government was going to let him keep his job at a third less money. His father was right. Something rotten was happening and he'd been too caught up in his own private world to realize it.

He remembered his own diploma from Johns Hopkins. No smiling photo. No photo at all. The Dean made sure of that. What was the phrase he used? Conduct unbecoming a Hopkins man. Maybe the Dean thought so. Paul thought his behavior was very becoming. A front page expose in the Blue Jay, the campus newspaper. A faggoty professor, one of the President's closest advisors, spilling classified information to his boyfriend of the month, and the boyfriend passing it on to HIS secret boyfriend, who, unbeknownst to just about everyone, was an Iraqi espionage officer. It had taken him over six weeks and a lot of surreptitious digging, some of it even legal, to piece the story together, and when it hit, without the sanction of the faculty advisor, Paul's career as a crusading journalist on the Charles Street campus came to an abrupt end. Happily for him, an editor on the Baltimore Sun noticed the article and hired him on the spot. By the time his diploma arrived in the mail that August in a plain brown envelope, Paul was already working the city beat on The Sun and starting to make a small name for himself. Not quite "wunderkind" but close enough. It was work he loved. He got up every morning feeling more alive than he'd ever felt in his short lifetime. If only it had paid a little more. More of the point, if only he had not stumbled across Mordecai Sheen.

Teresa tapped him on the shoulder, rousing him from his thoughts. "Paulie, on the phone. It's Lucy."

He got up quickly. "I'll take it in the living room."

"Daddy?"

That squeaky little voice he loved so much. "It's me, sweetheart. How are you?"

"I'm good. Robert has a cold." Robert was her stuffed zebra.

"Oh, I'm sorry to hear that. Did you take him to the doctor?"

"No. He's just sneezing a lot. If he gets a cough, we'll take him to the doctor."

"Well, that's very smart, Luce. We don't want you catching anything bad from him."

"I'll be okay. Did you know its Poppa Vic's birthday?"

"I knew that. We're having a party for him. I know he wishes you were here. We all do."

"Me, too. I can't come because I can't miss school." Paul chuckled. Yes, missing a day or two of first grade, that could really put a blot on one's academic transcript.

"Say, weren't you going to be in a class play or something?" Paul recalled.

"Daddy!" his daughter said reprovingly. "That was last month. I was a sunflower. I was very good, too."

"I'll bet you were."

"And after the show Mommy and Bert took me to Chucky Cheese."

Bert? Who the hell was Bert?

"I dont think I remember Bert, sweetheart."

"Oh, he's Mommys new friend."

Paul heard a voice in the background, then Lucy. "I have to go now. Mommy wants to say hello."

"Okay, Luce. Love you."

"Love you, too."

Amber came on the line. "Paul?"

"Hi."

"Your Dad sounds great," she said. "How's he getting along? I mean, really."

"He's good. Tough as ever. He may bury both of us."

He heard her chuckle. Then a more somber note. "Look, Paul, about July. I know that's your month with Lucy but we may have to change things around a little."

"Now wait a minute, Amber—"

"Calm down. All I said was MAY, okay? It's just that, Bert's mother and father rent this condo in Hawaii the first two weeks in July and they want us, and that means Lucy, too, they want us to vacation with them. I said I'd let them know after I talked to you."

Paul felt a tight fist clutching at his innards, old resentments gorging up into his throat. "Okay, you're talking to me and I've got problems. July is my month and I've already laid out plans," he lied.

"What plans?" she asked, knowing he'd lied.

"They're not set in stone, not yet," he said

"I'll bet they're not."

"And who's this Bert anyway? I don't know anything about him."

"And you don't have to," she replied.

"I do if he thinks he's taking my daughter to Hawaii."

There was a moment's silence. "Look, Paul, don't do this. Don't make me play bad guy. You know what the agreement says. I go way past what I have to because Lucy loves her father and I don't want to get in the way of that. But bottom line, if I want to take her to Hawaii, that's where she's going."

"And where does Lucy want to go?"

Another pause, then: "Lucy wants to go to Hawaii."

"Sure, after you brainwashed her. Jesus Christ, Amber—"

"It's her choice, Paul. She says I can see Daddy when I come back.

Now you want me to put her on the phone so you can tell her she can't go?"

A rock and a hard place. "No, forget it. Go. Have a good time."

"Paul, I'm sorry—"

"I'm sure you are. I'll try to work something out for August. Anything else?"

"Not really."

"Say goodbye to Lucy for me." He hung up.

So now it starts. Another year older. More demands from school and friends. More guys named Bert crawling into her life. Three thousand miles away in beautiful downtown Pasadena. She might as well be in Khazakstan.

He gathered himself, then started for the kitchen. "Mom! Pop! I gotta get going."

He let himself into his darkened apartment, suddenly feeling very tired, though the trip back from Queens had been easy. No traffic, no tie ups, no accidents. Not a world's record but close. The little red light on his answering machine was blinking furiously. He checked it out. Three messages. He hit play. Silence. Hit it again. More silence. Same for number three. "You have no further messages" the machine intoned.

Damned telephone hucksters, he muttered yanking off his tie. No, he did not need a new credit card or a million dollars of life insurance for two bucks a month, or slippers that glowed in the dark so you could find them easily when stumbling out of bed.

He went into the bedroom, yanked open the closet to grab a hanger for his chinos and sport jacket. His eyes fell on the slacks and cashmere sweater hanging in the corner. Who the hell belonged to them? Tina? No, too small. Tina was nothing if not zoftig. Yeah. The kid. The little brunette from accounting, the one who'd never heard of Sylvester Stallone or The Eagles. They hadn't had much to say to each other but then conversation wasn't the bedrock of their relationship, such as it was. What Paul remembered it was, was maybe three dates over a ten day period. He couldn't recall who got tired of who first. Not that it mattered.

The phone rang. What the hell. Not at this hour. He picked up the receiver ready to give vent to his spleen.

"This better be good," he growled.

After a pause, a feminine voice. "How good do you want it?"

"Excuse me?"

"I said—never mind. I called three times, hung up three times. I said I'd give it one more try before midnight or the hell with it. So here I am."

There was something oddly familiar about that voice. "So here we are, uh...." Groping for a name which was not forthcoming.

"You don't remember. Christ, Castelli, you sure make a girl feel special."

Castelli. There was a clue. Someone from the old days, or just a smart ass?

"Getting old," he protested. "Little black holes eating into my brain, more and more every day. Drooling to follow."

"Okay, its been a while but I love busting your balls. Always have. A balmy day in October on the Eastern Shore, picnic for two, crabs and chowder and then late that night, on a woolly rug in front of a fireplace at the Sea Breeze Inn—"

"Jesus, Jennie Bovano."

"The one and only, in person," she said, sounding like a broken-down ex- vaudevillian. "So I see its going pretty good for you, Castelli."

"Good enough," he replied, "and how's by you, Bovano?"

"Getting along, boss. Getting along." At the Sun she'd spent a summer interning, mostly following Paul around, until she had to get back to Law School in New Haven.

"Doing what? Chasing ambulances? And by the way, how did you get this number? It is top secret."

"I have my sources. Don't worry, I didn't sell it to the Enquirer."

"You know, you are being very enigmatic."

"I am," she said. "I'm also very sleepy so here's the deal. I'll be jogging in the Park tomorrow morning. Around 6:45 I'll swing by the Tavern. See you there."

"At six forty five I am usually wrapped in a warm blanket, dreaming erotic thoughts about Julia Roberts—"

"Oh, you're into older woman now."

"Or Hannah Montana. You didn't let me finish."

"Pervert. Listen, Castelli, six forty five and don't be late because if you are, at seven o'clock I call Geraldo Rivera. Sleep tight."

She had hung up. Paul hesitated momentarily, then went into the bedroom, picked up the alarm clock and dialed in a wake-up time with which he was totally unfamiliar.

CHAPTER FOUR

Paul cupped his hands to his mouth and blew hard. His breath, its vapor visible in the cold morning air, did little to warm up his stiff unresponsive fingers. In the shadow of the glass and timber edifice that was fast becoming one of New York's premiere tourist traps, the only restaurant he knew of where a dining room had been built around a live elm tree. He felt himself alone and pretty much vulnerable, though he knew that he wasn't. A decade or so earlier he wouldn't have dared enter Central Park at West 67th Street at this hour of the morning but Giuliani had made good on his promise to oust the muggers and the rapists and turn the city back to its citizenry. Bloomberg had followed in his footsteps. An overweight guy in a Dior running suit struggled by, dragged along by a copper-toned Irish setter who seemed to be endowed with boundless energy. A kid wearng an NYU sweatshirt cycled by from the opposite direction and veered off onto a path that led deeper into the park. So far he'd seen no pack of teens that looked like extras from 'West Side Story'. He started to relax.

Paul checked his watch, started to jog in place when he heard her voice.

"Hi, stranger!"

He turned as she emerged from behind a large sagging conifer.

bundled warmly in grey sweats which tried unsuccessfully to hide what Paul knew to be a dynamite figure. Her ash blonde hair was pulled into a pony tail and held in place by a blue and yellow silk bandana. Her running shoes were worn and scuffed but top of the line. On her wrist she wore an oversized timepiece which probably did everything but make her breakfast. It had been seventeen years since he'd last seen her, but time had not diminished her wholesome beauty. To the contrary.

She glided up to him, encircled him with an affectionate hug.

"Long time no see, old buddy," she said.

"You look terrific, Jennie."

"You should see me in a bikini," she grinned.

"I'd like to."

"Actually, you have. And a lot less than that."

"I remember."

She grabbed his left hand and checked out the ring finger. "Still divorced?"

"Happily so."

"Seeing anybody special?"

"Not lately."

She smiled. "Yeah, I know. I'm just busting your chops, Castelli. I know all about your miserable private life."

"I'm flattered," he said.

"Don't be. Every now and then I even check out your website. I also force myself to watch your television show. Not often, however."

"Really? Not interested in the trials and tribulations of your fellow man."

"Not the ones you trot out."

"Thanks for the four star review," he responded testily. "The last I looked you were about to graduate from law school. Did you ever attain that so-called lofty status?"

"Later, Castelli. Right now, I need breakfast. Your place or mine?"

He laughed. "So that's it. You've missed my rockhard body all these years—"

"Whoa, my old friend. You misread my ever pure intentions. I am sweating like a stevedore and unfit for public display. Did you drive here?"

"Cab."

"Then we'll make it my place. My car's right outside the gate."

She started off, turned back. "Come on, Castelli. I won't bite. At least not for a while."

Bemused and a little bewildered, he fell into step beside her as they started for the 67th Street entrance.

Jennie's apartment was part of an old brownstone on West 49th Street. It was small, cozy, very tidy and looked well lived in. Jennie tossed her car keys on a table near the door.

"I'm going to take a shower," she said. "You can fix the coffee. The machine's in the kitchen. So simple a TV host could figure it out."

"I'll do my best," he called after her. "You look very settled in here. How long have you been in town?"

"Ask me over toast," she called back, shutting the bathroom door.

Paul mastered the coffeemaker easily, found bread for toast, some eggs and a few other ingredients for an omelet. He opened a fresh carton of orange juice and dug out a half-empty jar of marmalade from the back of the fridge.

Later, when they were sitting down with their food, Paul reiterated his question.

"So how long have you been living here?"

"About a year."

"Guess I wasn't at the top of your to-do list."

"Guess not," she said.

He nodded. "And you're working as a lawyer? Big firm?"

"Maybe THE biggest," she replied. "I'm assistant to Deputy District Attorney Leon Goldman."

Somewhat surprised, he smiled approvingly. "Very nice, Jenn. Very, very nice. I hear Goldman's at the top of the list to replace Vanderhoven when he runs for Governor."

She nodded. "You and I hear the same thing. Leon's taking the UP escalator and I'm going right along with him."

"Well, you always knew what you wanted."

"So did you, Paul, or so I thought." The lightness had left her voice. "What happened?"

"What do you mean?"

"You know what I mean."

"I'm sorry, Jenn. It wasn't you. Things got sticky and I had to make a midlife course correction."

"I know. I kept the Sun coming by mail even when I went back to New Haven. I followed your byline for months, then suddenly no byline. No Paul Castelli. I phoned the business office trying to find you. They said you'd quit. No forwarding address. Gone from the face of he earth. Just like that."

"Honest, it had nothing to do with you—"

"Forget ME. Come on, Castelli, give."

He shrugged. "It's a long story."

"I've got time."

She was staring at him intently. He felt himself getting annoyed.

"Last night on the phone, you hinted at some story tip. You even threatened me with Geraldo."

"You first, Paul. I want to know what turned a really talented investigative reporter into a poor excuse for Jerry Springer."

"Come on, Jenn, it's really—"

"None of my business? I think it is my business, Paul. We spent some wonderful weeks and months together. I was proud you were my friend, proud of who you were and what you did. Now, if what we had together, however fleeting it might have been, meant anything at all, then yes, it damn well IS my business."

He sipped at his coffee, stalling for time, then sat back pensively. "Okay. Maybe I owe you that much." His mouth was suddenly dry. For the first time in fourteen months, he thought he needed a drink. How to tell her. How to tell anybody what he'd been trying to forget for seventeen years. How to recount what a coward he had been. How, when faced with possible ruin, perhaps something worse, he had flinched and backed off. Backed off? Hell, he had run for his life.

"Did you ever hear the name Mordecai Sheen?"

She shook her head, poured hot coffee into her empty cup, topped off Paul's.

"He was a lieutenant in the Baltimore police department, working vice. Something of a minor celebrity on the force. Tough as nails. Took no crap from anybody, especially the low lifes he had to deal with day after day. Funny thing about Sheen. He didn't live in Baltimore, he had a four bedroom house in Towson just west of the city. He rode around in a new Jaguar. His wife drove an even newer Ford Explorer. His three kids all went to private school. All this on a police lieutenant's salary. To a 22 year old kid with burning ambition, this didn't feel right, so I started probing. Not digging, just probing a little. I found out he had a couple of brokerage accounts, one in his name, one in his wife's. He was also part owner of three apartment houses in an upscale section of the city. A run of the mill crooked cop just like hundreds if not thousands all over the country. But of course to this 22 year old's naive, pea-sized brain, this was shameless crime at the highest level, a betrayal of the public trust and so on and so forth."

He paused, sipping at his newly warmed up coffee.

"And naturally you felt you had to something about it," Jennie said.

"Well, I did, but my editor didn't. He told me to let it be. I thought then he was probably on the take. Later I realized he was just being a realist. It was not a fight the paper could take on without great risk. Not just money, but access to the cops, and who knows, maybe even physical harm."

"So what changed things?" she asked.

"Spider Grozak," he said. "A low life dealer who worked the black neighbor-hoods in East Baltimore. One night he ended up in the county hospital from a beating he'd taken. I was there on another story but I stopped by Grozak's bed just out of curiosity. He told me Sheen had tried to rip him off, then beat the crap out of him when he wouldn't fork over. I wasn't shocked, not even surprised but I doubted I could turn it into a story. It was a he-said, he-said kind of thing. I told Spider as much. He just smiled. You think I'm lyin'? I got his button, he says. His button? Yeah, I ripped it off that fancy coat of his while he was wailing on me. Spider opened his hand and there it was, a fancy leather-covered button right off the front of Mordecai Sheen's thousand dollar cashmere overcoat."

Paul smiled at her. "Then I went and did something very stupid. I went back to the paper. The night editor was on the desk. He didn't know about the no-touchy policy. I wrote it up and it appeared in the morning edition at which point, you can guess, all hell broke loose. Editor number one wanted to fire me on the spot, but for what? Doing my job? And we were getting a lot of calls. Positive calls. Ordinary folks who didn't like the way Sheen operated. The Managing Editor hauled me into his office. The City Editor was already there, looking like he'd just been sentenced to thirty years in Chateau D'If.

But he wasn't any happier with me either. Who the hell was I to go off on my own, disregarding orders from the desk, writing up a story I knew was going to put the paper at risk? What the hell kind of a team player was I anyway? I kept my mouth shut because I wasn't and we both knew it."

He fell silent. Now came the tough part. Jennie pointed to his coffee cup, silently asking if he wanted a refill. He shook his head.

"To its credit, the paper let me follow up with the story. They checked and double-checked my facts until the lawyers gave the green light. For a couple of days I had Sheen squirming. The Chief of Police was in front of the TV cameras twice a day, crying foul and setup and anything else he could come up with to protect his boy as well as the department. Then on a Friday evening, I got a call from a guy, said he'd been following the story. He also had knocked heads with Sheen but he'd been smart enough to wire himself up. He told Sheen about the recording and after that Sheen laid off of him. He didn't need to show the tape to anybody, just having it was enough, and if he had to turn it over to someone, who could he give it to? The State Police? Maybe. But then if Sheen wriggled out, the informant would find himself a couple of months later with two broken legs. And that's if he were lucky. Anyway, the guy says he wants to give me the tape so I can nail Sheen for good and would I meet him at this HoJos just north of Bowie on Rt 3 in Anne Arundel County. So, me, being so experienced and sharp as to the ways of the world, charges down there, hoping to get back in time to make the morning edition.

"Well, it was about two miles out of Bowie when I pick up this squad car behind me, lights flashing and its whooper whooping. I pulled over. Two county cops approach the car, one of them telling me I'm driving with a busted taillight. No surprise since I'd heard one of the cops bust it just before he reached my window. Anyway, bottom line, they drag me out of the car, fortuitously find a couple of ounces of skag in my jacket pocket, throw the cuffs on and haul me down to the station house for an extended conversation.

"The room was about six feet by six, no windows with a lot of padding on the walls. Soundproofing I think they call it. I'm in a chair, still cuffed, while they take turns rearranging my facial features. After about ten minutes, another cop sticks his head in the door, whispers something to one of these goons and they leave. I was just starting to wonder what sort of good fortune had befallen me when the door opened and in walked Mordecai Sheen with a wide but not so friendly smile on his face. He didn't say anything. He just hauled off and slugged me, loosening two teeth in the process. He grabbed my shirt front and lifted me out of the chair and slugged me a half dozen times in the belly, then shoved me back into the chair which tipped over and I crumpled onto the floor. Then he kneeled down next to me, his face close to mine, his breath smelling of Tic-Tacs. 'Listen to me', he says. 'I'm going to tell you this once. They've got you photographed and printed and booked. You're looking at 2-3 years for dealing, resisting arrest and a dozen other charges too numerous to mention. You will be tried, you will be convicted, you will go to prison and when I get you behind prison walls, you will be killed by a fellow inmate, how and when to be determined by me. Do you understand me?' I mumbled that I did. He continued on. "There is one and only one way for you to avoid this tragic end. I will arrange for you to be released in your own recognizance. All records of your appearance here will be expunged. You will drive straight to your apartment, pack up your things and drive away from this city. Far from this city. You will tell no one, you will call no one and you will never set foot in Baltimore again as long as you live. Am I clear?" I remember nodding. In twenty minutes, I was out of there, running for my life, so scared I'd pissed my pants. I never looked back."

Paul looked up into Jenn's eyes. "That's it. All of it. Paul Castle, fearless, crusading journalist who has no trouble picking on terrified women but quails at the sight of anything a little more dangerous."

Jenn reached over and took his hand. "And what were you supposed to do? Let him kill you? And for what? The sake of a story about a two-bit crooked cop, a story nobody wanted you to write in the first place."

Paul shook his head violently. "I turned tail. It took nothing to get me to run. Nothing."

"And if the same thing happened today? What would you do?"

"I don't know. I honest to God don't know." he replied.

She got up from the table and went to get her purse. She rummaged around inside, extracted a freshly opened pack of cigarettes. She tapped one out, lit it, inhaling deeply. "One of my many vices," she said. "The one I can't get myself to quit." She proferred the package. He shook his head. She returned to her now-cold coffee.

"You know, at one time I worshipped you," she said. "Sounds corny but I mean it. You had all your shit together. Pulitzer Prize? It wasn't a question of whether or when, it was how many."

He shook his head. "Jenn, please, that isn't helping—"

"And when I saw your show and all the freaks and misfits and watched you put them through your hoops, it hurt, Paul. It really hurt."

"It's a living, Jenn. I gotta eat. I've got a little girl I have to put through college someday."

"You don't have to do this."

"What then?"

"What you started out doing," she said.

He smiled wanly. "Little late for that, kiddo."

"Is it? Suppose I put you onto a story, I mean a real story. Not the schlock you're involved with now."

"What kind of story?"

"The best. With all the elements. Could you handle it? Would you try?"

He pondered it. "Yeah, maybe. If it was right."

"Even if things got a little hairy. Not like that lieutenant, but it could get rough."

"Like I said, I could try."

She crushed her cigarette out in the remains of her omelet.

"I told you, I watched your show last night. The woman in green. What's that all about?"

"The last time I looked? Sex."

"And that's it?"

"Come on, Jenn. So it isn't the Pentagon Papers. Uptight bachelor Congressman from New Jersey has secret tryst with mystery woman in luxury hotel. Straight arrow Boy Scout type dies in the saddle. Friends and neighbors scandalized and nobody has any idea who this woman is. Yeah, I think that's a story."

"And he died in the saddle, as you so graciously put it. Of what? Stroke? Heart attack?"

"Natural causes, according to the medical examiner," Paul said.

"Well, the medical examiner's rethinking his position. He's ordered up a new tox screen."

Paul's eyes narrowed. "Why? What did he find?"

"He missed it first time around. A small puncture in his left arm pit, somewhat obscured by body hair."

"Which means—"

"Which means we are left with two options and since Johansson was left-handed, suicide seems hardly likely."

"Murder."

"That'd be my guess, Castelli. Not just a sex story anymore, is it?" She smiled at him coyly.

In the kitchen of her neatly ordered postwar ranch home in Grafton, New York, just a few miles east of Troy, Mary Ellen Chaffee poured fresh hot coffee into her husband Don's dented scratched up but still servicable thermos. The thermos went into a little basket into which she had already placed a couple of sliced pork sandwiches, an apple, a banana, a pear and three crisp and crunchy chocolate chip cookies. The size of the menu was a good indicator of the length of the trip Don was about to take. Today's would be an all-day run. If she was lucky, she'd see him tonight before midnight.

Don Chaffee came into the kitchen. A tall scrag of a man with a still-full head of white hair, he inspected the basket and found it acceptable. He gave his wife a firm pat on her rump and a kiss at the base of her neck.

"I still think you oughta get Otis to go with you," she said. "Utica's a long trip and besides, a full load of sheet rock, that's a lot to handle."

"I told you, Mother, I'm not loading and I'm not unloading. I'm just driving."

"Well, just hope you don't have any trouble along the way. And quit calling me Mother. I feel old enough already without you helpin' out, thank you very much."

"You old? You'll never get old. You can't take the time. Why, if Jesus himself came to carry you away, you'd still put up a ruckus. Can't go, O Lord, my baby granddaughter Emmy hasn't graduated from high school yet, and Rory and Bess'll be havin' a baby any year now. Don't want to miss that. And then after that, let's see—" He made a show of deep thought.

"You quit your laughin' AND your blasphemin'." she grumbled.

"As you wish, my dearest. Just trying to brighten your day." He took the truck keys from the hook on the wall and grabbed up the basket. "I'm aimin' to be back by ten," he said, "but if I'm not, don't get all freaky about it."

They headed out the back door to the driveway where the semi was parked.

"You got your cell phone?" she asked.

"I do, but I'm not always in a place that gets good reception."

"But—"

"But me no buts," he said. "On the odd chance, one in ten million, that something happens, you're going to be the richest widow in Grafton. Now I know that ain't saying much but it's better than being the poorest."

"Now will you quit that—"

He took her by the arms. "No, Mary Ellen Chaffee, YOU quit it. We have this conversation every time I'm going out on the road for more'n three hours and I'm telling you, I'm getting damn sick of it. Now you know where the bankbooks are and the safe deposit keys. Josh knows all about the insurance and Wilfred knows about the lawyering requirements. Now kindly give me a kiss goodbye so I can get this pathetic show on the road."

She leaned in and hugged him tight. He responded in kind, whispered in her ear. "Goodbye, my darling wife," he said giving her an extra special squeeze. Then he was in the cab of the truck and backing out of the driveway.

Mary Ellen watched him drive away.

Why did he have to go? In his condition. He should be retired now, just as they'd planned, but somewhere, somehow, something had gone very wrong. He couldn't earn enough to keep up. Their retirement account which they'd contributed to every year since they were married was wiped out in the stock market debacle of '08 and '09. Whatever had happened, she thought, it shouldn't be like this Not for her and Don. Not for their friends who were struggling worse than they were. It just wasn't fair.

Maybe if he wasn't feeling so poorly. Maybe if Doc Weathers hadn't up and quit the HMO. Not that she blamed him, the way things had changed. The new doctor, Dr. Rovich, he was all right but he was always so busy, a lot of times you couldn't get in to see him. Maybe if Don didn't have to wait three or four hours every time he went to the emergency room. Maybe if one time he could talk to the same doctor two visits in a row.

She shook her head and started back toward the house. Too many maybes in their lives these days. And in their friends' lives. Too many of a lot of things.

The truck rumbled down the dirt road to Route 2. At the crossroads, instead of turning right to go west to Utica, Don Chaffee turned left and headed east toward Vermont.

He reached Rutland shortly after two o'clock. One of the sandwiches was gone along with the apple and the banana. The coffee had been used up first but replenished at the first pit stop just outside of Bennington. If he'd been in the mood he could have allowed himself to be awed by the magnificent mountain greenery of Vermont in spring, but he had other things on his mind. Important things that could be put off no longer.

He reached into is pocket and took out the small notebook that had been given to him several days earlier. There was the address. He double-checked the Rutland city map. The yellow highlight showed him where to go and the best way to get there when entering Rutland on northbound Rt 7.

He checked the fuel gauge. No problem there. He fired up the diesel engine and pulled into traffic, lumbering toward the downtown area. He found the building on a lightly used cross street a block down from Rutland's main drag. The sign outside read "Offices of Ruth McCormack, 2nd Congressional District."

He moved on down the road, found a deserted dirt lot, pulled in and parked. He walked back to the Congresswoman's offices and went inside.

The woman at the desk looked to be sixtyish, plainly dressed, working with difficulty on a computer which seemed to be getting the better of her. She looked up with a smile.

"Can I help you, sir?" she asked.

"Well," Don said, clearing his throat nervously, "I'd be obliged for a minute or two with Miz McCormack. I heard she's back in town for the day."

The woman smiled. "That she is, but she's not in the office."

Don knew that but was just confirming. He feigned disappointment. "Well, that's too bad. I sure am sorry to have missed her. I think I heard somebody say she'd come back for her grandson's birthday or something like that."

"You heard right. She'll be heading over there in a little while and then she has to catch a plane out for the Capitol first thing in the morning."

"Oh, she's at her home then. Right now."

"Yes, she is, but I wouldn't want you going there and bothering her none."

Don grinned. "Couldn't rightly do that, ma'am since I don't know where she lives." He tipped his hat and headed for the door. "I thank you kindly, ma'am. You have a real good day."

Out the door, he hurried down the street to his truck and hopped in.

But Don Chaffee DID know where she lived and now that he had everything confirmed, it was just a question of watching and waiting,. He fired up the big engine and roared down the street toward the exclusive residential area just to the north of the city.

Her residence was clearly highlighted on the map as was his vantage point. There was only one way in or out of the McCormack home, a long dirt driveway that could have passed for a county road in lots of backwater states. She drove a silver Mercedes sedan. It would almost certainly be the only automobile exiting the property at that time of day.

He maneuvered the cab into a clearing overlooking the driveway. He had a clear view of the driveway for over seven hundred yards and a clear shot from this crossroad to the intersection below. He checked his watch, then dug in the basket for a chocolate chip cookie. No sense letting them go to waste. He snapped off a bite. Crisp and delicious. Mary Ellen worked magic in that kitchen of hers. He'd miss it. The fawning and the special attention she always paid to his meals. He'd miss her, too, if "missing" were possible where he was going. Which brought up another question. Just exactly where WAS he going? He'd never had doubts before. Now he wasn't so sure.

Out of the corner of his eye, he saw the dust rising far off from tbe driveway. He slipped the cab into gear and sped down the hill. At the intersection he turned right and started up the two-lane road, gathering speed.

When he saw her she was a speck moving toward him in the other lane, looming larger with each passing second. Her headlights shown automatically, as if that ineffective safety device would be much help on this balmy spring day.

Chaffee, who had not been nervous all day, felt a cold tremor go down his spine. Closer she came, now less than fifty yards away. He saw her behind the wheel, confirmed that it was the same woman whose photo was enclosed in the notebook.

At the last possible moment, he yanked the steering wheel left and careened into the oncoming lane. Congresswoman Ruth McCormack had no time to react. There was a horrible screeching of metal on metal, glass crashing, two giant globs of crumpled steel, skidding as one down the narrow asphalt road, then suddenly flipping to one side and tumbling, as one, down a steep embankment to the rocky crags below.

A spark, gas ignited, a yellow fireball erupted.

And then it was over. Two human beings were no more.

CHAPTER FIVE

It all looked so easy on television when Rockford did it, or Kojak or Columbo. Nose around, ask a few questions, wave a few Andrew Jacksons about and the information spilled forth like water over Hoover Dam. Somehow these guys missed the Westin Hotel in midtown Manhattan The way people were eyeing him, you'd think he was there to steal the silverware. The desk clerk was particularly surly. Paul figured if he was ever going to do an expose on hotel rip-offs of tourists, Blinky with the bad hairpiece would be a good place to start.

"I'm sorry, sir," said the desk clerk with the nervous tic in his left eye, "I have already told you, I cannot give out any personal information on hotel employees, especially not home addresses."

"Okay, then can you confirm for me that this chambermaid Consuela Ochoa was on duty the night the Congressman died?"

"Sir, please. I'm very busy."

Paul looked around. He was the only one standing at the desk. "Excuse me, madam," he said to a phantom guest standing behind him, "I was here first. Now please, quit shoving." He turned back to Blinky. "Now, you were saying?"

"You needn't be rude, sir."

"I know, but I'm so good at it." Paul said.

Blinky sighed. "Perhaps if you spoke to the manager—"

"Portly fella, kind of bald on top, dressed in black like an undertaker? Forget it. He shined me on over an hour ago."

The clerk reached for a phone. "I believe this is something security should handle."

"No sense getting testy. I can tell when I'm not wanted." He started off, turned back. "Just so you know, I'm in charge of booking hotel rooms for my college class's twentieth reunion. I'm sure you won't be surprised not to see us here this fall."

He turned, pleased with his well-honed zinger and left the hotel for the bright sunshine of a warm May afternoon. Only the smell of diesel fuel and carbon monoxide spoiled the perfection of the moment.

He checked his cell phone, hoping vainly that he had somehow missed a call back from the city's Chief Medical Examiner. He'd called twice, left two messages. No response. Now that was rudeness on a grand scale. Well, if the mountain wouldn't come to Mohammed—

He stepped off the curb, hailing a cab.

On the way to the city morgue at 520 First Avenue, he started reviewing what he knew. Not much. He was pretty sure that Consuela Ochoa had gotten a good look at the woman in green on the night of the murder. Bill Bates on Channel 7 had reported it and Bates always had the goods. Which means the cops have got her on ice or she's skipped the country for Tijuana or parts south. And yes, it had to be murder. There was too much bullshit floating around for it to be a simple accidental death. He felt lost. What was the next step? Even knowing about the needle mark, he had no place to go. He'd already talked to Johansson's staff and some of his close friends. They seemed to be leveling with him. Not a clue as to who this dark haired babe in green was. The only thing he'd picked up was why, ostensibly, Johansson had been in New York in the first place. Something about an exhibit of rare old coins. Originally, he'd dismissed it as a feeble cover story for a night of philandering, but now, maybe there was something to it. He nodded inwardly. Good idea. Right after he cornered the M.E., he'd check in at the library and look over some newspapers from last Friday. If there was an exhibit, somebody must have been promoting it.

The morgue wasn't a bad place to visit if you stuck to the upper floors. It was when you got into the subterranean areas that the place took on an olfactory charm uniquely its own. Normally the Chief M.E. would be upstairs shuffling papers and calling important people and saying just the right things. It was what you got paid for. This particular M.E. was a different breed. He liked getting down and dirty. He loved solving puzzles. And best of all, he loved the smell of fermaldahyde.

Paul didn't but he soldiered on, peering into open doorways, checking out the autopsy rooms for some sign of his elusive quarry.

"Mr. Castle!" a voice boomed behind him.

Uh-oh. Busted.

He turned to see a shortish, heavyset man wearing wire-rimmed glasses approaching quickly. For a beefy man, he seemed surprisingly light on his feet. Paul didn't need to see the holstered .38 snub-nosed Smith and Wesson in a holster peeking out from under his left armpit. His clothes said it all. Cheap cotton sport coat, a shirt that seen too many washing machines, a wrinkled tie with a couple of unruly stains, sensible shoes. Wardrobe by Cop.

"I was afraid you'd leave before I caught up with you," he said.

"Your lucky day."

"I understand you've been trying to reach the M.E. Can I ask what for?"

"You can ask," Paul said.

"Ooops, sorry. It's been a tough day." He fumbled about in his pocket, brought forth his tin and flashed it. "Aaron Kovacs. Lieutanant. Homicide."

"Whatever it is, I was never near the place."

Kovacs smiled. "I'll put that in my report. Now about the M.E."

"I'm working a story. Just following up on a lead."

"And what story would that be, Mr. Castle?"

"I don't think I'm obliged to tell you that."

"Good point," Kovacs said. "However, there is a civil and cooperative way we can deal with each other, sir, and there is another way. I despise the other way but sometimes I'm left with no choice."

"Ah, the old rubber hose gambit."

Kovacs looked genuinely insulted. "Certainly not. Look, can we get out into the fresh air. My sinuses can't stand much more of this."

Paul swept his arm toward the exit.

"Lead on."

The atmosphere outside was considerably fresher and Kovacs inhaled deeply. "Better." He indicated a pocket park across the way. "Do you mind if we sit on a bench for a few minutes? I 've got to get these shoes off."

"I'm at your disposal, Lieutenant," Paul said.

Kovacs smiled." Thats real nice of you, young man. Well, as long as you offered, I could sure use an ice pop from that fella on the corner over there. Meanwhile, I'll be working on the shoes."

Paul smiled as the cop crossed the street, exaggerating a limp. Two ice pops coming up.

Kovacs had both shoes off and was kneading his left foot when Paul arrived with a pair of frosty looking red ice pops.

"I got cherry and raspberry. Take your pick."

Kovacs looked them over. "Which is which?"

"Damned if I know," Paul said.

Kovacs grabbed the nearest one and chomped into it. "That sure hits the spot," he said.

"Which is it?"Paul asked.

"Damned if I know," Kovacs replied, laughing. The cop took another bite. "So, about the rubber hose thing, I don't operate that way."

"I'm impressed. A moral policeman."

Kovacs considered that thoughtfully. "No, I wouldn't say that. Just too damn many things to go wrong. Always having to look over your shoulder for some prissy little nancyboy from the ACLU trying to get you bounced from the force. Not for me. I can, however, take you down to the station for questioning and check you for outstanding warrants. Then after you've called your lawyer, I can move you to another precinct for additional questioning which might take several hours, unless you made some sort of overture to resisting arrest—and it wouldn't take much—and then I could probably keep you overnight which means you'd miss your broadcast tonight without so much as a word to the network since you had already used up your alotted phone call." He paused, taking another bite of the pop, then fixed Paul with firm stare. "Or we could handle this like two gentlemen who are, I suspect, working from the same page."

Paul smiled, making a note to himself. Do not ever underestimate this cagey old fox.

"As I said before, I am at your disposal," he said.

"Good," said Kovacs. "Now what did you want to see the M.E. about?"

"I was told he was ordering a new tox screen on the death of Congressman Johansson at the Westin the other night."

"And who told you that?"

"Not at liberty to say."

Kovacs nodded. "And why do you think a new tox screen was needed, if indeed, such was the case?"

"Same answer. Privileged source."

Kovacs thought about that for several moments, digesting it. Then he said, "Is there any particular reason why Jennifer Bovano would impart that information to you and you alone as opposed to any other television reporter?"

Paul's eyes narrowed. Cagey didn't even begin to describe this guy.

"Look, Lieutenant, I don't know what you think you've heard—"

"Spare me, please, son, or we'll be sitting here all afternoon. The girl's in no trouble. I'm just trying to sort out the pieces." Kovacs was kneading his other foot now.

"All right, I'll take your word on that. Jennie worked with me over seventeen years ago when I was a reporter for the Baltimore Sun. She thought I needed a fresh lead for my story. She was just doing me a favor." A thought. "And how did you know it was Jennie?"

"Mr. Castle, I'm a detective. It's what I do." He slipped into his sock and replaced his shoe. "Allright, now aside from the M.E.'s office, there are three of us that know the Congressman was murdered by the little honey in green."

Paul could sense what was coming. "And in light of that, it is my patriotic duty to say nothing on my program tonight, to take the scoop of the year and bury it six feet underground."

Kovacs expressed surprise. "On the contrary, Mr. Castle. I want you to lead with it tonight. I want you to shout it from the rooftops. 'O wondrous thing, how easily murder is discovered.'"

"Shakespeare? You surprise me, Lieutenant."

"We surprise each other, Mr. Castle."

"Reward? What kind of reward? What are you talking about," Murray sounded more harried than usual.

Paul was sitting in the back of a yellow cab that was crawling northward toward the Times Building. In a race between the cab, a snail, a tortoise and a centipede, the cab would be lucky to finish in the money.

"I mean, reward leading to the arrest and conviction of. You know the drill. The cops can draw on their snitch fund for ten thousand, but if we want to make a splash, we're going to need at least forty thousand more from The Old Man."

"Wait a minute. Why would the cops put up ten grand for the conviction of what, for Christs sake?"

"Murder, Murray. Good old fashioned murder."

A momentary silence. "No shit."

"No shit," Paul echoed.

"Not a maybe murder. The real thing?"

"Dead bang, "Paul said. "That's why this police lieutenant and I have to meet with the Old Man at five o'clock."

"I'll set it up. What else do want to cover tonight?"

"I don't care. Whatever you got set it up. I'll use the prompters, but figure twenty minutes on the big one."

"Right," Murray said. "I still got that story on the Congressman who got whacked in that restauant on Tuesday." He paused. "That's weird. Don't you think that's weird, Paulie? Two Congressmen getting iced within a couple of days of each other."

Paul thought about. "Yeah, very weird. But look, hold off on the Washington thing. I don't want to split focus on this."

"Right. You comin' in?"

"Going to the library. Do a little research."

"Yeah? I thought that's what we hired Big Tits for?"

"We did, "Paul said, "and heaven forbid we make her feel unwanted, but this is something I have to do myself."

"I'll break it to her gently," Murray said.

The cab dropped him off at the main entrance and he hurried inside. The New York Times wasn't much of a newspaper these days if you were interested in an unbiased view of the nation's ups and downs, but it was still a pretty good source for information on people, places and public goings-on. It took him less than twenty minutes, but there it was. "Public Exhibit of Ancient Coins and Other Antiquities." It was far down in a list of city-wide Friday night events. Open from six to ten. Public welcome. The address was a gallery in Greenwich Village. Having found no other competing event of a similar nature, Paul headed for Washington Square.

Deveraux's Antiquities on West 10th Street was considerably more than a shop but not quite a museum. The square footage of the main floor was substantial and just about all of it was devoted to the display of ancient objets d'art. Or maybe just high priced junk. Paul was well aware that he could not discern the difference between a 16th Century chamberpot or a Taiwanese knockoff, if there were such things.

"Not to worry," the little man said. "Whatever help you may need, Mr. Castle, I am here to provide it."

His name was Phillipe Deveraux, five foot three at the most with a glistening shaven head and a pencil thin moustache decorating his upper lip. Paul felt a twinge of self-satisfaction that the man had recognized him.

"Thank you, Mr Deveraux, but I'm not here to buy."

"Alas, I suspected as much, but no matter. What can I do for you?"

"Congressman David Johansson. Did you know him?"

A look of pain crossed Deveraux' face. "So sad what happened. A fine man, a most gentle man."

"Then you knew him?"

"Oh, yes."

"And can I assume, perhaps, that he attended the exhibit here last Friday evening?"

"You can, sir. He is....he was a most valued customer and if I may say, also a good friend. I'm afraid I disappointed him, however."

"Oh? How so?"

"He thought we had a certain piece on hand. The April 8, 1762, New Jersey Colonial 30 shilling." Off Paul's puzzled look: "Paper currency. He has an extensive collection of old paper currency and coinage from early America. I'd been trying to find that particular piece for him since early January."

Paul nodded. "When he came Friday, was he alone?"

"Oh, yes, as always. I personally saw him arrive."

Paul pondered that. "Is it possible he met someone here? Did you see him with anyone during the evening?"

"Oh, many people. He was after all a member of Congress, though perhaps not as popular as he once was. Several times I heard voices raised, not always favorably."

Paul frowned. "What were they upset about?"

Deveraux shrugged. "I'm really not sure. I do know that Dr. Franklin, he's a very well known heart surgeon, he was so loud and obnoxious to the Congressman that I almost had him removed."

"Why was he so upset, do you know?"

"Not really. Something to do with tort reform. Congressman Johansson killed a bill a few months back that would have made it harder for lawyers to get these huge multimillion dollar jury verdicts. In a way I could hardly blame Dr. Franklin for being angry. I mean some of the stories you read in the paper. A couple of million dollars because some doctor prescribed Tylenol instead of Excedrin or some such nonsense." He stopped, and then said apologetically, "Forgive me, I'm getting political, answering a question you did not ask."

"No problem, Mr. Deveraux. We all have our favorite lawyer jokes. So, did you notice the Congressman with a woman?," Paul asked. "Young, dark haired, wearing a green dress and a floppy hat."

Deveraux started to shake his head, then stopped. "Yes, there was such a woman. Toward the end of the evening, I noticed them together at the juice bar we had set up near the entrance."

"Do you know her name?'

The little man shrugged. "No, I'm sorry. She was not a regular customer. I don't believe I'd ever seen her before."

"I see. Do you have a surveillance system?"

"We do, but it recycles every 72 hours." Damn.

"Did you have a guest book, where people sign in as they enter?"

"Yes."

"Okay if I look at it?"

"Certainly." He started off toward a large antique desk standing in the corner. Anachronistically, there was a credit card machine on top of it. Deveraux dug in the desk drawer, drew out a black leather bound register. "It may not be much help. A lot of guests don't bother signing in."

Paul flipped through the pages until he reached the Friday night date. "I see about fifty names here."

"There were probably twice that in reality."

"Mind if I copy these?"

Deveraux hesitated." May I have your word you won't be hassling some of my best customers?"

"You have it," Paul said.

They went into the backroom and Deveraux copied the three pages of names.

"So Johansson didn't introduce you to the young woman."

"No."

"But maybe he did to someone else. One of these names."

"Very possible, of course."

Paul regarded the list. "Not a really big turnout, Mr. Deveraux. The cost of the notice in the Times couldn't have come cheap. How are you getting along?"

"Not as well as we once were. This is well below half of what we had last year, but...." He shrugged. "The taxes, the new regulations, the never ending paperwork. I've had to lay two of my people off." He laughed. "I may be next."

Paul smiled. "I doubt that."

"That's because you don't own a small business, Mr. Castle. We're fast becoming an endangered species like the dodo, to pick a very apt example."

Deveraux led him toward the entrance, a sad smile of resignation on his face. "They say unemployment checks aren't half bad and if you play the system the right way, you can keep collecting forever."

At the door, Paul grasped his hand. "One last thing, if you ever saw this woman again, do you think you'd recognize her?"

Deveraux nodded. "Oh, yes. I'm starting to forget many things, but the face of a beautiful woman? Not yet."

At precisely five p.m. the three of them trudged into The Old Man's office. Fritz Schoenfeld was leaning back in his chair, perusing that day's edition of The New York Post. He was tall and barrelchested with wavy whitish-blonde hair just a shade on the long side, just a little unruly as if he really didn't care much about his personal appearance. It was a carefully cultivated facade and his barber came in once a day to help him maintain it. His levis were stone washed and nearly white though he'd stopped short of wearing holes in them. His boots were lackluster and needed no special treatment. He just avoided polishing them.

The room was small for a man of Schoenfeld's status. Three TV monitors were lined up on the wall opposite his desk, sound muted. On a side table were piled stacks of newspapers and periodicals and a couple of dozen file folders. A corkboard filled the wall behind him.

Affixed to it were at least three dozen scraps of paper, held in place by pushpins of various colors and sizes. As he looked up, he noticed Aaron Kovacs staring at the board.

"Those are important notes to self, Lt. Kovacs. I find if I start to file things away, I tend to forget about them and lot of damned good ideas have been lost that way." He gestured to the three chairs that fronted his desk, uncomfortable armless wooden things that looked like rejects from a Long Island City yard sale.

"A good thing you gentlemen didn't bring along a lawyer or somebody'd be standing."

Paul and Murray hesitated momentarily. Kovacs plopped down in the nearest chair and started kneading his shoed foot.

Murray cleared his throat. "Uh, thanks for seeing us, Mr. Schoenfeld. Paul was very insistent we have this meeting and I, uh—"

"Never mind covering your ass, Mr. Bellson. Sit down." A look toward Paul. "Okay, let's have it."

As succinctly as possible, Paul laid out everything they had including the new, and as yet unannounced tox screen. The Old Man took it all in, looked over at Kovacs.

"He says murder. What do you say?"

"I say he's probably right but you want guarantees, go to Sears, Roebuck."

Schoenfeld leaned forward and peered down at Kovacs' shoe.

"Something wrong with your foot?"

"A few aches. Arches, I think."

"You want to take your shoe off?"

Kovacs nodded. "If you wouldn't mind."

"Go ahead. Got bunions myself. They can be buggers." He hesitated thoughtfully. "Where were we? Oh, yeah, my wonderboy wants me to put up forty thousand dollars on the off chance that a murder has been committed and if a murder really has been committed, we can cash in if we get the scoop. Something like that?"

"Exactly like that," Paul told him. Out of the corner of his eye, something on one of the monitors caught his attention. A wooden area, what was left of a big truck and maybe a car. The streamer below read CONGRESSWOMAN VICTIM IN FATAL CRASH. In front of the scene, a smashing blonde with not a hair out of place was reporting the event. Her mien was suitably somber. Paul wished he could hear the details.

"And WILL you, Mr. Castle?"

Paul turned to him sharply. "Sir?"

"You seem to be losing the thread of this conversation. Are we boring you? This meeting was your idea, I believe."

"Absolutely and damn fine idea it was, sir."

"Then I will repeat my question. If this harebrained idea failed to pan out, will you have any objection to my trading you to station KRAP in West Cesspool, Montana, for a used copying machine and a half-dozen ball point pens?"

"No objection, whatsoever, sir." Paul smiled amiably. "I understand the female population of West Cesspool is more than a little attractive."

"Oh, really?"

Paul nodded. "If you like moose," he deadpanned.

The Old Man shook his head and then broke into a hearty laugh and then waved them away. "Out of here, all of you. And this better work—"

"I know," Paul said, "you're down to your last ninety million."

"Out!"

The broadcast, all thirty minutes of it, was a knockout. Paul was right on point. The interview with Kovacs, while not specifically revealing, said a lot about cop thinking and procedures. And the announcement that Congressman David Johansson had been murdered, the studio audience (if there had BEEN a studio audience) would have come out of their seats. The security tapes were reshown, the reward offer was made. the network phone number was given out (over Kovacs' strong objections) and two of the office secretaries were put on overtime to handle the expected avalanche of calls.

The A.D. behind the camera held up five fingers, four, three, two, then one. The red light went out. The director's voice boomed from the control room. "That's a wrap. Nice show, Paul."

Kovacs sauntered onto the set. "So this is how it's done. You'll pardon me, young man, but frankly, it doesn't look that difficult."

"You want to take it tomorrow? I'll go out and shoot bad guys."

The cop smiled. "In that event, I reconsider. I would be forever humliated and the crooks would rob the city blind."

They walked off toward the rear of the studio. Paul said, "I don't suppose you noticed the news item, it was on one of the other channels, about some Congresswoman dying in a car accident."

"I caught it a couple of minutes ago in your relaxing room."

"Green room."

"It's painted yellow."

"It's still called the green room."

Kovacs shrugged philosophically. "I'll take your word for it. Tell me something, my young friend, do you believe in coincidences?"

"Not that kind." Paul said.

"Nor do I."

"Serial killer?"

"Not possible, but some maniac hiring hit men going from Washington to New York to Rutland, Vermont, in less than a week? Possible."

"Well, the trail is heading north," Paul said. "If someone knocks off the Prime Minister of Canada we'll know we're on to something."

"Just so. Well, even though there's not a direct connection, at least not yet, I'm going to chat up the Sheriff in Rutland tomorrow morning and compare notes."

Paul nodded. "I'm going to stick around here for a while in case we get a live one on the hot line."

'What you are going to get, Mr. Castle, I am very much afraid, is a motley collection of useless calls from neurotics, psychotics and other forms of God's warped children. But I could be wrong. So good luck."

Kovacs left and Paul went back to his office after checking with the two volunteers. He noted that one of them was Miss Big Tits, Crystal Huggins.

"Anything good come in?"

"Not unless you want a date with a big hunk of man who can do you right, Mr. Castle," Crystal said.

"Pass. I'll be in my office if anything breaks." Paul smiled at her. "Love your outfit."

"Thanks," she smiled coyly.

On his desk Paul found no urgent pink slip phone messages. He picked up the phone and punched in a number.

"Assistant District Attorney Goldman's office." The voice sounded young and pleasant.

"Jennifer Bovano, please."

"I'm sorry, sir, she's left for the day."

This he did not expect. Goldman was not known for tolerating nine-to-fivers on his staff. Improvisation was called for.

"Oh, that's too bad. This is Doctor Enright and I've just gotten back her lab reports. Neither of us expected any serious complications but, well, I'm afraid the news is not as encouraging it could be. I'm well aware that the D.A. has a policy against releasing home phone numbers, but in this one case. I'm afraid I must insist. These results could have dire consequences."

There was silence for a moment, then a very hushed titter of laughter.

"Is this Mr. Castle?" she asked.

"What? Oh, no, I mean—uh—"

"Ms. Bovano, on the odd chance you might call her, asked me to give you her cell number."

"Oh, that's very nice," he said.

"But I sure did like that story about the lab reports."

She giggled again and gave him the number, he thanked her and then called Jennie.

"Hello," she answered.

"Hello, yourself. It's me."

"It's me could be any one of a dozen guys."

"It's your favorite television host," Paul said.

"My God," she shrieked. "Regis! How did you get my number?"

"Honey, I've had your number for years."

"You think," she snorted. "Listen, Castelli, I'm in the tub and the water's turning cold so whatever this is, make it quick."

"Want some company?"

"No. As soon as I dry off, I'm going to curl up in bed with Patricia Cornwell."

Paul feigned shock." I had no idea you were that kind of woman."

"It's come to me late in life. I have James Patterson and David Balducci lined up behind her on my nighttable."

"Well, I was going to suggest a quiet time over drinks in some secluded bistro or a riotous night of drinking and dancing until the wee hours of the morning. Your choice."

He could almost see her smiling on the other end of the line. "I'll take a raincheck."

"On which one?" he asked.

"I'll decide when we get to it."

"Fair enough," she said. There was a long pause, then more seri ously. "Look, Castelli, I did not track you down just so we could pick up where we left off seventeen years ago."

"I know that," he said. "So which will it be, the quiet bistro or a TNT sized hangover the morning after?"

She laughed. "Okay, tomorrow looks pretty good but call me, in case the bossman has night duty planned for me."

"Will do."

"And Paul..... the show tonight. It was wonderful. I'm glad you're running with it."

"Sleep tight, my angel," he said.

He hung up, stretched with a yawn. He was tired. In a way he was grateful she'd passed on his invitation. His batteries definitely needed a charge.

The intercom buzzed. He flipped it on. It was Crystal.

"Mr. Castle?"

"Yes," he replied. Who else did she think it could be?.

"There's a man on the first line. I don't know. Maybe it's nothing but I think you ought to talk to him."

"What's his name?"

"He wouldn't give it."

Paul picked up the phone. "This is Paul Castle. Who are you?"

A thin reedy voice responded. "Just now, you don't need to know that. I saw your show tonight. First time. It was pretty good."

"Then keep watching."

"Can't," the man said. "Where I live cable don't carry your channel."

"I'll make a note. Where do you live?"

The man ignored the question. "Is that for real, I mean, the reward?"

"It is. Do you know that woman in the green dress?"

"I sure do."

"What's her name?"

"Not so fast, Mr TV man," the caller said, "I want to make sure I get the reward and no funny business."

Paul had a pad on his desk, pencil poised. "You have to give me something, my friend."

There was a short pause. "You know Rt.8 in Connecticut going north toward Waterbury?"

"No but I can find it."

"Just a little bit north of Naugatuck, on the right hand side, there's a White Castle. I'll be there around ten, sittin' outside, probably havin' a burger."

"Wait a minute, fella—"

"You want the woman, I want the fifty thousand and I don't want my ass in a grease fire over it. You comin' or not?"

"I'll be there. How will I know you?"

"I'll know you," the man said, breaking the connection.

Paul hung up. Just what he was looking forward to. A day in Connecticut. He wasn't sure his car, a city beast through and through, would agree to go there.

CHAPTER SIX

The vintage red Mustang turned onto the Cross Bronx Expressway and then, a few minutes later turned north on the Throgs Neck heading north on I95, once known as the Boston Post Road. Paul loved the throb of the V8 engine, the sensation of all that power under the hood. Like a little kid he wanted to let it out but the turtle-fast diesels that crowded the highway made that impossible. Just as well. He was recovering from a recent speeding ticket which had landed him an all day session at traffic school which was a total bore except for the twenty minutes of film looking at drivers and passengers mangled and mixed with blood and glass on the highways and byways across the nation.

The radio gave him a choice of heavy metal, business news, country and western, Alan Colmes or Rush Limbaugh. All five were designed to throw sane men into fits of depression. He slipped an old Credence Clearwater into the car's cassette player (CD's hadn't been invented back in '94) and hummed along tapping his hands on the steering wheel.

Kovacs' words from early that morning still rang in his ears.

"You're going WHERE?" he half-shouted. Paul told him again. "Young fella, you are getting your chain yanked, sure as God made walnut shells and peas."

"Sorry you can't join me."

"I'm grateful you didn't ask. While you're playing ring around the rosey I'm going to try to contact some of these people on the list you gave me from the exhibit. Might get lucky."

"We could use a break."

"Well, that's mainly what police work is, Mr. Castle. Asking a lot of questions and looking for a break. Speaking of which, we got one. The second tox screen came back. Tetrodotoxin. Almost impossible to spot unless you're specifically looking for it."

"Good to know we actually have an honest to God murder on our hands."

"Yes. Good to know. Well, I've got a call in to the Sheriff in Rutland about that car crash. If anything comes of it, I'll let you know."

"Right."

"Do the same for me if this Connecticut creep turns into a lead."

"Will do."

The trip north was uneventful. Paul stayed with the traffic and managed to average out at 69 miles per hour, even though it was posted at 65. The Nutmeg State they called it. So far he hadn't seen a nutmeg tree though he wasn't sure he'd recognize one if it fell on him. Plenty of fast food joints, however, and even more service stations boasting about $7.00 a gallon gas. And that was only if your car wasn't fussy about how much octane it guzzled.

Just outside of Naugatuck, he spotted the White Castle and pulled into the parking area. Sitting on one of the outside benches was a solitary black man in work denims, eating a burger and sipping coffee. Paul exited his car and approached the man who looked up.

"You're late, Mr. TV man," he said. "I was fixin' on havin' you buy me breakfast. You forced me to feed myself. Things have been going that way a lot lately."

"Sorry to hear it," Paul said. "I think I'll get myself a coffee."

The man smiled. "Long as you're buyin' I could sure use another burger."

Paul squinted at him. First Kovacs puts the bite on him for an ice pop, now this No-Name wants a free burger. Did he have a Kick Me sign tacked to the back of his jacket?

In a few minutes, he returned and slid the hamburger across the table.

"Appreciate it," the man said.

Paul nodded. He took a swig of coffee. It was hot and it tasted good.

"Okay," he said, "for starters, what's your name?"

"Let's not get into that."

"If I don' t know your name I can't pay you any reward."

He thought about that. "Evers. Robert Evers though folks call me Twig on account of I'm so big and brawny."

Twig looked to be about five-five and if he weighed more than a hundred pounds he'd been cheating on the Nutri System.

"All right then, Twig, who is she, why are you so sure its the same woman, and where do I find her?"

Twig raised a hand. "Hold on there, Mr. Castle. I told you on the phone, I want to make sure I don't get cheated out of no reward."

"I won't cheat you, I promise."

He broke into a big grin, revealing yellowed and uncared for teeth. "Last person told me ' promise' was nine years ago. Girfriend of mine says, you don't need no protection. I got it all covered. Promise. Nine months later I found myself bein' called Daddy."

Paul smiled. "Well, I ain't no two-bit ho."

Twig's smile faded. "I married that two-bit ho." he said.

Paul reddened. "Sorry, I meant no offense."

The smile returned. "S'alright, a year later she walked out on me flat. Got me a better woman now. A lot better."

"Married?"

Twig shook his head in disbelief. "Do I look like a man who would make that mistake again?"

"I guess not," Paul said.

"I guess not," Twig echoed.

Paul paused. "Look, you know I haven't got fifty thousand dollars on me, and even if I did—"

Twig put that hand up again. "That's okay, I'm cool with that. I want a paper."

"A paper."

"A paper that says how I'm the one that gave you the tip, you know, the information that got you to the lady."

Paul nodded. "I can do that."

"Then do it and stop wastin' time, or I'm gonna be needin' another hamburger."

Paul went to his car, brought back a pad of yellow-lined paper from his attache case and set it on the table. He started to write. "I, Paul Castle, attest that the man known asTwig—"

Twig pointed to the pad. "Better make that Robert. Robert Evers. It'll be more officIal that way."

Amused, Paul said "And we wouldn't want to confuse you with any other Twig Evers." He turned back to the pad.

"..... known as Robert Evers identiified to me a woman named—" He looked up. Moment of truth.

"Her name is Rose Temple."

".....Rose Temple who Mr. Evers claims is the same woman on the hotel security tapes seen running from the Westin Hotel on the evening of May 7 of this year." He paused, looked up. "By the way, why are you so sure it actually IS this Rose Temple? Her face was pretty obscured."

Twig smiled "Cause of her outfit. That dress and the dumb looking hat. She wore 'em both to the Town Meeting a couple of weeks ago."

Paul nodded. "Good enough for me." He started to write. "... signed for the National Heartbeat Channel..."

Twig grabbed for his pen. "Hold it. Don't that have to be witnessed?"

Paul pointed to the White Castle. "Get the fry cook, tell him there's a twenty in it for him."

Twig scurried off, returned in less than a minute, accompanied by a rotund senior citizen wiping his hands on his greasy apron. He snatched up the twenty Paul had placed on the pad. "Whereabouts?" he asked. Paul pointed, the fry cook signed and waddled back toward the building.

"Okay?"

"Guess it'll have to be." Twig picked up the sheet of paper, double folded it and put in his back pocket.

"So where do I find this Rose Temple?"he asked.

"Town of Bergensberg. Little bitty place. I oughta know. I live there. You go up the road here to 63, take it east to around Woodbury. Just ask anybody. They know where it is."

"If you're driving back, maybe I could follow you," Paul suggested.

Twig's eyes took on a dark hue. "I ain't going back, mister. I came down here lookin' for work. Stayed at a motel last night. Thats how come I saw your show. Like I told you, Bergensberg cable don't carry you."

"Things tough up there, Twig?"

"Tough don't even begin to describe it. Used to be a nice little town. Not much left now,"

Paul nodded. "Sorry."

"No need," Twig said. "That son of a bitch in the White House is screwing everybody. I don't take it personal."

Paul nodded. "So, how do I find this Rose Temple?"

"She and her Mom run an antiques shop on main street. You can't miss it."

Paul reached across and shook the man's hand. "I hope this pans out for you, Twig. I'd like to see you get the money."

Twig smiled. "Appreciate it," he said.

Twig Evers apparently had a talent for exaggerating for effect. Bergensberg was hardly a little bitty town. The roadsign entering the town limits announced a population of 2,260 and Paul spotted the usual amenities. A public school, town hall, police station, post office, myriad traffic lights, and a five block long shopping area. A majority of the storefronts seemed to be open for business which put Bergensberg light years ahead of many small towns who were basically shut down and boarded up. Not a new phenomenon but one that had been become more prevelant the past several months as the dollar continued to collapse.

Anna Marie Temple's antique store was easy to find, but the sign in the doorway read "Hours Noon to Six, Closed Monday." It was only 11: 15. Forty five minutes to kill. Paul spotted a restaurant down the street on the opposite side. Margie's Home Cooking. Having avoided the burgers at the White Castle, he was starting to feel the faint rumblings of hunger. He decided to chance it.

Margie's place was on the small side but neat and clean and the aromas coming from the kitchen were inviting. On a counter near the entrance there was a stack of newspapers. The Waterbury Weekly. A small sign said TAKE ONE. He did.

The woman behind the counter smiled warmly. "Morning." Paul returned the greeting. "Just sit anywhere," she said.

Paul slipped into a booth by the front window where he had a clear view of the antique shop. The woman approached with a menu, a mug and a pot of coffee. The name "Margie" was stitched on her uniform.

"You look like a coffee man and I'd guess black, no cream, no sugar," she said.

"Right on all counts," he said.

She poured the coffee and laid the menu on the table. "We got everything except fresh fruit. Delivery man broke down about an hour ago. Not surprised, that rattletrap old truck he drives. You looking for breakfast or lunch?"

"You tell me."

"Well, if you're real hungry I'd say wheatcakes and sausage topped with a fried egg. Otherwise I got a pretty good cobb salad or a bowl of turkey mushroom soup to die for."

"How about I try the soup AND the salad," he smiled handing back the menu.

She nodded. "Good choice. And then I guess you'll be having the hot apple pie for desert."

"We'll see. Depends on the soup and salad," he said with a twinkle.

She nodded and continued writing. "I'll just add the pie to the check." With a wink, she turned and walked off toward the kitchen.

Paul looked around. He was alone in the restaurant. Granted, he was there between mealtimes, but instinct told him Margie wasn't enjoying a robust business. Outside a dozen or so cars were scattered here and there. A truck was parked by the hardware store. The driver was getting help loading some wire fencing onto the truck bed. Two doors down a mother was shepherding two towheaded moppets into the barber shop. One of them didn't seem anxious to go. An elderly woman emerged from the grocery store pushing a cart with a solitary brown paper bag in it. As she proceeded down the street, no one came rushing from the store yelling 'Stop, thief.' It was a small town as small towns have always been only less so.

He turned his attention to the newspaper. The front page was dominated by a story concerning water rights, something about a difference of opinion between farmers and the non-agrarian citizens of Waterbury. Below the fold was an item that hinted, but did not guarantee, that a Wal-Mart might be erected a short distance from town. Sad. It was the last thing the people of Bergensberg needed. A boon to the economy, the article said. Wal Mart will be hiring. But if Twig Evers was right, they would be hiring people to sell to people who had no jobs. The logic escaped him.

The soup and salad arrived simultaneously. "Try the soup first," Margie advised. "Tastes real good when it's real hot."

He did and it was. He wondered why New York no longer had places like this instead of the overpriced chichi clip joints he was used to eating in. Probably because he was looking in all the wrong places.

Paul turned to the inside pages of the paper and he spotted her immediately. A posed shot of six people attending the Town Hall Meeting in Bergensberg. She was standing at the left wearing the green dress and the floppy hat. Next to her was a stern looking woman in a severe shapeless sack of a dress. The caption identified them as Rose and Anna Marie Temple.

Paul felt the rush of adrenaline. It was like the old days at the Sun when something fell into place and you knew you could be on to something big. He hadn't had a jolt like this in years and it felt good. He thought about calling Kovacs to crow a little, but realized that was probably premature. Besides he had a salad to finish.

A few minutes later he spotted a car pulling up in front of the antiques store. Two women got out and went to the door, unlocked it, went in. Paul slipped out of the booth, folded the slim periodical into his jacket pocket and moved to the counter.

"What? No pie?" Margie said.

"No room. The food was fabulous, Margie ." He laid two twenties on the counter. "Will that cover it?"

"Sure will. You come back soon, now."

"I'll try," he smiled and hurried out the door.

As Paul pushed open the door to the shop, a bell tinkled overhead. On the way over he'd mulled the approach he would take, decided to come at the young woman obliquely. If indeed he was facing down a murderess he didn't want to spook her into silence from the start. He looked around. The mother was busying herself behind a counter. Rose was nowhere in sight.

"May I help you?" Anna Marie Temple asked, forcing a welcoming smile.

"Just thought I'd look around, if you don't mind." Paul said.

She waved a hand. "Take your time."

Paul slowly started to peruse the wares. The majority of it was run of the mill junk, probably collected from barns and attics in the local area. There were a few interesting pieces like a vintage ice cream maker which looked to be in mint condition and a grandfather clock which was keeping perfect time.

His eye fell on a framed photo of a smiling sandy-haired GI standing next to a jeep. From the background it looked like Nam. A set of dog tags hung from a hook above the photo. Paul inspected them. The name indented on the tags was Elroy Temple. There was a serial number and a blood type. Next to it was a second photo, this time in civvies, his arm around a blondish, maybe red-haired woman. A quick glance at Anna Marie told him this was Rose's father. The woman was holding a baby in a blanket. Presumably, that would be Rose.

Then he spotted it. A glass case against a far wall, displaying all sorts of antique coins and paper currency dating back to Colonial days. He suspected some of it could be valuable. Not being a collector, he couldn't be sure.

"This looks interesting, "Paul said.

Anna Marie moved in beside him. "I suppose. Don't know much about it. Belongs to my daughter. She's been collecting this stuff for years."

"For sale?"

"Mister, everything here's for sale though Rose is a tough bargainer. You won't get anything cheap."

Paul nodded. "I collect these things myself. Just getting started, actually." He concentrated. His memory didn't fail him. "I don't suppose you've got a specimen of the April 8, 1762, New Jersey Colonial thirty shilling."

She paused. "You know, I believe we do. Rose and me were talking about that bill only a couple of weeks ago. It should be right here." She looked in the corner of the glass-topped case. "Now, that's funny. I'm sure that's where it belongs."

"I've got it, Mom." A woman's voice caused them to turn. Rose Temple approached. "I took it out last week to show someone. It's still in my purse."

Anna Marie nodded. "This gentleman was asking after it. I'll let you talk to him." She moved off to busy herself once more.

Rose Temple was a pretty enough woman, not striking, not beautiful, but with violet eyes that drew you to them immediately. Her smile was genuine revealing perfectly aligned white teeth, marred only by an occasional tic near her mouth. Her roundish face was encircled with lustrous black hair. For all of that, for all of her outward warmth, Paul felt there was a tinge of sadness about her. Maybe it had something to do with Bergensberg or maybe the absence of a ring on her left hand.

"So you're into old currency," she said. There was just the slightest slur in her speech pattern. Paul wondered if she'd been drinking. Pretty early in the day. Maybe they got started early here in Bergensberg.

"In a very small way," Paul replied. "When I was a young stud I drove a beatup Ford sedan but what I really wanted was a vintage Packard or a Mercedes coupe from the '30's. Seems I'm a slave to nostalgia but since I can't afford the cars, I'm settling for old bills and coins."

"And what makes you so interested in the 30 shilling?"

He shrugged. "I've got most of colonies, but no Jersey, and somebody told me it's a good piece." He hesitated, screwed up his face curiously. "Excuse me but have we met before?"

"I don't think so. Would you like me to go in the back and get the bill?" She had pointed to the rear of the shop. For some reason her hand was trembling.

"Sure." Then: "Wait a minute. Last Friday. The exhibit at Deveraux's. Didn't I see you there?"

She smiled. "No, I don't think so."

"No? I could swear....... I don't know. You have a twin sister you don't know about?"

This time she laughed and called across to her mother. "Mom, is there something I should know about a twin sister you might be hiding from me?"

Anna Marie shook her head at the foolishness. "Hardly likely. You were trouble enough all by yourself."

"This gentleman thinks he saw me in New York City last Friday?" Rose said.

"Be hard to do," the older woman said," seeing as how you were here with me all weekend."

Rose turned back with a smile.

"Sorry, my mistake," Paul said.

"Not a problem. Would you like to see the 30 shilling now?"

He glanced at his watch, feigned disappointment. "You know I really have to run but I'll try to get back. I saw some business cards on the counter. Mind if I take one?"

"Not at all."

They walked to the counter. "I sure like that grandfather clock over there." As she turned her head, Paul scooped up four or five cards from the display. Each featured Rose's face.

"It's priced to go," she said.

"As I said, I'll try to get back."

He moved to the door, opened it, the bell tinkled. He turned back to her. "You know, I'm curious about something. When I asked if you'd been at Deveraux's Friday I didn't say anything about New York City."

For a moment her face blanched. She exchanged a quick look with her mother. Anna Marie jumped in. "You can't be in the antiquing business in this part of the country, young man, if you don't know about Phillipe Deveraux."

"No," Paul said thoughtfully. "I suppose not."

But the nerve had been struck. He knew it. They all knew it.

On the way back to the city, he finally got a chance to crow to Kovacs on his cell phone.

"You're sure it's her?" the cop asked.

"Positive and I filched about a half-dozen business cards with her picture on them."

"Excellent, my young friend," Kovacs said. "We'll make a policeman out of you yet. Two of the people at the exhibit besides Deveraux are positive they'd recognize her. And we've got Consuela Ochoa, the chambermaid, on ice. She's staying with a cousin on Staten Island."

Paul laughed. "And how did I know that? You homicide fellas are a tricky bunch."

“Muddle around long enough and you start getting things right.” , the policeman said. “By the way, if you’ve been avoiding the radio and television, your broadcast last night has caused an uproar. You are either a lying muck- raking son of a bitch or a courageous fighter for the values that made this country great.”

“I like Door Number Two much better.” , Paul said..

“I think the party in power is starting to squirm a little,” Kovacs said. “Even they recognize that the murder of two of their most lefty of the left wing is more than coincidence.”

Paul hesitated. “What about McCormack? Or was she just an accident?”

“No accident,” Kovacs said. “Some kids were playing on a hill over looking the crash site. They said the semi-cab swerved into her lane deliberately at just the last second.”

“But she was a Republican.”

“Apparently not Republican enough. She voted with the Democrats about seventy per cent of the time and the way the district has been laid out, she didn’t have to worry about re-election.”

“Just like Tolliver and Johansson, “Paul said. “I smell a pattern here.”

“Smell is a good word, Mr. Castle. I think perhaps we have uncovered some kind of cesspool that goes far beyond my little homicide case.”

There was a long pause. They were both thinking about that.

“What do we do next?” Paul asked.

“That may be out of our hands, “Kovacs replied. “Why don’t you try to pick up a news station and I’ll talk to you when you get back.”

“Roger.”

“Wilco.” Wilco? Just how old was Aaron Kovacs?

It took Paul about a minute to bring in a strong signal news broadcast. He settled on it when he heard the familiar voice of the Speaker of the House of Representatives, Harry Bomford.

"......not a question of whether the bill's going to pass, just a matter of the vote margin and how many Republicans we can get to support it."

"Very few, Mr. Speaker, according to our sources. At least not the way the bill is currently written. The NRA is weighing in heavily against this legislation. I'd be surprised if you didn't have significant defections from your own ranks."

"Not a problem. Firearms are a major concern to the American people. They have a right to know their government intends to keep them safe."

"Yes, but this requirement to have taxpayers list all weapons on their tax forms and then have to fill out registrations and pay, what, a hundred dollars per year per weapon? It smacks a little of Nazism if I may use that term."

Bomford chuckled. "That's nonsense, Walter, and you know it. Using the tax form as a vehicle just makes for efficiency and saves the taxpayer the cost of even more paperwork. As for the fees involved, we know the Treasury can use all the help it can get and I believe that all right thinking Americans want to be a part of that help."

"That may or may not be, Mr. Speaker, but many people look on this effort as the latest step in a nationwide program of weapons confiscation."

"'That, too, is nonsense. This administration has no intention of executing any such plan."

"I see," said the host. "Then let me ask you this. We've been hearing that you are planning to introduce a bill which would call for a universal identity card which every citizen would be required to carry at all times."

"Yes, it's under consideration. I've asked Congressman DiNapoli and Congresswoman Thatcher to work up a bill and we'll take a look at it. I personally believe this is something long overdue."

"Forgive me, Mr. Speaker, but don't you think this is something that also smacks of Nazism?"

Bomford laughed. "Honestly, Walter, you've been watching too many old black and white war movies. I doubt the card would include much more than name, address, social security number, blood type, allergy warnings, maybe date and place of birth to alleviate this problem with undocumented workers. But nothing more than that."

Walter was not about to be put off so easily. "But of course, once the law is in place and the card's usage becomes mandatory, there would be little problem in adding other data. For instance, complete medical history, bank accounts, insurance policies, voting registration. That sort of thing." Bomford tried his best to reflect good nature but it was hard. "No, no, we would never support anything like that." The reporter started to ask another question but the Speaker cut him off. "Really, Walter, this whole thing is in the formative stages and I really don't think it serves any purpose to discuss it prematurely. Now, anything else? "

"Well, I would like to get your thoughts on the recent deaths of two of your colleagues. Congressmen Tolliver and Johansson."

"Tragic,"the Speaker said. "My heart goes out to their families, a feeling I am sure is shared by most Americans."

"It's been speculated that their deaths may be linked in some way. Any thoughts about that? Any speclal relationship that you know of between the two men?"

"If you're insinuating something of a sexual nature—"

"No, not at all."

"They knew each other. They worked together. Worked hard too. Beyond that I have no thoughts. As far as I'm concerned, these are two unrelated events."

Paul almost laughed out loud. Two unrelated events. That's my story and I'm sticking to it.

CHAPTER SEVEN

Paul swung by the Homicide Division before heading for the television station. He traded Kovacs the antique store business cards for an update on the Rutland crash that killed Congresswoman McCormack.

"The driver of the truck was a man named Chaffee. Donald Chaffee. He ran a one man trucking firm from his home in Grafton, New York. Last year he had three drivers working for him but the economy killed his business. Up to his neck in bills. Having trouble with the mortgage. Wife thought he was headed for Utica. Had no idea what he was up to, she says. I tend to believe her."

"The kids who saw it, their story checks out?"

"To a tee," Kovacs said.

"What's the sheriff like? Think he'd come on camera for me?"

"Might. He was sucking up to the local papers pretty good. You could probably get him."

Paul nodded. "Good. I need something for tonight's program. You know, this woman from the antique store, even if we get a positive ID, we still don't have much, do we?"

Kovacs smiled. "Son, we don't have anything. We can put her at the hotel, maybe even in the hotel room but as far as charging murder, let alone proving it, we've got a long way to go."

"Which means I can't use any of it on the broadcast tonight?"

"You could keep it general, dance around, mention no names. The last thing you want is to alert her in any way."

"I may have already done that."

"Can't say that'll help," Kovacs said. "I think the next step is to find a connection, if there is one, between the lady, this trucker and the fella in Washington DC, Leonard Philby. I'll start with phone records, see if anything pops up." Kovacs heaved himself out of chair and crossed to the water cooler in the corner of his office He took a bottle of pills from his pocket, downed two and followed them with a chaser. He turned back to Paul. "Start of an ulcer, the doc said. Getting old's hell, son. Avoid it if you can." He paused thoughtfully "You remember a while ago I told you this case might be out of our hands. Could be sooner than later."

"F.B.I?"

"Most likely. They might be a little behind us, but they'll catch up and when they do, you don't want to get in their way."

Paul frowned, anger welling up. "This is my story, Lieutenant. If I hadn't been chasing it the last few days, they'd have nothing."

"They won't see it that way. I'm just telling you, and it's the best advice I can give you, when they butt in, you butt out."

"We'll see," Paul said. He turned and left the office, avoiding an irresistable urge to slam the door.

The pink phone slips were piled up on his desk like fallen oak leaves on an autumn afternoon in New Hampshire. As usual Murray was his calm convivial self. "What the hell are we supposed to do for a show tonight? For Christ's sake, Paul, its four-thirty and we have nothing. Are we now making this stuff up as we go along?"

"Calm yourself. We'll have a lineup. Not to worry."

"Oh? You mean that lead in Connecticut actually panned out?"

"It did, "Paul replied, "but we can't use it yet, not without risking serious litigation."

"Then what—?"

"Lt. Kovacs is trying to tie in some loose ends. We should have something for Monday for sure."

"Yeah, thank God for weekends. So now I know what we don't have, just what DO we have?"

Paul consulted his memo pad. "The Sheriff in Rutland, Vermont. Name's J.R. Tyler. See if you can set up a remote with the guy through one of the local stations."

"Wait a minute! Now we're covering car crashes?"

"There may be a connection. The Rutland thing was no accident.."

Murray pulled up short. "You're shittin' me."

Paul shook his head. "Nope."

"And you think what, that there's a tie-in with the Johansson murder?"

"Maybe."

Murray started to pace, more annoyed than Paul had ever seen him. "Jesus, Paul, what kind of show are we doing here? America's Most Wanted? Murder, politics? We're an electronic sleaze show. It's why the folks tune in. They get their civics lessons from Fox and CNN, not us."

"Sorry, Murray, it's important."

"Tell it to the Old Man. He wants to see you. Immediatamente."

"About what?"

"Let him tell you." He started for the door. "I'll call that Sheriff in Rutland just in case we still have a show tonight." He fixed Paul with an unhappy look and went out.

Fritz Schoenfeld got right to the point. "Well, am I out forty thousand or not?"

"Not sure. I'd say yes. Whatever it is, we can't reveal anything publicly, not yet."

"Litigation?"

"Precisely."

He nodded. "Allright, we'll set that aside for the moment. You're numbers went up a little last night. I figure tonight they'll spike seeing as how you have become a minor celebrity, at least for the moment. What have you got planned for the broadcast?" Paul told him. He pondered it. "All right, go with it but understand something, Paul, this murder business, it's an anomaly. It isn't "Playback" and it sure isn't National Heartbeat. In a couple of days, unless your numbers go through the ceiling, we're going to drop this business and get back to reality."

Paul knew the Old Man meant it. He'd been hired to look under rocks and toadstools. As long as he'd stayed within Schoenfeld's parameters, he'd had no trouble, but it was painfully obvious that the Old Man was uncomfortable with this new direction. "I understand, but—"

"There are no buts, Paul. Actually I think it's kind of interesting, you playing Woodward and Bernstein but this thing's going to get bigger, too big for us to fool with, and I don't intend to have the federales come in here and start tearing apart my business. Do we understand each other?"

No sense arguing, not at the moment. "Absolutely."

Schoenfeld leaned back in his chair, put his scuffed boots up on his desk. "On the other hand, I see no reason why we shouldn't cash in on some valuable publicity for the channel. CNN wants an on-air interview tomorrow morning with Vera Staley. I told them you'd be delighted."

"Oh, now wait a minute—"

Schoenfeld shook his head. “We can use the press to put us on the map and a little personal publicity won’t hurt your career, either.”

“For God’s sakes, boss. She’ll chew me up and spit me out like four day old hamburger.”

“Naw, you can handle her.”

“If I can get a word in. Vera isn’t a reporter, she’s one of their opinionated hacks who equate run-on volume with erudition. I’ll look like a jackass.”

Schoenfeld leveled a cold stare. “I want it done, Paul. No arguments. Eight o’clock tomorrow morning at their studio.” He waved him away. “Now go put on a program.”

Paul returned to his office and absent-mindedly starting leafing through his phone messages, over half from people he’d never heard of. Toward the bottom of the pile was one from Jennie Bovano. “Call me,” it said. He did.

“Have you decided yet?” he asked her when she came on the phone.

“About what?”

“Last time we talked we set a tenative date for tonight with two wildly contradictary agendas.”

“I remember,” she laughed.

“And?”

“And what?”

“How about tonight?” he suggested.

“Tonight’s good,” she said, “but we’re going with Option C. Come by after the show tonight. I’ll fix us a light supper.”

Paul grinned. “This I like.”

“Don’t over-rev your motor, sport. For various reasons it’s best I not be seen with you in public.”

“Understand completely,” he said. “Should I wear my black outfit with the shiny cape and the Zorro bandana or just the glasses with the bushy eyebrows and the big nose."

"I'm a sucker for big noses," she said. She gave him her address. "Oh, and bring brownies. They bring out feelings in me you wouldn't believe." She hung up the phone and spun around in her office chair, staring out at the windows of the building next door. Her joviality had faded. She felt depressed just as she had for the past several weeks. All those little boxes across the way. Hundreds of them. Thousands more in the blocks nearby. Boxes just like the one she was sitting in right now. She'd thought long and hard before calling Paul Castle. Even now she wasn't sure she'd acted wisely. The one thing she knew, the thing that she'd always known was that she loved him. She'd had half a dozen lovers in the seventeen years since the day he disappeared from her life. Some were interesting. Some made her laugh. Some were agile and practiced lovers. But none had caused a spark. None had measured up, not even close. Was it because, having lost Paul, she had idealized him? They had been so young. Had there been anything real about their relationship? Had they just been playing at being love? Jennie didn't know but now she had to find out. Thirty six years old. Motherhood had become more and more an unreal option. She'd always been sure that her work would sustain her, no matter what. Now she wasn't sure. She'd become increasingly bored, she'd start to cry for no reason. Her apartment was a lonely cage at ten o'clock at night with only 'Law and Order' for company. And now here he was, Paul Castelli, back in her life and to what purpose? To recapture days gone by or to put the lie to a well-remembed fairy tale? Jennie didn't know but she was determined to discover the truth.

Paul's broadcast that evening was marginally acceptable. He danced around the identity of the woman in green. The usual nonspecific folderol. ".....a person of interest.....invaluable help from an informant close to the situation.....police following up on several leads... an arrest may be imminent....blah, blah, blah." The segment with Rutland sheriff J.R. Tyler was more productive. The man loved the camera and knew how to respond to it. He was somewhat verbose but his replies were non-evasive and what information he could divulge was fascinating. Paul stifled an instinct to suggest a tie-in between the three Congressional deaths. Those with an ounce of intelligence would get it. The rest would wonder why he wasn't covering Britney's latest fling with the twice-divorced NASCAR driver from Kentucky.

By the time he got to Jennie's, it was past nine. Flowers under one arm, brownies under the other, he rang the door buzzer. She opened the door, Paul's temperature rose a half-degree over the next three seconds. Her hair was down the way she used to wear it. Her white silk lounging outfit clung to her like paint on a new Mercedes. Her smile was warm and inviting. Paul wanted to hug her then and there but he had his arms full. Maybe later, he thought, as he whisked by her into the living room of her small but well appointed apartment.

"I got the brownies with nuts," Paul said.

"I like nuts," Jennie said.

"Well, I'm glad we've got that settled," he said, putting down his packages. The aroma of sizzling steak was coming from the rear of the apartment. "By the way," he continued, sniffing the air. "just how light is this supper?"

She shrugged. "Steak, salad, fries, asparagus."

"What? No soup? No fried calamari?"

"I would have but I couldn't help but notice the extra poundage you've acquired since last we met."

"They call that prosperity."

She snorted. "They call that a six pack of beer after dinner every night. Come on, let's eat. Everything's ready."

She'd set the small kitchen table with good china and real silver and crystal goblets filled with bottled ice water. The tablecloth was quality damask as were the napkins. And wonder of wonders, the food was just as good, if not better, than the trappings. Where did she learn to cook? From her grandmother. Her mother could barely brew tea, she told him.

For an hour they traded war stories. I went through this. You think that was bad, let me tell you what happened to me in Cedar City, Utah.

I thought maybe he was the guy but deep down he'd never left his mother's tits. He was a pretty good boss but whacked out over God and politics, which he never could seem to separate in his mind. Ronald Reagan was a latter day archangel; Jimmy Carter was Beelzebub.

Later in the living room, munching on brownies and sipping coffee, Jennie got around to business.

"My boss is on a witchhunt to find out who leaked the second tox report," she said.

"Is he onto you?"

She shook her head. "He's not as bright as Lt. Kovacs. Unless he finds out we have a history, I'm not worried."

"And if he does?" Paul asked.

"I could be out on my ass."

"Jenn, I'm sorry—"

"Don't be, I came to you, remember?"

She took his hand." The Lieutenant says you may have found the woman."

"It looks that way'

"Then I'd say it's worth it."

He shook his head. "Not if it costs you your job. Job, hell. A career."

"It won't come to that but there's something you should know. We had a half-dozen suits from Justice in the office today. The FBI won't be far behind, and they'll be talking to you."

Paul shrugged. "It'll be short and one-sided. You know I'm not going to give you up."

"I know, but I'm not talking about just that. When I fed you the lead on Johanssen, I had no idea it was going to blow up the way it has. I'm proud of the way you chased the woman down, Paul, I really am, but this thing may be a lot bigger than either of us can imagine."

"Meaning what? A vast right wing conspiracy?"

"What do you think?" she asked.

He looked at her helplessly. "Jenn, you know me. I'm not political. I thought this was a juicy sex story. Then a juicy sex story with a murder attached. Now I've got this bear by the tail and he's got me by the throat and I don't know where the hell I am or what I can do about it."

"Maybe just leave it alone," she said.

Paul poured himself another half cup of coffee. "Part of me says 'Amen to that'. The other part says 'You've got something here, something most reporters would die for. Maybe a Pulitzer. At worst a decent job in the majors. Do I just walk away? Should I? More to the point, CAN I?"

"You may have to. Look, this isn't just about your television show. This isn't about you calling the shots because you're in charge. You're not. A giant tidal wave called Washington is bearing down on this. You'll be swamped. I don't want that for you."

He smiled. "Hah. You care."

Her look was dead serious. "I've always cared."

He hesitated only for a moment, then got up and sat next to her on the sofa. He took her in his arms. She responded immediately, her arms tightening around him. He felt her nails digging into his back. Under the shiny white silk he could feel the softness of her skin, her supple responsive body. He leaned forward pressing her down, his mouth hungrily engaging hers.

And then just as quickly, she was pushing him away.

"No," she said hoarsely.

Paul backed off. "What is it? What's wrong?"

"It's me. I'm wrong." She sat up, smoothing her clothing. "I'm sorry. I didn't mean for that to happen."

"Dressed like that?" Paul asked dubiously.

She looked away. "You're right. I didn't know what I wanted." She paused. "Look, seventeen years ago you just up and disappeared. I know, I know, we were younger then, a different time, we were different people. Six months ago I went through another breakup. It hurt. Badly. I realize now I'm not cut out for anything casual."

He wanted to stand up and walk away, but if he wanted to maintain his dignity, Mother Nature was having none of it. He slid away from her. "With you, Jenn, it would hardly be casual."

She smiled, savoring the irony. "Oh. yes, I'm very aware of your slavish adherence to commitment." She took his hand. "Look, Paul, I'm not shutting any doors, believe me on that. But for now, I'd like to go slow. If that's a problem—"

"It isn't," he interjected quickly.

"I'm glad," she said.

Mother Nature, having returned him to normal, he stood. "I'd better be going."

She walked him to the door.

"If you want a laugh, tune in CNN tomorrow morning. I've got a date with Vera Staley. Round One starts at eight o'clock sharp."

"Can't wait, Castelli," she said and kissed him gently on the lips.

He left, disappointed at the waste of a half-dozen thick chocolaty brownies. With nuts.

Paul slipped quietly into the CNN studios with several minutes to spare. The regular host was interviewing Congresswoman Mary

Mae Thatcher who was extolling the many virtues of the universal identity card they were hoping to enact into law. It eliminated the need for cumbersome multiple ID's. It would be readily acceptable by everyone as the definitive piece of identification. Incorporated into the card, among other things, would be your date of birth, social security number, passport number, real estate owned including second and third homes, complete credit history from the age of 18 to the present, and a detailed run down of your medical history since birth. The medical information could help save your life. If you were a sportsman no need to carry a separate fishing or hunting license. It could be incorporated into the card along with the number of guns in your possession. Perhaps with the cooperation of the states, there might be a nationwide driver's license along with a detailed profile of your driving record. No need to carry a voter registration card and best of all, the UIC might even supplant your ATM card if your banking information was coded in along with the number and location of any safe deposit boxes you might rent.

The host listened intently. Unlike Walter, who had interviewed the Speaker, this host had no problem whatsoever with the concept. It was innovations like this that would help the government better serve the people.

"Good morning."

Paul turned. Vera Staley greeted him with the sort of warm smile usually reserved for beloved and doting grandparents. The stiletto which she was known to keep on her person was nowhere in sight.

"I wish you'd gotten here earlier, Paul. We could have sketched out what we're going to chat about." Nice word that 'chat', Paul thought. Benign as all getout.

"Might be better if we were just spontaneous, Ms. Staley," he said.

"Perhaps so, but don' t accuse me of ambushing you. And please call me Vera."

Paul smiled politely. The CNN studios were massive compared to National Heartbeat. Dozens of people scurried hither and yon looking busier than nuns at a church bake sale. Monitors were everywhere. Cameras stood quietly, readying themselves for action in front of darkened sets for some of CNN's most popular programs. They would come to life as the day wore on.

"What would you like to drink?" Vera asked. "Water? Coffee?"

"How about a Bud?"

She forced that warm smile. "Now, now, Paul. That's a no-no and you know it.."

"Just coffee then," he said.

She led him to the set, indicated a comfortable leather covered chair. "Please sit. We still have a couple of minutes."

He sat. Strong lights glared in his eyes. He was reminded of an old Cagney cop movie, him sitting on a bare wooden chair in his undershirt, sweat pouring from his glands while a goon with a rubber hose kept making slapping noises against his leg. He wondered if all CNN guests got the same wattage or was he just extra special.

Vera sat down opposite him. Her dark hair was swept up atop her head. It flattered her as did her conservative beige pants suit over a pale green silk shirt. Only her eyes gave her away. He'd seen them before. In a film called "Jaws."

The red light went on, Vera did the introduction and they quickly got down to business.

"You've made quite a splash with the revelation of Congressman Johansson's murder, Mr. Castle," she said. So now it's Mr. Castle. What happened to just plain Paul? She'd paused. It wasn't a question.

"I suppose so," he mumbled.

She smiled. "I think the country is well aware of your program—uh—"Playback"—"

"On the National Heartbeat channel," Paul embellished, fulfilling his obligation to The Old Man.

"Yes, of course. It seems to me, and others as well, I'm sure, that you've gone a little far afield from your usual material with this story. Does this mean Playback intends to take on more serious subject matter, perhaps cover the political scene?"

"Well, you know, I hadn't really thought about that, Miz Staley, but it might not be a bad idea." The smile never left his face.

"And it might get you invited to a better class of parties." The smile never left HER face, either.

"I'm sure you're right," he said, "but I seldom get out to parties. Aside from my natural tendency toward hermitism, I might miss Jeopardy."

A hint of annoyance flashed in her eyes. She didn't want to play this game, especially when she was being one-upped by a third rate anchor from a fourth rate cable network. "What can you tell me about this mysterious woman in green? You hinted on your program that you'd identified her."

"Did I? I don't think so. Anyway, if and when we can make an on-air identification, I think we'll save it for Playback. That's on National Heartbeat. America's Channel. 288 on your satellite dish."

Vera's voice took on a sharp edge. "You intimated last night that you thought there was some connection between the deaths of Congressman Tolliver in Washington and Congressman Johansson and the accidental death of Congresswoman McCormack in Vermont."

"That was no accident, Miz Staley. Check with the authorities."

"They've made no definitive finding, Mr. Castle. Until they do, we'll deal with facts, not wild speculation. You can't seriously believe there is some widespread plot in motion to kill off Congress."

Paul smiled. "It doesn't matter what I believe. We just report the facts as best we know them and let the people decide what they mean. I suppose we could spoon-feed them our own opinions but

National Heartbeat, 288 on your dish, doesn't operate that way."

Her eyes were ablaze now. She was losing her grip. She glanced sideways to the right of the set, looking for help. When none was forthcoming, she unsheathed the stilletto. "My research tells me you used to work as a reporter for the Baltimore Sun and that one day, you suddenly failed to show up for work and literally dropped off the face of the earth. Care to tell us why?"

"Not really," he said.

"One of your former editors says he remembers you well, that your work ethic was not up to their standards."

"No doubt," Paul agreed amiably.

"I really think—"

He interrupted her. "Miz Staley, I really think that all this has nothing to do with the subject at hand and furthermore my past employment is none of your business."

Her voice rose. "And if I were to suggest that you are withholding important information from the American people—"

"Ma'am, I don't care what you suggest or what you think. Wield your hatchet at somebody else's head. I've got better things to do with my time than playing pincushion of the day. Thanks for the lukewarm coffee."

He unclipped his microphone and walked off the set. If she had said anything in the wake of his departure, he didn't hear it and he didn't care.

He left the studio and hurried down the hallway toward the main entrance. Two men in dark blue suits stood by the doorway. As he approached, they intercepted him.

"Mr. Castle?" The taller of the two produced his identification and flashed it under Paul's nose. "Fowler Briggs, Federal Bureau of Investigation. We need to talk."

CHAPTER EIGHT

Someone once told Paul that FBI agents were divided into two categories, lawyers or accountants. Fowler Briggs looked like a one time pulling guard for the Minnesota Vikings. He was well over six feet tall, probably tipped the scales at 250. His expensive worsted suit was perfectly tailored for a body blessed with wide shoulders, thick chest and a well-tapered waistline. His skin was the color of milky coffee and his head was meticulously shaved. Gold-rimmed glasses rested comfortably on his nose. Everything about him screamed "gentleman" but Paul suspected that beneath the civilized facade was a grizzly bear who'd never met a meal he didn't like. Yet when Briggs smiled, as he did now, he exuded nothing but bonhommie.

"We only need a few minutes of your time," Briggs said leading him to a dark sedan parked at curbside. The other man had been introduced as Special Agent Duncan McIlroy. Duncan had nothing to say for himself.

"Where are we going?" Paul asked.

"Our office here in town," Briggs said, opening the rear door.

Paul balked, albeit pleasantly. "Well, if it'll be just a few minutes, why not chat here and save ourselves the trip?"

"We prefer doing it our way," Briggs replied softly. Voice quiet, eyes hard. Paul's trust level was plummeting.

"You do understand I am a member of the working press."

A look passed between Briggs and his cohort. Was that disdain he'd just spotted?

"And as such," Paul continued, "I am entitled to certain rights of confidentiality."

"I understand," Briggs said.

"Am I under arrest or something?" he asked.

"Of course not."

"Good, because stuffy government offices give me the willies, sort of like those small Southern police stations during the mid-Fifties. Of course, if you insist I can call my lawyer and we can sit around your office staring at each other for the next two or three hours."

Another look passed between the two agents. "What do you suggest, Mr. Castle?" Briggs asked.

Paul pointed. "There's a coffee joint down the street. Capuccino and Krispy Kremes. I'll even buy."

When they'd settled in at an outdoor table with what passed for Paul's breakfast (the agents settling for black coffee), Briggs got right to the point.

"We need to know what you know," he said.

"And I'll tell you," Paul replied, "up to a point. You have to remember, fellas, I'm working on a story here."

"Your story is of no importance to me," Briggs said, "nor to your government. You are required to tell us whatever you know about this case, without reservation or evasion."

Paul's pleasantry faded away. "I don't believe it works that way."

"It does, Mr. Castle, and don't fuck with me." Briggs, too, stowed away his winning smile.

"All right," Paul said slowly and cautiously. "In a nutshell. Congressman Johansson was murdered in his hotel room with an injection of tetrodotoxin. In all likelihood it was administered by a young woman whom he had met at an event earlier that evening. Whether they had a prior relationship, I do not know. Having injected the Congressman she ran from the hotel where she passed by several security cameras none of which captured a definitive image. She was also seen by a chambermaid who in all likelihood can make a positive identification. The woman is not local, she lives several hundred miles from here, and as to any motive, I am clueless."

Briggs was writing on a pad. He looked up. "The woman's name?"

Paul shook his head. "For the time being I'm going to keep that to myself."

The FBI man slipped the pad into his jacket pocket. "Mr. Castle, do you have the slightest clue who you are fucking with here?"

"You like that word, don't you? Hoover would have been horrified."

"I was told you were a wiseass. Not a very bright one either."

Paul shrugged. "We try for perfection. Often we fail."

Briggs flared with anger. "Now, Goddammit, you listen to me, mister. We've got three homicides here, three United States Representatives and it's no Goddamned coincidence. Now if you think the American government is going to let a bunch of red-necked fascist traitors murder its leaders with impunity, you are dead wrong."

"Then you've made the connection," Paul said.

"What?"

"The guy in Washington, Philby, and the trucker from New York, you've been able to tie them together as red-necked fascist traitors."

"That would be none of your concern, Mr. Castle." Briggs said. "Now I asked you for the woman's name."

Paul eyed the agent with skepticism. Redneck fascists? He pictured Rose Temple. She hadn't seemed much like a bomb throwing, wild eyed traitor. Whatever had driven Rose Temple to this act, it was not politically bred hysteria. There was a reason why a young reasonably attractive young woman with her whole life ahead of her would risk everything in the commission of a murder. Briggs was wrong. Very wrong, at least about Rose Temple. And probably the others as well. "You have no idea, do you?" Paul said. "You don't know if you're dealing with terrorists, fascists or Unce Sam's Aunt Tillie."

"Her name, Castle. Now."

"No." Then: "Look, Briggs, I'm not alone in this. What I know Lt. Kovacs of NYPD Homicide knows. If you have to, get the woman's name from him, but as long as I'm able, I'm going to protect my access to this story."

"We've been looking for Kovacs. Today's his day off. We can't find him."

"Then I can't help you."

Briggs dredged up his phony smile. "There's always my office," he said.

Paul reached into this pocket and took out his cell phone, waggling it for effect. "There's always my lawyer." he said.

Briggs glanced over at McIlroy. McIlroy shook his head subtly. The man still had yet to say something.

Paul leaned forward. "Don't be pigheaded. Here's the deal. Give me the rest of the day to cobble something together for a broadcast. If you still haven't gotten ahold of Kovacs, I'll give you what you want."

After a moment Briggs stood. So did McIlroy, still mute. Briggs reached over and clapped Paul on the shoulder. Hard. Very hard, delivering an unmistakeble message. "I'll give you until midnight tonight. Then I'll come knocking at your door."

Paul smiled, dragging out a corny German accent. "And as the Nazis used to say, we know where you live."

Briggs was not amused. He and McIlroy strode off toward their car. Paul took a bite of his donut. It tasted like hell. What had he gotten himself into?

"Where are you?" Paul asked.

"Yonkers," Kovacs replied.

They were both on cell phones.

"I thought today was your day off," Paul said.

"It is. I'm contributing my limited skills as a police detective to a good cause."

"What's in Yonkers?"

"A couple named Feldman. They were at the Deveraux exhibit, chatted with the Congressman, met the young lady who by then was hanging on his arm. They seem to remember her name being some kind of flower. Daisy? Violet?"

"Rose?"

"Close enough," Kovacs chuckled, enjoying his small joke. "You remember my telling you we might lose a handle on this case once the Feebs marched in?" "

I do."

"There's a flag on that play, young man. The Chief got an early morning visit from one of their guys, big black fella—"

"SA Fowler Briggs."

"That's him. Said agent tried to throw his weight around. The Chief shined him on, then told me to keep on the case, and if I got any interference from agent Briggs to arrest him for impeding an investigation."

"Can you do that?" Paul wondered.

"No, but I could have fun trying," Kovacs said.

"Just so you know, Lieutenant, he's looking for you."

"That figures. Well, I'll let him find me when I'm good and

ready."

Paul hesitated, mulling his options. "I think I need to talk to Rose Temple again."

"We've got enough to bring her in ."

"And lose her to Briggs? No, thanks. I need to know what's going on with her. Right now, I have no story."

"And that's your priority, Mr. Castle? Your story?"

"At the moment, yes. But if I get some answers, you'll get them. We're not at odds on this."

"No, we're not. You want company?"

"I don't think so. To her I'm just a potential customer. You're a cop and frankly, Lieutenant, it shows."

"You think?" Kovacs laughed. "Keep me posted."

Paul drove back to his apartment for a quick pit stop to pick up his attache case and a small mini-recorder. Whatever Rose Temple had to say, if anything, he wanted to get it on the record. He quickly scanned his e-mail, surprised to find the name of an old broadcast buddy from the Utah days. The message was terse and urgent. "Important you call me ASAP about your broadcast last night. Something you should know." He'd included a phone number. Paul had a few minutes. He called it. A familiar voice answered. "This is Dixie Boggs. If you're trying to sell me something get off the phone now. Otherwise, state your business." It was a recording.

"Dixie, it's Paul Castle. Pick up." Silence. "Pick up, you deadbeat. You don't owe me money."

Dixie clicked in. "Paul, my man," he said exuberantly." A pleasure hearing your voice once more ."

"The pleasure's all yours, old buddy. Last thing I remember you were supposed to give me a ride to the airport."

"An unfortunate circumstance, but a testament to your powerful memory. A thousand apologies. I was tied up with a young lady—

literally tied up, as I recall—one of those things over which I had no control."

"Are you still hustling the Grand Poobahs of Cedar City or have you moved on?"

"Moved on, upwardly, I'm happy to say. Prime time anchor for a decent little station in Port St. Lucie, Florida. Discounting the occasional hurricane, it is Nirvana on earth."

"I'm happy for you, Dix. I knew if anyone could make a career out of undiluted bullshit, it would be you."

"Speaking of which, you're not doing so badly yourself," Boggs said.

Paul glanced at his watch. "I hate to cut this short, amigo, but I'm in a kind of a bind for time."

"Right. The ominous deadline. I'll make it quick. On your broadcast last night you indicated that the hotel killing was third in a series of three murders."

"As far as I know."

"Well, technically, you're probably right but you should know, there was a botched attempt here in Port St. Lucie eleven days ago."

Paul reacted sharply. "Tell me," he said.

"Representative Hector Villanueva. One of those wacko socialists from the, uh...I forget what district. His housekeeper, a woman named Elsa Galesko, tried to split open his head with a fireplace poker. If his administrative aide hadn't walked in at just that moment, she probably would have succeeded. As it was, he was treated in the hospital for severe head trauma, or so its rumored."

"What do you mean, rumored?"

"I mean, all records of the Congressman's stay were expunged from hospital records. The housekeeper is being held somewhere incommunicado. Not a word in the local papers.. Only reason I know is from an EMT who was on the ambulance and who has since disappeared."

"What do the police say?"

"They don't know a thing about it. It may be nothing, but when I heard your broadcast, I thought it was something you should know about." "You did right, Dix. Look, I really do have to run." "If I get anything more on the housekeeper, I'll let you know. "

Paul hung up, then dialed another number. His call to Murray's house in Sheepshead Bay revealed his producer was at work in the city. "An emergency," his wife Reena complained. "The man's fifty-eight years old. How many days off does he have left? What emergency is so important?"

"Not a clue, Reena. Did he drive in or take the subway?" Paul asked.

"He's got the car. That's another thing. How am I supposed to take the kids to see their Nana Rachel in Wantagh without a car? You tell him, Paul. You tell him. He has to slow down. More widows around here we don't need."

"I'll tell him," he promised and hung up.

He slipped behind the wheel of the Mustang, pulled into traffic and made the short trip to the studio. It was Saturday. Traffic was light.

Paul found Murray in deep conversation with George Godfrey, the channel's business reporter. Murray spotted him, waved him over.

"If you're planning to go home this evening, bring flowers. Reena's on a tear." Paul said.

"Flowers won't begin to cover it." Murray shook his head. "Thirteen percent unemployment and my wife thinks I should tell the Old Man what to do with this job."

Godfrey smiled apologetically. "Sorry I have to borrow your producer, Paul, but Ben's on vacation and a big China story just hit. We're trying to assemble a special report for ten o'clock."

"What's the crisis?"

"Two hundred and twenty billion dollars in treasury notes the Chinese government is not going to roll over."

"Sounds like a big hit."

"Devastating. Seems they don't like the way our government has shredded the Yankee dollar into green confetti. And if we don't get them to change their minds, we'll be looking at junk bond interest rates or a still bigger deficit or still bigger taxes or maybe all three."

Paul nodded ruefully. "Or we could just keep printing money which seems to be this Congresses' answer to everything."

"You're up on your economics," Godfrey said.

"I'm up on the dwindling value of my paycheck, George. When it hits me personally I become an expert real quick." He turned to Murray. "I need your car for a few hours."

"What's the matter with yours?" Murray asked.

"Nothing. It's in my spot in the parking garage. I want to leave it there while I run an errand.."

Murray's eyes narrowed suspiciously. "What now?"

"The Feds. They promised to leave me alone for the rest of the day but I believe them like the Pope believed Galileo."

Murray took the keys from his pocket. "Don't bring it back with bullet holes."

Paul took the keys. "If anybody comes looking for me, I just stepped out for a bite to eat." He hurried out of the studio, down the stairs into the parking lot where he found Murray's drab but sensible Toyota Corolla. Within minutes Paul was out on the city streets, once again headed for the Throgs Neck Expressway.

While Paul was speeding north through Connecticut, retracing his steps to Bergensberg, a variety of things were happening across the country.

In a small room in a medical facility some distance from Port St.

Lucie, Florida, a woman sat quietly on a narrow bed staring vacantly into space. Her name was Elsa Galesko although she had been admitted to the facility under the name Jane Doe. Aside from an initial examination by the medical staff when she first arrived, she had received no treatment. Her meals which were good by institutional standards were delivered three times a day. Her mood was docile. Her attitude uncooperative. She hadn't uttered a word since being placed in the room. To the outside world, she no longer existed.

In Washington, Leonard Philby was being questioned for the sixth time since his arrest in the restaurant for the shooting death of Congressman Jerome Tolliver. Philby had made no move to run, no effort to resist. When the police arrived he had been sitting quietly by himself at a small table, the pistol lying on the floor where he had dropped it. Like Elsa Galesko, Philby had nothing to say when taken into custody. He did not wish a lawyer. He maintained his silence throughout every interrogation.

In Houston, a small unheralded website named SST made its debut on the internet. Not many people noticed. Those who did, if they had wished to, would not have been able to discover the entity behind the site, so cleverly had it been masked by routing and rerouting and other obfuscations. The content was off-beat, eerily so. Photos of Americana as it once had been flashed on the screen: GI's returning from WWII, Armstrong's moonwalk, fields of wheat on a Kansas farm, stunning views of the snow-capped Rockies, children at play in public parks, city kids dousing themselves from an open hydrant on a hot summer's day. The variety was endless, and interspersed from time to time, a legend that read "It Is Not Too Late." There was no Contact link, no E-mail address. They wanted no feedback. A message was being delivered. Nothing else mattered.

And in Chicago, at a luncheon sponsored by the Knights of Columbus, their honoree for the year, Speaker of the House Harry Bomford, was just settling in at the dais, anticipating with little enthusiasm, the warmed over chicken dinner that was sure to be served. Seated to his left was Daniel Cardinal Pritzker, an austere and humorless man whose rise in the church had been more a case of longevity and political savvy than any gift for compassion or understanding. He would have made a dandy Inquisitor.

To Bomford's right sat Joshua Jefferson, chairman for the day's festiivities, and president and CEO of a non-profit community action group known as PADS, People Allied for a Democratic Society. Jefferson was the Speaker's kind of civic leader. The past two city elections had resulted in Democratic pluralities which surpassed even the Daley years of yore. Their tactics were the same, only more so. Jefferson no longer bothered with the so-called "cemetery vote." All he needed were platoons of well-paid "volunteers" to blanket the poorest neighborhoods, signing up any and all who could walk and talk, regardless of residency, age, or citizenship. When the sheer numbers of these people cascaded down on the polls on Election Day, abetted by gangs of brown shirted civic organizers protecting the polls from 'disruption', the opposition had no defense. How else to explain the junior senator from Minnesota and others who were ostensibly swept into office by a tidal wave of blind adoration for the current occupant of the White House.

Adoration, rigged voting machines, intimidation at the doorsteps of polling places. It was all part of the package. Investigations were threatened but in the real world of elections, what is done is done and there are no second acts.

A pleasant woman in her middle years wearing a black and white waitresses uniform slipped a tepid bowl of chicken and rice soup in front of the Congressman. He smiled up at her. She smiled back. He sipped a spoonful, then another, turned to the Cardinal to compliment him on the excellence of the cuisine. Oddly, he was unable to get the words out. His throat constricted. A sharp pain stabbed at his innards. He tried to rise, couldn't. He grasped at the table, succeeded only in getting his hand on the tablecloth which he brought down on top of himself as he fell to the floor.

A hush suddenly filled the jammed room. A woman screamed. Cardinal Pritzker jumped up as if gored and stared down at his fallen guest of honor. Jefferson quickly kneeled by Bomford's side. "Doctor! We need a doctor!," he called out, but as he looked into Bomford's eyes staring vacantly into his own, he knew no doctor could possibly help.

The waitress continued to stand behind Bomford's chair, her face stoic and expressionless as she watched the man die. In the audience those with hi-tech cell phones were photographing the event as was a remote unit from one of the local TV stations. Two burly security officers rushed to the dais, seizing the waitress who made no effort to resist. To the contrary, she raised one hand above her head and made an odd little wave to the crowd as she was being lead away.

Paul eased off the gas as he entered Bergensberg. The speed limit sank from 50 mph to 25 in a matter of feet. To Paul's right, a few yards off the road was the hulk of an abandoned vegetable stand. Excellent cover for a patrolman looking to nab unsuspecting speeders and swell the coffers of the town treasury. God knows, it probably needed swelling. Sure enough, a blue and white with a fancy light bar on its roof was lurking in the shadows.

He pulled up in front of the antiques store. A sign on the door read CLOSED which was odd. One forty-five on a Saturday afternoon. Tourists should be abounding and in fact, Bergensberg seemed more crowded than the day before. He got out of the car, peered through the front window. No lights, no signs of life. He turned, pondering his next move, when he spotted Rose Temple exiting the bank a few doors up the street and then climbing in behind the wheel of her car. She looked harried as she yanked her car door shut and pulled into traffic, heading north out of town.

Paul quickly returned to the Toyota and began to follow her.

County Road 47 consisted of two lanes in hilly terrain. It was hardly a venue for through traffic and Paul was having trouble keeping her in sight without making himself obvious. Twice Rose came upon a slow-moving farm vehicle and twice she wheeled around them at a high speed, crossing a double line, with little or no regard for her own safety. Paul played it more cautiously and he almost lost her.

He sped forward around a turn, didn't see her, then glanced back over his right shoulder. She had turned onto a dirt driveway and was kicking up tiny rocks and debris racing toward a small white clapboard house that sat about a hundred yards off the road. He wheeled around, then paused at the head of the driveway, watching as she hurried onto the rickety porch and through the front door.

He turned in toward the house, pulled up behind her weather-beaten sedan, and exited the Toyota. Whatever Rose Temple was up to she planned to be quick about it. Most likely she'd decided to run, he thought.. She wouldn't succeed. The FBI cast too wide a net for her to escape. Her only chance, as Paul saw it, was to get her story out before the Briggs dragged her into the dark maw of federal custody.

He knocked on the door No response. He knocked again. Continued silence. "Miss Temple," he called out. "Please open the door. It's important that speak to you." And still no answer. He tried again. "Miss Temple, I have no intention of hurting you but we must talk. If you don't answer this door, I'm going to lift the hood of your car and remove the distributor. Do you know what the distributor is, Miss Temple? It makes the car go."

He waited. After a moment, the door opened. She looked at him without expression. "Tell me, Mr. Castle, are you here to purchase the Jersey thirty shilling or should we save that for another day?"

"Look, I'm sorry, I really am—"

"I saw the broadcast on CNN this morning," she said coldly. "I hadn't realized you were such a celebrity."

He shifted his weight uncomfortably. "May I come in?"

"No." She started to close the door, clumsily. Paul wondered if she'd been drinking again.

"I could have given you up this morning. I didn't."

"And should I be grateful?"

"I bought you some time. That's something you don't have a lot of." She hesitated, then opened the door to admit him. The front door opened immediately into the small living room which was furnished with older pieces, perhaps items the store had been unable to move. To the right was the door to the kitchen, to the left a closed door apparently leading to a bedroom. An open door to a second bedroom revealed Anna Marie clearing out a dresser drawer. He took this all in at a glance, then his eyes fell on two leather suitcases standing off in a corner.

"Packed and ready to go, I see," Paul said.

"A short vacation. Three or four days."

"I'm sure," Paul said, buying none of it. "What happened in that hotel room that night, Miss Temple?"

"I don't know what you think—" He interrupted her sharply.

"You know what I think! I think you killed a man for reasons only you can tell me and if you don't tell me, you'll be telling the authorities."

"I wasn't there—"

"You were there. The police have found at least three people who can put you at Deveraux's exhibit on the arm of Congressman Johansson. A chambermaid can put you in the hotel and the medical examiner has identified not only the needle mark but the name of the poison you used." He nodded toward the suitcases. "If you think you can run, think again. You'll be in custody inside of twenty-four hours and a jail cell is not where you want to spend the next few weeks, let alone the rest of your life."

Fear welled up in her eyes. "I can't go to jail."

"Then let me help you," he said.

"You can't." She shook her head nervously, from side to side, looked back into the open doorway toward her mother. "Mom!," she called out. The older woman looked back at her. "I warned you," she said quietly.

Paul pressed her hard. "About what? Warned you about what? Look, Miss Temple, you've got only one way to protect yourself now. Tell me what's going on? What's your connection with Leonard Philby?"

She looked at him blankly. "Who?"

"Leonard Philby and the trucker from New York, Donald Chaffee."

"I don't know what you're talking about."

He was fast losing patience. "Please—"

She shook her head violently. "Whoever those men are, I do not know them!"

"They killed two congressmen," Paul said. "You killed a third."

"Oh, God," she said, turning away. Her face was starting to twitch.

He moved to her, taking her gently by the shoulders." Who are they, Rose?" he asked her gently. "You must know them."

"No," she said. Then: "No one knows."

"No one knows what?"

She could only shake her head. She looked at him, then past him through the front window, out toward the driveway. Her eyes widened in sudden panic. Paul turned his head. A dark sedan followed by three State Police cruisers was speeding down the driveway. Rose backed away, turned toward her mother. "Mama!!!" she cried out.

Anna Marie came out of the bedroom The cars had skidded to a stop on the loose dirt and gravel. Fowler Briggs was bounding up onto the porch followed by his partner and three state troopers. Two other staties hung back by the cars. Both had drawn their weapons.

"Rose, it's okay. I can talk to them." Paul said.

She backed away like a wounded animal. "No talk, not now." she said. "Too late."

He reached for her. She wriggled from his grasp and clumsily fell to the floor. She struggled to her feet and stumbled toward the kitchen. He chased after her. She reached up, opened a wooden cabinet door and took down a small white box. Her right hand was shaking violently as she struggled to rip it open. Paul grabbed for her arm. She slipped his grasp.

Briggs was pounding loudly on the front door. "FBI. Open the door, ma'am!" he shouted.

Rose looked past Paul to her mother who was standing in the kitchen doorway. "Mama!" she shreiked once more. "I love you! It's not your fault!" The older woman met her eyes, then nodded almost imperceptibly. Rose tore open the box and managed to remove a single gel capsule. She jammed it into her mouth and crunched down on it just as the crash of splintering wood told Paul that Briggs had smashed through the front door.

As the FBI man dashed into the kitchen, Rose crumpled to the floor, splaying uncontrollably like a rag doll. Paul tried to kneel beside her but rough hands yanked him away. Briggs knelt down, putting his ear to her chest, listening intently, then began administering CPR.

Paul looked down at the sad, nearly lifeless face of Rose Temple, then at Briggs. "You son of a bitch," he said. "You miserable son of a bitch."

If Briggs had heard him, he gave no sign.

The House Majority Leader was settled comfortably in a padded leather chair, sitting across from his inquisitor, Seth Baxendale, news anchor for one of the major television networks. Francis X. Mackey, D-Rhode Island, was a portly man who had lived the good life for many years, starting about the time he had first been elected to the House eight terms ago. He reached for the logo-ed coffee mug, subtly hawking this particular afternoon news program, and sipped down a healthy swig of coffee that had been laced with Tia Maria. Those Mexxies, he thought, they weren't good for much but they sure did know how to make booze.

Baxendale was saying: "Then, Congressman Mackey, if I read you correctly, you're saying that you have enough votes to pass the House version of the Universal Health Care proposal."

"Not a problem, Seth, and let me add that there will be no delays. The man in the White House wants this done immediately and I quite agree. The longer we wait, the more at risk we place the American people. We can no longer afford this crisis in our health care system."

Baxendale smiled disarmingly. "May I remind you, sir, that a House bill very similar to the one you are now proposing was brought up last year in the President's first year and, forgive me, soundly defeated."

"A different time, a different bill," Mackey harrumphed.

"All the same," Baxendale pressed him, "many people will say that we cannot afford the monumental cost of this legislation."

"Not true," the Senator said. "What with savings from the abolishment of medicare and an increase in efficiency, the cost to the taxpayer should be negligible."

"The Congressional Budget Office apparently disagrees with that assessment, Senator."

"The CBO has no idea what is in the bill," Mackey bristled.

"Nor does anyone else, sir. But our sources have told us, above and beyond the projected cost, that there are key provisions for the rationing of care, particularly as it affects the elderly."

"Not true," Mackey said flatly, his irritation becoming more apparent. "Yes, there are certain limitations on procedures, the sort of common sense safeguards that even the private sector would have to enforce. For example, say a man or woman in their 70's might live a few years longer with a heart transplant. Perhaps so, but assuming these people have lived full rich lives, would that really be the best use of our resources? I think not."

Baxendale nodded. "Then I assume this philosophy would extend beyond something dramatic like a transplant. Restrictions might also be placed on expensive testing procedures like MRIs."

"Only in the interest of fairness. Can we be realistic for a moment? Our medical system is so advanced that people are living well beyond the span that might have been expected even twenty years ago. For the most part these people stopped working, stopped contributing to the general welfare years ago. I don't mean to sound callous but, yes, in some cases hard choices will have to be made."

"In other words," the newsman said, "as ex-Colorado Governor Lamb once put it, old people have a duty to die."

Mackey said,"I wouldn't phrase it that way." He took another swallow of his booze-laced coffee, wondering how long he was going to have to put up with this nosy asshole. As recently as a month ago, this jerk was kissing his ass for an interview. Hell, he'd always been a reliable cheerleader for the Party and now, what? The guy suddenly thinks he's a newsman? And a stupid one at that. Didn't he know that old people tended to vote for old ways. Young people, with stars in their eyes and their hearts on their sleeves, voted for the new and for all intents and purposes the Party had the young people sewed up, And of course, there was always that pool of true believers or, as they liked to call them in the White House, the "useful idiots." And most obviously there were the blacks, with no place else to go. It was an awesome coalition and once the country was locked into this new direction, there was no limit to what it could accomplish. And Francis X. Mackey, he was proud to say, would be right there to share in the spoils.

Hundreds of miles away, in a six bedrooom, six bath colonial style residence situated on six acres overlooking Massachusetts Bay, a tall spare man of 88 years with handsome chiseled features and a full head of snow white hair was watching Mackey's performance with interest, if not approval. He moved to a nearby desk and dialed a number.

"Have you been watching?" he asked. As he talked, he fingered a worn gold wedding band that he wore on a chain around his neck." Yes, I think something had better be done." Another pause. "Yes, I agree, and the sooner the better. Get someone on it now." The man frowned in annoyance. "I know we had it planned for later this week but this idiot has to be dealt with now. Get one of those people lined up and let's get it done." Angrily, the man replaced the receiver, then lifted the remote and with a click, obliterated the image of House Majority Leader Francis X. Mackey, D-Rhode Island.

CHAPTER NINE

Paul was seated in the waiting room of the small county hospital, his left wrist handcuffed to the arm of an uncomfortable wooden bench. The facility was crowded with people, official and otherwise. Rose Temple was dead. She'd expired in the ambulance despite the heroic efforts of a team of EMTs. She's dead because of me, Paul thought. I should have been more careful. He winced as he remembered the smug smile on Briggs' face as he'd retreived the homing device from under the collar of Paul's jacket. The agent had placed it there when he'd clapped him on the shoulder at the outdoor coffee cafe. For all his supposed cleverness in switching cars, Paul never had a chance. He was an amateur playing a professional's game.

He stared across the room at Anna Marie who was speaking quietly and intently with an older white-haired gentleman in a three-piece suit. Someone had called him 'Doctor' but he didn't seem to be staff. The Temple family physician maybe. He seemed possessed of a small town bedside manner, the kind you didn't see much of any more. He was holding Anna Marie's hand in consolation, and yet, if Rose's mother was feeling grief, she gave no sign. There were no tears, just that same look of blank stocism he'd witnessed back at the house. Rose had called out to her tearfully at her moment of greatest terror and Anna Marie had nodded, almost as if giving permission for the self-destructive act that was to follow. What kind of mother was capable of that, Paul wondered.

Nearby, a television set was tuned to a local station that had broken into its regular broadcasting to report the death of House Speaker Harry Bomford. The sound was muted but the streamer said it all. The tape of his death recorded by the local Chicago station was apparently being shown everywhere. Paul felt his stomach tighten and he shivered reflexively from a sudden chill. His Pulitzer Prize story, like a gulf hurricane, had suddenly gathered immense force, spinning out of his control. One after another, someone or some group was systematically killing off members of Congress and the killings had to be connected. And yet as he remembered Rose's denial, he knew she was telling the truth about Philby and Chaffee. There was no connection, at least not one that was obvious. On screen, the Chicago waitress was being led away by security, waving awkwardly toward the camera.

"What's that supposed to mean?"

Paul looked up. An orderly was standing beside him staring at the television.

"Did you say something?"

The orderly, whose name was Buford according to his name tag, nodded. "Just trying to figure out what that woman's trying to say."

"What are you talking about?"

"She's signing, man. You know, like for deaf people. I know 'cause I studied it for a year. Figured it might come in handy some day."

Paul looked back at the screen. "What's she saying?"

Buford shrugged. "She ain't sayin' nothin'. S-S-T. That's all." He mimicked her with his right hand. "S-S-T. Don't seem to make much sense."

Just then a crotchety nurse came by and took him by the arm. "Need a cleanup in number four, Buford. Let's go."

He protested. "C'mon, I'm off in twenty minutes."

"Right, but for twenty more minutes, young man, you belong to me. Move it." With a last puzzled look at the television, the orderly followed her out of the waiting room.

Paul looked back at the television screen. Two split-screen talking heads were now blathering to one another, undoubtedly no more informed than he was. S-S-T. The storm was growing .

Briggs waded into the room followed by three of his minions." I want that house tossed from top to bottom. "He gestured toward Anna Marie." Get permission. If she won't give it, toss it anyway. I'll have one of staties get us a warrant. Where's that damned chopper?"

McIlroy checked his watch. "Should be here in about fifteen minutes."

Briggs nodded. "Who's on board?"

"Jameson, Olivet and a local guy. I don't know him."

"Put Jameson on phone records. Olivet can handle the bank."

McIlroy hesitated. "It's Saturday, Fowler."

"I don't care if it's the fucking Fourth of July. I want everything on my desk by eight o'clock tonight. Put Reese in charge to coordinate. We're going back on the chopper and we're taking him with us." He nodded his head in Paul's direction.

"Excuse me," Paul piped up, "but I'd like to contact my office and I believe I'm entitled to a phone call."

Briggs whirled on him angrily. "You're entitled to nothing, Mr. Castle, except maybe a lengthy stretch in a federal prison."

"On what charge?"

"For starters, obstructing an official investigation," Briggs said.

"I'm still entitled—"

"Shut up, mister. Just shut up. Have you bothered to read The Public Safety Act of 2009? Hell, I don't even have to feed you. Now sit there, keep your mouth shut and pray I don't get more pissed off than I already am."

With that Briggs and the others left the room. Paul looked up at the clock on the wall. Nearly two o'clock. Kovacs might be wondering where he was, might phone him. And then he remembered, his cell phone had been confiscated. He felt alone, isolated. He thought of Franz Kafka. The weird little Czech from Prague would have reveled in this misery. "Excuse me. Mr. Castle?" Paul looked up. The white-haired doctor who had been consoling Anna Marie Temple was hovering over him.

"Sorry for the intrusion," he said. "Grayden Walsh." He put out his hand. Paul shook it.

"That would be DOCTOR Walsh?" Paul presumed.

Walsh smiled. "It would." He looked toward the doorway where Briggs had just exited. "You seem to be in a bind. Is there anything I can do?"

"You can, thanks. Call my office, ask for Fritz Schoenfeld."

"Just a minute, let me write this down." He took a small note pad from his pocket. Paul repeated the name, gave him the phone number.

"They'll be taking me to FBI headquarters, 26 Federal Plaza. I'll be there by 3:30. If he could have a lawyer meet me there—"

Walsh nodded. "I'll call right away. Anything else?"

"I borrowed a friend's car. It's sitting in the Temple's driveway."

Walsh smiled sympathetically. "That's inconvenient."

"There's an orderly here named Buford. He gets off work in a few minutes. There's five hundred dollars in it for him if he'll drive the car back to New York. Five hundred and plane fare back."

"I'll pass along the proposal," Walsh said.

Paul gave him the station address and Murray's name.

Dr. Walsh put away the pad and sat down next to Paul. "It's not your fault, you know. Rose's death."

Paul shook his head in disagreement. "I led them to her."

"They would have found her sooner or later," Walsh said. "What she did she did of her own volition."

"But why?" Paul asked.

"I know she was terrified of jail, but to kill herself like that, she must have had other choices."

"Perhaps she didn't think so." Paul glanced across the room at Anna Marie who was leafing through a magazine. "Another thing," he said. "I don't get her. That's a cold, cold woman. It's as if she didn't care."

Walsh looked toward the older woman sadly. "She cares deeply, Mr. Castle, but she's not one to display her emotions."

"No, its not just that, it's something else. Something she's got hidden away."

"I've known Anna Marie for almost thirty years. She lost her parents at Dachau, her only son in Viet Nam. And yes, you're right about one thing, she lives within an impenetrable shell. I tried to give her comfort but I was only going through the motions. She's a good woman, but damaged, Mr. Castle. Badly damaged."

"How's her health?" Paul asked.

Walsh shook his head. "You know I can't discuss that. She's a patient."

"Someone told me that Rose moved back to Bergensberg about eight months ago to take care of her."

Walsh considered that for a moment. "Whoever told you that was wrong."

Paul smiled "You wouldn't lie to me, would you, Doc?"

Before Walsh could respond two state troopers entered the room. The burlier of the two unlocked Paul's cuffs. "Chopper's here," he said.

As he was being led out, Paul turned to Doctor Walsh. "You won't forget."

Walsh patted the pocket into which he'd placed the notepad. He smiled reassuringly. "I won't forget."

Within three hours of the death of Speaker Bomford, the American political landscape changed dramatically. Under the direction of the Department of Homeland Security, armed personnel were assigned to protect every member of Congress including members of the Senate. The FBI and Secret Service were stretched to the limit; city and state police were commandeered to fill in where needed. Protection for the President doubled around the clock; his public appearances were cut to the minimum.

In the offices and corridors of the country's major media outlets, one thing was thought certain. The people behind the rash of assassinations were unquestionably right wing zealots. There could be no other explanation. Special reports on the crisis flooded the airwaves, pushing regular programming off the air. Bloggers of every description were waxing hysterical. Newspapers, caught between editions, tried to play catchup on their web sites, but the truth was, for all their so-called journalistic prowess, the print media as well as electronic were clueless. No one knew who or why and certainly not when. None of this, however, seemed to deter the familiar media experts from chewing up airtime with ill-informed analysis, backed up by a total absence of facts. The speculation centered mainly on the politics of the four victims. All were rabid socialists. All had been elected from safe districts, sure to return them to Congress for years, if they so chose. All were also powerful committee chairmen whose influence on the country spread far beyond the confines of their own particular districts. It was not beyond the pale of reason to suspect that the culprits were God and his Bible-thumping bigoted emissaries on earth. Wild accusations and unbridled conspiracy theories choked the airwaves, but the truth was, no one had a clue.

That was particularly true of the man who stood by a large window in his richly furnished office, looking out over the city that had been his home, personally and professionally, for the better part of forty-two years. Levi Zwick, the present day successor to J. Edgar Hoover, was both angry and frustrated. He'd written off the attempt on Congressman Villanueva as an isolated incident and taking his cue from the Attorney-General, had managed to smooth over the attempted murder. He wasn't quite sure why but he was aware the DNC had put pressure on the President who in turn squeezed the AG. Elections were on the horizon. The attempt on Villanueva's life could only be a negative in the upcoming campaign. It was politics as usual. He'd learned not to question it. But when Congressman Tolliver was gunned down in the local restaurant, Zwick sensed immediately that these were not unrelated incidents. The full force of the Bureau was brought to bear on any possible connection between the housekeeper Zalesko and the industrialist Philby. Two days of intense sifting through bank records and phone logs netted nothing. The same for interviews with neighbors and co-workers. Then came the killing of Congressman Johansson in New York City and the brutal murder days later of Congresswoman McCormack a short distance from her home in Rutland. Efforts were redoubled. The agents assigned worked diligently. They, too, came up with nothing. No contacts of any sort, by phone or by computer. The perpetrators were all separate entities, seemingly having nothing to do with one another. And yet, members of Congress were being systematically liquidated by apparent strangers, all law abiding citizens without criminal records, not the sort who would engage in political assassination. Elsa Galesko, widowed, no children. Leonard Philby, also widowed, sole owner of a small manufacturing plant in upstate California, father to four sons. Donald Chaffee, age 63. Self-employed trucker. Married to his high school sweetheart. Three children. All successful, all living in other states. And now Rose Temple. Pertinent data to come but Zwick was sure the pattern would hold. A nobody from small town America with no criminal record, no past to hide, no overseas bank accounts stuffed with illgotten money, and most puzzling of all, no contacts or connection with the other three. As for the waitress at the Chicago luncheon, to date they knew only her name.

The intercom buzzed and his secretary's voice came over the speaker box." The Attorney General is on line one, sir," she said.

Zwick stared at the phone, then reluctantly went to the desk and picked up the receiver.

Meanwhile, across the country, the number of hits on the tiny Houston website known as SST had expanded a hundred fold. Still a miniscule amount by internet standards. The graphics had remained basically the same but the message had morphed into something more specific:"Men and Women of Common Sense and Good Will Can Restore Our Freedom. It is Not Too Late. Act Now."

On orders from the Director, an agent of Homeland Security had tried to contact the website. He was totally unsuccessful. Five hackers based in different parts of the country and acting independently of one another tried to trace the ownership of SST. One thought it was based in France. Two others were sure it linked through a small country in Africa. A fourth was convinced it was a front for the current administration, operating in some sort of perverse reverse logic which he couldn't explain. The fifth had no clue.

The powerful black government helicopter swooped down over the city, hovered momentarily and then descended onto the heliport at West 30th Street. On the street below an unmarked car of approximately the same color was parked at curbside in a loading-only zone. On orders from higher up, uniformed policemen on traffic duty stayed clear. Paul, flanked by Briggs and McIlroy and a third agent, was hustled into an elevator. At ground level, helplessly cuffed, he was shoved out the entrance and into the waiting car which pulled into traffic. At the corner, it turned left and headed north on the Avenue of the Americas. To reach FBI headquarters, the driver should have turned south.

"Excuse me, but we seem to be going in the wrong direction," Paul said. No one responded. "You do know FBI headquarters is the other way." From his seat by a rear window, Paul looked into the rearview mirror which framed Briggs' eyes staring at him icily. Briggs looked away, saying nothing.

The car proceeded north to 57th Street, turned east, then swung north again on Madison Avenue. It was late afternoon now. The movers and shakers of New York City were starting to pour out of the office buildings, heading for their homes. Tourists, most of them from overseas taking advantage of the anemic Yankee dollar, were strolling along the outskirts of the park, sampling chili dogs and stocking up on miniature Statues of Liberty to take home to relatives. Hunter College loomed up on their right and a block later the car turned east onto 70th Street headed toward New York Presbyterian Hospital. They crossed Second Avenue, then First. Just before reaching the cluster of hospital buildings, the car turned into an undergound parking area that serviced an overhead structure identified only as "Medical Clinic."

The driver pulled into a reserved spot near a stairway door. The agents got out, opened the rear door and half dragged Paul to the doorway. They went inside, hurried down a dimly lit staircase until they reached a door which was marked "Entry Prohibited." Briggs pushed a button next to the door handle. Faintly a bell could be heard ringing from within. A moment later a panel in the door slid open and a woman peered out. The panel slid closed and the door opened. The woman stepped aside as Briggs entered without acknowledging her. McIlroy had Paul by the elbow. They moved quickly down a corridor, then through a set of double doors that opened into a large, sterile-looking room. It could, in fact, have been a medical clinic except there was no receptionist, no patients and apparently no doctors. Three hospital beds were positioned against a far wall separated by curtains. In another corner of the room were several pieces of medical equipment including x-ray machines and an MRI. Nearby was a glass enclosed cabinet displaying drugs of every sort imaginable.

McIlroy pushed Paul down into a chair near the center of the room and removed the handcuffs, then his jacket. Gratefully, he massaged his wrists which had grown numb over the course of the trip from the hospital. He had no idea where he was and if he had any notions about why he had been brought here, he tried to ignore them. He knew nothing pleasant was going to come of this. He thought about Fritz and a lawyer waiting vainly for him at FBI headquarters. He belonged to Briggs now and he dreaded what might be in store for him. Had this been two or three years ago, he would not have been so fearful, but much had changed since the election sixteen months ago. Freedoms once taken for granted had been buried under an avalanche of new laws and regulations, implemented quickly and with little thought. Paul had heard the stories of lost liberties, hinted at, rumored. Water cooler speculation. Like most Americans he'd sloughed them off as aberrations, glitches in an imperfect system. Certainly no one could believe that such affronts to the Constitution were orchestrated. But were they? He'd never been political and basically had no use for politicians of either party unless he could exploit their bizarre escapades for a juicy story. Decades ago, in a land that perhaps never was, citizen-legislators were selfless patriots who put country ahead of all else, but not today. With some exceptions the average Congressman was an egotistical, self-serving idealogue who put nothing ahead of his or her own avarice and ambition. Were these the people who were going to save the nation from the strangling grasp of Socialism? Paul doubted it and now as he sat in the chilly silence of the cheerless room, alone and vulnerable, he knew what it was like to be afraid.

The sliding doors opened again and a balding man in a white lab coat entered, giving Paul a passing glance. Briggs moved to him and for several minutes they conversed quietly. At one point one of the agents appeared from an adjoining room and handed Briggs a slim manila file folder containing a sheaf of papers. He perused it as he continued talking to the white-jacketed man. Finally Briggs nodded and as the man moved to busy himself at the drug cabinet, Briggs grabbed a nearby chair and swung it around so he could sit straddling it, facing Paul.

Briggs opened the folder, again studied the contents. Finally he looked up. "Mr. Castle," he said, "I am going to ask you one final time. What do you know about this rash of politically motivated homicides?"

"Nothing," Paul replied. "Not a thing."

Briggs nodded thoughtfully, as if to himself. After a moment, he continued "You knew the identity of a woman who murdered a United States Congressman. You refused to divulge her identity to lawful authorities. Not only did you refuse to cooperate, you deceived me and attempted to contact this woman without my knowledge. When I caught up with you. you were on the scene when the woman took poison to avoid capture. That says to me, Mr. Castle, that you know a great deal and before you leave this room, you are going to tell me what that is."

Paul responded firmly, trying to keep the anger out of his voice. "I told you, I was working on a story. That's all she was, a story. Just a lousy sex scandal or at least that's the way it started out."

"Until you found out from Jennifer Bovano of the District Attorney's office that Johansson's death was murder," Briggs said.

Paul looked at him sharply.

"Yes, we know all about your relationship with Miss Bovano dating back to your employmentat the Baltimore Sun. So, Mr. Castle, you discover murder is involved, and then what?"

"Then I've got a bigger story. A major story, Agent Briggs. A career maker and I'm not about to let it go."

"Go on."

"I had learned from one of the Congressman's friends in New Jersey that he'd been in NewYork that night to attend an exhibit of antiquities. Old coins, paper currency. That sort of thing. He was a collector. I checked the back issues of the Times, found the event, learned from the owner that Johansson had hooked up with the woman seen running from the hotel. When our station offered the reward for information, I received a call from a man who lived in Bergensberg who knew her. I drove up there, met her, we chatted, I satisfied myself that she was the woman in green and came back to New York to figure out the next step."

Briggs eyed him coldly. "And it never occured to you to turn this information over to the authorities."

Paul snapped, "I was working with the authorities. Lt. Kovacs. He was heading up the homicide investigation. What I knew, he knew."

"But you withheld her identity from me."

Paul hesitated. "Yes."

"Because?"

"Because I didn't want you trampling all over my story."

"Which you put ahead of the safety and security of this country."

"I wouldn't put it that way, "Paul said.

"I would," Briggs replied. Paul fell silent. The agent referred to the file folder. "You father's name is Victor. He operates a taxi service in Queens."

Paul frowned warily. "What's he got to do with this?"

"Mother's name Deanna. A sister named Teresa, a brother named Ernest."

"They are not involved with this, "Paul said angrily.

"We'll see, won't we?" Briggs smiled.

Paul stared at him, trying to make sense of it. "Why are you doing this to me?"he said.

"Because I don't believe you, Mr. Castle. Do you grasp that? I believe you are a liar, that you are hiding something." A quick glance at the folder. "Did you know that your brother was a member of the Atlanta Conservative Association—"

"No, but—"

"—and that he was arrested two years ago for disturbing the peace outside a polling place."

"Ernie's very active—"

"I'm sure he is. The Atlanta office is questioning him now about his ties to several political organizations."

"Damn it, I told you, he's got nothing to do with this!"

Briggs ignored him, glancing again at the file folder." Your sister was arrested twice for shoplifting—"

"Wait a minute, Those were juvenile offenses. The records were sealed—"

"Do you know the name Louis Marchetti?" Briggs asked.

Paul shook his head.

"Did you know that he owns a 33% interest in your father's business?"

"That's not true—"

"Did you know that twenty years ago, your father remortgaged the family home so he could pay off a $75,000 loan to Mr. Marchetti?"

"No, I would have—"

Briggs overrode him. "It aggravates me no end, Mr. Castle, when people like you assume that people like me are either stupid or ill-informed."

"I've never thought that."

Briggs exploded. "No? Then tell me how and when you and Rose Temple first met, how you were able to secretly communicate, and what you know about Leonard Philby and Donald Chaffee." The FBI man leaned forward. "Tell me now. Tell me everything. Don't make me take this another step further."

Paul shook his head." I've told you the truth. I've told you everything I know."

Briggs hesitated. Then: "Very well." He turned and nodded to the agent who was standing directly behind Paul's chair. The man grabbed Paul under the arms and lifted him. A second agent moved in to assist. They dragged him kicking and squirming to one of the three hospital beds, pinned him down and strapped him in with heavy leather belts.

"You son of a bitch! You can't do this!"

The white jacketed man approached carrying a hypodermic needle while one of the agents rolled up Paul's shirt sleeve. He pressed against the restraints vainly as sweat poured from his hairline. He tried to catch his breath, gasping for air. The agent was holding his arm rigid now as the man with the needle probed for a vein.

Across the room, a phone rang. The woman who admitted them answered it, then signalled to Briggs, holding out the receiver. She mouthed the words 'The Director.' Irritably Briggs took the phone from her. Paul was too busy struggling to note that the conversation was one-sided with Briggs doing most of the listening. After a moment or two he handed the phone back to the woman and turned toward the bed.

"That's enough!" he called out.

The other men backed away as Briggs strode to the bedside and stared down at the quivering Paul. "You have friends more powerful than perhaps you realize, Mr. Castle." He smiled icily." We'll just postpone this until some future date."

CHAPTER TEN

The room was bright, blindingly so. He tried to close his eyes but he couldn't. Strong arms were clamped on his arms and legs and he felt himself being carried. He struggled helplessly. A familiar voice rasped in his ear. "Son of a bitch. I'll show you who's a son of a bitch." He tried to turn his head, caught a fleeting glimpse of Fowler Briggs' bald brown head. Then suddenly he was crashing through a set of double doors onto a balcony. The blinding light vanished as he looked up into a grey-black sky, roiling with ominous rainclouds. Moisture pelted his face. A shard of lightning stabbed through the sky and he could see he was high up over the city. The rough hands that held him raced him toward the balcony railing, righted him, pushed him forward until he was staring into an abyss a hundred stories below to a rain-soaked street. "No," he screamed, "please don't kill me!"

Briggs smiled at him broadly. "You will die, you son of a bitch. You will die today. You will die now!" The hands shoved forward, letting go. He felt himself plunging downward. From far away he heard a soft ringing. Over and over. Unceasing.

Paul rolled over in the bed. He was no longer plummeting toward certain death. His body was soaked in sweat. Groggily, he tossed the bedcovers aside. He was wearing only his skivvies and a teeshirt.

The room he was in was darkened. The shades had been lowered but he could see sunlight peering in from the edges of the window frame. He looked around. The room was unfamiliar. Meanwhile, the ringing had stopped. He heard a muted voice coming from an adjoining room.

He got to his feet unsteadily. His head was pounding, and his mouth was dry. If he didn't know better, he'd say he was suffering from a hangover but that couldn't be. Or could it? Across the room he saw the open door to a bathroom. He went in, turned on the tap and sloshed cold water on his face. He remembered that bright, sterile clinic and Briggs and then, then he was at FBI headquarters, being met by Jennie and Fritz Schoenfeld and another man. A lawyer? Yes, that's who he was. Within minutes he was free of the place out on the street with Jennie. Where was the Old Man? That's right. He'd wanted Paul back at the studio, to do an on-air report of his ordeal. Paul had refused. The Old Man had gotten angry. "If it wasn't for the fact that the Attorney General and I go back forty years to a North-South bowl game, you'd still be locked up." Paul was grateful but adamant. He wanted to be left alone. "You still work for me," Schoenfeld had said. To hell with the job, Paul had told him and to hell with you, as he'd walked away. So he was now unemployed. So what?

He strained to remember. He'd gone somewhere. He and Jennie. Somewhere. It was all a blank.

He moved to the bedroom door, opened it, stepped out into a hallway. The muted voice was louder now. Jennie. She was talking on the phone. He moved down the corridor into the living room. She was curled up on a sofa, cell phone in hand, talking intently. The television set was on, the volume muted. Jennie looked up and saw him, said a quick goodbye and broke the connection.

"Good afternoon, stranger." she smiled.

Paul frowned. "Afternoon?"

She glanced at her watch. “Seventeen hours. Obviously you needed the rest.”

“Looks that way,” he said. He spotted a bottle of water on the coffee table. “You mind?”

“Help yourself.”

He took three deep swallows, then sat on the arm of the sofa “I don’t remember much.”

“I’m not surprised,” she said. “After we ditched your boss and the lawyer, we headed for the nearest bar. Well, you did. I tagged along so you wouldn’t ditch me, too.”

“I drank.”

She laughed, highly amused. “Oh, yes.” Then more seriously: “From what you told me, I think you had good reason.”

He shrugged. “Well, there goes my five year chip.”

“Oh. Sorry. I didn’ t know.”

He nodded, then looked at the television screen. “What’s the latest?”

Her face darkened. “Do you really want to know?”

“What?”

“Three more.”

He looked at her in disbelief. “Three?”

“Whatever it is,” she said, “it’s escalating.”

She filled him in quickly. A Congressman from Oregon and a Congress-woman from Ohio. Both had traveled back home over the weekend. Both had been making political appearances, one at a shopping center opening, the other at a testimonial for a Bnai Brith contributor. The Secret Service has always maintained that if an assassin is willing to lose his own life, it is almost impossible to stop a bold public attempt. Such was the case in both instances. Although accompanied by security people, both politicians insisted in mingling with their constituents. The two assassins carried small caliber automatics loaded with hollow-point ammunition. Both were arrested on the spot. Neither had anything to say. The Congressman from Oregon, Randall Ames, was a Democrat and a self-identified Marxist and had been representing his district for seventeen years. He had become embroiled in party politics immediately upon leaving Gonzaga University, first as an organizer, then a fundraiser, then a successful candidate for mayor of his home town and finally, the big prize, the seat in Congress. His district was 66% Democrat and the chances of unseating him had been nil. He had clung to his seat for the better part of two decades because he liked getting rich, he liked the feeling of power, and perhaps most importantly, he knew were he to lose an election, he had absolutely no way to make a living. The same, sad to say, could be said about scores of his peers. The Congresswoman from Ohio, Mary Mae Thatcher, was a Republican who had served her district for twenty five years and had hoped to serve it for twenty-five more. She was a spinster of questionable sexual orientation who loved to see her name in print or, preferably, carved in granite. Among her achievments, the Mary Mae Thatcher Bridge connecting one town of 210 people to another town of 86, the Mary Mae Thatcher Research Center for Plant Disease, the Mary Mae Thatcher Museum of Native American Culture and so on and so on. Ninety six edifices in all which over the years had cost the taxpayers something like ten billion dollars. Also located in Mary Mae's district was a giant aircraft manufacturer who, through her efforts, had been snagging lucrative defense contracts for years. Six months ago, she managed to ram through a bill requiring the Defense Department to purchase thirty-six experimental fighter planes with enough bugs in them to populate a Philadelphia slum, The Air Force didn't like them, didn't want them and if pressed to the wall, wouldn't fly them but to Mary Mae, that was irrelevant. She was saving thousands of jobs (and ensuring thousands of votes). Her district was 59% Republican and showed no signs of changing. She, too, had no observable skills outside of politics.

The third victim was Oscar Kurkow from Virginia who chaired a key subcommittee with oversight of the nation's Medicare program. He had been out on his small cabin cruiser, powering along the Severn River when he was hailed by his close friend and neighbor, Jack McGreavy, a spry octogenarian who was out in his skiff trolling for rockfish. As McGreavy approached, Kurkow's security people moved to the cruiser railing warily, but the congressman allayed their fears. He and McGreavy had known each other for years. As the skiff pulled alongside, McGreavy calmly put down his fishing rod, picked up a shotgun and blew a six inch wide hole in Kurkow's belly. One of the security people, a local part-time traffic officer, was so incensed that he took out his weapon and blew a two-inch wide hole in the middle of McGreavy's forehead. If there had been an questions to be asked of him, they would remain unanswered.

Paul made an instinctive move to reach for his phone, then realized how he was dressed, or more properly, undressed.

"Thanks for putting me to bed," he said.

She smiled. "I would have joined you but you were in no condition."

He laughed, snapping his fingers in mock frustration. "Just my luck." Then: "Did I get any calls?"

"I turned off your cell phone. It's in your jacket pocket. Clothes are in the closet." She pointed toward the bedroom.

"I don't feel hungry but maybe I should eat, "he said. "Someplace close by?"

"Sure," she said. "My kitchen."

"You don't cook," he said incredulously.

"Is that a question or a statement?"

"Not sure."

"I make a mean cheese omelet, I can toss a helluva salad, and my french fries turn out golden brown and crispy, just like McDonald's."

"Sold," he said. Then, "I think I need a shower."

"I think so, too "she responded, "but out of politeness I wasn't going to say anything."

He went into the bedroom, leaving the door partly ajar and stripped down, half hoping he'd catch her peeking. No such luck. The shower was quick and though his underwear was dampish when he put them back on, he felt halfway human again. He reactivated his cell phone and punched in his brother's number in Atlanta. It rang four times before Ernie answered. "Little bro, it's Paulie."

"Hey, are you okay?" Ernie asked.

"Sure, why not?"

"The Atlanta goon squad's been telling me you're about a gnat's hair away from a thirty year stretch in Leavenworth."

"Bastards."

"My thoughts exactly," Ernie said. "You sure have raised a lot of hell, brother."

"Too damned much for my own good," Paul said. "Seriously, Ernie, are you alright?"

"Far as I know. They came to the house, asked me a lot of questions which made no sense. I answered as stupidly as I could and after a while, they got tired of asking and left."

"They may be back."

"I know that."

"Is there any way you can get in hot water?"

"Not that I know of." He paused. "Paulie, you gotta call Pop. He's been trying to reach you all day?"

"About what?"

"He wouldn't say."

"I'll call him," Paul said. "Ernie, these characters give you any more trouble, let me know. I might be able to help."

"I can handle it."

"Ciao." Disconnecting, Paul called home. His mother answered. "Paulie, where are you? We were worried."

"I'm fine, Mom. Ernie says Pop's been trying to reach me."

"We thought maybe you were hurt or something."

"Mom, I'm okay. Promise. Put Pop on the phone."

"He's not here. He had to go into the office."

Paul frowned. "On a Sunday evening?"

"I don't ask questions, Paulie." No, she didn't. She never had. Vic Castelli was the rock, the foundation on which the family was built. He was blunt and tough and honest and if you didn't like him or the way he did things, that was your problem, not his. He was a man to be respected, and in Deanna Castelli's case, a man to be loved.

He said goodbye to his mother and went into the kitchen. The eggs for the omelet were on the counter, as yet unbroken. "I need a raincheck on that." He looked at his watch. "Two hours at the most. I have to see my father."

She turned off the flame under french fries. "I'll go with you," she said.

"I'd rather go alone."

"I don't think you're fit to drive and besides it's my car. Yours is still back at the studio, remember?" She took her keys from a nearby hook and waggled them under his nose. "If you insist I'll wait in the car."

He hesitated, then nodded. "Let's go."

They were quiet as they sped crosstown and entered the Queens Midtown Tunnel at E. 42nd Street. Traffic was relatively light as they emerged onto Long Island and followed the signs to 495 East.

"So how does it feel to be unemployed?" Jennie asked, breaking the silence.

"Good, I think," Paul said.

"I don't think you meant it." she said. "Neither did your boss. I think he's heard it before."

"He has, but this time it'll stick. I'm tired, Jenn. Tired of these killings, tired of being pushed around by bullies with badges like Fowler Briggs."

"So you're backing off."

"Call it that if you want. I know I never want to be manhandled again the way I was today. There were moments when I was sure he was going to kill me."

"Why would he do that?"

"Because he can."

She glanced over at him for a fleeting second, taking her eyes off the road. "All right, maybe you had a right to be afraid," she said.

"You're damned right I did," he snapped. He looked at her. She didn't react but stared through the windshield. He looked away, out his window. It was starting to rain. Not hard. A light mist if anything but it did nothing to raise his spirits.

"So what will you do now?"

"I don't know. Find a job in some small station nestled in the Rockies. I've done it before. It's not a bad life. Better than this."

He fell silent. She said nothing.

"Exit at Woodhaven Boulevard and go south," he said finally. She nodded. "You probably think I should stay with this."

"I never said that."

"It's not my story anymore, Jenn. The world owns it, from every first year copyboy to the overpaid pundits at the Times."

"You're right."

He stared out the window and again they didn't speak except for directions. Seven minutes later, Jennie pulled her compact Nissan into the parking area outside the Grey Star Taxi company and cut the engine. The outer doors to the garage area were open. Inside two cabs were getting cleaned out and hosed down. A third had its hood up. A mechanic was checking it out. Paul looked up to the second floor. A light was burning in his father's office.

"Better stay here," he said as he got out of the car." I'll try to make it quick."

"I'm not going anywhere," she said.

Paul cut through the garage and hurried up the staircase in the rear. He knocked on the office door and entered. Vittorio looked up, forced a welcoming smile. "Paulie, I've been trying to reach you."

"I know. Ernie told me."

The old man nodded. "You talked to him. Good. They're busting his balls. Good kid like that, busting his balls'" He gestured toward the ratty chair by the desk. "Sit. Sit. You want some wine?"

Paul shook his head. Vittorio fiddled uncomfortably with the pencil in his hand. His face was drawn. Paul suspected he'd gotten a big headstart on the vino. "What is it, Pop?"

"I got troubles, Paulie. Maybe not the kind I can handle by myself," he said.

"Louis Marchetti."

"You know."

"Enough. The FBI filled me in."

Vittorio's eyes flooded with hate. "Schwartze bastard."

"Special Agent Briggs."

The old man reached into the bottom desk drawer, took out a bottle of wine and filled the empty glass sitting in front of him. "He came to see me at the house. We talked in the backyard. I didn't want your mother to hear."

"Hear what, Pop? You have to tell me. I know you borrowed money from this Marchetti guy. What else?"

Vittorio hesitated, took a sip of the wine. "Years ago. A lotta years.

Times were hard. Ernie was getting ready for college. The scholarship didn't cover enough. Not nearly enough. What could I say to him? No? I had money for your brother Paulie but not for you? I talked to Herb, we took out a loan through the company figuring to pay it back when things got better. Marchetti was a good customer, always used our limo service. He heard of my trouble, offered me money to pay off the bank so the company didn't run into credit problems. After a few months, he wanted his money back."

"With interest."

"Yeah, interest. Lots of interest. That's when I remortgaged the house, but it wasn't enough. He wanted a piece of the business.."

"How big?"

"A third. A third for him, a third for Herb, a third for me."

"And this has been going on, how long?" Paul asked.

"Do the math. Your brother's out of college thirteen years now."

"Jesus," Paul muttered under his breath. "A third, Pop? How can you make a living. The company, it's not that big, not for a three way split."

Vittorio averted his eyes, started to again fiddle with the pencil. "We get help."

"What kind of help?"

"From Marchetti. He puts cash into the business, enough so we stay afloat and make a decent income."

Paul nodded as the picture became clearer. "Dirty money in, clean money out, is that how it works, Pop?"

"Paulie, I swear to God, on the soul of my mother, I didn't know. I never would have let him near me. I was stupid, okay. Just stupid." Tears were welling up in his father's eyes. He turned away in embarrassment.

"And Briggs knows it all." Paul said.

Vittorio nodded.

"And what does he want?" Paul asked.

"He didn't say. He said you'd know."

The old man put his hands to his face, then looked up into his son's eyes. "Paulie, I'm sorry. If there's anything I can do to make this right, I'll do it. You just tell me."

Paul came around the desk, leaned down and kissed his father on the cheek." It's okay, Pop. I can fix it. You don't worry about it."

"Yeah, sure," Vittorio said. "I'll be okay." Then, half-laughing: "Don't tell your mother."

Paul smiled and walked quietly out of the office.

The trip back to Manhattan was driven in silence. When they emerged from the tunnel, Paul said, "I think you'd better take me by the studio."

"If that's what you want," she said.

He smiled ruefully. "You know what I want but tonight's not the night."

"What am I going to do with all those soggy french fries I left sitting in the pan?" she said.

"Got a dog?"

"Nope."

"Too bad."

Even though he was trying to keep it light, Jennie knew that Paul had been severely shaken by the meeting with his father. She had kept silent, leaving him to his thoughts. But she wanted him to know she was there for him, whatever the problem.

"Will I see you tomorrow?" she asked. "I'd like to."

"I don't know."

She looked away, hurt. He immediately regretted his brusqueness.

"I'm sorry. I didn't mean it that way. Look, Jenn, you gotta understand. I'm radioactive. Anybody gets near me, they're in the way. You can get hurt."

"I'll be all right," she said.

"No, you won't. Briggs—"

"Briggs has already tried," she said, cutting him off. "He called my boss at home first thing this morning, told him I was the one who leaked the information to you about the second tox panel, that you and I were lovers years back, that I was unstable and unreliable. He told Leon that I was a detriment to his department and to the investigation, that everyone would be better served if I were terminated or, at the very least, suspended."

"Doesn't miss a trick, does he?" Paul said in disgust. "I'm really sorry, Jenn."

She smiled. "Not to worry, passionate lover from years back. Leon is made of sterner stuff than I imagined. He told Briggs I was his brightest and most reliable assistant, that every one of my performance evaluations had been A+, and beyond that, I was the only female on a staff of eleven and that the last thing he needed was a gender discrimination lawsuit, not to mention an avalanche of phone calls from the ACLU and NOW."

"Good for Leon." Paul said. "I'd like to meet him."

"You will." A pause.

"You're sure you want me to drop you off at the studio?"

"Positive. But I will call you and thanks for inviting me, dinner at your place tomorrow evening will be just dandy."

She reached over and squeezed his hand. He squeezed back.

A few minutes later she dropped him off at the studio. He bypassed the offices and went straight to the garage. There'd be no one upstairs he wanted to talk to. He needed to be alone with his thoughts, to sort out his options, if, in fact, he had any. He unlocked the door to the Mustang, slid behind the wheel and tilted his head back against the headrest.

What the hell was he supposed to do, he thought. He knew nothing that Briggs didn't know though the FBI agent showed no signs of believing that. He could beg for understanding. Appeal to reason. Neither of these seemed likely to be fruitful. He could go on the attack, use his broadcast to expose the tactics used on him at the FBI safe house. But what good would it do, and in fact, it would probably cause more harm. His father's relationship with the mobster Marchetti was fact, not fiction, and Vittorio was in grave danger of being arrested and tried on money laundering charges. In truth, there really was no way Paul could protect his father if Briggs followed through and Paul had no idea how to stop him.

The dream that had awoken him earlier was still vivid in his mind and he again wondered if, deep inside, he wasn't basically a coward. He certainly had run away in fear from the threats of Mordecai Sheen seventeen years ago. Wryly, Paul considered that Sheen and Briggs had a lot in common when it came to abuse of the badge, the only apparent difference being that Briggs seemed to be a zealot in the mold of Inspector Javert while Sheen had been nothing but a nickel and dime crook.

To stay. To run. To fight. To cower. He felt like a sixteenth cousin to the Prince of Denmark. And if he ran, where to? Could he really pack it in and flee westward to bury himself in a third-rate job in a sleepy little town no one ever heard of? But as Hamlet was loath to say, Ay, there's the rub, because Fowler Briggs could and probably would find him no matter he went.

He felt the pangs of hunger, reminding him that he hadn't eaten in more than twenty-four hours. He needed food and then sleep, a deep sleep that would help him escape the mass of quandries that were assaulting his mind.

He leaned forward and started the engine

As Paul slept that night, the largely unknown Houston website known as SST was continuing to receive increased attention. As word of mouth had spread, the number of hits per hour had climbed to over a thousand and seemed to be growing at a faster and faster rate. Additionally, the format had changed. Appearing alphabetically were the faces and abbreviated voting records of 396 Congresspeople. Notably missing were the eight who had gone on to meet a Maker they probably didn't believe in, plus 19 Democrats, 7 Republicans and 1 Independent who was in fact an avowed Marxist from the Bay Area of San Francisco. The message seemed to be that the 396, some liberal, some conservative, most moderate, were generally patriotic citizens who believed first and foremost in the rule of law as laid out by the Constitution. None of them were perfect. They were a mixed bag of lawyers, farmers, teachers, businessmen, ex-military, former pro athletes, a veterinarian, a one-time nightclub singer, and twin sisters representing adjoining districts in Iowa. There was not a radical among them and none were entrenched professional politicians. The message seemed to be a permission to vote for one of these Representatives, regardless of party affiliation, if one so chose.

As for the 27 not featured on the site, one might wonder if they were aware of SST, whether they would be as eager to appear in public as they had always been or whether they should appear at all.

CHAPTER ELEVEN

Except for him, the vast office crowded with desks was empty. Through the glass windows that faced on the East River, he could see the sun just beginning to rise over the roof of the Beth El Medical Center. The coffee which he had made over an hour ago was growing cold in the mug by his elbow.

Unable to sleep in his hotel room, Fowler Briggs had taxied to headquarters, hoping to get a jump on the day's work. Hoping, perhaps, for some magical clue to drop into place, to suddenly reveal with clarity the truth behind the insane events of the past week. And they were insane. Nothing about these murders was rational unless you believed that someone, some group of people, was intent on killing off the entire Congress of the United States of America. And to what end? So that the American public, in its infinite wisdom, could elect another 435 Representatives who would probably be no better and perhaps a lot worse than those currently sitting in Washington.

He tapped the keyboard of his computer. A familiar list filled the screen. Five men, three women. A businessman, a truck driver, a housekeeper, a shopkeeper, a waitress, a retired Navy captain, a pet store owner and a retired school janitor. Not crazed Muslim fanatics, but ordinary American citizens who committed murder in plain view, knowing they would be caught, knowing they would pay a severe price. Insanity. Yes, that was the word. Eight people totally unconnected. The intensive background searches had proved that and yet, something tied them together. Briggs was no seer, but he dreaded what he knew this Monday would bring. Another killing, probably more than one. The carnage seemed to be multiplying.

And so was the pressure on him and those under him to produce results. He'd spent over an hour last evening getting reamed by the SAC. He'd taken it stoicly. The SAC was a top agent and Briggs knew that he'd been summoned to Washington earlier in the day for a meeting with the Chief. No doubt there'd been a lot of SACs in that meeting. Here's an ass-kicking, boys. Pass it on.

For a few fleeting moments, he longed for those easier days in El Paso. His job had been pretty low key; it was the Immigration guys who'd been taking the body blows. Except for the damned heat, Briggs had liked El Paso. During those two years he'd made a lot of friends, something he hadn't been able to do previously, hopscotching on temporary assignment from one crisis to another. A month here, eight weeks there and before he knew it, six years had passed. Always a loner, Briggs hadn't minded much but El Paso had shown him a new kind of life.

He thought of Marisha. She could have been a big part of his future, but he'd been so wrapped up in work, so driven to not only succeed but to prevail, that he failed to see her drifting away. And when he did, it was too late. She flew to Seattle for a job interview and never came back. Lonely, angry with himself, he threw himself into his work even harder than before. Results, that's all that mattered. Accept your assignment, do the work, make no excuses and if anyone gets in your way, push them aside any way you can. It had worked in the Manzito case. He had stumbled onto a counterfeiting ring, worked his way into the gang hierarchy and in the end, had supervised the arrest. It was the case that brought him to the attention of the Chief, and weeks later, to Washington. Not bad for a dirt farmer's kid from Mississippi.

"Did you make this coffee?" He looked up to see Duncan McIlroy staring down at him, holding his very special "FBI Guys Do It Under Covers" coffee mug.

"And how are you this morning, Duncan?' Briggs smiled.

"This shit tastes like—shit," he said.

"Brilliantly put."

McIlroy grabbed a chair from a nearby desk and pulled it over next to Briggs. "I've got a full load this morning, Fowler. The boss wants me to run down to Houston to check out some damned website." He shook his head in annoyance. "No, don't ask, please. But before I go, I want you to understand something. You are never, ever, to put me in that kind of situation again."

"What are you talking about?," Briggs asked.

"You know what I'm talking about. Paul Castle."

"That was an interrogation."

"You went way over the line and you know it," McIlroy said.

"The revised Public Safety Act gives us the authority—"

McIlroy overrode him. "You know where you can shove that Public Safety Act. A wet dream thought up by a handful of Commie wackos in Congress. For God's sake, Fowler, we're the FBI, not the Gestapo."

Briggs shook his head. "Castle knows something."

"I don't think so," McIlroy said. He rose. "You're a nice guy when you want to be and you're a damned good agent but whatever you were pulling in El Paso, it doesn't go here. Keep it up and you'll be topic number one in my next report."

Briggs hesitated, embarrassed. He wasn't used to being chewed out by subordinates and he didn't like it. But he also realized that

McIlroy was probably right. He had crossed the line.

"You're right," he said. "I just lost it. It won't happen again."

Meanwhile, across town in a conference room in the news department of one of the so-called Big Three networks, news chief Daniel Federer was excoriating the troops. There had been a lot of excoriating going on lately, increasing in intensity through the weekend. Federer was suffering from major frustration brought on by a total lack of information about the deaths of eight Congressmen. Of the surviving perpetrators none had made a statement, none had been interviewed, none had retained an attorney, none had a family member who would speak for the record. All they had were vacuous comments from neighbors, all of which boiled down to the usual: "He (She) was so nice, so pleasant, so quiet, it's all so hard to believe."

Federer glared around the room at his cadre of producers and reporters led by the nightly news anchor, Harvey Cantrell, a handsomely coiffed but internally empty ex-Journalism professor whose meliflous tones threatened to put his viewers to sleep each evening between six and six-thirty.

"I'm tired of this damned tap dancing," Federer said." Tonight I want to open the broadcast hard. I want a lead-in to an expose that will put these right-wing sons of bitches in their place. We've got to get people mad, folks. We've got to spell it out in terms a chimpanzee could understand. Any questions?"

Those seated around the table who wished to keep their jobs wisely had no questions. The news anchor who probably thought he was too vital to the operation to be fired leaned forward and voiced a hesitant query.

"I'm not sure how we do that, Dan, I mean, without much to go on."

Federer glared at him. "It's very simple, Harvey. We line up two or three experts to analyze, pontificate and speculate. I'd include blovi-ate in that lineup but O'Reilly's got the word copyrighted. The son of a bitch."

One of the younger female correspondents at the far end of the table raised her hand tentatively. Federer recognized her. "Tammy?"

"Elliot Randall's agent called me last night. Randall's got a new book coming out next week on the fascist threat posed by evangelicals. I'm pretty sure we could tailor his appearance any way we wanted."

Heads nodded around the table. Elliot Randall was certainly a major "get."

"Sign him up, Tammy." He turned to the manager of on-air pro-mos. "Irv, put together a twenty second spot, plug it all day, every show." The man nodded, making a notation on his yellow pad. "One other thing, ," Federer said, opening the file folder in front of him. "I just got a copy of a Rasmussen poll regarding these assassinations. Make sure we use these numbers tonight."

He slipped on his reading glasses. "According to the poll, 85% of Americans believe these killings are politically motivated. 72% think the killlings are wrong while only 11% believe they are justified. These are good numbers to play up."

Harvey Cantrell, well-known ex-Journalism professor who passed high school math with flying colors, cleared his throat." Excuse me, Dan, but doesn't that seem to mean that in addition to that 11%, another 17% have no opinion as to whether it's proper to kill off Congresspersons?"

Federer glared at him again.

"Just asking," Harvey said with a shrug.

Paul was sitting on a chair outside the Old Man's office perusing a month old copy of US. He'd been there over a half-hour when the elevator door slid open and Schoenfeld emerged. Their eyes met and as Schoenfeld moved to his office door, he nodded to Paul to follow him.

"Why are you here?" Schoenfeld asked.

"I came to un-quit," Paul said.

"Don't be stupid. I never took that seriously."

"Happy to know I'm so convincing," Paul said. "You think my viewers see through me as easily as you do?"

"Not yet. Now as to my question, you shouldn't be here."

"I've got a show to put on tonight."

Schoenfeld shook his head. "Bill Farnum's filling in. It's all arranged."

"No."

"Don't tell me no, young man. You've been through a helluvan ordeal. I want you out of here for at least a week, settle down, recharge your batteries."

"I can't, boss," Paul said. "If I don't show tonight, it says I've backed off, that I can be bullied. I went down that road many years ago. I won't do it again."

"Those FBI guys don't like being challenged, Paul."

"I'm not worried about them. Are you?" Paul looked him squarely in the eye.

Schoenfeld laughed. "Is that what you think? That I'm going to back off because of some arrogant cop from Washington?"

"Just checking."

"Check no further."

Paul smiled, straightened to attention. "Permission to broadcast, sir?"

"Permission granted, mister. Dismissed."

Paul headed for the door, turned as the Old Man said seriously, "Paul, watch your back."

Paul nodded and went out.

Murray was on the studio floor going over the lineup for the noon hour show "Spotlight on the Stars," or as it was known around the network, "Slime on My Hands." Paul clapped him affectionately on the shoulder.

"Get your car back, old buddy?" he asked.

Murray smiled venomously. "Oh, yes, and thank you so much, old buddy. My day was going relatively well with only a few major catastrophes when this nitwit comes up to me looking for five hundred bucks and plane fare back to Connecticut in exchange for my car which he has parked downstairs."

Paul smiled. "I knew Buford was my man."

Murray ignored him. "Not only do I not have five hundred bucks in my pocket, it is after all the weekend and the business office is closed, but I also do not have an airplane ticket to Watertown—"

"Waterbury."

"Whatever—sticking out of my back pocket. And guess what else I do not have? A car. Because said nitwit parked in a loading-only zone and when we finally get downstairs we learn that said vehicle is now being held in the city auto impound."

"Oops."

"Yeah, oops."

"Murray, I'm sorry. I mean it. My checkbook's in my office, I'll write you a check to cover whatever and I'll personally go to the impound and get your car back—"

Murray waved him off with a smile. "Forget it. The Old Man covered the whole thing and Reena picked the car up first thing this morning."

"Excellent. No hard feelings then?"

"We'll see," Murray deadpanned. "So what are you doing here? Bill Farnum's got the show tonight."

"Not any more. Check with the Old Man."

Murray nodded. "Okay. Any ideas?"

"I'm mulling things over."

"Don't mull too long. I'm a producer, not a mindreader."

Paul nodded. "When you get a chance, give me a rundown on anything you've got, the gamier the better."

"What about these killings? Are we off that?"

"It's one of the things I'm mulling." Paul said as he walked away. When he got back to his office, his secretary was missing, no doubt powdering her nose which she was wont to do at least a dozen times a day.

The phone was ringing. He picked it up. It was Aaron Kovacs. "I'm down the street having a bagel. You wanna join me?" he asked.

A "schmear" is a glob of an edible substance (almost always cream cheese) which is spread upon a toasted bagel. Aaron Kovacs knew how to schmear. He took a healthy bite and chewed with satisfaction. Two hundred calories. No, maybe only one-eighty. Well, so what? Who cares? Buck naked, he'd looked at himself in the full length mirror that morning and forced himself not to be depressed. So he was no longer a dashing sexual animal. Was it so bad? Years ago, about the time he'd gotten his gold badge when he'd been working vice in the Bronx, he'd been a player. The girls were all over him like ticks on a beagle. Forget dinner tonight, Alma, Big stakeout near the stadium. Won't be home tonight, Alma. ' Round the clock surveillance on this pusher from Harlem. What he didn't know was, the only thing he was pushing was his luck. The drug boys had him tied up in a strait jacket. Photos he never knew were being taken suddenly showed up in his police locker. Where should we send these first, your wife or the Chief? First he got sick and then he got mad. He was an honest cop, never took a dime and all of a sudden he's getting threatened with this sleaze, just because he had an eye for the ladies. He wanted to strike back but he knew it would be futile so when the slot opened up in Manhattan Homicide, he grabbed it, and after a couple of false starts, he got pretty good at it.

Sure, there were more women along the way, lonely women looking for a man to warm them up on a cold winter's night. He steered clear of them. Rebecca was twelve, going on sixteen and she needed a father more than he needed a jump in the sack with some hot divorcee from the Upper East Side. That's when he started putting on the pounds. Maybe it was genetic. Maybe it was self defense. All he knew was he slept better at night and over the years he remembered more and more why he'd married Alma in the first place. At his last physical the police force doctor told him he was packing far too many pounds. Pounds of contentment, Doc, he'd told him. Don't worry about me. I've got three more years until I'm outta here. I can't drop dead before that. Alma won't let me.

He looked up as Paul entered the diner and looked around. Kovacs waved to him. smiling inwardly. Three more years of duty like this babysitting assignment, that he could do in his sleep. Paul slipped into the booth opposite him. The waitress came by. Paul ordered black coffee and an English.

"What is it that goyem see in English Muffins?" he asked.

Paul shrugged. "It's hard to believe that Jews are the chosen people when they choose to eat bagels." Kovacs nodded solemnly. "Well, now that we have the racial humor out of the way, good morning."

"And to you."

"I hear the Feebs gave you a rough time yesterday."

"You get around."

"Your friend Miss Bovano. She thought I ought to know. Are you okay?"

"I'll live."

"All we can hope for in this helter-skelter world," Kovacs opined. "So, to keep you in the picture, the FBI knows nothing, we of New York's Finest probably know less, but I can pass along a few rumors that might be helpful."

"Shoot."

"Homeland Security's getting ready to enforce some of the lesser known provisions of the Revised Special Powers Act. They've already taken several family members of the perps into custody."

"Charged with?"

"Material witness. Nobody knows exactly who or how many. The Commissioner's all over it but they're telling him nothing."

Paul shook his head violently. "No, no, they can't get away with that."

Kovacs almost laughed. "They can and they will. Where have you been for the past year and a half, buddy boy, besides looking up Madonna's dress? This omnipotent, all-powerful Congress—"

"That's redundant," Paul interrupted.

"Screw you, college boy," Kovacs replied. "This Congress pretty much does what it damn well pleases when it comes to power grabbing. Not always that obvious to the laity like yourself but we minions of law enforcement, we're pretty much up to our asses in their bullyboy tactics."

Paul smiled." Whoa. That's tough talk, Lieutenant, Almost subversive."

Kovacs shrugged. "Well, brown never was my favorite color in men's shirts."

"It can't be that bad," Paul said.

"Not yet," Kovacs responded. "So shall we get on to more news of the day? Item two. Early this morning a man broke into the bedroom of Congressman Jacoby of Michigan and put two twenty-two slugs in his brain. His wife had awakened and saw the whole thing. She was too scared to scream. Apparently the man just looked at her and said, "I'm sorry." He sat down in a chair and waited for the security people to come pounding through the door."

"We didn't pick anything up on the wire. I checked."

"It's being sat on. Nobody knows, not even the DC police."

Paul shook his head hopelessly. "Another perfect start to another perfect day."

"Elsewhere," Kovacs said, polishing off the last trace of bagel, "I followed up on that tip you gave me about Port St Lucie. Had a long chat with a sergeant there. Nice guy. Good cop. Not much affection for the Feebs. He knew something about the Villanueva thing because the locals had been on the scene for a couple of hours before the political guys got involved and shut it down. The police report disappeared from the files almost immediately but the sarge remembers seeing the name Elsa Galesko."

Paul grinned. "You know, for an old guy, you're a pretty good cop."

"I'll ignore the compliment. On a hunch, I started calling hospitals, clinics, sanitariums all around the area in every direction. After a dozen misses, jackpot!" He consulted a slip of paper he took from his shirt pocket. "The Sunland Gardens Convalescent Home for Senior Citizens."

"She's there."

"I'll assume so. I asked to be connected to Elsa Galesko. The woman on the other end seemed flustered, admitted to be filling in temporarily. Then she said,' Oh, yes, here she is' and then there was a long, long silence. Then she said, 'No. My mistake, there's no one by that name admitted here'. When I got a little pushy, she transfered me to the administrator. Same story. I have the wrong facility. They have no such patient."

Paul slowly nodded. "I don't suppose I could use this for my broadcast this evening."

Kovacs shrugged. "Why not? I don't own the copyright. Just be sure you leave my name out of it. All of this was strictly extra-curricular."

"I'll phone my buddy Dixie, get him to call. He'll get the same runaround and I can put him on the air. He'll jump at it."

"I would think so," Kovacs said, then more seriously. "You know, if Briggs is unaware of this, he's going to be more than a little pissed."

"Briggs knows or at least he should," Paul said. "When they started supplying security to every member of Congress, which includes Villanueva, it had to come out. Trouble is, whether he knows or he doesn' t know, he's going to wonder how I found out."

Kovacs nodded thoughtfully. "This does not bode well for your next encounter."

"Well, fuck him," Paul said.

"My thoughts precisely," Kovacs agreed as his cell phone rang. He took it out of his pocket. "Kovacs.......Uh-huh—When?—Uh-huh—What about the perp?—No kidding, that's a first—Okay, keep me posted." He flipped the instrument shut.

"Second one today?" Paul ventured.

"And the first one without a perp. DiNapoli from the Pittsburgh area."

Paul nodded knowingly. Among Washington politicians, Phil DiNapoli was legend. Thirteen years in the House, first elected at the age of 26, dubbed the wunderkind by the media. He had risen to the post of majority whip and was considered an odds on favorite to get the nomination for the Senate seat opening up upon the retirement of the incumbent. He was also the architect of the Carbon Usage Reconciliation Act of 2009, a misbegotten piece of legislation that had in a few short months resulted in higher prices for everything from fuel oil to produce to appliances and everything in between. The only legislation in memory that had ever caused more dire unin tended consequences was the Volstead Act of 1918, a so-called noble experiment which had given birth to Al Capone and a decade of booze and gangsterism.

"How'd it happen?," Paul asked.

"He slipped away from the security guys to see his girlfriend," Kovacs said. "They found him parked outside her apartment house with two slugs in his head. Girlfriend says she never called him. Matter of fact, she already had company, not the kind she'd want DiNapoli to find her with unexpectedly."

"You know, Lieutenant, these guys may be nuts but damned if they're not well organized."

"Oh, yes, but it makes you wonder how since they apparently didn't know one another." Kovacs glanced at his watch. "Well, I've got to get back to work."

"Me, too. Thanks, Lieutenant. I owe you."

"Good. Pay for breakfast." They went out onto the street. Kovacs' unmarked car was parked half a block away. Paul started in the other direction. The policeman called after him. "Paul. Just one more thing."

Paul turned. "You sound like Columbo."

"Did you ever hear of a website called SST?" Kovacs asked.

Paul shook his head.

"A friend of my grandson's found it. It's ..uh.. interesting. You might want to take a look before Big Brother has it shut down."

"SST."

Kovacs nodded. "Check it out."

Back at the office, Paul called Dixie Boggs in Port St Lucie. His old friend was on another call but promised to call back immediately. While he was waiting, Paul booted up his computer and typed in SST. Instantly the website flashed onto his screen. The parade of Congressional faces and resumes had not changed in the past twelve hours. Across the lower part of the screen, various messages streamed. "It's Not Too Late......Honest Men of Good Will Can Find a Way to Come Together...... The Time is Near. You Have a Vote. Cast It Wisely.......Your Freedom Came at a Terrible Price. Do Not Dishonor Those Who Sacrificed by Throwing It Away." There had been one other alteration to the format. In the upper right hand corner was a small box labeled: To Download Click Here.

Paul stared at the screen in confusion. What exactly was this? Obviously it was tied at the hip to the killings but was it an unrelated afterthought posted by some conservative zealot after the carnage had begun or had it been intrinsic to the murders from the onset?

His phone rang. It was Dixie. Paul filled him in quickly. Glad to help, his friend said. Live interview tonight? No problem. "I'll try to record my conversation with the telephone receptionist, "he said. "Call you back when I've got the goodies."

Paul hung up, stared at the screen. SST? Suddenly it came back to him. The hospital waiting room. Buford, the orderly, who had studied sign language, watching the waitress being led from the K of C hall. SST. The woman had signed SST. This website was no Johnny-Come-Lately. It was a major piece in the grand design.

At twenty minutes to six, Paul picked up the phone in his office and dialed FBI headquarters. He asked for Agent Briggs. Within moments he was put through.

"Are you planning to watch my broadcast this evening?"

"Mr. Castle?"

"You've accused me of being uncooperative and withholding information. All right, I'm cooperating. Do you know anything about a website originating in Houston called SST?'

"Houston?" Briggs said in puzzlement, then remembered McIlroy's destination.

"We're checking it out. What do you know?"

"Almost nothing. Watch the broadcast. Question two, what do you know about the attack on Congressman Villanueva about two weeks ago?"

Briggs leaned forward in his chair, totally alert. "Say again?"

"Congressman Hector Villanueva. Two weeks ago his housekeeper tried to cleave his head into two equal parts."

"Didn't happen. We'd know about it."

"Not if the local politicians covered it up with the help of the cops. He invented some bullshit story about falling down a flight of stairs. Sound familiar?"

Briggs tensed. It DID sound familiar though he knew no details. "Where'd you get this?"

"It's all in the broadcast, Briggs. The woman who made the attempt is named Elsa Galesko. She's being held at The Sunland Gardens Convalescent Home for Senior Citizens. They're going to deny it, of course, but since when did a silly little thing like that ever get in your way?"

"Could you repeat—"

"No. You people tape every incoming call. Play it. The time is now five-forty-nine. You've got eleven minutes to make a couple of phone calls to make yourself look good. I suggest you make them."

"If this is some kind of scam, Mr. Castle—"

"Fine. Wait for the broadcast. Make your calls when half the country already knows about it." Pause. "Briggs, by my count, you owe me one."

"We'll see about that," the agent said, disconnecting. He hesitated for a moment, then pushed a button for internal communication." This is Briggs. Is the SAC in the building?"

Two hours later, Paul was sitting cross-legged at Jennie's coffee table helping Jennie devour several cartons of asiatic delicacies from Uncle Wu's Family Restaurant. Jennie, sitting beside him, was a little miffed that her second offer of cheese omelets and fries had not been seized upon, but truth be told, she was exhausted from a harrowing day and Wu and his family could always be counted on to deliver the very best in stick-to-the-ribs eating.

They were watching the final minutes of Jeopardy, each fighting to out -answer (or rather, out -question) the other.

"Who is Andrew Johnson?" Paul shouted.

"No, no. Who is Alexander Stephens?" Jennie countered.

The contestant piped up." Who is Alexander Stephens?"

"Correct!" said Alex Trebek.

Paul screwed up his face in disbelief. "Alexander Stephens? Who the hell is Alexander Stephens???" he said.

"The Confederate Vice President, Castelli. Pay attention to the category," she chided.

"Shhhh,"he said, "if you keep talking I won't have a chance to get the next one wrong." They laughed. Jenn had a great laugh, Paul thought. Nothing phony about it. A truly happy person and in that, he envied her. He slipped his arm around her and pulled her close. He kissed her cheek and nuzzled her hair. "Down, Rover," she said, wriggling away, "I'm still working on the Moo Goo Gai Pan." And she was. He watched in wonder as she piled a couple of huge spoonfuls onto her plate. Two platefuls, working on three. A true trencherman, this girl. And where the hell did she put it? At five five and a hundred and twelve pounds she should have been eating like a bird. Well, in a sense she was. A California Condor.

Suddenly, Jeopardy disappeared from the screen. The graphics read BREAKING NEWS. A voice-over announced: "This a special report. From the WSAC newsroom, David Carpenter reporting." A solemn looking man wearing grey looked into the camera. "House Majority Leader Francis X. Mackey, the most powerful man in the House of Representatives and the man thought most likely to succeed to the vacant Speaker's chair, is dead. He died (a quick look at an off-camera clock) twenty seven minutes ago in the lobby of the Metropolitan Opera House, the victim, like so many of his Congressional peers, of a gunshot wound. We believe, though we cannot confirm, that a single bullet struck Congressman Mackey in the heart and that death was nearly instantaneous."

Paul looked over at Jenn whose eyes were concentrated on the set, all thoughts of food forgotten.

Taped footage from the Opera House filled the screen. "We have been able to obtain raw, unedited footage of the shooting which we are showing to you now. Several media outlets were on hand as tonight's performance of Otello marked the finale of the current operatic season. Mr. Mackey was accompanied to the closing by three security people two of whom were Secret Service, the third believed to be an ATF agent. If you look closely on the right of your screen you will see a white haired lady in a pale blue evening gown—yes, there she is—approaching the Congressman. You can see that she is holding a clutch purse in her left hand. The Congressman seems to know her. He steps toward her even as one of the security people is trying to pull him back. He wraps her in his arms and there, there it is, he stiffens slightly, stumbles awkwardly and falls to the floor. As you can see we have no audio to go with this footage but as you might imagine the entire scene turned chaotic."

Jenn spoke slowly under her breath, in disbelief. "My God. Betsy," she said.

"You know her?"

She nodded. "Betsy Wallenberg. Her husband founded Wallenberg Financial. When he died about eight years ago, he left her something like nine hundred and fifty million. She's on the Board of just about every major charity in the city including the Mayor's Council on Inner City Poverty." She looked over at him, shaking her head. "Her grandaughter Lisa and I were sorority sisters. We attended law school together. I was a guest at the Wallenberg house a half-dozen times this past year. That woman on the screen is gentle, thoughtful, generous—." Words failed her.

"Dare I ask? Republican?"Paul queried.

Jenn looked at him, her face ashen. "That's just it. Lifelong Democrat. Twenty years ago she ran for the Senate and lost the primary by a handful of votes."

Paul looked back at the screen in bewilderment. Now, truly, nothing made any sense at all.

CHAPTER TWELVE

Standing by the desk in the wood paneled den of his rented home in Georgetown, Representative Duane Delroy Rogers, a powerful member of the Black Caucus and a longtime resident of southern Ohio, stared nervously at the screen of the HiDef television he'd had installed in the opposite wall. The local network outlet, having belatedly come upon the existence of SST, was reporting in great detail the names of those Representatives who had been conspicuously omitted from its roster of acceptable candidates for the November election. Those ignored included Rogers himself as well as many of his closest colleagues on the House floor. Unused to being challenged under any conditions, he deeply resented being targeted by this bunch of fanatics, whoever they were. He fancied himself a committed champion of the people, particularly those least able to fend for themselves, and his position as the most senior member of the Black Caucus gave him enormous power and influence that went far beyond his small Congressional district located a few miles outside of Cincinnati.

He was not a Socialist, he'd made that very clear at every one of the $1000 a plate dinners held in his honor throughout his nineteen years of service. Yes, it was true that on many occasions he had voted with a majority of his colleagues for progressive legislation that would strengthen the power of hard working union members or teachers or trial attorneys or whoever. And yes, all these groups had supported him with generous financial contributions. But that's the way the game was played. It always had been. It always would be.

He'd been elected to Congress a threadbare lawyer. Today his net worth topped sixteen millions dollars, much of it in ventures proposed to him by wealthy and powerful constituents, anxious to solidify an amicable relationship with him and with the Caucus. A major bank had allowed him to finance his home back in Ohio at a ridiculously low rate. Several manufacturing plants that employed black labor working under substandard conditions had been more than generous and he had turned a blind eye to their practices. No one forced these blacks to work in these factories. If they didn't like the conditions, they were free to quit. That was the American Way. No, he'd done nothing wrong, of that he was sure.

Then, he wondered, why were his nerves so on edge, why had he been unable to hold down food last night, and why had he suddenly decided to take a hiatus from legislative duties to spend a week, perhaps longer, at his rustic riverfront cabin just outside of Frederick, Maryland? Almost no one knew of its existence, most particularly his wife. For this week's getaway, however, romantic idylls were the last thing on his mind. He needed time to kick back, reflect and relax, spend some quiet daylight hours fishing and evenings by the fireplace catching up on his reading. And of course, there was the safety factor. Not that he believed he was in real danger. From what he'd been told Homeland Security was only hours away from making significant arrests. No, his personal safety was far down on his list of priorities and, who knew, perhaps within a day or two this national nightmare might be over.

A tall black man with close cropped grey hair and who carried himself with a rigid military bearing appeared in the doorway. "The luggage is packed in the car, sir. Ready to go when you are."

Bert Yancey, former Green Beret and ex-vice cop formerly attached to the Cincinnati police department, had been assigned (at his own request) to be one of three security people responsible for Rogers' safety. As a constituent he'd felt it his duty to volunteer.

"Ready now, Bert," Rogers said. "What about the others?"

"I left them a note. When they get here, we'll be long gone."

"You do think we're right about this, I mean, I'm sure you can handle it—"

"Sir," he overrode him. "These people are pussies, old men and women. I can certainly handle anything they can bring and as I told you, I firmly believe that the fewer people who know where we are, the safer you'll be."

They headed outside.

"And we're still scheduled to pick up Congressman Bowles?" Yancey asked.

Rogers nodded. "At exactly eight-forty-five at the rear exit to the restaurant. He's going to slip his security people by going to the men's room and then ducking through the kitchen." Rogers looked into Yancey's expressionless face. "I know you don't approve, Bert, but I really would like to have company, no slight to you intended."

"None taken, sir."

He smiled and slipped behind the wheel as Rogers got in the passenger seat and buckled up.

Paul was in his office by nine-thirty after having spent a chaste evening at Jennie's apartment. He was going slow and she showed no inclination as yet in speeding him up. He awoke on her living room sofa to the aroma of freshly brewed coffee and the sound of sizzling bacon coming from the kitchen. He sat up, wearing only his skivvies which was starting to become a habit. He donned his clothes which were draped over a nearby chair and went into the kitchen, hoping that the aroma and the sizzle might be accompanied by a pair of well- turned eggs and perhaps an English Muffin.

The chef was hard at work at the stove. He put his arms around her, kissed her on the neck, and pinched her in the butt, all in the name of a friendly good morning. In response she jammed an elbow into his ribs and told him to sit down.

Plans were made for the day which included dinner that evening at an out of the way Italian ristorante in the Village which had come highly recommended to both of them. As for the rest of the day, Paul had leads to follow up and a program to prepare for. More importantly, perhaps, Jennie was going to try to reach Lisa Wallenberg and see if she could find out anything at all about her grandmother's involvement in the Congressional killings.

As he was leaving, Paul kissed her, a deep lingering kiss which, had they not had people to see and places to go, might have led directly to Jennie's bedroom. As it was, the kiss held out great promise for later that evening.

A quick trip to his apartment, a shave and shower and a change of clothes had then brought him to his office where he flipped on his computer and clicked to the SST site. The faces and the resumes flashed by, one after the other, the content basically unchanged. Although Paul had no way of knowing it, the number of hourly hits to the website was now nearing 2500. Slowly but surely, America—all of America—was beginning to get the message.

As Paul sat pensively studying the screen, Lt. Aaron Kovacs wandered into his office carrying a container of coffee and a small paper bag. He sat down, making himself at home.

"Good morning," Paul said with amusement to his uninvited guest.

"Good morning," Kovacs responded, reaching into the bag and taking something sort of brownish and white and red, possibly edible, wrapped in waxed paper.

Paul eyed it suspiciously. "That is not a bagel," he said.

"Keen observation, young man. The hallmark of good detective work. This is a blintz. It is better than a bagel," Kovacs responded.

"Lieutenant, ANYTHING is better than a bagel. And don't you have anything better to do than crowd up my office?" Paul asked.

"Now that you ask, no. You might as well know, the Commissioner has assigned me to keep you up to speed on any developments in the case."

"And why, pray tell, would the Commissioner do a dumb thing like that?"

"Because—" Kovacs took a bite of the blintz and a blob of cream cheese fell onto his freshly cleaned trousers. "Shit!" Paul got up quickly and poured a cup of water from his cooler, grabbed a paper towel and handed them to the detective.

"Thanks," Kovacs said, trying his best to maintain his dignity while he scooped up the cheese and with a wet towel scrubbed around his crotch area. "Because," he continued, "as I was saying, you have a popular broadcast and you are covering these events and the Commissioner believes that you will characterize the efforts of the NYPD favorably as opposed to anything you might have to say about the FBI."

Paul nodded appeciatively. "Well, that makes sense. So tell me, what up to date developments do you have for me this morning?"

"Well, for starters, your lady suspect has been whisked off from the Sunland Gardens Convalescent Home to Never Never Land or wherever the local pols decided to stash her. Happened around 7:30 last night, about an hour after your broadcast. The Feebs showed up at 8:00 with a warrant—"

"A warrant? Well, that must mean Briggs wasn't involved."

Kovacs wagged a finger. "Uh-uh. Bitterness does not become you, my young friend."

Paul threw up his hands in frustration. "This is great. I give Briggs a tip. It turns out to be a big nothing and I'm back at the top of his personal hit list."

"Won' t happen," Kovacs said. "One of the hospital's candystripers tipped one of the agents. She saw Galesko being taken out the rear entrance and put into a Port St Lucie ambulance. Where it was headed she had no idea."

"Thank God for that little girl," Paul said and then sharply, leaning forward: "What the hell?"

"What the hell, what?" Kovacs said.

"The website. STT. It suddenly disappeared." He swung his computer screen around so that Kovacs could see. Sure enough. Gone were the faces and the resumes, replaced on screen by a single sentence: "THIS WEBSITE MAY NO LONGER BE ACCESSED," and lower down in small type: "By Order of the Department of Homeland Security."

Kovacs snorted. "Hmm. Love this administration They may not be very bright, but they certainly do work slowly." He lumbered to his feet. "Well, I'll leave you to ponder this latest wrinkle while I go back to headquarters and await further developments." He moved to the door, tossing his waxed paper and the brown paper bag into Paul's trash basket.

"Lieutenant, what about last night at the Met? Anything?"

"The lady is in custody. Some time today she may be released on her own recognizence. Depends on how expensive her lawyer is." He smiled. "Ain't it great to be rich and shoot any damned person you please?"

With that he went out the door.

Paul smiled and turned his attention back to his computer just as the intercom buzzed. He pressed the button on his phone console.

It was the Old Man. "My office. Now. Chop chop."

Schoenfeld was standing at the large corkboard, rearranging some post-it notes into some semblance of order when Paul walked in.

"We got a phone call about twenty minutes ago from your tipster pal, Twig Evers." , Schoenfeld said.

"You gonna try to stiff him out of his 50Gs?" Paul asked.

"Technically, I could," Schoenfeld said, "since technically there's not much arrestin' and convictin' going on. But no, we're not going to cheat the guy."

"Happy to hear you won't make me look like a schmuck."

"First of all, he delivered. Second, reneging shows bad faith and could lead to bad publicity. Three, we're going to want to get him on the show live, hopefully tonight. Oh, yes, and fourth, he tipped us to the funeral for Rose Temple. St. Bartholomew's Church. One o'clock. I want you there. "

Paul glanced at his watch. "We'll never make it on time."

"With a camera crew," Schoenfeld continued. "I've chartered a plane at La Guardia. I want you in the air by ten-thirty. Bring this Twig guy back with you and the woman's mother, if she'll come."

"She won't."

"Try."

Paul shook his head. "I'll be lucky if she doesn't spit in my face. If it hadn't been for me, Rose would still be alive."

"Then maybe we should send a female reporter to interview her." A pause: "Too bad we don't have one."

"Maybe we can borrow one from Fox News. They've got more than they need." Paul managed a smile. "Just kidding, boss. We both know no self-respecting female journalist would be caught dead around here."

The Old Man waved him away. "Do the best you can."

"I do have someone that might pitch in, that is, if I can get her loose from her job for a few hours," Paul said.

Schoenfeld fixed him with a squint-eyed stare. "Your lady lawyer friend?"

"And why not?"

"What does she see in you anyway?"

"Haven't the slightest idea." Paul said.

Schoenfeld shrugged. "Her problem, not mine. Take whoever you like. Just remember, wheels up by ten-thirty."

As churches went, it was no cathedral. White clapboard, a tall steeple that overlooked the town, St. Bartholomew's Episcopal Church was not unlike thousands of others scattered in small towns throughout New England. The sign at roadside read, in part, Established 1803. Old as it was it showed little evidence of aging. No sagging, no listing. Despite the cloudiness that hung over the town, threatening rain before night fall, the church exuded a gleaming, comforting exterior, thanks to a recent paint job. Inside, the two dozen pews could accomodate around 250 parishioners if need be. The need had not arisen in years, although the turnout this grey afternoon probably exceeded the expectations of the Reverend Jonathan Constable who was intoning an over-written eulogy to Rose Temple, describing her as a loving daughter, a caring neighbor, and a devout Christian. No mention was being made of her homicidal activities. Paul and Jennie were seated on the aisle in the rear pew, isolating themselves by choice from the townspeople. Above them was the choir loft which was not in use, most probably because the choir members had jobs they needed to hang onto. A hefty woman with an amazing contralto voice had opened the service with two hymns with which Paul was unfamiliar, being a Catholic and a lapsed one at that. With Twig Evers help, the cameraman was elsewhere shooting a B roll for tonight's broadcast: the Temple residence, the main street of town, the front of the antique store, and anything else that seemed appropriate. He was under strict orders to be back in time for the gravesite internment which would take place at the small cemetery located next to the church.

Anna Marie sat in the front pew, accompanied by Doctor Walsh. They were by themselves. No other family members, if there were any, were present. When she'd entered the church on the doctor's arm, Paul had momentarily caught her eye. She showed a momentary sign of recognition, then looked away. This is going to be a long and difficult day, Paul thought. Very difficult. He looked over at Jennie as she squeezed his hand, as if reading his thoughts. Having Jennie here might just make this bearable.

The graveside ceremony was short. A prayer by the Reverend, then a few words of compassion whispered into Anna Marie's ear. She clutched the clergyman's hand in gratitude, then rose and moving to the casket, placed a single red rose atop it. The other mourners followed suit as she moved away from the grave, Dr. Walsh holding her arm. Paul and Jennie intercepted them.

"Mrs. Temple," he said, "please accept my deepest condolences. Your daughter's death is truly tragic. I am very sorry."

Anna Marie looked into his eyes. "Thank you," she said without emotion, walking past him.

"I wonder if we might get together later," he called after her. "There are things I'd like to learn from you."

Dr. Walsh turned back toward him and shook his head. He mouthed the words 'Not now'. Paul watched them go, a heavy feeling settling in his chest. He turned, looked over at the gravesite, then walked over to stare at the coffin, now hovering over the six foot deep hole, waiting for the gravediggers to lower it into place and cover it with dirt. The finality from which there was no return. Ashes to ashes, dust to dust.

In his mind, Paul again replayed the agonizing sequence of events that had led to this moment. If only he'd been quicker. If only he hadn't let her slip from his grasp. If only he'd been able to snatch away the lethal pill. He hesitated, knowing the truth. If only he hadn't walked into that house in the first place. He was responsible for her death and nothing would ever change that. Tears began to trickle down his face. He felt Jennie beside him, squeezing his arm in a comforting gesture.

"I killed her," he said.

"No." She moved around to face him. "Paul, look at me. It's not your fault. Do you understand? It's not your fault." He reached out. She fell into his arms. He held her close, his tears continuing to flow. The cameraman moved toward them, looking for new instructions. Jennie waved him off and he walked off toward the SUV they'd rented at the airport, lighting a cigarette as he put down his equipment and leaned against the car. Twig Evers stood nearby, shifting his weight impatiently from foot to foot.

After a few minutes, Paul composed himself and he and Jennie moved toward the car. Just then a burgundy Lexus pulled up behind the SUV and Dr. Walsh got out.

"Anna Marie asked me to apologize for her rudeness, Mr. Castle," he said.

"If she was rude, Doctor, I didn't notice it. I was just hoping to learn something that would help our viewers better understand Rose. Most of the news outlets are describing her as some sort of monster. You and I know that isn't true."

Walsh smiled. "Of course it isn't. And if this were a few days from now, I suspect Anna Marie would be willing to talk with you. But, really, not today. It's all been too much for her." Paul nodded, then realized Jennie was at his side. He introduced her. Walsh smiled warmly. "You'll be heading back to New York then," he said. Paul nodded. "Well, if there's anything I can do, any questions you need answered, just call," the doctor said. "I'll do what I can. I know this wasn't your fault."

Walsh went to his car and drove away. Paul watched him go. "There's someone else who says it wasn't my fault." A puzzled look crossed his face, as if he'd thought of something. The cameraman stomped out his cigarette and walked up to him. "Well, boss, what-dayasay? Do we get this show on the road? It's past two o'clock."

Paul glanced at his watch. Ten after two. Time was getting short. He beckoned to Twig. "Twig! Come over here!" The diminutive black man, anxious to be paid, was just as anxious to please. He hurried toward them. Paul turned to the cameraman.

"We're going to do the interview here and now. Bud, let's get the church at my back and if we can Twig in front of the cemetery."

Twig scowled. "Does this mean I'm not goin' to New York?" he asked.

"Not today, but the check'll be in the mail, I promise."

Twig glowered. "I've heard that before."

Paul turned to Jennie. "Can you stay the night?"

She shrugged. "I guess so. Why?"

"I can't go back without talking to Anna Marie."

She scanned his face. "You're on to something."

"Maybe." he said. "Dr. Walsh was the second person to tell me it wasn't my fault. You were the first. And then I remembered. In the house. Rose. Just before she took the pill, she looked at her mother and screamed something like 'Mama! It's okay! It's not your fault!" Jennie looked puzzled." What's that supposed to mean?"

"That's just the point. I don't know. Maybe nothing. But, I don't know, it could have been something she just let slip out, something that might give us another place to look." Jennie nodded. "But even if you're right, especially if you're right, do you think she's going to talk to you?"

"Maybe not," Paul said, "but I can't leave without trying."

An hour later, Paul and Jennie were seated in a booth at Margie's drinking coffee. He was also picking away at a slice of hot apple pie which Margie had put in front of him." It was on your tab last time, mister. You paid for it and if you don't eat it, I'm going to be mighty insulted," she told him. "Fine, fine, I'll eat it ," Paul said, raising his hands defensively. Jennie watched the byplay with amusement, not quite getting it.

He'd called Murray, explained the situation with as little detail as possible. Bill Farnum was on hand and ready to sub for him. There was plenty of decent material to fill the thirty minutes. Jennie called her boss and got a dispensation for another day. And finally, Paul had called Dr. Walsh to ask him to intercede with Anna Marie for an interview the following morning.

"It's the only reason I'm staying, Doc," Paul said.

"I'll do what I can." Walsh replied.

"Thanks. I'll take that as a yes. See you tomorrow," Paul said, shutting down his cell phone. On the strength of that, he called the Hilton Garden Motel they'd passed on the way into town and made a reservation for that night. Listening to the room clerk, Paul looked at Jennie. "One room or two?" he queried. She smiled, held up one finger. After a moment: "One king or two queens?." Jennie stroked her chin, pretending deep thought. Then again held up one finger. Paul grinned, then after a moment: "A view of the parking lot will be just fine. The name's Castle. We'll be checking in before six." He slipped his phone into his shirt pocket. "I swear to you, Jenn," he said, "I did not entice you up here for a night of wild and lurid sex."

She looked disappointed. "Oh. But that's the only reason I came."

He looked at her with mock seriousness. "I'm feeling very vulnerable now. I hope you won't take advantage."

"I'll be gentle, "she said.

At that moment, Jennie's cell phone rang. Nothing special. Just the first eight bars to the theme from "Now Voyager." On the sentimentality scale, Jennie was a pushover. "Lisa? Hi. Hey, thanks for getting back to me." Paul gave her a little wave of understanding, pointed toward the restrooms and left the table.

The men's room was neat and clean, two booths, three urinals. A balding man with a beer belly was washing his hands at the sink when Paul walked in. For a moment, the man stared at him as Paul went to a urinal to expel several hour's worth of black coffee.

"Hey, ain' t you that fella?" the man asked.

"What fella's that?" Paul replied over his shoulder.

"A couple of days ago, didn't I see you on TV with that bimbo from the news channel?"

"That was me," Paul said, zipping his fly and moving to the sink.

"Well, you sure laid her out, partner. Nearly busted a gut laughing, I did. Good on you."

"Thanks."

The man extended his hand. "Chester Potts. Potts Feed and Grain."

Having dried off with a towel, Paul grasped the man's hand with a firm shake. "Paul Castle."

"Castle," the man nodded. "Yeah, that's it. Guess you were here for the funeral." Paul nodded. "Terrible business," Potts continued. "Real nice family, the Temples. Terrible luck. Now this. Hard to figure."

"What do you mean, terrible luck?" Paul asked.

"Oh, I guess it started when the Daddy walked out them. Then the business sort of went to hell, and Rose getting sickly and all."

Paul looked at him sharply. "Rose sick? I thought she came back to take care of her mother."

Potts laughed. “Anna Marie? Let me tell you, mister, even flu germs steer clear of her.” He started out. “Well, nice meeting you.” He paused at the door and turned. “Say, since you were at the funeral, you might not have heard.”

“Heard what?”

“They got another one. Fella from Alabama. Can’t remember his name, but he’s the one had a couple of hundred thousand dollars stashed away in a refrigerator in his basement.”

“Pickens.”

“That’s him. I recall as how they were gonna toss him out on his ear, and here it was three years later and he was still down there stealin’ big as life. Guess he won’t be doin’ much stealin’ now.”

“Be honest with me, Mr. Potts, how do feel about that?,” Paul asked. “I mean, not only Pickens but the rest of them as well.”

Potts lost some of his folksy good humor as he took a step toward Paul. “How do I feel? I’ll tell you how I feel. I didn’t fight two years in ‘Nam to turn this country over to a bunch of Socialist crooks like that bastard Pickens. People like him get in Congress for a few years and pretty soon they think they’re entitled to a lifelong job and what you think and what I think don’t mean diddely.”

“Then you approve?”

“Hell, yes. Son, I’m 63 years old and I’ve seen this country crumble year after year until there’s hardly anything left to proudly call the United States of America. The way they got it rigged, your vote don’t mean a thing anymore, so what’s left. I call it the Second American Revolution and I just wish I was a part of it.” A shrug. “Maybe some day soon I will be.”

And with that Chester Potts walked out of the men’s room. Paul followed a moment or two later.

Margie was leaning on the booth table, chatting up a storm with Jennie as Paul approached. Self-consciously Margie looked up and saw him coming, then scurried away with the empty dishes as Paul slid into the booth. “What was that all about?” Paul asked. “Basically, she wanted to know if we were making it, and if not, why not. I think she's got a crush on you,” Jennie said.

He shrugged. “I could do worse. She makes a mean bowl of soup.”

“Well,” she smiled, “if your stomach is your number one priority, I can see I'm wasting my time hanging around this place.”

Paul laughed. “Ah, but can she make a cheese omelet? So, tell me, how's your friend Lisa Wallenberg?”

Jennie shook her head sadly. “Crushed. She and her grandmother were really close.”

“Did she tell you anything helpful? Anything we can use?”

Jennie shook her head. “Only that Betsy was 83 years old, her health was failing badly, and her closest friends were dying all around her. As for motive, she'd been talking a lot about the way the Democratic Party had sold itself off to the lunatic fringe. Lisa said that she was very bitter about that, but as to why she would commit such a heinous crime in full view of hundreds of people, Lisa had no clue.”

“You think its possible she knew some of the other people involved in the killings?”Paul asked.

“I don't think so. When I told Lisa we were in Connecticut for Rose Temple's funeral, it meant nothing to her. And she was sure her grandmother didn't know her. She said that, actually, except for the occasional public appearance, Betsy was pretty much housebound and the only people she saw or talked to were old friends of many years.”

“And the music goes round and round,” Paul hummed sarcastically.

Jennie stared out the window, drumming her fingers impatiently on the table. “Do you think it's too early to check into the motel?” she asked, turning and looking at him square in the eye.

“No, I don't,” he said without a moment's hesitation.

They were barely into the room, slamming the door behind them, when they found themselves entangled in each other's arms, They hugged and kissed and caressed one another, hands and arms groping and searching as pent up hormones exploded between them. She ripped at his shirt as he pulled her sweater off and tossed it on the floor. She unbuckled his belt and whipped it through the loops, sending it flying against a wall. She reached for the zipper on his fly as he swooped his hands up under her skirt and yanked down her panties.

"Are you sure you don't want to hold out for committment?" he asked hoarsely.

"Screw committment," she said, biting him on the neck and wrestling him onto the bed. Within moments all clothing had been dispatched elsewhere. Their bodies meshed. The moment of passion could not wait. They conjoined inelegantly and lay back, spent.

Thirty minutes later, they tried again, more successfully. The passion was there but so was the tenderness and as Paul buried his face in the luxuriance of her hair, he despised his stupidity in walking away from her those many years before. He held her tightly, as if afraid she would suddenly morph into a wraith and disappear from his grasp. Before long they were both asleep, still holding one another close.

It was a few minutes past midnight and in the Oval Office, the lights were burning brightly. Six tired and jittery Democratic Congressmen were attempting to formulate some sort of strategy with the help of the President and his Chief of Staff. Over the past several days the House had lost its Speaker, its Majority Leader and its Majority Whip and the question before them was, who to elevate to the Speakership, presuming of course that the individual would accept the job. Three of the Congressmen were on SST's "acceptable" list, three were not. Who best to shepherd the President's agenda through the House? The Chief of Staff opted immediately for a radical left-winger from Wisconsin who had declined an offer to participate in the discussion, preferring instead to remain in the safety of his Georgetown home with security people posted at the front and rear doors. One of the Congressmen put forth the name of a moderate from Texas. The Chief of Staff immediately vetoed the idea. The Congressman looked to the Pressident for support, but the President merely yawned, stood up and stretched and announced he was going to bed. Whatever the Chief of Staff wanted, he told them, would be just fine with him. And he was gone.

Without further discussion, the left-winger from Wisconsin was tapped as the heir apparent and he would be invited to the White House in the morning. Those invited to the White House rarely if ever refused a Presidential request, even if the President hadn't actually requested it.

The Congressmen rose to leave. The Chief of Staff bade them sit. There was one more matter on the agenda. These events of the past week had stirred up a flurry of dissent around the country. (Flurry? one Congressman thought privately. More like a blizzard.). In light of this the Chief suggested it might be helpful if patriotic Americans, receiving e-mails and such criticizing the Congress and the Administration, might forward these e-mails to the White House for examination and study. Perhaps even criticism made in casual conversation might be worth checking out.

The Congressman from North Carolina, more a libertarian than a liberal, stared at the man in utter disbelief. Had he lost his mind? Did he know nothing about the law? Or was he so arrogant that he felt that he and the President were above the law. Did they not remember the lesson of Richard Nixon?

Inwardly, the North Carolinian sighed. He was very, very grateful that the SSTs, whoever they were, had labeled him acceptable.

CHAPTER THIRTEEN

Bubba Conroy's huge diesel-powered semi rumbled up the slight incline on Virginia's Route 210, heading north toward the Beltway and beyond that, the Nation's capitol. It was a few minutes past six. The commuter traffic had not yet begun to jam the roads. With luck he'd arrive at the wholesale produce market by six-thirty. He was tired and hungry. He thought about the flapjacks at his favorite IHOP. His stomach growled. As he crested the rise, an unusual sight greeted him. His favorite billboard featuring a bikini clad babe hawking the sun and sand of the Bahamas had been papered over. The new message was brief and to the point. Against a solid white background were the bold black words, Sic Semper Tyrannis, and underneath, the translation from the Latin, "Thus Always to Tyrants." Across the bottom in bold red lettering was a single sentence: "It Is Not Too Late." Unknown to Bubba, throughout the night dozens of volunteers had worked until daybreak, repapering 65 billboards strategically placed alongside state and county roads leading into Washington D.C. Some faced north, some south, some west. Anyone entering or leaving the capitol could not avoid seeing the message at least once and more probably many times. This in response to the government's shutting down of the Houston website. The owners of the four outdoor advertising firms who had accepted the business were not fussy about where their income came from and happily accepted cash from a man they would variously describe as being tall, short, old, young, blonde, grey, brunette, with a limp, without a limp, blue-eyed, brown-eyed and in one case, eyes of different colors.

By six-thirty most news outlets were aware of the billboard campaign. At seven o'clock the so-called big three networks were leading with it as they opened their morning shows. Shunted down their list of priorities were the killing of Joshua Pickens, he of the cold cash in the refrigerator, and Rory Crimmins, who was dispatched to his final reward on the sixteenth fairway of the Congressional golf course. Crimmins, a 17 handicapper, was about to attempt an eighty yard pitch shot when a golfer on an adjoining fairway calmly withdrew a 30.6 rifle from his golf bag and plunked the Congressman in the middle of his backswing. Possibly these deaths were starting to become less and less newsworthy. Also possible was the idea that America was getting very tired of the biased network commentary accompanying these reports. A new Rasmussen poll now showed that only 74% of Americans were outraged by this assault on Congress, a decline of seven points, while 16% were inclined to think it wasn't a bad idea, an increase of five percent.

Paul awakened shortly past seven, morning light peeping through the window. Jennie was fast asleep, scrunched up, arms encircling her pillow, a trace of a smile on her lips. Paul brushed his teeth with a hotel-supplied toothbrush, then dressed quickly, wondering what he was going to do about his shirt which had popped two buttons and showed a slight tear around the collar. (Vicious wildcat! he thought).

He slipped out the room quietly and went to the lobby where a sign had promoted a continental breakfast starting at 6 a.m. He grabbed a tray, two O.J.s, two black coffees and four fruit danish. By the time he got back to the room, Jennie was in the bathroom, showering.

He flipped on the television, caught the end of the SST billboard story and then sat through a law firm's interminable commercial fishing for victims of rickets, promising a class action suit that would reap millions. (For the lawyers, of course; the victims would have to fend for themselves).

At that moment, Jennie emerged from the bathroom, buck naked and toweling off her hair. As if reading his thoughts she said, "Don't even think about it, Castelli. I'm starving."

He pointed to the tray of goodies on the dresser. "I came bearing gifts," he said.

She smiled. "Why, thank you, sugar daddy. Your reward will be bestowed at some future time." She took a terrycloth robe from the closet and wrapped herself in it, then attacked the tray with a vengeance. Maybe I should have brought up more than four danish, Paul thought to himself, recalling her assault on the Chinese food.

He turned his attention to the television which had just gotten around to the fatal attacks on Pickens and Crimmins. The on-camera reporter solemnly noted,"Their deaths now bring the total of Congressmen and women murdered by right-wing extremists to fourteen. In addition, sources at Homeland Security have told us that four others are missing or unaccounted for. They include Duane Delroy Rogers, Democrat of Ohio; Max Bowles, Democrat of Tennessee; Edwina Thurgood, Democrat of Georgia; and Blanton Phelps, Republican of Maine. All four were among the so-called "Omitted List" from the former SST website, making them, in the view of law enforcement officials, primary targets of the group behind the rash of Congressional killings. Homeland Security now believes that twenty-one Representatives remain at high risk. Law enforcement has asked them to keep as low a profile as possible, limiting themselves to work at their offices, on the floor of the House and otherwise to keep to their residences. Security details for the twenty-one have been redoubled. When asked how long he felt this crisis would continue, FBI Director Levi Zwick said arrests could possibly be made within the next 72 hours."

Paul looked at Jennie. "Right. And my sister's spayed cat will give birth to quintuplets by noon," he said.

At that moment the phone on the nightstand beside the bed rang. Paul got up to answer it. "Hello......Oh, good morning, Doc.......Uh-huh......... Ten o'clock. That's great......Wait minute, let me write that down." He grabbed a pen and a piece of notepaper from the nightstand drawer." Uh-hh...........I'll find it....... Right. See you then." Paul turned to Jennie. "Ten o'clock. Doctor's office. She's not happy about it. Doc says he can't guarantee how helpful she'll be ."

As it turned out, Anna Marie Temple wasn't helpful at all. In fact after a few polite preliminaries and several innocuous questions, she became downright hostile.

"It's not your fault?" Anna Marie looked genuinely puzzled." I don't remember Rose saying that. Or anything like that. You must be mistaken, Mr Castle."

"I don't think so, ma'am," Paul said.

Her back stiffened visibly. "Are you saying I'm lying?"

"No, I'm not. Things were hectic. You weren't close by. You probably didn't hear her properly."

"My hearing is just fine, Mr. Castle."

"I'm sure it is. But let's say for the sake of argument, she did say it. Do you know of any reason why she would say it?"

Anna Marie glared at him. "What you mean is, did I have any part in abetting or encouraging her actions? Is that what you're trying to get at?"

"I'm just asking the question, Mrs. Temple. I don't presume anything. I just thought it was an odd thing for her to cry out just before she took her own life. Blame me for being a nosy newsman but that's what it is. Curiosity."

"And I told you," anger rising in her voice, "I heard her say no such thing because there is no reason why she would have said it. What Rose did, she did on her own and without my knowledge."

Paul nodded, then switched the subject abruptly. "How's your health, Mrs. Temple?"

"Are we talking dementia here? Alzheimers? Would you like me to dodder for you? My health is fine and I believe this conversaton is at an end." She rose. "I told you this was going to be a waste of time, Grayden," she said to the doctor who had remained silent throughout, puffing on a pipe at his desk.

Walsh got to his feet as she headed for the door. "I'll see you to your car," he said.

"And your daughter, Mrs. Temple," Paul asked sharply as she pulled the office door open. "How was HER health?"

Paul was aware of Walsh's eyes flicking toward him sharply as he passed by. Anna Marie glanced toward the doctor, then back at Paul. "Aside from a recent cold, Rose was in excellent health, Mr. Castle, not that it's any of your business."

On that note, she and the doctor left the office. Paul turned to Jennie who had also remained mute during the interrogation. "Funny," he said. "I think it's very much my business."

He rose from his chair, crossed to the window and looked out toward the street. Anna Marie and the doctor were deep in animated conversation. Finally she got in her car and drove off. Walsh started back toward his office.

"I apologize," he said, coming through the door. "I was hoping she'd be more helpful. She's not really like that, you know. Just the strain of the past few days."

"I understand, Doc, but maybe you can be of some help. About

Rose, what about her health? How was it?"

Walsh smiled, raising his hands helplessly. "I'd like to help, Mr. Castle, but she was a patient. I really can't discuss her."

Paul scoffed good naturedly. "Oh, come on, Doc. Not the old medical confidentiality game. She's dead. What's to hide?"

Walsh pondered that for a moment, then shrugged." Nothing, actually," he said. "Aside from slightly elevated blood pressure she was in excellent shape."

"Really?" Paul said somewhat dubiously. "I thought I noticed some facial spasms and once in a while a tremor in her hands."

"Oh? And are you a certified M.D., young man?" Walsh asked with a twinkle. "The woman has just murdered a United States Congressman, she's about to take her own life and you are concerned about a few reflexive motor symptoms?"

Paul salaamed apologetically. "That's one for you, Doc. Think I'll stick to reporting."

"Wise choice. Will you be heading back to the city, then?" Walsh asked.

Paul glanced at his watch. "Right away," he said ." We've got a plane to catch in Waterbury."

Walsh showed him and Jennie to the door, wished them well, and repeated his offer to help further should the occasion arise. Paul thanked him, giving Walsh not only his cell phone number but his unlisted landline number at his New York apartment.

As they walked down the path toward the rental car, Jennie took his arm and said, "You seem troubled."

"Not troubled," he replied. "Unconvinced."

They got into the car. "Where to now, boss? Airport?" she asked.

"Airport," he said, "but first I need to make a quick stop."

He drove north several blocks, turned onto Main Street and

pulled up in front of Margie's Home Cooking while Jennie made plane reservations on her cell phone.

"I won't be long," Paul said, as he headed inside.

At that moment a burgundy colored Lexus pulled up to the curb a half block away. Grayden Walsh watched Paul enter the little restaurant. He drummed his fingers nervously on the steering wheel, wondering what he should do next.

During the short flight back to LaGuardia airport, Paul stared out the window at the vista below but his mind was not on scenery. He squirmed restlessly, his mind elsewhere. Jennie leafed through a magazine, reluctant to interrupt his thoughts. She knew he was trying to sort something out. When he had, he'd tell her. She could wait.

A few minutes from touchdown, Paul took out his cell phone and punched in Kovacs' number. The lieutenant, who had caller ID, answered. "Good morning, Mr. Castle," he said jovially, "and I hope—no, I pray—that you are calling with some major break in the case."

"No such luck, Lieutenant,"Paul said, "but I may be sniffing around a minor lead. I need a favor."

"Speak."

"Rose Temple's blood type. Probably included as part of the autopsy report."

"Most likely, but it was performed in Connecticut. I have no jurisdiction. If I get it, it'll be as a courtesy."

"Will you try?"

"Of course, "Kovacs said, "but if I strike out, I know someone who can get it for you. Agent Briggs."

"I'm not proud."

"And if he asks why?"

"Tell him the same thing I'm telling you. It it turns into something, he'll know and you'll know."

"Good enough," Kovacs said. "I'll get back to you."

Jennie put down her magazine as Paul disconnected. "Blood type?"

The "Fasten Seat Belts" sign flashed overhead. Quickly he filled her in on his theory. As he explained, he realized it sounded a little far fetched.

Jennie smiled in encouragement. "I'm with you, but this tree you're barking up, I hope it's the right one."

Agent Fowler Briggs hopped onto the elevator and took it two floors down to the nerve center of the FBI building. He and six other Washington-based agents had just spent an unpleasant twenty-five minutes with the SAC learning about the incompetence of the yokels doing security duty in the current crisis. By yokels, the SAC really meant locals, i.e. non-FBI. Two Congressmen, Rogers and Bowles, had flown the coop, hiding out God knows where while the yokels scratched their heads without a clue. A Cincinnati vice cop assigned to Rogers had left a short note saying the two men would be safe but the SAC had heard that many times before. The two other missing Congresspersons were still missing. The only good news was that as of noon, there had been no attempts on anyone. Maybe the increased security and the enforced low profiling had finally put an end to the carnage.

Briggs sat down at his desk next to McIlroy who was busily going through some heavy-duty paperwork. "Nice job in Houston" he said, "shutting down the website."

McIlroy looked up at him with an amused smile on his lips. "You think? Well, Fowler, they may have been shut down but they haven't been quieted. You know about the billboards?"

"I heard."

"Well, have you heard about My Face, My Space, My Achin' Ass and a dozen other people-sites on the internet?"

"Yeah, sort of," Briggs responded uncertainly, not being the computer maven his partner was.

"It seems a few thousand, hell, it could be a few hundred thousand, people downloaded the SST programming and now it's sprouting up like weeds all over the country. It's everywhere you look and I don't care how ballsy Homeland Security thinks it is, it isn't about to shut down the entire country."

Briggs leaned back in his chair, shaking his head. He looked at McIlroy. "Dunc, what the hell is going on?" he asked seriously.

McIlroy shook his head. "No clue."

"Housewives, shopkeepers, an 83 year old socialite, for Christ's sake. They're coming at us from every direction, no rhyme, no reason, no sense at all. Why not some woman in a wheelchair or a Catholic priest, or—I don't know. They sit down, they hand over their weapon, they say nothing, they want nothing, not even a lawyer. They know they could be facing the needle and they don't care."

McIlroy smiled again, almost permitting a laugh. "Not to worry, Fowler, the Director promised we'll have someone in custody within 72 hours." With that he made a big show of checking in and around his desk, as if looking for a hidden bug.

Briggs laughed just as his phone rang. He picked up.

"Briggs." Pause. "Oh, sure, Lieutenant, how can I help you?" He listened intently, made a couple of notes on a desk pad. "Did he say why?" He listened some more. "All right, I'll see what I can do." He hung up and looked over at McIlroy. "My favorite television reporter needs a favor. I suppose I could just ignore him."

"You could," McIlroy said, "but the last time Castle called he gave you something pretty good."

Briggs pondered that for a moment, then reached for the phone and pressed a button. "This is Briggs. Get me the number for the coroner's office in Waterbury, Connecticut."

Paul was in his office at ten after two, hovering over his computer logged onto a site that was telling him more than he really wanted to know about blood typing. Somewhat lost in a sea of allelles and antigens, he thought he had a grasp on the big picture when the phone rang. It was Kovacs.

"The young lady was Type A." he said. "Now what the hell are you up to?"

"Type A." Paul mulled it, checked his screen again, and then logged out. "You never met the lady's mother, did you, Lieutenant?"

"You know I didn't," Kovacs said.

"A tough old bird with red hair. The real thing. Not a dye job because as she's gotten older a lot of grey has crept in and she's not trying to hide it."

"So?"

"In the antique shop, there's an old photo of her husband from his tour in 'Nam. He's a blonde. And what I ask myself is this. How do a blonde and a redhead give birth to a daughter with jet black hair?"

"I don't know. How? "Kovacs asked, playing it dumb.

"They don't," Paul replied. "Hanging next to Daddy's picture were his old GI dogtags which said he was Type B-Negative, which also means, Lieutenant, that Daddy wasn't Daddy at all."

"You sure about that?"

"The science doesn't lie. Anyway I got clued in by one of the locals that Anna Marie did a little dallying on the side. I confirmed it with a very nice lady who's a hell of a cook besides being a charter member of the town's Gossip Central. Some twenty eight years ago the husband was on the road a lot selling industrial supplies. Anna Marie was home alone, bored out of her mind. She met this guy, a

Latino—Margie doesn't remember his name. They went at it hot and heavy for a couple of weeks and then the guy left town. Home comes the husband. Nine months later Rose makes her debut. The husband takes one look, puts two and two together and a few days later, he's gone."

"I assume you're going somewhere with this," Kovacs said.

"I am. Rose Temple, contrary to what her doctor told me, was not a well woman. At times her speech was slightly thick and slurry. She had occasional tics on her face and often her hands trembled badly. Now here's where you have to make a leap of faith. There are certain debilitating diseases that are inherited. If that were true in Rose's case, she wouldn't have gotten it from her mother because Anna Marie is in good health and certainly shows none of Rose's symptoms. Ergo—"

"Ergo??"

"Ergo, she got it from her biological father who Anna Marie slept with bringing forth Rose and chasing off her legal husband, leaving the two women alone and forcing them to survive on their own for twenty-eight years. Rose, suffering from a disease given to her by a man she never met because of Anna Marie promiscuity, forgave her mother in those last moments of her life. Mama, she cried out, it's not your fault."

There was a long silence.

"That's pretty damned farfetched," Kovacs said.

"It is," Paul said, "but it explains a lot, particularly why a young woman like Rose would commit murder. Because that disease wasn't just debilitating, it was terminal."

"And the why?" Kovacs asked.

"I don't know."

Kovacs leaned back in his chair and stared at his water-stained ceiling, pondering it. It sounded plausible if you had a vivid imagination. On the other hand...... He shook his head. "Wait a minute. The autopsy. If the Temple woman had something really wrong with her, they'd have caught it."

"Maybe they did, but we didn't ask. Or maybe they missed it. I'm not a coroner," Paul said.

"Maybe this, maybe that."

"And maybe I'm full of crap. Entirely possible. I'm just trying to find something—anything—that begins to make sense." There was another long silence from Kovacs' end as he weighed it. "I wonder what kind of shape that trucker was in before he put the nose of his semi into the Congresswoman's grille?"

"Wouldn't hurt to find out," Paul said. At that moment Murray appeared in Paul's doorway waving his arms with urgency and pointing skyward. Someone apparently needed him urgently and it was either Fritz Schoenfeld or God.

"I'll take a swing at it," Kovacs replied, "though I'm beginning to think I'm just as loony as you are." He hung up.

Murray stood in the doorway, a grin stretching from one of his oversized ears to the other. "We have got a live one, Paulie," he said.

And they did.

Before Paul could get through Schoenfeld's door, the Old Man was talking. "You're needed in Washington NOW, Paul. You and the camera crew. Round 'em up. You've got to be there no later than five-thirty. We go live at six."

"Live with what?

Schoenfeld looked over at Murray who said,"I didn't tell him, boss. Saved that for you."

"Leonard Philby. He wants to talk on camera. With you, Paul. Only you. I think he likes your style."

Paul was stunned. "My God. And how does the FBI feel about

this?"

"They're pissin' bullets but what can they do? He won't say squat to them. I guess they figure you're better than nothing."

Paul shook his head. "I can't do an interview with them hanging all over me."

"I told them that. It'll be just you and Philby, camera and audio in one room. After the broadcast we give them a copy of the tape."

"Preconditions?"

"None. If he doesn't like the question, he'll tell you so and you move on."

Paul nodded. "I'll need to see the files to know what to ask."

"You can look at it, take notes. You can't keep it and you can't copy it." , Schoenfeld said.

Paul looked at Murray. "You coming?"

"I'll be liaising with a local station. They're supplying the dish and the van in return for the live feed through their outlet. I'll be at the controls with the director."

Paul shrugged, satisfied. "Well, as Jackie Gleason used to say, 'Away we Go!'"

They reached La Guardia at quarter past three, parked in the private avation sector parking lot and then hustled across the tarmac toward the waiting 8-seater Lear Jet. The stairway was already lowered, a flight attendant stood by the open door. The pilot was visible in the cockpit doing a last minute instrument check.

As Paul hurried up the steps and entered the small cabin area, a familiar face smiled in greeting. "Good afternoon, Mr. Castle," said Agent Fowler Briggs. Paul hesitated momentarily before moving to a nearby seat.

"Good afternoon, Agent Briggs," he said. "Don't need a body-guard, but thanks for thinking of me."

Briggs smiled and patted the seat next to him. "You'll be more comfortable here."

"I don't think so," Paul said.

"But I insist," Briggs said, still smiling. Paul hesitated for second, then got up and took the seat next to the agent. Briggs clicked open the attache case on his lap, took out a manila envelope which he handed to Paul. "Reading material for the flight. If you have any questions, that's what I'm here for."

Paul slipped the twelve page report from the envelope. It was the case file on the murder of Congressman Jerome Tolliver. He leafed through it quickly. It was packed with detailed information. Say what you will about the FBI, they knew how to investigate. As the plane's engines roared to life, Paul tightened his seat belt and leaned back. He opened to the first page and started reading.

After forty minutes, he put the report down and rubbed his eyes.

"Tired?" Briggs asked.

"Small print. I'm getting a headache."

Briggs nodded "I talked to Kovacs. About the woman's blood type. He filled me in on your theory. I don't think it flies."

"Probably not," Paul said. "You got anything better going?"

"You know us FBI guys don't talk to the press."

"Hell, I hear you don't even talk to your wives."

"That would be the married ones," Briggs said. "I don't even talk to my mother," he continued without cracking a smile.

"Well, if you did talk to your mother, is there anything you might tell her, anything at all no matter how insignificant, off the record, of course."

Briggs looked at him. "Not a thing," he said. "Not a damned thing."

Washington's Central Detention Facility is a large but basically dreary looking building located at 1901 D Street SE, home to miscreants of every descripton. For some it's a way station on the road to Leavenworth or some other state or federal facility, for others a temporary residence of three to six months after which they will be released back into society to ply the anti-social behavior that landed them there in the first place. Many will return and if they return often enough, the gates of Leavenworth will beckon. The CDF is also the temporary home of Leonard Philby for want of a more appropriate facility because no one really knew what that facility should be.

A modest sized visitor's room on the first floor had been set aside for the interview The ambience was prison deco, that is to say, non-existent. A single table had been set up in the middle of the room with facing chairs. The lighting was harsh and untextured. Paul found it serviceable. Bud Wollens, the cameraman, set up two cameras at cross angles to cover the participants. The audio would be captured by a small boom mike manipulated by the sound man. A pitcher of ice water had been placed in the center of the table alongside a short stack of paper cups.

Per Paul's request Philby was led into the room at ten minutes to six. He was wearing prison garb, a bright orange jump suit, but was unshackled. Two guards would be positioned outside the door in case of trouble. Paul doubted there would be.

Philby was tall, maybe six-one, and thin. Very thin. Almost gaunt. Paul wondered if he was on a hunger strike. No, that would have been in the file. Philby looked at Paul, smiled almost imperceptably in greeting and sat down in his chair. At the sound man's request, he recited 'Mary Had a Little Lamb' so the sound levels could be locked in.

Paul checked his watch. Two minutes to go. He sat down. "Thanks for the opportunity," he said. "May I ask why me, Mr. Philby?"

"Ask anything you like, Mr. Castle, on camera." Philby said. "Just try your best to act like a reporter and not a cop."

Agent Briggs, watching a television monitor in a nearby office, gritted his teeth. He didn't approve of any of this. Men like Philby were supposed to answer to the law, not get their faces and their opinions plastered all over the country on some second-rate television show. The Director had suggested that Philby and the others were a different kind of criminal. Briggs didn't buy it. A perp was a perp.

In the interview room, the second hand swept by six o'clock and Paul started talking. Without larding it on too thickly, Paul opened by describing the broadcast as groundbreaking, unprecedented and unique, all redundant ways to let America know that National Heartbeat had scored a great big coup.

Paul opened with a dozen or so innocuous questions. Where was Philby born, reared, where did he go to school, military service, marriage, the untimely death of his wife, raising four sons on his own, working hard to make a success of a small software company. Philby's answers were concise if not illuminating. He spoke quietly in measured tones. If he had a sense of humor he didn't show it.

"In my opinion," Paul said, finally, "everything about you, Mr. Philby, bespeaks a typical American upbringing, a conventional life in most regards, certainly a successful business career and yet here you are, in custody, charged with the murder of a United States Congressman. I am curious, as I'm sure all America is, as to how you reached this point."

"This program isn't long enough to detail all my reasons. The short answer is, yes, I had a typical upbringing. I was privileged to serve my country when she needed me the most, I was lucky enough to marry a woman whom I loved deeply, who blessed me with four wonderful sons, and fortunate enough, also, to have the freedom to pursue a career that would allow me to provide my sons with the best this country had to offer."

"And yet, despite all that, in a local restaurant packed with patrons who witnessed it, you shot and killed an unarmed man in cold blood."

"In cold blood is your characterization, Mr. Castle, not mine," Philby said.

"And how would you characterize it?"

"Cold blood implies a lack of feeling. That wasn't the case." Paul nodded, then referred to the file. "According to the file," he said, "you and Congressman Tolliver were old friends."

"I wouldn't say that."

"But you attended college together. You knew each other."

"Yes."

"And you were not close."

"No. At school, we were acquaintances. Since then I'd seen him only twice. Once at a reunion many years ago and two weeks ago at the restaurant."

"This meeting. Who initiated it?"

"I did."

"And you brought a gun to the meeting. Does that mean you intended to kill him right from the start?"

"I had hoped I wouldn' t have to." he said, then quickly shook his head. "No, erase that. It was necessary. It had to be done."

"Why?"

"Because he was destroying the country."

"Explain that."

"Certainly. In addition to being a self-serving thief, Jerry Tolliver espoused a Communist philosophy which threatened to tear apart the fabric of this country."

Paul looked at him askance. "Communist. Don't you think that's a little over the top. Socialist, maybe."

Philby smiled. "You know what my definition of a Socialist is, Mr. Castle? A Communist who doesn't have the guts to admit what he really is."

"So even though Tolliver was legally elected to his seat in Congress by the people in his district, you still felt you had the right to murder him."

"Yes, even though," Philby said. "Mr. Castle, you are not a stupid man and you are not blind. You know exactly what's been happening to this country since the national election a year and a half ago. Government takeovers of the auto industry, banks, investment houses, insurance companies. Over a trillion dollars in so-called stimulus that only stimulated the bank accounts of tens of thousands of corrupt politicians throughout the country. A second trillion a real possibility. Scores of regulations eating away at our personal freedoms, freedoms we've enjoyed for centuries, freedoms guaranteed by the Constitution. A once proud military, defunded and gutted. School systems throughout the country that now seize your children at the age of three and put them into indoctrination centers posing as day care. And worst of all, nationalized health care. A year ago, the President's original grandiose scheme was defeated by the narrowest of margins and now here it comes again, as ugly and as dangerous as it ever was. This is not the America I fought for. This is not the America I love. This is not the America I am willing to leave to my four boys. You may call it murder, Mr. Castle. I call it war and in war there are casualties. When Jerry Tolliver declared war on our traditional way of life, his fate was sealed."

Paul sat, fascinated. He'd been too caught up to interrupt. Not once had Philby raised his voice and yet he had been mesmerizing. Whether you agreed with him or not, you knew the man was a true believer.

After a pause, Paul found his voice. "But why Tolliver, Mr. Philby? Why not start at the top because if he is anything, the President is more of a Socialist, or Communist according to you, than Tolliver could ever hope to be."

Philby smiled. "Don't be naive. First, assassinating the President is not something easily done. Second, his death would make him an instant martyr. If you know your history, and I'm sure you do, John Kennedy's death led to an outpouring of grief which permitted Lyndon Johnson to push through every piece of controversial legislation that Kennedy had left undone, laws that might not have been enacted if he had lived. And thirdly, Mr. Castle, rightly or wrongly, the President was elected by all the people, not just the few."

"You lost me there." Paul said.

"You may believe that the President was elected because of mammoth vote fraud in several key states. You may believe that he was elected because he was opposed by a confused, indecisive old man who ran an unbelievably inept campaign. And you may believe that he was elected because he spent the last sixty days spewing out one lie after another to convince the public he was a moderate. But even if you believe all that, he was still voted in by a substantial majority of the voters. That's the American way and no one has the right to subvert it.

"On the other hand, there are a handful of Congresspersons, less than ten percent, who are able to exercise power far beyond the confines of their Congressional districts. People like Tolliver with their influential committee chairmanships. And like Tolliver, representatives from 'safe' districts, so heavily weighted to one party that it becomes impossible to unseat them. The powerful lobbies hold sway over them, billionaire contributors buying influence, but when it comes to you and me, our single vote is totally meaningless."

"And why just the House?," Paul asked. "Why not the Senate as well?"

"It may come to that, but for now, the House is the body closest to the people. There is an election in November. If the people of this country wake up in time to really understand what's happening to them, we may be able to reverse this takeover immediately. Pray God we're right."

"You say 'we.'"

"Did I? By that, I meant all patriotic Americans."

Paul nodded. "Let me ask you about Congressman Johansson. A woman named Rose Temple—"

Philby interrupted sharply. "I'm not here to discuss anyone else. Mr. Castle. Just myself and Congressman Tolliver."

"I understand. I just wondered if you had known her prior to—"

"If you persist, this interview is at an end. Now do you have any further questions about me?"

Paul shook his head. "No." Then he looked up sharply. "How's your health?"

Philby was momentarily caught off guard. "What?"

"I said, how's your health?" Paul repeated.

"My health is just fine," Philby said, collecting himself.

"You look a little thin," Paul persisted. "When was the last time you saw a doctor?"

"If there's nothing else—"

"I really don't like your pallor, Mr. Philby. Kind of yellowish."

Philby stood, unnnerved, and called out, "Guard!"

"You know I'm not sure I blame you," Paul said." Don't care for doctors much myself. They're always giving you bad news. Sometimes really bad news."

The two guards opened the door and stepped inside. Philby brushed by them. "Let's get out of here," he growled.

Bud had been alert enough to grab one of the stationary cameras when the two men stood and he caught the entire exchange. Now he swung from the doorway to Paul's face.

"Well, there you have it, America," Paul said. "Leonard Philby, dedicated patriot or raving lunatic, or somewhere in between? You make the call."

In the nearby office, Briggs was staring at the screen. Castle did a good job, he thought. No doubt about it, Philby was a certifiable whack job. And that question about his health. Very sharp. He leaned back, thinking he might want to give a little more thought to Rose Temple and her Type A blood.

Meanwhile at a sub-station of the Maryland State Police located just outside of Frederick, the phone rang. The officer assigned to desk duty for the evening, picked up the receiver. A man's voice spoke.

"I want to report a double homicide," the voice said. He gave directions to the location and hung up. Fifteen minutes later two state police cruisers appeared, turning into the driveway of the rustic hideaway retreat located on the banks of the Monocacy River just north and east of Frederick. The cars skidded to a halt on the oyster shell driveway and four troopers got out, guns drawn, approaching the cabin cautiously. Two men were sitting sprawled on rattan chairs on the small front porch. Half empty beer bottles rested on the table sitting between them. Each man had a quarter-sized hole in the middle of his forehead. A light shone from within the cabin. The lead trooper, a sergeant, carefully pushed the door open and peered inside. A black man with a grey military haircut was seated at a small table in the kitchen area playing solitaire. A .38 police special lay on the table next to the man's ID which was propped up and easily readable. The sergeant approached, gun at the ready, peered down at the ID.

"You on the job, Lieutenant?" the sergeant asked.

"Was," Bert Yancey replied without looking up.

"The two guys on the porch?"

"Couple of Congressmen."

"You're the one called it in?"

"Uh-huh," Yancey nodded.

"You know who did it?" the sergeant asked.

"Uh-huh," Yancey said, pointing to the pistol.

The sergeant picked it up carefully by the trigger guard. "Yours?"

"Uh-huh."

The sergeant was puzzled. "I guess that means I'm going to have to take you in."

Yancey finally looked up at him and smiled. "Hell, Sergeant, if you don't you're not much of a cop, are you?"

Yancey was cuffed and put into the rear seat of one of the cruisers. A call for an ambulance and a homicide detective had been sent out (Take your time, boys, they ain't going anywhere). The troopers waited for them to arrive.

From the back seat of the cruiser, Yancey stared at his handiwork still sprawled uncovered on the porch. Two less leeches to worry about. Rogers had been a hopeless case, crooked to the core, his vote for sale on any issue, any time. The socialist crowd paid best. That's where he went. Bowles was another thing altogether. More zealot than thief but in the end, a despicable hypocrite. When one of the really decent Congressmen from North Dakota tried to tack on an amendment to the new health care bill to require all members of the Congress and the Adminstration be covered by the same regulations they were forcing down the American gullet, Bowles marshaled his forces in committee and killed the amendment dead. This one didn't even require a payoff. The people-loving socialist members of the House were scared shitless of the totalitarian regulations they were about to impose on everyone else. Bert Yancey couldn't help but smile. Bowles would no longer need health coverage of any kind. On the other hand, he thought ruefully, neither would he. According to his doctor, his body was riddled with bone cancer. If the doc was right he had less than six months to live.

CHAPTER FOURTEEN

He'd started to sag on the flight back to the city. By the time they landed at LaGuardia, Paul's energy level was registering near zero. When the cab pulled up in front of his apartment house, the cabbie had to wake him from a sound sleep. He trudged into the lobby, grunted an obligatory greeting to Sasha, the night security guy, and rode the elevator up to the third floor. As tired as he was, he knew he'd done a good day's work. Anna Marie and Dr. Grayden Walsh were at the top of tomorrow's "To Do" list. He had a pretty good idea what they were hiding. The question was, why? And the interview with Philby. It couldn't have gone any better. The look in Philby's eyes when he was pressed on his health. Paul knew he was very close to something, something he couldn't quite get a grip on.

But first, blessed sleep. He turned the key in the lock, stepped inside and flipped the light switch. Nothing happened. He flipped it again, up and down. Suddenly someone grabbed him from behind, pinning his arms to his sides. He struggled, lurching forward, stumbling, slamming into a table and knocking a lamp and the phone to the floor. He tried to kick backwards but whoever had grabbed him was too strong. As he tried to twist away, he was aware of someone else close by. A bag of some sort, maybe a pillowcase, was pulled down over his head and wrapped tight with some sort of cord. He struggled for air. A steel hard fist buried itself in his belly and he doubled over in pain. Nausea flooded through him. Another blow, then another and then he was tossed roughly onto the floor. He tried to curl up in the fetal position. A shoe slammed into his ribs. Twice, three times, each kick more vicious than the one before. He was able to breathe but just barely. He gasped, tried to scrabble away on all fours and then felt a man's foot pressed into the small of his back, pushing him down, freezing him in place. He was suddenly aware of a man's head leaning in very close to his own. The man's voice was unhurried and quiet, almost a whisper. "We don't want to kill you, but we will if we have to," the man said softly. "If you love your country, you will stay out of this. Nod if you understand."

Paul nodded.

"Good. You won't be warned again, Mr. Castle."

Paul, his head reeling dizzily, felt the man move away. Whoever had his foot in Paul's back removed it. A few seconds later he heard the apartment door open and shut. All was silence except for insistent buzz-buzz-buzz from the phone which had been dashed to the floor. He tried to crawl to the phone but found he couldn't. A sharp jagged pain stabbed at his ribs. He reached up, felt the cord holding the sack over his head. He yanked at it vainly, then an inky black wave roiled up from the back of his head and enveloped his brain. The sleep that he had so craved only a few minutes before wrapped him in its arms.

Later (he wasn't sure how much later) he was aware of a knocking on his door and then the bag was being removed and soft hands were holding his head. A woman was speaking his name. In the background he could hear a man with a decidedly Russian accent on the phone, calling for an ambulance.

At the hospital, the birddog had become the quarry. A dozen or so reporters, print and electronic, were camped outside the main entrance waiting for the arrival of someone, anyone, who could give them a quote or a sound bite. They knew that Paul Castle was inside, the victim of a vicious beating, but the how, the why and the where were unknown. Following the interview earlier that evening with Leonard Philby, Paul Castle had suddenly become a celebrity of national status and instant fodder for the talking heads that infested cable news channels. Was the beating connected to the broadcast? Only a fool would think otherwise. CNN praised Paul's incisive shredding of the right wing fascist murderer. FOX thought the interview even-handed and while deploring the idea of murder to resolve political issues, did suggest that some citizens, fed up with the direction the country was being led into, might be irresponsible enough to resort to tactics that were clearly beyond the pale.

Inside Paul was resting uncomfortably in bed in a private room where he was sent after a thorough going over in the emergency room. The verdict was two cracked ribs (now neatly taped up) and a truckload of bruises. The ribs would be painful for a week or two; the bruises would take care of themselves. Over his objections they'd dosed him with Demerol to help him sleep, but he was determined to go cold turkey starting in the morning. He needed a clear head if he was going to keep after this story and that he was going to do, despite the ominous warning. He wasn't afraid any more. He was pissed.

Jennie was sitting next to him. She'd tried to call several times, kept getting a busy on the land line and no answer on his cell. Worried she'd taken a cab over and talked Sasha into opening his door.

Paul reached out painfully for his plastic cup of water. Jennie handed to him. He sipped slowly and put it down. "One way or another, I'm going to get those bastards, I swear to God."

"And you've got no idea who they were?"

"That's what I told the cops," Paul said.

"That's not an answer."

"It'll do."

"You recognized a voice?"

"No, but I have some ideas."

"I'll tell you an idea you ought to have, Castelli. Moving. You pay big bucks for that apartment and the security that goes with it. So how'd they slip by Sasha?"

"Probably through the basement garage. If you can get through the staircase door, you can bypass the lobby."

"Swell," she groused.

"I know, I know. I'll complain to the management. By the way, I forgot to ask you. How'd you make out with Lisa Wallenberg ?"

"She couldn't tell me much more than she already had. When I pressed her, she gave me the name of her grandmother's doctor—his name is Hammond Chambers—but she doubts he'll tell me anything. She says he's a tight ass who goes by the book."

Just then Paul's mother appeared in the doorway. There were traces of tear stains on her face as Deanna Castle hurried to her son's bedside. "Paulie," she wailed. She started to cry again.

"I'm okay, Mom," he told her.

"I heard from the doctor already about how okay you are."

"A couple of cracked ribs, that's all."

"Like it's nothing," she said. "You could be dead."

"I'm not dead. If you stop crying, I'll be over for lasagna next Sunday. Where's Pop?"

"Parking the car." Deanna looked over at Jennie as if seeing her for the first time and appraising her instantly.

"Mom, this is Jennie Bovano."

"It's very nice to meet you, Mrs Castelli," Jennie said pleasantly.

Deanna caught it right away. "You know Castelli? You must be special." She hesitated thoughtfully. "Jennie Bovano. You're the one from Baltimore, the one he told me was the one and only."

"My God, Mom, that was seventeen years ago."

"Yes, and I'm still waiting for those grandchildren," Deanna said. "Remember one thing, my son, a mother never forgets." She smiled at Jennie. "It is a pleasure to meet you, Jennie, and let me apologize for my son who at times can be a blind self-centered idiot."

"And pig-headed, too," Jennie added.

"Exactly," Deanna agreed.

Just then Vittorio strode into the room. "Where's my boy? Hey, Paulie, you look like crap but they say you're gonna live."

"Afraid so, Pop," he said, "and don't give me one of those bear hugs or they'll hear me screaming in the lobby."

Deanna came around the bed and took Jennie by the arm. "You boys talk your man stuff for a few minutes. Jennie and I are going to have coffee in the waiting room."

When they were alone Vittorio's tone became more serious. "You okay, Paulie? Tell me."

"I'm going to be fine, Pop. Word of honor," he said.

"Your insurance, that's okay?"

"Pop, don't worry."

"I just want to help." The old man's eyes moistened slightly.

"I know, I know. Listen, Pop, about your trouble. I think it's going to be okay."

"The FBI guy?"

Paul nodded. "I'm helping him, he's helping me."

"I can't testify against Marchetti. I'd be dead," Vittorio said.

"I know that. He knows that. Just don't worry, Pop. I'm working it out." Vittorio reached over, took his son's hand and gently squeezed it.

"Now go on, Pop. I gotta sleep. Say goodbye to Mom and Jennie for me."

Vittorio nodded. "Ciao." He moved to the door, flipped off the lights and closed the door behind him. Paul stared up at the darkened ceiling. Within minutes he was dead asleep.

Paul was awakened three times that night. Once by an insistent bladder, once by a nurse under orders to record his temperature and blood pressure and third time by a very young nurse who, misreading his chart, woke him to give him a sleeping pill. He then managed to sleep uninterrupted from five a.m. until nearly seven-thirty. When he awoke he found Lt. Kovacs munching on a pathetic looking roll which he had obviously filched from the breakfast tray sitting on the table next to the bed.

"Apparently, Lieutenant," he said, "you will eat just about anything."

Kovacs nodded. "I almost drew the line at this. You people seem to have no standards at all."

Paul peered at the tray. "I see tiny crumbs of bacon on the plate next to the overcooked eggs."

"You do, indeed. I have a motto. Never let a good pig die in vain. My rabbi disagrees. If you're hungry we still have eggs, juice and diced potatoes."

"I'll pass," Paul said. "Hand me a coffee."

Kovacs passed it over. "You should have told me you were going to Washington yesterday. I like that city."

"So do I, what I saw of it. Sightseeing was not on the list of activities. So, Lieutenant, have you arrested my attackers yet?"

"Sorry, no. We did a thorough sweep for fingerprints. Found a lot of yours. None of the obvious clues you see on Perry Mason: cigarette ashes, match book covers, muddy shoe prints. These fellas knew what they were doing. By the way, we found jimmy scratches on the lock on the basement door to the staircase."

"Figures."

"We've got a few uniforms canvassing the building and the neighborhood. I don't expect much but you never know. You got any ideas?"

Paul nodded. "One pretty good one. Except for the office, nobody knew my address, not even my parents. When you do a sleazy tabloid show like mine you tend to piss people off which was why I kept it secret. When I was leaving Dr. Walsh's office yesterday, I gave him both my cell number and my land line."

Kovacs nodded in understanding. "And with the phone number and a backwards directory, he gets your address. I don't know. You made him seem like a pretty nice old guy ."

"Who lied through his teeth about Rose Temple's health."

"Also doesn't sound like a guy who'd resort to muscle."

"These guys who jumped me were young, hard. Paid goons."

"You know, someone could have followed you home one night from the studio," Kovacs suggested.

Paul shook his head. "I've been watching my back for over a year now. Nobody followed me. What about the trucker's doctor? You get anything out of him?"

"Nope." He consulted a small note pad. "Name's Jacob Rovich, works for an HMO in Troy. That's pretty close by Grafton. I got that much from Chaffee's wife. Rovich was pretty close-mouthed. The usual doctor- patient runaround. I was pushing him on the phone so I didn't have much leverage but I got the feeling if I drove up there, I'd get the same story."

"And the local hospitals?"

"Worse. Warrants, warrants, warrants. That's all they could talk about." He slipped the notepad back into his pocket. "So let me guess. You're headed for Bergensberg to wring the truth out of Doctor Walsh."

"Give that man a kewpie doll," Paul said, tossing back his covers and gingerly lowering his feet to the floor.

Kovacs said, “You know, you’re in no condition—”

“I’ll be fine,” Paul snapped, steadying himself.

“I was going to say you’re in no condition to drive. This time I’m going with you and my presence is not optional.”

“No, I—”

“I’ve got a badge and you don’t, son, and while it isn’t worth diddely in Bergensberg, we might be able to put a little fear into the good doctor. Not the fear of God, of course, but maybe one of the twelve apostles.”

Paul looked at him and couldn’t help grinning.

If Paul had awakened a half hour later and if Lieutenant Kovacs had not appeared in his hospital room and if he had not checked himself out early and if he had had the television set tuned to a certain well known network morning show, he would have been treated to six minutes of intriguing television journalism. Andrea Wilkes, the waitress who laced the soup of the Speaker of the House with cyanide had decided, on the heels of Paul’s interview with Leonard Philby, to add her own perspective to the national debate. The morning show host was more than willing to handle the segment but the network brass wanted a harder edge to the questioning. A subtle stirring of understanding among the populace for these anarchists was starting to be felt throughout the country and it had to be stopped. People like Andrea Wilkes had to be shown for what they were, cold blooded killers of respected unarmed American patriots. Jason Gerardi, an outspoken contributor to many of the network’s weekend news specials was tapped for the assignment. Jason was in rare form.

“So, Mrs. Wilkes, “he asked, “how does it feel to murder a man, I think our viewers would like to know.”

Andrea looked at him coldly. "Actually, it felt terrible. It's a mortal sin."

"Ah," he smiled. "You sound like a Catholic. Well, as a Catholic, how do you justify it?" Gerardi asked.

"I don't. Deep down I believe it blackened my soul for eternity but in time of war there are casualties."

"Oh, you believe we're at war? With who? Each other? Or maybe you think God has ordered you to kill people you don't agree with, progressive people with fresh new ideas who won the last election and not you people who lost."

"What do you mean, 'you people'?"

"You know exactly what I mean, Mrs. Wilkes."

"Actually, I don't. I'm a mother, I was a wife until my husband died, I was a homeowner until the bank took my house away, I was a bookkeeper with eighteen years experience until the company I worked for was forced to accept unionization even though the employees didn't want it and as a result went out of business. After that I was a janitor in an office building, moonlighting as a waitress whenever I could to pick up some extra income. Now which of those 'you people' do you want me to be, Mr. Gerardi?"

"Just your average hardworking American, is that what you're trying to say? And you poisoned Congressman Bomford on what? A whim?"

"Hardly. The man was responsible for a great deal of misery in this country. It is certain that he was trying to turn us into a Socialist state. Every legitimate poll showed that the majority of Americans opposed him. He was an arrogant little man who felt he owed nothing to the people and who exercised a warped power that extended far beyond the boundaries of his Congressional district."

"And so that's what it comes down to," Gerardi sneered. "Not a holy war but good old fashioned impersonal political assassination."

Andrea stiffened and her eyes started to moisten. "No, Mr. Gerardi, not impersonal. Not at all. Ten months ago my husband had a good paying job in an automobile assembly plant, but the company couldn't meet the competition from the government owned factories in Michigan so they went out of business. For two months Jack was out of work. He finally found a job ninety miles away. He commuted every day—"

"Yes, yes, I'm sure—" Gerardi tried to interrupt.

Andrea ignored him, managing to supress her tears. "Up at 4:30, two hours to work, home by 7:30, dog tired. Week after week until one late afternoon he was so exhausted he fell asleep at the wheel and smashed into a bridge abuttment."

"You have my sympathy, Mrs. Wilkes, but you're evading my question—"

"Six days later I got a call from a clinic in a neighboring town. They said my daughter was there. I needed to come right away. When I got there she was in a great deal of pain. She'd lost a lot of blood, but the procedure had been successful. Do you know what kind of procedure we're talking about here, Mr. Gerardi?"

Gerardi was losing his temper and it was showing. "Again, Mrs. Wilkes you are totally off subject—"

"It was an abortion clinic, funded by the government—"

"Madam, I really have no time nor the patience for an anti-abortion tirade from a fanatical right-to-lifer—"

Andrea overrode him. "I am not anti-abortion. I had one myself when I was twenty-three and I had no choice. I am anti-abortion when it comes to a thirteen year old girl who is ordered not to notify her parents of her condition, so scared out of her mind she would have let them do anything to her."

That stopped Gerardi momentarily. "Yes, I can sympathize—"

"No, you cant. Do you have children, sir? Well, no, of course you don't." Gerardi was an avowed homosexual and proud of it. "Without children you have no idea what I'm talking about."

"Please!" Gerardi half-shouted. "The issue here is the murder of Congressman Bomford. Surely you can't blame him for your personal setbacks."

"But I can and I do. The Speaker, more than any other individual aside from the President, is most responsible for the mess this country is in and for the misery he has caused. "

"You don't solve political problems with a bowlful of poison—"

"Be grateful, sir, that it was only one bowl and one man. Last year the people showed great common sense in blocking the original Congressional health care proposal. Now they've brought it back and even though a majority of the country is opposed to it, the Speaker said last week that he was bound and determined to enact his program whether the people liked it or not. We were, in his words, too stupid to know what was good for us. "

Gerardi shook his head helplessly" I'm sorry, it's time to end this farce—"

"So, yes, Mr. Gerardi, I eliminated Mr. Bomford before he could do any more harm to the country and if need be, I would have done it again. And again. And again."

At that point, the network cut away to a weather report.

"Slow down before you get to that old vegetable shack up there on the right," Paul warned as they approached the town limit sign for Bergensberg.

Kovacs noted the sudden drop in the posted speed limit. "Humph," he said." I thought that sort of thing went out with 8-tracks."

"Not up here."

They crept by at the posted speed. On this day, the town police car was apparently busy elsewhere. Kovacs proceeded toward Main

Street taking it all in. "Looks like a kinda nice little town," he said. "Kinda like where I was brought up."

"Where was that, Lieutenant? "

"Little speck on the map in Illinois. You never heard of it. Two traffic lights, a dozen stop signs. If you sneezed going through, you missed it."

"Never would have taken you for a small town boy."

Kovacs grinned. "I'm not. That's why I left."

Paul pointed. "That's the shop, there on the left."

The policeman pulled into an empty parking spot. There were a lot of them. They got out of the car, Paul gingerly. The long ride had done nothing to ease the discomfort in his rib cage. Even though it should have been open, the shop was again closed. Paul peered in. Empty. The door was locked.

Just then one of the locals approached, a wizened grey-haired lady moving slowly with the aid of a cane. "You lookin' for Miz Temple?" she asked.

"We are," Paul said.

"Don't believe she's in town," the old woman said. "Heard she left town this morning to visit kinfolk."

Paul and Kovacs exchanged a quick look. "You wouldn't know where, by any chance?" Paul asked.

"No. I think maybe somewhere in Maine. Might be staying there a while. Looked like she'd packed a lot of luggage in her car."

Kovacs looked at Paul. "Might have left a forwarding address at the post office."

The old woman shook her head. "No, didn't do that. William would have mentioned it. William's my grandson. He's the postmaster."

Paul nodded. "And no one has any idea where in Maine these kinfolk might be living?"

"No, most folks here in Bergensberg try to mind their own business." She smiled as she tottered off. "Well, you two boys have a nice day now."

Kovacs watched her go. "You think maybe this doctor fella decided to retire and moved to Arizona this morning?" he asked dryly.

"Well, aside from chasing after Granny and asking her, there's only one way to find out," Paul said.

There were three cars parked outside Dr. Grayden Walsh's home/office. Two people were sitting on chairs in the waiting room, an Hispanic young man with a bandage on his left hand and a plumpish looking woman who sniffled a lot. Walsh's receptionist-nurse was seated behind a desk at the far side of the small room.

Paul approached. "Excuse me, but I need to see Doctor Walsh."

"Are you a patient?"

"No, this is personal. If you'll just give him my name—"

"I'm sorry, but Doctor is very busy today. Perhaps if you came back after hours—"

"I'm from out of town. I can't wait that long."

"I'm sorry, sir, unless you're in need of medical assistance I can't help you."

Paul thought about that for a moment, then untucked his shirt, lifted it to his neck revealing his bandaged ribs. "Will this do?" he asked.

The woman hesitated momentarily, then handed him a clipboard with several blank forms on it. "Fill these out. I'l try to fit you in." Kovacs, who had been wandering around, admiring the Norman Rockwell prints on the wall, watched in amusement as Paul started to fill out the paperwork.

Thirty minutes later they were in Walsh's office. Paul introduced Kovacs. "You're quite a long way from your jurisdiction, aren't you, Lieutenant?" So much for intimidation with a badge.

"Just here to see the sights, Doctor," Kovacs smiled, "and to keep my good friend company."

Walsh nodded pleasantly. "And you, Mr. Castle, you have some sort of medical problem?"

Paul lifted his shirt again to display his bandaged torso.

"My, that looks nasty," Walsh said.

"It ought to," Paul replied. "Those goons you sent to warn me off knew what they were doing."

Walsh's face clouded over. "Goons I sent? What are you talking about?"

"My apartment. Last night. Two guys lying in wait. No one knows where I live but you could have found out when I gave you my home phone number."

Walsh responded indignantly. "That's absurd. Why would I want you hurt you, Mr. Castle?"

"Because I caught you lying about Rose Temple and her physical condition and you knew I'd caught you. What did she have, Doc? Lupus? Parkinson's? Huntington's?"

There was an inadvertent flash in Walsh's eyes at the last one.

"Right. Huntington's? Was that it?"

"As I told you, I really can't discuss—"

"She inherited from her father, her real father, who's probably dead by now. Hell, he'd have to be. So what was she, Doctor? Incurable? Terminal? How long did she have ? A couple of years? Maybe less?"

Walsh leaned back in his chair, twiddling his thumbs as he thoughtfully considered his answer. "A year," he said. "Probably less."

Kovacs was wandering around the office, inspecting all the certificates and diplomas, photos and memorabilia, collected over a long career. But he was listening intently.

"Why did you lie, Doctor?"

"Out of respect."

"Why? She was a victim. She hadn't done anything wrong."

"Out of respect for her mother. Anna Marie had been through enough in her lifetime. In my opinion, this was a burden best kept private."

"So let me see if I've got this right. Rose killed Congressman Johannson, knowing that even if she were arrested and even convicted, it would be meaningless because she was going to die anyway. That would explain her bravado."

"I suppose," Walsh conceded.

"Then the only question remaining is, why?"

"I wouldn't know."

"Was she political?"

"No."

"Are you sure? Did you know her that well?"

"She was no more political than you or I, Mr. Castle."

"And just how political are you, Doctor?" Paul asked.

"I'm not."

"Wow! This is something." It was Kovacs' voice.

"Paul, you should see this. Dr. Grayden Walsh, Doctor of the Year,2004, honored by the Connecticut Medical Association. Congratulations, Doctor. A tiny little town like this has the Doctor of the Year. This is really something."

Walsh smiled. "Thank you, Lieutenant. I think its mostly because I've outlived so many of my contemporaries."

Kovacs snorted. "I seriously doubt that. Look here, Paul, signed by the chairman of the association, Dr. Hammond Chambers."

Paul looked sharply toward Kovacs, then back to Walsh." Do you know Dr. Chambers, sir?"

Walsh shrugged. "I've met him. Know him? No, not well. I doubt we've run into each other more than four or five times in the past twenty years."

"He's a pretty well known society doctor in New York these days.

But I guess you knew that."

"Actually, I didn't." He rose from the desk. "And now, I hope you gentlemen will let me get back to my patients. I have a busy afternoon scheduled."

"I understand," Paul said, shaking his hand. "Thank you again. Sorry if I sounded inquisitorial. It's part of my job. And my nature, too, I guess."

"No offense taken, Mr. Castle. Nice meeting you, Lieutenant Kovacs," Walsh said, leading them out the door into the waiting room which was empty. Odd, for such a so-called busy afternoon.

Outside on the sidewalk Paul and Kovacs compared impressions. "Lying through his teeth," Kovacs grumbled with certainty.

"Probably so."

"Walsh and Chambers. Rose Temple and Betsy Wallenberg. This is the first real link we've come across in this plate of spaghetti."

"I'd say there's more," Paul said.

"You bet your sweet ass," Kovacs responded.

"You think there might be a library in this town? I need to get my hands on a computer."

Kovacs snorted. "Well, how about if I just drop you off. Think maybe I'll just buy me a big bag of peanuts and feed the squirrels in that park we passed comin' in."

"Ever think about joining the twenty-first century, Lieutenant?" Paul asked.

"Not if I can help it."

CHAPTER FIFTEEN

To tell Briggs or not tell Briggs, that was the dilemma. They argued about it all the way back to New York. They didn't have much and what they had was thin. Walsh knew Hammond Chambers and Chambers knew Walsh. According to the records of the New York State Medical Association, Chambers also knew Jacob Rovich, the physician who treated Don Chaffee, the trucker from Grafton. Rovich and Chambers had served together on the association's board of directors in 2007, according to the association's website. Whether Rovich knew Walsh, that connection couldn't be made.

"None of this means a thing," Paul said. "Briggs will want hard facts, not a lot of guesswork. And suppose he runs with it because he has nothing better. Do you really want a few dozen FBI agents trampling all over this case with no idea where they're going?"

"Good point. On the other hand," Kovacs said, "we've got to find out the names of other doctors that might be involved. That's the only way we'll be able to construct the web and without Briggs I don't know how we do it."

Paul glowered as he stared out his window. "Shit," he muttered. If he and Kovacs were on the right track, then the perpetrators wouldn't give up the names of their doctors easily and the doctors wouldn't give up their patients at all. On the other hand, teams of federal agents could question friends and neighbors and within a few hours, probably pull together most of what was needed.

"Maybe we should sleep on it," Paul said.

"Good thinking," Kovacs agreed.

A few miles out of New York City, Paul flipped on a drive-time news program. There wasn't much out there. A recap of Andrea Wilkes' morning interview (the first Paul and Kovacs had heard of it), meaningless statements from the NYPD and the FBI, filling air time, saying nothing. There was a three car pile-up on the Long Island Expresssway, the Governor was fighting the Legislature over a proposed tax hike, and a famous teen idol was either getting married or she wasn't, either pregnant or still a virgin, making a deal for a new movie or getting busted for smoking a joint on the steps of Gracie Mansion. Take your pick.

Paul turned off the radio and looked at Kovacs.

"Kinda quiet out there," he said.

"It is," Kovacs agreed.

"Hard to believe." Paul nodded. "The day's only sixteen hours gone and nobody dead yet."

"Strange. Really strange," Kovacs said with mock solemnity.

Paul walked into his office at five-fifteen. Murray was waiting for him, pacing nervously, but not frantically. On the Murray-scale, there was a big difference between the two. Murray faked a smile. "The Prodigal returneth. Tell me, wandering one, have you arrived bearing programming for the evening or do we just go with the usual crap?"

"I bring you the Big Zero, Lord and Master," Paul said. "Now what?"

Murray sighed. "Well, it's not as bad as it could be. We've got about seven minutes on the Wilkes interview this morning along with 30 seconds of their tape, credited of course, though I'm not sure how proud of it they are." He filled in Paul with the short version. "Brad Pitt punched out some paparazzi who was hassling his kids in a public park. Pretty juicy. Pitt's got a helluva right hand. Some female high school teacher in Oklahoma's in the slammer for servicing the high school basketball team after a heartbreaking loss in the state championship game. She bills herself as the consolation prize. We've got a crocodile race from Australia. Numbers on their backs. Bookie wagering. Fascinating stuff."

"It all sounds just peachy," Paul said, flipping on his computer.

"Nothing at all on the big story?"

"Nothing I can use." Murray nodded. "You want Bill to fill in tonight. You could use a night off."

Paul shook his head. "My show. I'll handle it."

Just then Crystal Huggins hurried into the office wearing a cashmere sweater, advertising the genesis of her affectionate nickname. She was carrying an 8 x 12 manila envelope. "A messenger just dropped this off in the lobby, Mr. Castle."

He took it from her. Printed on the outside in magic marker were his name and "Open by 5:45."

"Will there be anything else, Mr. Castle?" she jiggled.

"No, Crystal. Thank you." He gave her a big smile. She smiled back. Murray, who had not yet met Jennie, thought he was missing the bet of a lifetime. Paul knew better.

He tore open the envelope, found a single sheet of paper inside. At the top was scrawled "For your six o'clock broadcast." The message below was short and to the point. Paul read it aloud.

> Beginning at twelve -oh-one Eastern time this morning, SST unilaterally ceased its activities against selected members of the United States House of Representatives. We believe that our actions to date clearly demonstrate the

seriousness of our purpose. The sixteen who have died to date represent the most egregious of our entrenched politicians who have abused their offices and betrayed the trust of their constituents. Their one overriding goal was reelection and to this end, they employed tactics that brought shame upon the Congress they were elected to serve. Our organization is non-partisan. It is true that this rush to a Socialist overthrow of the American way of life basically emanates from the Democratic Party, but many Republican members of the House are equally guilty of indecent, illegal, and indefensible behavior. They, too, face our judgment.

The moratorium on our activities will extend for 72 hours beginning this evening at 6:00 p.m. Eastern Daylight Time. During this period of truce we expect that the 21 Congressmen whom we find most at fault for the outrageous behavior of the House of Representatives will resign their seats immediately. There will be no modification of this demand. Resign and make room for others who, by the grace of God, may prove to be wiser, more capable and more honest and who will put the will of the people above personal ambition.

We have no wish to resume these killings but if our demand is not met, they will continue. For each one of you we have a thousand patriots unafraid to face the consequences of their actions. For each one of those thousands there are tens of thousands more who believe in our cause. Ignore us at your peril.

Murray stood there, dumfounded. “Holy crap,” he said.

Paul agreed. He punched the intercom button. “Tell Crystal to get back in here.” He went to his computer’s copying machine and ran off two copies.

Crystal hurried into the room. “Sir?”

Paul handed her the copies. "Take one of these to Mr. Schoenfeld right away. Take the other one to Fred in graphics, have him set it up for broadcast tonight. If he has any questions, have him call me." He waved her away. "Shoo, shoo." He was smiling. She smiled back as she hurried out the door.

Murray shook his head. "These guys. The gift that keeps on giving. If they could just keep this up for six months, you could make Geraldo look like a copy boy."

"Murray," he said with no little sarcasm, "I like the way you grasp the big picture." The intercom on his desk buzzed him. "Call for you on line one, Mr. Castle. He wouldn't give his name."

"A crank?"

"He said to ask if you got the envelope."

He looked at Murray, then reached into his desk drawer and took out a mini tape recorder. "Murray, check the switchboard, see if we have a number through caller ID."

"Will do," Murray said, hurrying out the door.

Paul pushed the power button on the recorder. "I'll take it," he told the switchboard operator. Then he punched line one on the phone.

"This is Paul Castle."

"Good afternoon, Mr. Castle." It was a man's voice, slightly distorted, probably electronically. "I assume you received our message."

"I did. Nice to know you're going to stop whacking away at Congress. What happened? You get a little bored with it all?"

"Not for a moment but we truly believe that our cause is best served by permitting the enemy an opportunity to leave the field gracefully."

"Very compassionate of you."

"And good business as well. The American people are starting to wake up, as all the polls show. Nothing would please us more than to avoid any further bloodshed. I will assume you're going to use our communication on your broadcast."

"Absolutely. And I'm also going to find a way to squeeze in a recording of this conversation."

"I assumed as much," the man said. "So far you are the only media outlet that has this information. The networks will get it at ten o'clock in time for the 11:00 news. The major newspapers will have it in time for their morning editions."

"And what makes me so privileged?" Paul asked.

"Two things. Your interview last night with Leonard Philby was pretty even handed, more so than what we could expect from the major networks. Secondly, it's by way of apology for the unfortunate incident at your apartment."

"Yes, I was going to ask you about that."

"Two of our supporters violated policy. They've been severely reprimanded. We're not in the business of harming the innocent. It won't happen again."

"I'm curious as to why it happened in the first place. Was I getting too close to the truth about your organization and how it operates?"

"We have nothing to fear from you, Mr. Castle," the man said. "Put on a good broadcast. The country will thank you for it."

Paul paused for only a second, then took a gamble. "And what about you, Doctor? Will you thank me for it?"

Silence. Then a click as the man disconnected.

Murray popped back into the room. "No ID. He probably used one of those throwaway cell phones." He checked his watch." We gotta get to the studio."

Paul held up a hand. "One minute." He punched in Kovacs number and waited for only a moment.

"Lieutenant, it's Paul. Drop what you're doing, turn on the broadcast. And call Briggs. He won't want to miss this."

The ratings for the previous night's broadcast had been up 12% over the previous night. On the basis of the Philby interview, the Old Man predicted that this evening's ratings would be up another ten to fifteen percent. Not O'Reilly numbers but pretty damned good. The broadcast aired without a hitch. Fred's graphics were outstanding, the message scrolling behind Paul as he read it off the teleprompter. When he played the recorded phone conversation with the alterted voice, Fred had put up a box with a black silhouette of a man. Paul played the whole conversation with the exception of his parting words. The notion that a gaggle of doctors was involved in this was something he was determined to keep to himself for as along as possible.

When the broadcast ended the switchboard was flooded with hundreds of calls. National Heartbeat Channel was becoming a major player in the cable game and Paul Castle had crawled out of the slime of sleaze and scandal. The tapes of Brad Pitt, the high school hooker and the Aussie crocodiles were stashed on the shelf. Feelers were sent out to FBI Director Levi Zwick and the Director of Homeland Security, inviting them to be interviewed the following evening. If they declined three Congressmen, two Senators and an ex-Presidential candidate had all contacted the Old Man volunteering their expertise in widening the national debate.

By morning, every major outlet had covered the story. The left-leaning press congratulated law enforcement for their diligent efforts in forcing the SST's to abandon their agenda. Apparently they forgot to read the second paragraph in the message or perhaps they didn't understand it, even though it was written in sixth-grade English.

Paul was invited by all three major networks to sit down for a taped interview with their prestigious evening anchors. The use of tape was obviously in play to avoid a repeat of the disastrous CNN interview conducted by Vera Staley. Paul wisely declined all three invitations, adhering to precept number one of modern electronic journalism. Never submit to an interview with a man who controls the editing machine.

Exhausted, Paul had slept soundly from eleven p.m until nearly ten. He was awakened by the sound of the super's power mower as he attacked what little grass there was in the apartment complex. Jennie, who had spent the night, was long gone, leaving behind a loving but borderline obscene note and a full pot of coffee. He dressed quickly, found his two dollar morning newspaper at his place at the kitchen table. He opened to the sports section, grimaced at the news that the Mets had lost, grimaced even more at the news the Yankees had won and flipped back to the front page which, predictably, was devoted exclusively to SST's announcement of a cease fire. A boxed commentary ran across the bottom of the page. It was written by the paper's resident disinformationist. Paul spotted his own name. It was spelled correctly. That was good. He was described as an apologist for a gang of brain dead anarchists. Not so good. He looked to see the latest pro/con opinion poll on the killngs and couldn't find it. Then he realized that the paper had printed only the first poll taken last week, They had ignored the subsequent ones showing a growing approval of what SST was trying to accomplish. He shook his head, almost amused. All the news that's fit to print. They still had the temerity to claim that. Amazing.

His cell phone rang, a pedestrian ring by any standard. He thought, well, hell, if Jennie could have "Now Voyager," he could program his own distinctive sound. He immediately thought of the theme to Mighty Mouse. ("Here he comes to save the day!") Good idea. I'll do it, he told himself. He flipped open the phone, checked the caller. Hah! His old pal Dixie Boggs. Was this possibly good news?

"I'm here," Paul said.

"Good," Dixie said. "I was afraid your new found celebrity had made you too stuck up to take calls from minions and other subserviants."

"Skip the flattery, Dix. What have you got?"

"I got your doctor for you and then some."

"I've always said, you are the best, my friend."

"The doctor's name is Hernan Oliva. He's been treating Elsa Galesko for the past eight or nine months. All it took was a little shoe leather and about two hours last evening. Believe it or not I'm kind a celebrity here in Port St. Lucie so I didn't get many doors slammed in my face. Anyway, some of these neighbors, once I got them started they wouldn't shut up. Seems Elsa started acting a little funny maybe nine or ten months ago. That's when she went to Oliva. Started having headaches, occasional blurred vision. The neighbor across the street, a Mrs. Fernandez, she and Elsa were close. One day Elsa comes over crying. Can't stop. Test results showed a star four carcinoma in her brain. Inoperable."

"God help her," Paul whispered quietly.

"She quit her job, moped around the house, waiting to die, I guess."

Paul's door buzzer sounded. And who the hell is that at this hour, Paul thought. "Hang on, Dix, some asshole's at my door." He looked through the peephole. The asshole was Lt. Kovacs. He opened the door and beckoned him in.

To Dixie on the phone: "It's my favorite homicide detective. And without food in his hand. Amazing."

"What?"

"Never mind. She's home waiting to die. And?"

"Two months ago she sees an ad in the paper and goes to work for Congressman Villanueva. Now get this, Paulie. A few weeks later Fernandez sees her coming home and goes over to chat. Right away she sees Galesko isn't doing very well so she says Elsa, you should be home resting. Why did you take that job with that Congressman? And Galesko just smiles and you know what she says? She says, I have to help him get where he has to go. How do you like that?"

"I like it just fine, Dix. Great job."

Kovacs had poured himself a mugful of hot coffee and was staring out at the tourists wandering in and out of Gramercy Park. He didn't know what Paul had on the other end of the phone line but he knew it was something good.

"So, listen, Paulie," Dix was saying, "if you hear of any of those big city stations up there that need a solid guy, put in a good word for me, huh?"

"Hah. If I put it in, you'll be dead meat, but I tell you what I will do. I'll talk to the boss here at the channel. You got anything against cable?"

"Hell, no."

"I'll be in touch."

He hung up. As he did, Kovacs settled onto a kitchen chair and started spooning sugar into his coffee.

"Morning."

"Morning," Kovacs replied. "So?"

"Like hitting a trifecta," Paul said. "Got the doctor. Got the patient. Elsa Galesko, inoperable brain tumor. Has a few months left at most."

"I detect a pattern developing here," Kovacs said. "I have to tell you, Paul, when you first came up with this notion I was sure you were nuts."

Paul grinned. "Actually, so did I."

"Well, the Chief's going to be ecstatic. He's lending me four rookies just out of the academy to do some leg work."

"Would that include putting a tail on Dr. Hammond Chambers?"

Paul asked.

"It would not," Kovacs said.

"Why not? It's the closest thing we have to a local perp and even I know you don't need a warrant for a tail."

"It's a question of manpower and money, young fella. The Chief proposes, I disposes. Now, back to these four nitwits from the Academy." He pulled out his scruffy notepad and flipped through the pages. "This Mary Mae Thatcher got iced by a woman named Cassandra Jellico, lives in Millville in South Jersey. The Oregon Congressman was shot by a Gregory Chang, probably Chinese ancestry, lives in Woonsocket, Rhode Island."

Paul nodded. "Well, we pretty much know what we're going to find out about the perps. The important thing now is to identify the doctors. If we can start tying them all together, we can shine a big bright light on this SST operation and put a stop to it."

"Not us, young fella. It's much too big for that. Probably too big for us city folk, too. They've probably got members in every state, every county. They were talking in the thousands and I don't doubt it. Think about it. Thousands of doctors recruiting people like your Leonard Philby, screwballs with nothing to lose."

Paul cocked his head thoughtfully. "You really believe that, Lieutenant, that they're screwballs?"

"No matter how you twist it around, son, it's not war, it's murder. Probably these people will never be tried, never be imprisoned, never have to answer to the law. It's the ones behind them, these doctors that we have to identify."

"No argument here. The big question remaining is, when do we tell Briggs?"

"When we've put it together," Kovacs said. "We've already got the names of four doctors, my guys may get two more. I know a Captain on the Cincinnati force might give me something on the ex-vice cop. And if we could get somebody into Philby's plant on the q.t. we might dig up something there."

Paul regarded him thoughtfully. "Yes, we just might," he said.

"I know that look. You got something cookin'?"

"You don't want to know," Paul said.

"Try me."

Paul nodded." Last year we did a segment on this kid. Gus Caramedes. Sixteen years old. A whiz with a computer. As the old TV show used to say, he can go where no man has gone before."

"A hacker." Kovacs said. "You're right. I don't want to know."

"The FBI file says Philby's company has health coverage for every employee. If Gus can get in—"

"I'm not hearing this, "Kovacs protested.

"Okay, okay. It's a bad idea."

"I didn't say that. I just said I'm not hearing it."

"Good enough. How soon before you think you might have something?"

Kovacs shrugged. "If my buddy in Cincinnati is on the job today, maybe late afternoon. The kids from the academy? Who knows?"

"And then what? We take it to Briggs."

"Let's see how it plays out. "

"Okay, but just one thing," Paul said. "Before we hand it over to Briggs, I get to break it on the air."

"If we can," Kovacs said flatly.

"Now wait a minute—"

"I said if we can," Kovacs said sharply. "Up to now you and I have been loosey-goosey with each other because we were just groping around. Well, groping time's over. Time to tend to business. The law comes first. Your program comes second."

Paul wanted to argue but he couldn't. He knew Kovacs was right.

On a side street off Lincoln Avenue close by the mall in Yakima, Washington, a battered dark green pickup sat unmoving, it's engine idling. The dashboard clock read 7:39. The sun had been up for over two hours. The town was just beginning to come alive. Behind the wheel sat Emanuel Childers, a barrel-chested man with piercing grey blue eyes, a wild untamed head of grey-white hair and a three day growth of beard. In his faded jeans and red checked shirt he looked every inch the apple grower he had been for the past 44 years. For nine hours he had been drinking and the more he had drunk, the angrier and more bitter he had become. It was time, he had decided, to finally teach that dumb son of a bitch a lesson.

Next to him in the passenger seat sat his oldest son, Adam. A carbon copy of his father, he, too, had been drinking. He was angry but only because his father was angry and anger was expected of him. Truth to tell, he didn't give a damn about the dumb son of a bitch. In his right hand was a bundle of three sticks of dynamite, fused and ready to be set off. "You sure you want to do this, Pa?," the son asked.

"Hell, yes, I'm sure," Emanuel replied.

"Probably be smarter to do it at night. Less chance of bein' seen."

"Suppose I don't mind being seen. Suppose that, Adam. These other folks doin' what has to be done, just walkin' up and poppin' those Congress people. Pure guts, that's what they got. Pure guts. Least we can do is show we're with 'em."

"I just don't feature goin' to jail, Pa, what with Emmy expectin' with the baby and all."

"Ain't nobody goin' to jail and ain't nobody gettin' hurt. The son of a bitch is back east and Missie Lorna don't get to the office til nine o'clock." The father looked at him with cold hard eyes. "You ain't afraid, is you?"

Adam glared back at him. "Naw, I ain't afraid."

"Well, let's get to it then," Emanuel said, slipping the gear shift into drive and tromping on the gas.

The truck roared up the alley and took a hard right, fishtailing onto First Street, narrowly missing an oncoming moving van. Emanuel raced by a couple of compacts and then edged right skirting the curb. "There she is, right there next to the bank. Light 'er up and toss 'er!"

Adam lit the fuse with his cigarette lighter, then leaned out the window as Emanuel slowed in front of the plate glass window that read: "Offices of Congressman Warren Simcox." Adam let fly with the dynamite. They, watched as it crashed through the window, then sped away. Several seconds late they heard a horrendous explosion and Emanuel watched in the rear view mirror as smoke and fire belched forth from the office. They were aware that several people had witnessed the incident, people who knew Emanuel and his son by sight. Emanuel didn't seem to care. He drove out of the city, heading for the Moxee Valley and the family home in the woods eight miles to the east. He was extremely pleased with himself.

Unknown to Emanuel, Lorna Beckenfeld, a warm-hearted woman of 55 known to everyone in Yakima as Missie, had decided to pick this morning of all mornings to come to work early. For the past several days, the volume of e-mails and snail mail had picked up considerably and Missie Lorna considered it her sacred duty to answer each and every one of them. Consequently she was sitting at her desk, composing a letter to an 86 year old constituent, Lydia Mayberry, a cultured, softspoken and ladylike spinster, who, each year, sent the Congressman a box of cookies for his birthday. This year, no box had arrived. In its place, Ms. Mayberry sent the Congressman a short letter. "No more Goddamned cookies for you until you do something about the price of sugar and flour."

Missie Lorna was about to forge the Congressman's name to a flowery letter of sympathy when she heard the crash of glass and turned to see the bundle of dynamite bounce across the floor and land at her feet. Missie Lorna had a strange thought. Why would anybody throw a bundle of red candles through the Congressman's window? It was to be the last thought she ever had.

CHAPTER SIXTEEN

The bully who had humiliated Gus Caramedes in front of his girlfriend the previous Saturday night was about to pay a terrible price for his churlish behavior. Not that Gus felt sorry for him. Not at all. The star defensive back on the school's football team was entitled to certain privileges such as surrogates to write his book reports, a new car from adoring but basically neglectful parents and the right to feel up any girl he chose, any where, any time. Which is why Gus had taken a swing at him and why Gus had ended up in the gutter outside the multiplex theater with a broken nose. But now it was Gus's turn and with a few quick strokes of his computer, he reduced Mr. Football's bank balance from a plus four hundred and eighty dollars to a deficit of seventeen dollars and fifty cents. His credit card account suddenly showed that he hadn't made a payment in over two months. And finally, hacking into school records, Gus magnanimously changed a D to a B and two C's to two A's. With those marks, colleges would be clamoring for the bully's enrollment. On the other hand, after a well placed phone call to the school district supervisor, the principal would be clamoring for his head.

Gus's cell phone rang. He answered his usual way "At the beep, leave a message, asshole."

"It's me, Gus. Paul Castle."

“Ah, my favorite asshole!” Gus grinned.” What’s up, bro?”

Paul started to explain his problem. The more he explained the broader Gus’s grin.

Paul hung up on Gus and leaned back in his office chair. He stared at his computer screen scanning Dr. Hammond Chambers personal website in the hope he might find something useful. There wasn’t much there. A lot of ego-boosting huffing and puffing and subtle encouragement to contact the doctor if you were in need of expert medical diagnosis and treatment. Procedures involving less than $25,000 seemed to be discouraged.

The phone rang. It was Kovacs.

“I divided the rookies up into two teams, one on the way to Rhode Island, the other headed for south Jersey. They’re under orders to get what they can today. Nobody’s paying for any overnight hotel bill.”

“Good. What about Cincinnati?” Paul asked.

“I talked to this Captain. Like I said, he’s married to one of my wife’s cousins. We see each other at Christmas. Anyway, it was enough to get him talking to me. He knows Yancey very well. Knew he was sick when he left the force. Very sick, he said. If he had to guess, he’d say the big C but he doesn’t know for sure.”

“How about the doctor?”

“The city’s got an HMO deal which means Yancey may have seen different doctors at different times. No way to pin down any one guy.”

“But if we could hack into the records—”

“Whoa there, young fella,” Kovacs interrupted. “Did I not tell you I don’t want to hear about it? Are you trying to get me bounced from my lofty positiion within the department with only three years left to go for my thirty years?”

"Sorry Lieutenant, I havent the slightest intention of violating this HMO's website, uh?—What did you say was the name of it?"

"Sohio Medical Associates."

"—violating Sohio Medical Associates website by tomorrow at the latest, trust me on that."

"Well," Kovacs chuckled, "if I can't trust you, who can I trust?"

At that moment, Murray entered the office, pointed to the TV set and crossed to it, turning it on. Paul knew immediately something important was happening.

"Gotta cut this short, Lieutenant. Some sort of disaster is looming on the horizon. I'll call you later."

He hung up as the picture came on: a bombed out storefront on a main street in some small city in the United States. A reporter with a microphone was standing off to one side. The legend "Yakima, Washington" appeared on the screen.

"...... at approximately 7:45 this morning. The truck, a grey green pickup, was identified as belonging to a local businessman named—" The reporter looked down at his notes." ....Emanuel Childers. Several witnesses have already identified Childers as the man behind the wheel. There was also a passenger in the truck, believed to be Childers' oldest son Adam. As yet we've been unable to talk to the Yakima Chief of Police, his name...." A glance down. ".....uh, Howard Urbanski. We believe Chief Urbanski is inside the burned out offices of Congressman Simcox with members of the fire department. We have also been told, unconfirmed at this point, that there has been one fatality. That would not be the Congressman who is back east in the Capitol. The speculation is, the victim is a Lorna Beckenfeld, his personal assistant."

Paul stood and crossed to the coffee maker, poured himself a cup, hardly noticing it was an inky black. He looked at Murray who looked back at him gravely.

"Here to my left......" The camera widened out to reveal a pleasant looking man in his late thirties with a cherubic face and a balding pate, ".....is Mayor Kenneth Coulter. Mayor, this is obviously a horrendous tragedy. What can you tell us?"

"Well, Marty, I can tell you I was one of the first ones here at the scene. The missus and I were just driving into town for a breakfast with the Lady's Flower Association. Heard the explosion, then saw the smoke. Got here right away but there wasn' t anything to do but watch, the flames were that fierce A couple of minutes later the fire boys showed up. Did all they could, I promise you that, but the place was too far gone."

"I've been told we have a fatality," the reporter said.

"Yep, Missie Lorna, most likely. Don't know anybody else who'd be in there this time of day. I can tell you, Manny Childers is going to pay a high price for this."

"Then you're sure it was him."

"Hell, yes, and everybody saw him. And everbody knew he had it in for the Congressman. I haven't talked to the District Attorney yet but if I have anything to say, we'll be looking for the maximum."

"I've been told the FBI has been asked to help with the investigation."

The Mayor scowled. "Nobody's asked them for anything. They're just coming. What with a Congressional office being involved and everything that's been going on these past couple of weeks, I'd guess they're coming whether we like it or not."

Meanwhile Briggs and McIlroy were driving south from the Upper East side having spent the best part of the morning interviewing friends of Betsy Wallenberg. None had the vaguest idea why Betsy would have done such a bizarre thing. Two deplored the killing as unconscionable. The third, who had never cared much for Francis X. Mackey, thought it was a damned shame a sweet old broad like

Betsy had to get mixed up in something like this.

McIlroy's cell phone rang. He answered it, grunted a couple of times in response and hung up. "The SAC wants us in his officc stat. Something just broke."

Something, indeed, had broken and the SAC couldn't have been happier. He filled them in. Yakima, Washington. Possible attempt on the Congressman's life. Firebomb. One fatality. Eyewitnesses galore. The perpetrator ID'd. Finally, something they could wrap their arms around. This might be just the break they needed to unravel this goddamned conspiracy.

"You don't think it might be a non-related incident?" Briggs ventured.

"The Director thinks not and he wants you two in the air within the hour. We don't want these locals screwing up this case. A couple of agents from Spokane are on their way to the scene, but the Chief wants D.C. carrying the ball."

Briggs wasn't satisfied. "This wasn't an attempted killing. These people are smart enough to know the Congressman's in the capitol. Something tells me this isn't connected."

The SAC glared at him. "And something tells me the Director doesn't want any pushback on this. Now get going and don't even think about coming back until you've got this mess sorted out."

Elsewhere in the country, there were those who did not regard the situation in the nation and particularly in Yakima as a mess. On the contrary, they were beginning to regard it as a long-overdue call to arms.

In a hardware store in a small town outside of Spokane, owner Jeb Kramer had watched the unfolding story with growing excitement. Concord and Lexington had started this way. A random shot, another, then return fire and before long the colonies were aflame with rebellion. Only through armed resistance could America ever hope to stop the erosion of their Godgiven freedom and personal liberties. Others in the town had laughed at their weekend exercises, the paintball war games, their makeshift uniforms. The laughter was about to stop, Jeb thought. Sooner than anyone thought.

Across the border in Idaho, in a small town near Lewiston, former Green Beret Lewis Dunlop addressed the cadre of his band of survivalists. He, too, was aware of the events in Yakima. Childers was the spark that had lit the fuse. There would be no turning back. The first target: town hall. His second in command had had a portion of his land stolen by the town government to make way for a WalMart. Not a school or a library or even a youth center. A fucking Walmart and the Supreme Court, those ninnies, had said it was perfectly all right. Well, maybe seeing their precious town hall reduced to blackened timbers might change their mind about that.

And in central Montana, Brigadier General Terence McCarver Ret., one of the state's largest cattle ranchers, watched the news with equal pleasure. The time, which once seemed so far off, was now. Today. He and his boys would see to it. His boys were his ranch hands who doubled as a security force, one hundred and twenty strong. Those without military background need not apply. According to the papers, a group of faggot greenies from Washington would be inspecting War Horse Lake to figure out some way to protect the habitats of some endangered mosquito. Or was it some kind of minnow. McCarver didn't know and didn't care. The way to the lake was an access road that ran through his ranch. Well, today there would be no access. He and the boys would see to that. Maybe they'd get lucky and the weenies would call in the local sheriff or maybe the National Guard. Oh, yes, today could turn out to be one helluva party.

By noon, sobered up by the television reports and pumped full of black coffee by his wife, Emanuel Childers was visibly shaken by the events that had transformed him from a grouchy, opinionated and generally disliked businessman into a vile, cowardly murderer of defenseless women. His son Adam, sitting across from him at the dining room table suppressed an urge to say 'I told you so'. He kept his mouth shut, as he always did, waiting for his father to decide what to do next. Emanuel's two youngest sons, Seth and Enos, were in the living room with their wives and children being led in prayer by Emanuel's wife Velma. What was needed now was divine intervention and if anyone could muster it up, Emanuel thought, it was Velma who has worn out two kneeling pads at the church and was working on a third.

If that damned fool woman hadn't come to the office so early, Emanuel was certain he could have worked things out. Judge Prouty had been seeing things his way for years. A big fat fine, rebuild the office, make a nice contribution to the Democratic Party (he cringed at the thought of that one) and soon things would be back to normal. But murder? Especially Missie Lorna. No, that was a pig from another sty. That'd be prison time for sure and at his age Emanuel knew for damned sure he wasn't going to let himself get thrown into any damn prison. At first Emanuel wasn't sure of what he was hearing. He lifted his head up, strained turning his best ear toward the door.

"I hear 'em, Pa. Damned sirens. It'll be Urbanski for sure. Maybe the whole damned police force," Adam said.

He was almost right. Four cruisers lit up like Disneyland and wailing to raise the dead turned off the county road and raced along the winding dirt trail that led to the front of Emanuel Childers' home. Riding shotgun in the lead car was Chief of Police Howard Urbanski, a ruggedly handsome man just past 40 with craggy features and a reddish brown moustache that matched his hair color. Urbanski had been told that federal agents were on the way to assist, but Urbanski figured that the day he needed help from the feds was the day he'd turn in his badge. He and his boys were more than capable of handling the likes of Emanuel Childers. Inside the house, Childers got up quickly from the table. He grabbed the .44 cailber pistol that was laying on the table and stuffed it in his belt. "Adam, you get in there, tell your brothers to grab the rifles and post themselves at the front windows. You cover the back. Tell your Ma and the gals to take the little ones into the spare bedroom and don't come out til I say so."

"Right, Pa." He scurried off.

As the four cruisers skidded to a halt in the small clearing in front of the house, Childers stepped out onto the porch, the massive .44 very visibly tucked into his belt. Urbanski got out of the lead car and approached the porch, hands held open non-belligerently at belt level.

"I don't want any trouble, Manny." Urbanski said.

"Me, neither, Chief." He leaned over, spit into the scrub brush in front of the porch. One of Urbanski's officers moved up nearer the Chief. He was the youngest man on the force. His holster was unsnapped. He was looking for a fight.

"You know I got to take you in." Urbanski said.

"You got a warrant?"

"Didn't think I'd need one. I can get it, though."

"Then get it."

Urbanski shook his head. "Don't make this hard, Manny."

"Hell, Howard, I don't think you even got jurisdiction here. Am I right?" Urbanski didn't answer. "Thought so. You're trespassing here, Chief," Childers continued. "Get the hell off my property."

The younger cop stepped forward reaching for his service revolver. "Hey, old man, we're the law here—"

A shot rang out and a bullet ripped through the policeman's leg, right above the knee. He spun around and fell to the ground screaming in pain.

"What the hell!" Urbanski shouted. "God damn it!"

Childers pulled out his .44 and leveled it at the Chief. Smoke was coming from the barrel of a rifle poking out of a front window. The old man shouted to his sons. "Next one pulls a gun, shoot him between the eyes!"

Urbanski was backing up now, hands raised in surrender. "Okay, Manny, you take it easy now. We're going." He shouted to one of his men. "Jocko, get the kid, put him in the car!" He looked back up at Childers. "We gotta come back, Manny. You know that. And this time we'll have our warrant. While we're gone, you think real hard about what you want to do. You handle this wrong, people are gonna get killed. That's all I gotta say."

Urbanski eased himself back into the cruiser. The young officer was loaded into the back seat of another one. All four backed up and then turned and sped away. Childers watched them go, then spit again into the scrub brush.

Gus Caramedes' call came shortly after four o'clock. Paul was in the office watching the Yakima fiasco unfold. The coverage on CNN and FOX was wall-to-wall and the fact that there was very little new information didn't stop them from filling airtime. Talking heads abounded, speculation ran rife. Following Urbanski's failure to arrest Emanuel Childers and the non-fatal wounding of the young officer, references to Ruby Ridge and Waco were already being floated. The FBI was on the scene and the connection to the Congressional murder rampage had already been drawn.

"Paul, my man," said Gus jovially, "yours to command, mine to obey."

"You've got something?"

"Was there ever any doubt?"

"Sorry, Gus," Paul said. "I lost my head."

"Mr. Leonard Philby, sole owner of Philby-Styles Electronics, located in Vista Valley, California. Thirty four hundred and seventy employees all covered by a company called Norcal Health Group. Norcal's records show that they were billed nine times over the past year by a Doctor Umberto Rossi, an oncologist. They were also bllled for various x-rays included two MRIs, a Catscan, and several weeks of chemotherapy. Sure sounds like cancer to me."

"Good work, buddy. What's the charge?"

"A hundred bucks 'cause you're an old friend."

"Deal. Got time for another one?"

"Sure, but no discounts for volume."

Paul laughed. "Get this one right, you might even get a bonus." He told him about Bert Yancey, the ex-vice cop and the Sohio Medical Associates.

"I'm on it," Gus said and hung up.

Paul leaned back. Umberto Rossi. One step closer. Maybe. And yet as he stared at the television screen, he realized his uneasiness was growing. The FBI seemed much too eager to tie Yakima to the SST operation. Get Childers. Mission accomplished. Case closed. Paul knew that wasn't true and he prayed to God the feds would see beyond this one instance.

And what to do about tonight's broadcast. Go along with the prevailing opinion about Yakima? Punch holes in it? Possibly. But then what? Offer an alternative explanation? He and Kovacs weren't ready for that, not yet. They had to get phone records. They had to get into computers to check e-mail traffic. To whom, from whom. Discussing what? They were very close but this last step was going to be the tough one.

Meanwhile, the news channel droned on. A plumber who last week had fixed Missie Lorna's kitchen sink told the world what a sweet loving and generous old lady she really was, even if she did throw coffee grounds into the garbage disposal.

On the rear patio of his home in Alexandria, Virginia, Congressman Hank Wilhelm D-Missouri, sat sipping a rum collins and contemplating his future. As one of the 21 House members out of favor with SST, he was an endangered species. Almost immediately upon watching Paul Castle's broadcast the night before, he had decided that retirement was certainly the smartest of options. Seventeen years was long enough for any man to sacrifice in service to his country. Yes, he'd miss the celebrity and the power, and the money, of course. Especially the money, but that could be handled. Plenty of lobbying jobs available to the right people. He'd have no problem on that score. And it would mean he could stay in the Capitol and not have to go back to, God forbid, Missouri. Oh, yes, God save him from that, he thought. Those clodhoppers and rednecks whose idea of culture was a Willie Nelson concert at the local junior college auditorium. Those people with their carping e-mails to which he always replied: "Thanks so much for your insightful thoughts. I will give them every consideration." And the snail mail. He loved to watch Geraldine zap the letters open and search for checks. Those people got a letter back by return mail. Basically these letters said "Thanks so much for your check and your insightful thoughts. I will give them every consideration." Letters without checks went into the shredder, unread.

Yes, retirement had definitely seemed the better option, but this business in Yakima seemed to be changing everything. The FBI was doing its job. Maybe he wouldn't have to give up his cushy seat after all. He picked up his cell phone and dialed Congresswoman Louise Baggett D-Michigan. Louise was a good friend. A very good friend. More of a good friend than Hank Wilhelm would want his wife to know about. Louise was also on the endangered list. She was a smart babe. She'd have the right handle on this. Too bad he had to do this by phone but between his security guys and hers, face to face was a real problem. Ah, well, he thought, this bullshit can't last forever.

In the cozy booklined den on the second floor of his home/office in Bergensberg, Dr. Grayden Walsh watched with growing concern the erroneous coverage of the Yakima bombing. He'd been afraid of something like this from the beginning. It was far too easy for some lunatic fringe groups to piggyback on SST's activites and change what Walsh believed to be a just and necessary cause into a national bloodbath without purpose or reason and resulting in the death of innocents, innocents like Lorna Beckenfeld. The more he watched the more agitated be became and finally he got up and went to his desk. He took out the untraceable throwaway cell phone he'd purchased the day before and punched in a number. He knew he was being overly cautious but something told him that Castle and that New York detective were not about to leave him alone. After three rings a man answered.

"Hammond, it's Grayden Walsh."

There was a moment or two of silence. "Good afternoon, Grayden. Are you calling about a patient referral?"

"Don't worry, I'm calling on a throwaway phone."

Another pause. "I'm in the middle of a consult now, Grayden. Why don't you give me that number and I'll call you back in a few minutes."

Walsh did so and five minutes later, the little cell phone rang. "You may have been on a throwaway, Grayden, but I wasn't. I am now. We've discussed this at length. Limited contact only when necessary," Hammond Chambers said.

"Have you been watching the news? I think we have a major problem."

"That man in Yakima has nothing to do with us."

"That's just the point. As far as the country's concerned he IS us," Walsh said.

"You're overreacting."

"Am I? I wonder how the others feel about that?"

Chambers hesitated for moment. "What do you suggest?"

"I think we should contact Galen," Walsh said.

"He won't like it."

"I know but it can't be helped. I called you because I didn't want to act on my own but I truly believe we need his input."

"All right, but you contact him. Make your own case. Let me know what he thinks." Walsh clicked off the phone, then went to his desk and started up his computer. He clicked on MAIL, then COMPOSE and then typed in: "Galen 22020"

Paul spent twenty minutes of his thirty minute broadcast playing contrarian to the prevailing wisdom. The events in Yakima were certainly serious but they might have nothing to do with the killing spree gripping the country. No killing was accomplished or even attempted. Simcox had been in Washington, everyone knew it. The other perpetrators had for the most part been unemotional, made little or no effort to run away or conceal their identities. By way of balance, Paul did a phone interview with FBI Director Levi Zwick. Politely and in so many words, Zwick told Paul he didn't know horsepuckey about what was happening, that his office was indeed zeroing in on the radical right-wingers like Emanuel Childers, and that arrests were imminent. Who, besides Childers, Paul had asked him. Zwick was not at liberty to say. With four minutes left to fill, the videotape exhibiting Brad Pitt's pugilistic skills versus the paparazzi was pulled from the shelf. It was an excellent exclamation point to an excellent program. Or at least Murray thought so.

Paul was back in his office by 6:45. Jennie was sitting in a chair, laptop computer in its carrier on the floor by her side. She gave him a thumbs up as he entered. He leaned down and placed a juicy kiss on her lips.

"I thought we'd order in. Chinese or pizza?" he asked.

"Pepperoni and sausage, double cheese, no onions," she replied. "And I think you've got mail." She pointed to his computer. "It beeped."

He went to the desk, opened up the latest from Gus. "Boss, Sohio Medical shows former patient Albert Yancey suffering widespread bone cancer. No hope. Three doctors saw him, but the primary looks like a guy named Alejandro Casals. He's from Miami. I'd bet his folks are Cubans who got out early. Need anything else? Let me know. "

"That makes six," Paul said. At that moment the phone rang. It was Kovacs. Paul listened. mumbled something and hung up. "And that makes seven," he said. "Cassandra Jellico, the one who shot Mary Mae Thatcher. Doctor named Theodora Bascomb, a GYN. Jellico has uterine cancer and it has spread."

Jennie shook her head in disbelief. "I can't believe this. Doctors. They're supposed to save lives, not take them."

Paul nodded. "You're right, but I'm beginning to get a feel for these people. They may believe they are sacrificing the few to save the many."

"Then it's all about health care. Doctors saving their own little corner of the American dream."

"Maybe. But I think they may see it as more than that. If we're on the right track, we'll find out soon enough. Let's get to work." Jennie reached for the case, slipped out the computer and placed it on the desk facing Paul. She clicked it on. "Ready when you are, Castelli," she said.

The streets of Yakima were cluttered with strangers and odd pieces of heavy equipment, satellite dishes, mobile vans and the like, along with working press from all over the country. More were expected. The top line hotels were booked solidly, the best restaurants had already stopped taking reservations. A two-star Mom and Pop motel on the outskirts of the city had raised their nightly rate from $85 to $150 and they were getting it. They weren't the only ones. Mayor Coulter, while deploring the terrible tragedy that had befallen the city, couldn't help but mentally calculate the amount of business it was bringing in. Besides that Yakima was on the national map and that in itself would be a boon to tourism. Now if only the Chief of Police or the FBI didn't go and do something really stupid. It was twenty past five when an alabaster stretch limousine sped into town and pulled to a stop at the entrance to the Ledgestone, one of the best hotels in the city. Harvey Cantrell, the distinguished news anchor based in New York City emerged from the rear and looked around, a trifle disapprovingly. Two minions followed him out of the vehicle and all three headed inside. A neatly dressed desk clerk with a winning smile greeted them. Yes, Mr. Cantrell, we've been expecting you. It is an honor to have you staying with us. Sorry, I'm afraid we don't have a Presidential Suite, but I'm sure you'll find the accommodations very much to your liking. Yes, we have a health club and a spa. Oh, yes, the restaurant features a most excellent wine list. Harvey looked around the lobby, sniffed the air, slightly less disapprovingly and decided this was the best he was going to do. After making sure that no other network anchor would be getting better accommodations than he, he signed the register card. The two minions signed in as well for a shared double room with a view of the parking lot.

Several blocks away in less elegant surroundings, Fowler Briggs was on his cell phone, reporting to the Deputy Director. Having watched Paul Castle's broadcast the night before, he was unwilling to risk the Director's wrath by confronting him with facts. The Deputy, a man of unusual common sense, could always be reasoned with, if not persuaded. Briggs described, from second hand accounts, Chief Urbanski's blundering attempt to bring in Childers without jurisdiction and without a warrant.

"Forget it, Briggs. You're in charge now. I hope this Chief knows that."

"He does now."

"What's the situation?"

"Childers lives a few miles from downtown in a place called Moxee Valley. His house is two story, wood frame, maybe four or five bedrooms, stuck off in the woods. There's a long dirt driveway off a county road that leads in but aside from that it's pretty inaccessible. He's holed up with his wife, three sons, their wives and five or six grandchildren. Not sure how many."

"Shit," growled the Deputy. "What's his mindset?"

"I'm pretty certain it's not surrender," Briggs said. "He's got a dead body in the explosion and a wounded deputy. He's also an arrogant bastard from what I hear and he hates authority. If we don't play this right, we could have a real mess in our hands." The Deputy, who'd been an ATF agent in Waco at the time of the Koresh fiasco, winced visibly.

"We'll start with talk, try to reason with him," Briggs said. "I'll bring along a couple of media people to watch and listen, make sure we get a good press."

"And if he doesn't want to talk?"

"We escalate. I'll be sure you sign off on it."

"Good enough."

Briggs hesitated. "Sir, I've brought this up before and been shot down but I have to try again. I am not convinced this man is behind the killings, I don't believe he's even part of it."

"Your point?"

“The Director’s gone way out on a limb with this guy. If he’s wrong, we’re gong to look like a bunch of damned fools.”

“You know that Simcox is one of the Congressman who’s been threatened.” the Deputy reminded him.

“I know, I know,” Briggs said, “but it just doesn’t feel right. And I guarantee you, every one of these reporters has already made the connection and they’re going to want me to confirm it. Unless you order me, I can’t do that.”

The Deputy hesitated thoughtfully, then: “How about ‘No Comment’?”

“That’ll be good for about twenty four hours,” Briggs said.

“Then that’s how long you’ve got to bring this guy in, Briggs. Do we understand each other?”

“Yes, sir,” Briggs said and hung up.

Twenty four hours, he thought glumly. He could already smell the cordite in the air. It was Waco all over again.

CHAPTER SEVENTEEN

It was past eleven o'clock when they finally got the break they were looking for. Paul and Jennie had been hunched over their computers since seven o'clock with only a short break for pizza and garlic toast. The night crew at National Heartbeat was pretty much congregated upstairs in the studio. The post nine o'clock schedule, except for five minute news breaks on the hour was all reruns of previous programming. The switchboard was manned by one receptionist, usually a college student intern. It was light work. People seldom called after midnight. A good time to catch up on studies.

Paul and Jennie had been logging onto every conceivable medical website, looking for membership rosters, conventions and seminars and lists of attendees. Anyplace where they could connect two or more of the seven names they had gathered. It had been slow going. Paul's expertise was minimal; Jennie was a whiz and her fingers flew over the keyboard. He suspected that if she ever developed a talent for hacking, she'd be very dangerous.

Here and there they'd made a small connection, usually two names, once in a while three, but the hits didn't prove much, especially if the geography involved was close. Then at eleven-oh-three, Jennie stumbled onto the mother lode. The American Association of Family Physicians had held their Congress of Delegates in Boston the previous October. Three names popped up: Grayden Walsh, Jacob Rovich, and Theodora Bascomb. Jennie noticed a link to AAFP's Family Medical Congressional Congress in March in Washington D.C. This was basically a series of informational panels and seminars on how to deal with Congress on proposed legislation, approaches to use, helpful do's and don't's. A quick perusal of the attendees revealed six of the seven doctors they'd been able to connect to SST. The seventh, Hammond Chambers, was a speaker.

Paul and Jennie shared a look. It was almost too easy. It didn't prove anything, of course, but if you believed it was a coincidence, then you also believed in Santa Claus, the tooth fairy, and Indiana Jones.

"Briggs'll buy this," Jennie said with certainty.

Paul nodded. "Yes, he will. If they let him."

Jennie looked puzzled. "You heard Zwick last night. He's a dog with a bone and he won't let go. I'm pretty sure if his agents get marching orders, they march."

Jennie was appalled. "But it's stupid. Childers is a right wing screwball acting on his own." She pointed to the screen. "This is SST. For God's sakes, Paul, they can't be that stupid."

"Not stupid, Jenn. They don't know what we know and they're under a lot of pressure. I think they're doing a lot of praying that they're right."

"We've got to talk to Briggs now." Jennie said.

"Absolutely now." Paul said, dialing the number for FBI headquarters in New York.

At that moment, as she was getting ready to shut down her laptop, she noticed that she had mail. She clicked on and saw that the sender was Dr. Hammond Chambers.

Meanwhile Paul was engaged in a frustrating conversation with the agent saddled with night duty. No, agent Briggs was not on duty. No, he did not have a phone number for him. No, he had no idea how he could be reached but if Paul would leave his name and number, he would see that Briggs got the message. Paul frowned. That last response sounded very contradictory. Probably government-speak for 'Get off the phone, we're busy here'. Nevertheless Paul left his information and asked the agent to stress that the call was urgent. The agent said he would certainly do his best and hung up. Jennie smiled at him. "You'll never guess who just politely reamed my butt. Dr. Hammond Chambers."

"You're kidding," Paul said.

Jennie read the e-mail aloud: "Dear Miss Bovano. I understand from Lisa's grandmother that you have been asking pointed questions about the state of her health. Your concern is laudable and understandable but I have been told by Mrs. Wallenberg on numerous occasions that she wishes to keep her medical condition private and I would hope that as a friend of her loving granddaughter you would respect her wishes. Sincerely, Hammond Chambers, M.D."

Paul leaned back in his chair, rubbing his chin thoughtfully.

"Interesting," he said. "That could be a warning."

"If he knows what we're doing," Jennie said.

"Or he may be oblivious which he might be if he hasn't connected you to me," Paul replied.

Just then Paul's cell phone rang. He flipped it open. It was Kovacs.

"Are you watching television?, Kovacs asked.

"No, Jennie and I are at the office. We think we may have pulled some things together."

"Tell me about it later. Meantime, turn on Channel 2."

Paul signaled to Jennie, pointing to the television set and holding up two fingers. She turned it on. There, filling the screen, was the face of unreachable FBI agent, Fowler Briggs. He was in the middle of an interview.

"We have agents positioned in the woods on all sides of the

Childers home. Two squad cars from the Sheriff's Department have blocked off the access road. No one in that household will be going anywhere tonight."

The reporter weighed in. "Then you are not planning any sort of action this evening, Agent Briggs."

"I'd like to avoid the word 'action' here. I very much hope to talk Mr. Childers into surrendering tomorrow morning. We've been trying to contact him by phone but he's not responding. Perhaps by daybreak he will appreciate the hopelessness of his situation and give himself up peaceably. The last thing we want is for any one else to get hurt."

Another reporter stuck his mike in Briggs' face. "There's widespread consensus that Childers is one of those involved in the SST organization."

"We have no evidence of that." Briggs said.

"But doesn't it seem obvious, I mean, Congressman Simcox is one of those being targeted—"

"Emanuel Childers is one man in Central Washington who we want to question about the bombing of a Congressional office. Whatever you may have heard or surmised, at the moment Mr. Childers is a suspect and only a suspect, entitled to a presumption of innocence. When we bring him in, and we will, we will be questioning him on a variety of subjects including any possible participation in the SST conspiracy."

A female reporter wedged herself in front of him. "Your boss FBI Chief Zwick says this incident is key to the investigation and that several arrests will be made over the next 24 hours."

"I have no information about that. And now if you'll excuse me, I have a long day tomorrow." '

Briggs struggled to free himself from the throng as questions continued to pepper him. How many men do you plan to use on tomorrow's raid? What contingency plans exist if Childers refuses to give up? Has the Director given you a free hand in this operation? The camera swung around to reveal a fourth reporter.

"There you have it. Special Agent Fowler Briggs of the FBI who tomorrow morning will lead a coordinated raid on the Childers home in Moxee Valley. Troopers from the state police as well as FBI agents being flown in this evening will comprise the strike force prepared to resolve this situation by any means necessary. Will there be a peaceful resolution to this standoff or will there be bloodshed? Tune in tomorrow morning for our special coverage starting at 9 a.m. Eastern Time."

Paul signaled to Jennie to shut down the TV. She did so. Paul still had Kovacs on the line. "Looks to me, Lieutenant," Paul said, "like Briggs has got himself in the jaws of a nutcracker."

Kovacs agreed. "Won't do us much good if he's out west chasing after that whacked out bomb thrower."

"Too bad because we're getting close. Very close." He started to fill the detective in on everything they had put together.

Jennie picked up the last cold slice of pizza and started to nibble on it as she stared intently at Hammond Chambers' e-mail.

Meanwhile, on the veranda of a stately home on Cape Ann in Massachusetts, a man sat quietly staring out over Massachusetts Bay. Far out in the water he could see lights from several fishing boats. The silence of the night was disturbed only slightly by the muffled clanging of buoys closer in toward shore. Overhead the night sky was clear. A million and one stars peppered the inky blackness. A gentle breeze wafted up from the shore line while dozens of fireflies danced across the delicately manicured lawn. The sweet smell of honeysuckle filled the air.

He should have been at peace but he wasn't. After 88 years he was entitled to spend his final years without stress, comfortable in the home that he and his late wife had built some thirty years ago. He wanted only to lose himself in the books from his extensive library and to enjoy the occasional visit from his daughters and his grandchildren. After years of service to his country, sometimes sacrificing family to the demands of his national obligations, he wanted nothing more than a quiet contemplative solitude. But apparently it was not to be. His country had needed him one more time and in its time of need he could not refuse.

As he absent-mindedly fingered the worn gold wedding band he wore on a chain around his neck, he thought of his five grandchildren and dreaded the kind of world they were facing. It was not the world he had been born into. He knew he'd been lucky. His family had survived a terrible Depression. He had fought bravely and survived the Second World War and Korea. He'd been free to attend the college of his choice, pursue a career that gave him great joy and satisfaction. His life had been lived on the bedrock of personal freedom but somehow over the years, that freedom had been eroding. People who believed that the individual should be subservient to the collective had been amassing more and more political power. Average Americans, busy with their own lives, had hardly noticed the encroachment on their liberty. Hidden in the shadows. the insidious crawl toward socialism had hardly been noticed. And now, in the wake of the election of a man they didn't fully understand, the nation's citizens were suddenly faced with a harsh reality. Demagogues who espoused the Marxist way of life were about to transform the country into a place where individual initiative was to be abhorred and individual freedoms did not exist.

No, he thought, if it takes my last breath, this cannot be permitted. I will not leave that kind of world to my grandchildren and the children who will follow them. With effort, the man who was known to many as Galen got up from his chair and headed into the house. The arthritis that racked his body had slowed him down but he took nothing for the pain. His mind was as clear as ever. He wanted to keep it that way.

He went to his desk, unlocked the bottom drawer and withdrew the laptop computer that he used only for SST e-mail communication. It was a precaution he had taken when he had formed the group. The others had followed suit. In today's world of exploding technology, you couldn't be too cautious. As for the situation in Yakima, Grayden Walsh and the others had a right to be worried. This fool Childers was threatening to undermine everything they had worked for. But what to do? He sat back, arms folded across his chest, pondering a half dozen alternatives. Those who, at great personal risk, had followed him deserved an answer.

Jennie had once again spent the night, She was curled up in the crook of Paul's arm as he sat up in bed, watching a television news channel. The sound was muted to barely audible. It was a few minutes past six, the sun was barely peering over the Triborough Bridge. On the streets below the city was just beginning to stir. He looked over at the clock. It was still a few minutes past six, still too early to call Gus Caramedes who might be an up-at-fiver or a sleep-tilnooner, Paul didn't really know which.

It was Jennie who had come up with the idea. Neither of them really knew what hacking entailed but it seemed to them both if you could gain access to a person's computer, you could discover a great deal. The trick seemed to be gaining access. Last night, when Hammond Chambers had e-mailed Jennie, his message had included his identifying e-mail address. It seemed simple and obvious. Hack in and check out the last three or four months worth of e-mail correspondence. With luck that would include the other doctors and

THEIR e-mail addresses. If there was something to be found, Gus would find it.

As he continued watching the TV set, suddenly "Breaking News" flashed onto the screen, then the image of a late model car turned on its side on a city street. Two police cruisers with lights flashing were parked alongside. The legend below the picture read CONGRESSMAN VICTIM OF DRIVEBY ATTACK. Paul picked up the remote and boosted the volume.

"........a few minutes past five a.m., according to witnesses. Congressman Tompkins was apparently on his way to an early breakfast meeting with constituents at a restaurant in Front Royal, Virginia, about sixty miles west of the Capitol. A newspaper delivery driver who was stocking vending machines was parked at the intersection of 21st and E street when he saw an SUV overtake the Congressman's Ford Taurus. Two shots were fired and the Taurus swerved and then rolled over. The SUV then sped away. The newspaper employee, identified as Anthony LaPresto, called 911 and then went to the overturned car to help. Congressman Tompkins, a moderate Republican from Virginia's Tenth District, was not hit by the gunfire and apparently suffered only minor bruises. He has been taken to George Washington University Hospital for observation. Further details at the bottom of the hour as they become known."

Paul stared grimly at the set. First Yakima, now this. The waters were becoming very muddied. He turned off the television, got up and padded into his den, picked up his phone and called Gus Caramedes. If he was still in bed, too bad. He could sleep tomorrow.

Fowler Briggs stamped his feet on the ground, trying to keep them from falling off. Somebody should have told him that southern Washington in May was only slightly warmer than Pt. Barrow, Alaska. His upper body was wrapped in a warm fur-lined parka and his head in a fur-flapped hat, both courtesy of the County Sheriff's Department, but the rest of him was in danger of death by terminal frostbite. Just as he was about to go back inside the motel, the sheriff's cruiser appeared, followed by a motorcade of other vehicles. All were carrying officers from various jurisdictions. All were armed. Bringing up the rear was a TV van carrying a pool reporter and a pool cameraman. Briggs did not want a media circus disrupting his operation; on the other hand, if he banned all press and something went wrong, the Bureau would be excoriated from coast to coast and the conspiracy theorists would run amok. The cruiser pulled to the curb and Briggs hopped in, sitting next to the Sheriff who eschewed a chauffeur, preferring to drive himself. Sheriff Wally Wilkerson was tall and thickly proportioned across the chest and shoulders. At age 41, he was a former linebacker for the Washington State Cougars and his weight hadn't changed by two pounds in the interim. He looked over at Briggs and smiled.

"A little too cold for you, Agent Briggs?" he asked.

Briggs tossed him a wan smile.

"I'll live."

"This is what we call around here a brisk day," Wilkerson said. "You get used to it."

Briggs shook his head. "No, YOU get used to it. My ancestors spent thousands of years adapting to an equatorial climate. They did not bargain for something like this."

Wilkerson grinned. "Well, I can understand that. You know, I'd lend you some gloves and some boots but I got a feeling if Manny Childers comes out on the porch to chat, he'll probably be wearing a cut-off T-shirt and shorts. Wouldn't want to see you put at a psychological disadvantage," he deadpanned.

Briggs looked over at him, figured he was being put on and laughed. Wilkerson laughed with him. Just a couple of good old boys on their way to a shootout.

It was twenty after seven when they pulled up to the head of the dirt road leading to the Childers home. One of the deputies on duty backed his cruiser up, giving the task force room to pass. The temperature was hovering around 30 and the branches of the pine trees lining the driveway glistened with nearly melted ice crystals. Wilkerson slowed as he approached the house. Grand entrances were reserved for hot dogs like Howard Urbanski who, in Wilkerson's opinion, was good for handing out parking tickets and little else.

The cruiser came to a full stop. The vehices in the rear also came to a halt. Wilkerson got out from behind the wheel and reached in the backseat for his bullhorn. He and Briggs had already agreed that Wilkerson would make the first effort. If need be, Briggs would try a tougher approach. Unwillingly, Briggs exited the warm car and fought off the urge to stamp his feet.

"Manny Childers. This is Sheriff Wilkerson. We need to talk." The sound of his voice, enhanced by the bullhorn, reverberated in the stillness of the surrounding woods. There was no response from the house. After a few moments he tried again. "Manny, there's no sense making this hard. You got women and children in there. Come out and talk. Nobody's going to shoot you."

Briggs looked over at the window to the left of the door. It had opened slightly. A rifle barrel appeared in the opening. Above and to the right, another rifle appeared in a second story window. He thought he saw the flash of a female face. If so, there was a lot more firepower in that house than they'd counted on. He knew he'd have to tread softly.

More silence. Then slowly the front door opened and Childers stepped out onto the porch. No T-shirt. No shorts. He was wearing heavy corduroy pants and a heavy grey wool sweater. His boots looked fur-lined. On his head was a baseball cap with a Mariners logo. In his right hand, held down at his side, was the .44 revolver. He looked over at Briggs, appraising him.

"Who's the nigger?" he asked.

"Special Agent Briggs of the FBI," Wilkerson told him, putting down the bullhorn. Childers looked back at Briggs, then leaned over and spit into the scrub brush.

"Guess they're takin' anybody these days." , he said.

Wilkerson looked over at Briggs who shook his head subtly as if to say, don't make a big deal of it. Wilkerson looked back at Childers. "I got a warrant here for your arrest, Manny, and it's my duty to serve it. You come along now, the rest of your family stays here. We'll leave 'em be. When you get to town, call yourself a lawyer, maybe the Judge'll let you out on bail. That'd be the smart thing for you to do and I hope you do it."

"Well, I'm not that smart, Wally. Isn't that what you're always tellin' me? But you know, I am smart enough to know I ain't gonna get no bail and I sure don't feature getting locked up in some tin can jail cell. "

"Manny, somebody's going to get hurt here." Wilkerson warned.

Childers nodded. "You're right about that." He called out. "Seth, train that gun on the Sheriff. Anybody makes a move put one between his eyes. Adam, you get the nigger."

Wilkerson looked over at Briggs as if to say, 'Your turn.'

"Mr. Childers, my name is Briggs. I represent the federal government and because the office of a United States Congressman was bombed, the Bureau has jurisdiction here."

Childers half-smiled. "Well, boy, I'm mighty impressed by that."

"First, I want to make something clear. Much as you and your sons might like to take a shot at me or the Sheriff, there's not going to be any bloodshed here today. Or any day, if I can help it."

"Well, in that case you can leave, Mr. FBI man," Childers laughed.

"But I'll tell you what we CAN do. First we can cut off your gas and electric power. Then we'll shut off your water supply at the main back on the county road. After that, come dark, we'll bring in a couple of dozen floodlights and aim 'em at your windows while a set of loudspeakers plays Godawful music loud enough to be heard back in the city. And if that doesn't convince you to cooperate, Mr. Childers, we've got a few dozen other things we can try. Or, as the Sheriff said, you can come back to the city with us and take your chances with the law."

"That being the case, I'll take my chances," Childers said and turned to go back inside.

Briggs called after him. "Mr. Childers, are you affiliated with the group that calls itself SST?"

He turned back, puzzled. "What are you talkin' about, boy?"

"SST. They're the people who are assassinating the Congressmen."

"No shit," Childers grinned. "Well, God bless 'em."

"Are you saying you never heard of them?" Briggs asked.

"Heard of 'em but don't know 'em. Don't care to know 'em." He took a couple of steps forward and again spit off the end of the porch. He stared down at Briggs, his eyes reflecting nothing but bigoted hatred. "Now get off my property, Mr. FBI man or I will, by God, blow your fuckin' head off." He turned and headed for the door. Briggs shouted after him.

"One more question, Mr. Childers. How's your health?"

Childers whirled angrily at the doorway. "Damn good, boy, and I sure as hell am gonna outlive all of you bastards!" With that he went inside slamming the door.

Wilkerson looked toward Briggs. "I told you he was a mean son of a bitch."

Briggs nodded in disappointment. "And the wrong son of a bitch at that."

A half-hour later Briggs trudged into the motel and assembled his task force. As he outlined his strategy, McIlroy booked three adjoining rooms on the second floor and had the connecting doors removed. A local Rent-All took an order for six desks, a dozen chairs, three tables, and other necessities for a temporary war room. By noon, everyone knew they were in for a long siege. Days at a minimum, maybe weeks.

The call from Zwick had come in just before eleven o'clock. What the hell was going on out there? He'd promised the country results and that's what he wanted. Now, not next week. Briggs listened to his tirade for several minutes and then pushed back. There was no way to take the man by force without getting a lot of people shot and maybe killed. Briggs had no intention of presiding over another Ruby Ridge and if Zwick wanted to replace him, that would be just fine. And he'd be just fine with the Laramie, Wyoming, field office, if it came to that. The two words Zwick hated most to hear were Ruby Ridge and while he had not yet joined the FBI when it happened, the killings had left an indelible stain on the good name of the Bureau. Zwick backed off. Briggs was probably right. But goddamnit, something had to be done about all these killings. Once again Briggs told him that he believed the killings were rising from a different source. Again, Zwick refused to believe it.

As he hung up, Briggs reminded himself that no Congressman had been killed since the SST had declared their unilateral truce. But that was yesterday and now there were less than 48 hours left before the carnage would resume, presuming, of course, that the 21 Congressman had not resigned in the interim. Briggs wondered how many would actually quit their seats. As a group they weren't known for their courage, moral or physical. He would have to check with some of the security people back in D.C.

Just then he noticed for the first time that an envelope had been slipped under his door. He picked it up, opened it. It was from headquarters and read: "Paul Castle trying to reach you. Says it's urgent." At that moment the phone rang. It was McIlroy. There was a problem with the electronics store supplying the temporary computers. Annoyed, Briggs stuffed the message into his side pocket and stalked out of the room.

CHAPTER EIGHTEEN

Paul and Kovacs were embroiled in a heated argument. Paul had stopped by police headquarters to get Kovacs up to speed. As soon as the Lieutenant heard what Paul was up to with Gus Caramedes, he grabbed him roughly by the elbow and steered him into the nearest men's room.

"Are you out of your goddamned mind?" Kovacs sputtered, his face turning color.

"Come on, Lieutenant, we're nowhere without access to their computers or their phone records, you said that yourself." Paul said.

"That doesn't mean you can willy-nilly go violating a half-dozen privacy laws. It's one thing to try to dig up the name of a doctor. It's something else to start pawing around in someone's private correspondence. Damn it, son, suppose you do find out something. What good is it ? Can't use it in court and anything else we get as a result, that's inadmissible too."

"We're not at the courtroom stage and you know it. We've got bits and pieces we can't put together and if we don't, a lot more people may end up dead. So to hell with your legal niceties."

Kovacs shook his head angrily. "You've got a real pair on you, son. You're just itching to get tossed in the slammer."

Paul glared at him. "If you think that's where I belong, do it. I need something for tonight's broadcast anyway. How about a remote feed from the city jail? Hi, this is Paul Castle reporting to you from Cell 69."

Kovacs waved at him in disgust.

"Come on, Lieutenant, there's got to be a way to get surveillance on these guys."

"With what?" Kovacs growled in frustration. "Say, Judge, I've got these seven doctors who know each other. Interesting, says the Judge, what else do you have? Nothing else. That's it. Oh, well, in that case, let me sign this warrant right away. Can I borrow your pen? Thanks. Was that quick enough for you, Lieutenant?" Kovacs raised his eyes to heaven.

Paul, slightly chastened, held his hands up in surrender. "Okay, I get it. Sorry, I'm not a cop and I'm not a lawyer, I'm just a thick-headed television guy out to maybe stop another dozen murders."

Kovacs eyed him closely, then said quietly, "I am, too, son. And just so you know, I've got a tail on our pal Hammond Chambers, not that it's doing anything for us." Kovacs angrily slammed his fist into his hand. "Damn it, Paul, I don't like being hamstrung any more than you do but the law's the law and without it we don't have much, do we?"

"Right."

Kovacs hesitated again. He started to pace nervously, then turned to Paul. "I'm not telling you this, but listen anyway. This hacker, this kid, you make sure he talks only to you. Only to you, do you understand? It's my job and my pension's on the line here. If I find out he's blabbed to anybody—that means his buddies, other hackers, his priest, even his mother, anybody—I'll walk him into a jail cell and toss away the key. And that presupposes he can still walk and I haven't broken both his legs."

"I'll tell him," Paul said.

"He's a teenage kid. Tell him twice." Kovacs said.

Paul decided to walk back to the studio. For one thing, he'd save the $3.00 subway fare. For another, he hadn't worked out in over a week and he was starting to feel it. A brisk walk was just what he needed but he soon realized his walk through midtown Manhattan was going to be anything but quick. With Mother's Day looming, the shoppers had swelled the ranks of the businessmen heading for their favorite lunchwagons or watering holes. Jostling and elbowing were the sporting events of the day. He passed by an appliance store featuring an array of big screen televisions. Regis and Kelly were joshing with a distinguished British novelist who looked as if he'd rather be anywhere else but sitting on a three-legged stool. Drew Carey was trying to give away an outdoor barbecue to a hyperactive housewife who looked as if she couldn't add two plus two. One would never guess the nation was in a state of crisis.

Paul continued on. If the store had been displaying one of the round-the- clock news channels, he would have learned that tiny pockets of rebellion were starting to pop up in various parts of the country. With events in Yakima temporarily frozen, the channel was reporting on the mugging of a Congressman in a men's room at a posh Washington hotel where he was having breakfast. Not being at risk, he had no security detail to protect him. In Nevada, a billboard featuring the smiling face of the local Congresswoman was sprayed with bullets from an AK-47 being fired by a man who was buck naked. He was also dead drunk. At a beach near Fairhope, Alabama, three men tried to abduct the teenage son of the local Congressman. The attempt was thwarted by a couple of off-duty police officers who drove into the parking lot just as the men were trying to stuff the boy into the back of a van. And in Georgia, a local preacher was staging a prayer meeting on the front lawn of a Congressman who believed that God should mind his own business and stick to his churches instead of trying to worm his way into every corner of the federal government. As he turned a corner, the offices of National Heatbeat ahead in the middle of the block, his cell phone beeped. "Yo," he said.

"It's me," Gus said.

"Who's me?"

"You know who. We gotta talk."

"So talk."

"Face to face. I got stuff I gotta show you."

"Come to the office. I'm just walking in the door now."

"No," Gus said. "I don't want to be seen there."

"Fine. I'll come to your place."

"No! My Mom's home sick. She thinks I gave up all this crap months ago."

"All right. You name it," Paul said.

"DeWitt Clinton Park. Southwest corner near Pier 92. Only a couple of benches there. Not too crowded."

"When?"

"In an hour. Maybe less."

"I'll bring peanuts and pretend to feed the squirrels," Paul said.

A moment's silence, then: "How do you pretend to feed the squirrels?"

"See ya, Gus," Paul said as he turned off the phone.

Forty minutes later, Paul was sprawled on a park bench tossing beer nuts in the direction of a quintet of bushy tailed squirrels who apparently hadn't eaten in weeks. If they felt slighted because no actual beer was being served with the nuts, they gave no sign of it. A minute later Gus Caramedes came up behind Paul, slipped around the bench and sat down, staring straight ahead, trying to give a casual observer the impression he didn' t have the vaguest idea who Paul was. Paul looked at him with amusement.

"The waters near Brataslava have big boobies," he said out of the corner of his mouth.

Gus jerked his head toward him." What?"

"If you don't know the password you're going to have to leave," Paul said in all seriousness.

"Stop yankin' my chain, bro' ," Gus said. "We might be into some heavy shit here. And something else—" He looked around furtively. "You never know who's hanging around, watchin' you. You know what I mean?"

"I know what you mean. So what have you got?" Paul asked.

"Basically, nothing," Gus said.

Paul frowned. "Nothing? What happened to the heavy shit?"

Gus undid two of the buttons on his shirt, reached inside and took out a brown manila envelope. "Here's how it went down," he said. "I e-mailed this guy Chambers with a teaser he couldn't ignore. As soon as he opened, I gave him a cold—" Seeing Paul's blank look: "—fed his machine a virus and a few minutes later I was all over his e-mail files like a wino at a tasting party. I got correspondence with four of those other doctors so now I have their e-mail addresses. So I get into those four computers and start hunting around and you know what? Unless they're talking in code, I'm getting a big zero. Patient referrals, birthday greetings, a couple of them talked about joint vacations. One of them warned the others to stay away from some crappy teen movie. His opinion, not mine. So do these guys know each other? Yeah, and very well too. Are they mixed up in some kind of spy ring? Not so's you could tell from their mail."

Paul sagged in disgust, tossing away the nuts, bag and all.

"Except—" Gus said, and let it hang.

"Except?"

"Except for these two e-mails I rooted out between Chambers and Dr. Grayden Walsh." He opened the envelope and took out two sheets of paper. Each was a copy of an e-mail. He handed them to

Paul who scanned them. Gus scooted close, peering over his shoulder. "I'm really curious about this top one." It read:

> Thanks for recent input. Your analysis was excellent. R.T. having possible second thoughts. May not go through with surgery. Her choice, of course, but I believe she is an excellent candidate for this procedure. May need additional persuasion. Any thoughts from you or Galen would be appreciated. Apologize for this contact.
>
> Number two is malfunctioning. Will have to replace.

It was sent from Grayden Walsh to Hammond Chambers. "Now get a load of Chambers' reply. You think he sounds a little steamed, or what?"

> Imprudent to contact me about your patient R.T. We have procedures in place for emergencies. Use them. Do not write me until replacement up and running.

"That's it?" Paul asked.

"That's it. I gotta tell you, bro, these guys are cagey bastards. See this. Number two malfunctioning. You know what that says to me? These guys all have second computers, just like throwaway phones. Whatever they're talking about among themselves, it's going back and forth between these other computers."

"And how do we get into these backups?" Paul asked.

"If all they use them for is talking to each other, we don't," Gus said.

Paul pointed to the sheet. "This guy Galen. Was he mentioned anywhere else, by any of these guys?"

"Nope."

Paul nodded. "From what you read, did you get any feeling about who might be in charge?"

Gus shook his head. "Not really. Chambers, maybe. Walsh, possible, but I don't think so. Except for these two e-mails there really wasn't anything there."

Paul hesitated thoughtfully. "One other thing. Let's just say that you're right, that they all have these secondary computers. Okay, so Walsh's crashes on him. He buys a new one right away. Does he trade in the old one?"

"That'd be pretty dumb," Gus said.

"Okay, but let's say he's not as smart as you. He trades it in. What if we could get our hands on it?"

Gus opened his hands wide. "Jackpot time, amigo."

"Even if he erased it?"

Gus nodded. "Even if. We devils of the keyboard, we have our ways."

Paul smiled, then folded the sheets and stuck them in his jacket pocket. "Really good work, Gus. I appreciate it." He reached n his shirt pocket and took out five $100 bills folded over and handed them to Gus. "Here. Go find yourself a hooker, take her to your bedroom and screw her brains out."

Gus looked at the money dolefully. "I told you, bro, my Mom's home with a cold."

Paul shrugged, smiling. "Sorry, man, I lost my head."

A few blocks away, at the New York office of Democratic Representative Bernard Steinmetz, a cautiously reflective man of 46, an ex-History professor, a gentle non-confrontational man with moderate views and great intelligence, a crowd was gathering. Untypically of New Yorkers, they were orderly and well-mannered and they liked Ben Steinmetz, but like most Americans over the past year, they had grown more and more disenchanted with the direction Congress was taking. They were quick to point out that they weren't picketing Ben, who they loved, but as constituents, they could hardly be expected to picket that wild eyed harridan whose district was fifteen blocks to the south.

Similar gatherings were beginning to form in towns and cities all across the country. Perhaps it was SST that had lit this spark. Perhaps, but less likely, the alcoholic anarchist in Yakima. Yes, they knew their Congressman (or Congresswoman) was in Washington but a protest rally was not to be ignored, wherever and whenever it occurred. People with something to say and an overpowering need to say it were starting to band together in common cause.

Was the sleeping giant at last arousing itself, starting to make noise that would be heard in every far flung city and town in the nation? Would it sustain like the uncontrollable rage of the summer of 2009, or would it eventually fizzle like the "tea parties" that had preceded it? The events of the next few days might very well answer that question.

Jennie was in her office when Paul barged in, unaware that she was chatting with her boss, Assistant District Attorney Leon Goldman. Paul excused himself and started to back out. Goldman smiled and waved him in.

"Come in, Mr. Castle. I've been looking forward to meeting you." He put out his hand. "Leon Goldman, Jennie's magnanimous boss who lets you borrow her any time you like."

Paul returned the smile and shook his hand firmly. "And don't think I don't appreciate it."

Goldman was a short little man, barely five feet four inches with a freckled face and a Donald Trump combover. He was nattily dressed in a three piece grey worsted suit. The vest did its best to disguise a slight paunch but failed miserably. "So, have we any exciting new developments on the medical front?" Paul reacted visibly but Goldman just smiled and shook his head. "Not to worry, Jennie's been filling me in. Whatever she says, I keep to myself."

"Good to hear," Paul said. "I'd hate to be the laughing stock of the D.A.'s office."

Jennie piped up. "No fear of that, Paul. Leon actually thinks you may be on to something."

Paul looked at Goldman. "Does that mean we might get a little help?"

Goldman shook his head sadly. "I'm afraid not. I told Jennie your theory was bizarre but not beyond the realm of possibility. You have a premise and a handful of maybes and could-be's. Get something solid, then come see me." He put out his hand and they shook again. "You've got a good mind, Mr. Castle. A good mind and a good program. Keep doing what you're doing." As he went out the door, he said to Jennie, "You I'll see later," and then with a look toward Paul, "Or maybe not." He was gone.

Paul moved to the door, closed it, took the e-mails out of his pocket and handed them to Jennie. "Gus thinks we've got something."

Jennie read the top one. "R.T. That's Rose Temple."

"Right. Has to be."

"She was starting to chicken out. Walsh didn't know what to do."

"Right again. So he e-mails Chambers for instructions."

"Chambers or Galen," she said.

Paul shrugged. "Whoever he is."

"Another doctor."

"Where do you get that?" Paul asked.

She shook her head. "Really, Castelli, you are woefully ignorant of Greek history. One of the great classical physicians, second only to Hippocrates."

"Sorry, I only go back as far as Dr. Kildare. You remember seeing any Galen in the stuff we went through last night?"

"No, but I'd be willing to bet it's an alias, some sort of a cover name. I mean, who names their kid Galen any more?"

Paul shrugged. "Who names their kid Hippocrates?"

"Funny," she said.

"Actually it was pretty lame," he said.

"So it was. "

He slipped his arm around her waist. "Then it wasn't my incisive wit that attracted you to me?"

"Hardly. Now, back off, tiger, Leon may come back through that door in any minute."

Paul shook his head. "Leon is gone for the day," he said and kissed her lingeringly on the lips. Before the moment could escalate into something less sedate, Paul's phone rang.

"Sorry," he said to Jennie. Into the phone: "This is Paul."

"It's me."

"Are we going to start that again, Gus?"

"Something maybe you should know. After you left the park, I just hung around a couple of minutes, scoping things out."

"I know. You can't be too careful," Paul said patiently.

"Good advice, bro. Take it. When you were leaving the park, there were these two guys about fifty yards behind you."

Paul's face darkened." Are you sure?"

"Hey, I'm paranoid. I'm not blind."

"What'd they look like?"

"One white, one black. Didn't see their faces. The black guy had a bulge in the small of his back under his jacket. Big. Maybe an automatic."

"Okay, thanks, Gus. I'll keep an eye out."

As he hung up, Jennie was aware of the concerned look on his face. “What is it?” she asked.

“My doctor friend lied. I’ve got company again.” , Paul said.

Jennie grabbed him tightly by the arm. “Paul, tell Kovacs. Now.”

Paul thought about it. “I could do that,” he said slowly.

“No, you WILL do that,” she said. “Don’t be stupid.”

“These two guys following me, they could be useful, Jenn, if I can find out who they are, they could lead me back to whoever hired them.”

“Oh, for God’s sakes,” she said. “Paul, you know what kind of people these are. If you get in their way, they could kill you.”

He shook his head. “No, I don’t believe that.”

She looked at him in disbelief. “Are you out of your mind? These people come out of nowhere, they kill in broad daylight. You’re not immune, Paul. You’re a target and the closer you get to the truth.....” She broke off, tears starting to form. She turned away from him in frustration.

He went to her, tried to take her in his arms.

“Let go of me!” She wriggled free.

“Jenn—”

She turned back to him, cheeks now stained with tears. “Call Kovacs. Let him handle it.”

He looked away. “I can’t. These people aren’t afraid of arrest. They’d just clam up. What good would that do?”

“It might keep you alive.” He turned away from her. She grabbed at his arm and spun him toward her. “Or maybe you think you have something to prove. Is that it? Years ago you backed away and now you’re going to prove what a brave man you are.”

“No,” he said.

“Not brave. Stupid and suicidal, yes. Don’t you have any feelings for me? I’m the one who got you into this. If you get hurt or killed, it’s my fault.”

"You're wrong. This is my choice, my responsibility. I know what I'm doing."

Her eyes blazed. "You don't know anything, you damned fool. All right, go ahead. Get yourself killed. I don't care any more!"

He reached for her. "Jennie—"

She pulled away from him and walked over toward her desk. "Get out of here. Just go! Go!"

He hesitated. He had no words for the moment. He turned and walked out of the room.

Fowler Briggs lay on his bed, hands laced behind his neck, staring up at the water-stained ceiling. The ugly brownish pattern was either a stein of ale or a bent over tomato plant or maybe a fat guy playing the harmonica. A psychiatrist could have a field day with this one. He had tried to sleep but he was too angry, too wound up inside to even relax. He tried to remember the last time anyone had called him nigger. High school, maybe, when he and a couple of his buddies had gone to nearby Biloxi for a traveling carnival. There had been four of them, hulking white boys in bib overalls. The biggest of the bunch "accidentally" bumped into him and then sneered, 'Watch where you're walkin', nigger'. Briggs didn't stop to think. He slammed his fist into the boy's face, breaking two teeth. Instantly the other three were all over him. People started yelling. "Fight! Fight!" and "Some white boys are beatin' the crap out of some nigger!!!" As the crowd gathered, he looked for his buddies, spotted them hightailing it through the throng, running for cover. He spent six hours in the hospital with a concussion and a broken hand. As best he could recall that was the last time anyone had used that name for him. At Oxford, at the University, many thought it but the epithet was silent, communicated only in body language and icy indifference.

No doubt that Emanuel Childers was a bigoted, arrogant and

contemptible bully, but one thing he was not was a mass murderer. Even if he had the guts, which Briggs doubted, he didn't have the brains. No, Childers was an anomaly hogging the national spotlight while the real perpetrators, this SST group, sat watching and waiting. And Castle, the TV guy. He was on to something. Briggs didn't know exactly what but as soon as this farce ended, he was going to find out. That is, if it wasn't too late. He checked his watch. If his math was right and the SST'ers weren't bluffing, they had about 30 hours before the killing resumed.

He realized he was thirsty and got up off the bed. There was a vending machine down the hall next to the ice machine. He dug into his pockets, looking for change, took out a small slip of paper. He glanced at it. "Call Paul Castle. Urgent."

He went back to the nightstand, picked up the phone and dialed 411. "New York City," he said. "Offices of National Heartbeat. It's a television channel." When he got through, Paul wasn't in his office so he left his cell phone number and a message: "Call me anytime. Day or night."

As anger escalated across the country, fifteen Congresspersons on SST's death list had decided that the core of all their problems lay with the right-wing maniacs who infested the great Northwest and who were personified by their leader, Emanuel Childers. Indeed, the FBI supported them in this. No, they had no intention of giving up their plush seats in Congress. It was only a matter of time before this national nightmare would end and they could go back to business as usual.

The remaining six Congressmen had a different view of things. The threat, they believed, was not quite so obvious nor the solution quite so simple. Three had been offered lucrative jobs in the private sector and had already announced their intention to resign. Between the pay at their new jobs and what they had already stolen from the national treasury, they would live in luxury for their remaining years which, by taking this action, might be quite a few. The remaining three, also sporting net worths in to the mid-to-high seven figures, were assessing their options. The anti-Congress protests sprouting up all over the country were getting angrier and noisier. People were actually starting to read the bills Congress was dead set on passing even though they had written upwards of 1000 pages, notably the proposed bill to establish the Universal Identification System, a special favorite of the President, which had come in at a whopping 1210 pages. How and why were these people reading these monstrosities when even they, Congress, couldn't be bothered? Fearful that Yakima was an irrelevant sideshow, these three had all but decided to throw in the towel in order to devote more time to home and family. In this case, that was actually what they intended to do.

The debate between the validity of Yakima versus SST had spilled over into the studio. It was seven minutes past five and Murray had put himself squarely into Paul's face.

"We are doing Yakima and that is that," Murray half-shouted. When he half-shouted you could hear him all over the studio. When he actually shouted, you could hear him in the executive offices, two floors up.

"It's a sideshow!" Paul countered.

"I don't care if its Ringling Brothers, Barnum and Bailey! We go with it just like FOX, CNN, NBC, CBS—Jesus Christ, Paul, are you trying to destroy this program?"

"This is a conspiracy involving a handful of doctors—"

"Yeah, yeah, so you've told me. Got any names we can use? Any kind of facts. Any evidence. A paper trail, maybe. Just what the hell do you think you can put on the air that won't have dozen lawyers in the Old Man's office first thing in the morning?"

"We have protests all over the country. We have attacks on Congressmen—"

"Even though your guy said they were going to cool it for 72 hours," Murray interrupted.

Paul ignored him. "Did you see the latest poll numbers? Only 52 percent condemn the killings. That means almost half the country has no problem with it. You don't think that's a story?"

"Look at me. Did not your FBI pal not thirty minutes ago leave you a message with his cell phone number on it. You know what that means? That means we get an exclusive interview, maybe remote, maybe by phone, with the FBI agent in charge. We got a big huge "get" and you want to babble about poll numbers. Yakima, Paul. Yakima!"

Paul shook his head. "I want to speak to the Old Man."

Murray moved in closer, nose to nose. "You ARE speaking to the Old Man. I spent a half-hour with him while you were out playing Jim Rockford, Private Eye."

Paul stared into Murray's face which was approaching a salmon pink. "I won't do Yakima," he said.

"What's that supposed to mean?"

"Bring in Bill Farnum. I'm done."

"What do you mean, done?"

"What does it sound like? The deal was, you and the Old Man let me run the show my way, no interference. Let Farnum be the trained seal." Paul turned on his heel and started off.

Murray shouted after him. "I swear to God, Paul. He'll fire you."

"Fuck him," Paul said over his shoulder.

Murray wasn't finished. "Where's that cell phone number for Briggs?"

"And fuck you, too!" Paul said as he strode out of the studio.

CHAPTER NINETEEN

Fritz Schoenfeld had hauled him up on the carpet which was a neat trick since there was no carpet in Schoenfeld's office to haul him up on.

"Damn it, Paul, you can't just walk off the show like that. You've got a contract."

"Which you abrogated." Paul replied angrily.

"Don't you start throwing those forty dollar words at me, young man. I'm the fella who rescued you from that 60 watt Utah station and made something of you."

"I might have had something to do with that myself."

"Damn little," Schoenfeld said. They were both standing, facing each other across Schoenfeld's massive desk. "We manufactured you, son. We took that good set of teeth and that schoolboy smile and that bull terrier persistence and we created another Geraldo Rivera, except maybe not as good. I mean, how talented do you have to be to scrape around in the bottom of a septic tank every night?"

The words stung. Inwardly, Paul cringed. "You've done all right by me."

"And we're going to keep doing all right, "Schoenfeld said, "starting tomorrow night."

"I don't think so," Paul said. "I quit."

He'd said it before he realized what he was saying. Oh, well, too late now.

Schoenfeld stared him down for a moment, then smiled knowingly. "I get it. You've got a better offer. All this, this rebellion, it's all about breaking your contract."

Paul shook his head."There is no better offer. Tomorrow morning I'm going to sleep late with nowhere to go and no one to see. I can't wait."

"More money? Is that it?" Schoenfeld asked.

"Not that either." Paul moved away from the desk, toward the door. "You know I came in here half-hoping we could work things out. But I see now, that's not possible. In your eyes I'm still a crap vendor and that's all I'll ever be. I'd like to think I'm something more than that. So, yes, Fritz, with no job and no prospects, I quit and if you want to take me to court, well, then, let's get it on." He walked out the door. Fritz stared after him, mentally calculating how big a raise it would take to keep him.

By the time Paul returned to his office "Playback" with guest host Bill Farnum was already underway. He flipped on the TV, plopped down in his chair. He took out his phone and called Jennie at the office. Not there. Not expected. He tried her apartment. The answering machine picked up. He didn't leave a message. Ditto her cell phone.

On screen from Yakima a local freelancer hired by Schoenfeld was trying to cover the story coherently but he was either out of practice or he'd never been much good in the first place. Paul flipped to a network station where wavy-haired Harvey Cantrell was interviewing three typical citizens of Yakima, expressing their unbiased opinions on the events of the last 24 hours. A hatchet faced woman named Dora (not identified as the chairman of the local Democratic Party) deplored the violence being wreaked on the country by Emanuel Childers and his crazy right-wing cronies. She did not identify specifically who these cronies were. Harry Somebody-or-other (not identified as the president of a union local that boasted a membership of 880) said Childers actions were going to cause the loss of good jobs in the Central Washington area. He didn't specify exactly how that correlated. The third member of the triad, a black man named Wallace, stated without reservation that Childers actions constituted a direct threat to the safety of the President which was precisely the sort of thing you could expect from a racist society. He proved his point by citing the murder of Congressman Duane D. Rogers, completely overlooking the fact that the vast majority of the Congressional victims were white. All the while Harvey Cantrell kept nodding his agreement, no matter what was being said.

The phone rang. Paul picked up.

An electronically altered voice asked, "Do you know who this is?"

Paul flipped back to Bill Farnum and the dummy from Yakima, keeping the volume low. "No, I don't, but we've talked before."

"Yes, we have," the man said. "I'm watching the broadcast of Playback."

"While you're having supper?" Paul asked.

"What?"

"Sorry," Paul said, "just my clever way of trying to determine what time zone you're in."

"Would it help if I said I was having a midnight snack?"

"That would put you in the Canary Islands. Not much help at all." Paul responded.

"Good. Now that we have the meaningless banter out of the way, why aren't you doing the program this evening?"

"Well, for one thing, you and I both know that the real story is not in Yakima, Washington."

"You are much sharper than your reputation, Mr. Castle,"

the man said. "I thank you for not adding to the proliferation of misinformation."

"By the way, you know my name, but I don't know yours. What do I call you?"

"It's unimportant."

"Yeah, I know, but it's awkward. I really don't want to address you as Old Robot Voice. How about if I call you, oh say—Galen."

There was a silence on the end of the line.

"You can hang up on me again," Paul said. "It's your nickel."

"Galen will be fine, Mr. Castle. You do realize that there are now less than 24 hours left before our unilateral truce comes to an end."

"I know, but you could extend it."

"In truth, I'd like to," Galen said, "but that wouldn't serve our purpose. Short of that, Mr. Castle, what would you suggest? We still have 15 Congressmen who have no idea of the danger they are in."

"Oh, they know," Paul said, "but they think Yakima is the key to their salvation. But listen, good friend Galen, speaking of danger, I thought we had an understanding. What's the idea of siccing those two goons on me again?"

"I don't know what you're talking about."

"Today in DeWitt Clinton Park. Two big enforcer types, one white and one black and both carrying cannons."

"They have nothing to do with us, I promise you. Who else have you teed off lately?"

"Good question," Paul said, trying to put together a mental enemics list.

"Mr. Castle, I called you this evening to ask you, no, to plead with you to use your influence, your program, anything at hand to try to convince the country, and particularly these remaining Congressmen, of the seriousness of our mission."

"Well, I'll try, Galen, but I've lost my bully pulpit. As of twenty minutes ago I am a man without a job."

"I'm sorry to hear that. I hope it wasn't because of your support for our cause."

"Hold it, buddy!" Paul said sharply. "I don't support your cause. I despise your cause and if I can find a way to help bring you down I'm going to do it. So don't go mistaking my quest for the truth as any kind of endorsement of your tactics."

"Fair enough," Galen said, "but I repeat, anything you can do to persuade America that we are dedicated and committed and that we want only to see these 15 holdouts give up their seats. Do that and you will be doing a service to your country."

There was a click. Galen had hung up.

Paul sat there quietly staring at the television which was airing a commercial for a sexual enhancement product. Having voiced it to Galen, Paul was suddenly becoming aware of the enormity of what he'd done. How was one supposed to eat on a devil-may-care gesture? Quit indeed. He was an idiot. He clicked off the television just as Bill Farnum's face reappeared. The atmosphere in his office was far too stuffy. What he needed was some fresh air.

An hour later he was getting all the fresh air he needed from the air conditioning unit at McNaughton's Irish Pub, a used-to-be-trendy watering hole a few blocks from his apartment. The decor was right out of 'The Quiet Man' with shillelaghs on the wall, along with clay pipes, ceramic shamrocks, unplayable harps, and so-called authentic photographs of real life leprechauns. The only thing missing was a good old fashioned brawl in the middle of the barroom. Paul was working on his third Guiness with a Bushmill chaser when a red-headed freckle-faced colleen sidled up to him at the bar and took the adjoining stool.

"I know you," she smiled. "You're the guy on TV, right?"

Paul grinned and raised his glass in acknowledging salute.

"I just love your show, Mr—uh—?"

"Castle," Paul said, "as in Camelot, a land that never was and never will be." He raised his glass again in an awkward toast and drank deeply. "Let's hear it for reality," he muttered. His diction was imprecise though he wasn't aware of it. If asked he was positive he could do a flawless recitation of the Gettysburg Address.

The girl kept on smiling. "I just loved that thing with Brad Pitt last night. Wow! Right in the face. I just love him. Don't you just love him? Brad Pitt, I mean."

A little blearily, Paul pondered his response which he was sure would be witty and concise. "Never thought about it," he said.

She leaned in closer. "Do you live around here, Mr. Castle, because I really like you. You know what I mean?"

Well, sure he did. He was pushing forty and she was, what, just out of high school. Maybe.

"Not tonight, honey. Maybe some other time." It came out 'may hee smother dime'.

She slipped her arm around his shoulders and leaned very close to his ear, whispering. "It'll be the best you've ever had and only two hundred. Satisfaction guaranteed."

Paul almost choked on the stout as he started to laugh. "Only guarantee I ever got in my life was from my high school principal who guaranteed I wouldn't amount to a bag of dog-do, and whatdayaknow, the old bastard was right. Take a hike, sweetheart, before your parents learn you snuck out the bedroom window."

The girl's smile disappeared and a few seconds later, so did she.

Totally blitzed and feeling sorry for himself, Paul paid the tab and wandered out of the tavern. What Jennie needed now was a good piece of his mind, and what he needed was a good piece of Jennie. Instead of turning north toward his apartment, he headed south toward Jennie's place.

When Jennie arrived home at a few minutes past nine, she found him sitting by the door to her apartment, head in hands, nearly asleep. When he became aware of her, he looked up with red-rimmed exhausted eyes. His voice was barely audible. "I'm scared," he said. "I am so scared."

She helped him inside and sat him up at the kitchen table while she brewed a fresh pot of coffee. She poured a glass of water from the tap, put it down beside him along with two aspirin tablets. Then she went to the bread box and toasted him two slices of dry rye bread. During all of this neither of them said a word. Finally, when the coffee was ready Jennie poured each of them a mugful. She sat opposite him, watching him intently as he tried to sip the steaming brew. Finally, he said, "I quit my job."

"All right," she said. They sat in silence for a couple of minutes longer.

"I won't be able to pay my rent," he said.

"Yes, you will," she said.

"I don't have a job," he said.

"You'll get another one," she said.

"Where?"

"Anywhere."

"With who?"

"Anybody."

"Doing what?"

"Anything."

He stared at her for several seconds. "Did you ever consider getting work as an employment counselor?"

She laughed out loud. So did he.

"I'm sorry," he said.

"About what?"

"This afternoon," he said.

"Oh, that," she said. "We're supposed to do that. We're in love."

"Are we?" Paul asked quizzically.

"I think so."

"Well, then I guess it's all right."

She got up and came around the table, leaned in and kissed him gently on the lips. "It's all right," she said.

"I'll call Kovacs first thing in the morning," he told her.

"Okay," she said. He pushed back in the chair unsteadily, got up. She helped him keep his balance. "I'll be alright in a minute," he said.

"Come on, lay down in the bedroom," she said leading him from the table.

She propped him up with two pillows, took his shoes off and threw a comforter over him. She sat down on the bed beside him, holding his hand.

"Does this mean we're getting married?" he asked

"Damned if I know," she said.

"I say it's a good idea," Paul said. "What do you say?"

"I say it's about time. My eggs have been waiting patiently for seventeen years ."

He reached out and pulled her close, kissing her gently. She responded voraciously. He groaned. "Not now, honey. I've got a headache. No, I mean it. I really have a headache."

Again, they started laughing and held each other very close.

Fowler Briggs was trying to figure out how to take the lid off his container of steaming hot coffee without taking off his gloves. He finally gave up, doffed the gloves and flipped the lid, all in one fluid motion and within nine seconds had his gloves back on, cradling the container as if it were a Faberge egg. Gonzo Burkhalter watched him with amusement, sharing a quick undetected look with Sheriff Wally Wilkerson who also was getting a laugh out of the FBI man's frustration with the cold night air.

Gonzo owned and operated a rolling lunchwagon which he drove back and forth between construction sites during daylight hours. The menu consisted of hot soup, cold sandwiches, coffee, tea, candy bars, cookies and assorted bags of chips, krinkled, kettled and otherwise. With upwards of forty officers staking out the Childers homestead, Gonzo saw an opportunity and with the Sheriff's blessing, was trying to keep the strike force as comfortable as possible. With the temperature hovering around 28 degrees, it was mostly a losing effort.

Briggs and Wilkerson were parked at the head of the dirt driveway next to the Gonzomobile, radio on, ready to respond immediately if there were any change in the situation. So far, total silence from the house. The electricity and gas had been turned off, the water stopped at the main. Floodlights shined from every direction, lighting up the rustic home like a Six Flags amusement park. Loudspeakers surrounding the home were belching forth long forgotten hits such as "Teensy Weensy Bikini," "Splish Splash," "My Friend, the Witch Doctor," the Best of the Chipmunks and others, each more annoying than the others. Periodically, Wilkerson would call the Childers number. No one ever answered.

Briggs had been standing out in the cold for eleven minutes now and he eyed the cruiser hopefully. Wilkerson had wanted to cut the engine and the heater for a while just to make sure they didn't run out of juice later that night.

"Uh, Sheriff, do you suppose, uh, maybe we could start her up again," Briggs suggested hopefully.

Wilkerson temporized. "Well, I'd been hoping to give it at least twenty more minutes, but if you've got a problem—"

Briggs shook his head manfully. "No, no. I'm fine. No problem."

Without really being aware of it, he'd started stamping his feet. At that moment, his cell phone rang. Damn. How was he supposed to dig out his phone from beneath the parka with his gloves on?

He signaled to Wilkerson. "Phone," he said and hurried to the cab of the lunchwagon. The heat wasn't on but it was better than standing outside. He managed to extract the phone from his pocket.

"Briggs."

"Briggs, it's Paul Castle." His voice was strong and clear. A potload of coffee and a couple of hour's rest had sobered him into coherence.

"Oh, yeah, well, this isn't a good time, Mr. Castle—," Briggs said.

Paul ignored him. "I happened to look at the clock. Almost eleven here in the east. That means we've got about nineteen hours before all hell breaks loose again."

"Well, there's not much I can do about that unless I want to storm this place, guns blazing and take out half the family," Briggs said.

"Bullshit," Paul said. "You know this guy's just a bystander. Your problem, Briggs, is the same as mine. We both work for a couple of assholes."

"Tell me about your asshole," Briggs said.

"Sure," he said. "I explained to him in one-syllable words even an eighth grader could understand that the people behind these killings are a bunch of doctors, not some loony government-hating survivalists."

Briggs came alive, forgetting the cold. "I'm listening."

"I think they have a big bank of terminal patients, people who consider themselves true patriots, who have nothing to lose because they'll be dead long before they can come to trial. I think they assassinate publicly and surrender peaceably to make the point that they are willing to sacrifice their lives for the greater good of the country."

"Which is not exactly true," Briggs said.

"You're right. It's not, but as long as the public doesn't know about their terminal illnesses, it makes for great theater. It's the kind of thing that can arouse a lethargic citizenry which is exactly what's happening. As heinous as these killings are, they are striking a chord in the hearts and minds of a lot of people."

"You approve?"

"No. But when you really examine who these victims were and what they've been doing to this country for the past couple of decades, you can understand what's motivating everyone."

"Can you prove any of this, Mr. Castle?" Briggs asked.

"Not yet, but we can with your help. Federal warrants, wiretaps. We've got a lot of names to work with and we can get more. The problem is the damned nineteen hours."

"Well, I'm stuck here for God knows how long. And it's a little late to bring anyone else up to speed." Briggs said. "Have you got any ideas?"

"Only one. There may be a computer up in Bergensberg, Connecticut, that might have some answers. It's a long shot but I haven't got anything else."

"I can't help you, Castle, but I can wish you luck," Briggs said.

"Matter of fact, you CAN help me, Briggs. When I go to Connecticut I'd like to go without the two gorillas that have been following me for the past couple of days. Maybe you could assign a couple of your agents to discourage them."

Briggs smiled, even though Paul couldn't see him do it. "Those two gorillas belong to me. I put them on you after that beating you took just to be sure it didn't happen again."

Paul hesitated, suddenly feeling a little foolish. "Thanks, Briggs. They scared the crap out of me. You want to call 'em off. I'm going to be safe enough."

"You sure about that?"

"No one's going to kill me," he said wryly. "I'm not a Congressman."

Just then Sheriff Wilkerson came to the window of the cab and rapped hard on the glass, frantically waving Briggs to follow him and then jogging off toward his cruiser.

"Sorry. I've got to cut this short," Briggs said. "You've got this number. Keep me in the loop." He exited the car and hurried towards Wilkerson's waiting cruiser. As he hopped into the front passenger seat, Wilkerson whipped the car into a tire-spinning one-eighty and roared down the road toward the house.

"There was a shot fired inside the house," the Sheriff said. "Adam Childers came out on the porch yelling for me."

The cruiser slid to a stop in front of the house. Wilkerson and Briggs jumped out and raced to the porch. Adam Childers was frantic. "Inside. My Paw." All three plunged through the doorway into the house. The power was still out but the glare from the floodlights provided ample illumination. Briggs could hear the sound of weeping women from another part of the house. Sprawled on the floor was the inert body of Emanuel Childers. His other two sons were hovering nearby. Seated at the dining room table was Childers' wife Velma. The big .44 was resting on the table in front of her. She was staring straight ahead, seemingly unseeing and unhearing.

Wilkerson knelt down, rolled Childers over on his back. His shirt front was soaked with blood. There was a massive hole where his heart should have been. His eyes, usually so filled with hate, now reflected only disbelief. Wilkerson looked up questioningly. Adam met his gaze, then looked over toward his mother. The Sheriff rose and walked over to her.

"Miz Childers?" he said.

Velma Childers looked up at him without expression. “He shouldn’t have killed that woman. A lot of things that man shouldn’t have done, but killing that woman, that was an abomination. The Lord cannot abide such men.”

Wilkerson picked up a napkin from one of the place settings and carefully wrapped the gun in it. He looked over at Briggs who just shook his head.

David Letterman was right in the middle of one of his stale ‘squirrel and his nuts’ jokes when the network interrupted for a dramatic newsbreak. From Yakima, Washington, word that anarchist Emanuel Childers was dead. Apparently, in a fit of despair or perhaps cowardice, Childers had taken his own life. As yet, no confirmation had been received but sources close to the situation say his death was due to a single gunshot to the head. Probably on orders from the network’s news department, the on-air reporter characterized Childers as a right-wing fascist and a traitor to his country who deserved to die.

In the White House, the President, propped up in bed with the latest Dick Morris book, breathed a sigh of relief. Zwick had come through. The national nightmare was over. He made a note to himself to make a speech tomorrow from the Rose Garden. Thirty minutes ought to cover it. He was positive the national networks would cooperate. Maybe he’d sweeten the presentation by awarding Zwick the Presidential Medal of Honor.

In Alexandria, Representative Nathan Halperin D-New York congratulated himself for having the courage to withstand the threats he’d suffered the past several days. Resign, indeed. Not likely. He was so pleased with himself that he phoned fellow endangered Congressman Jimmy Ray Cobbler R-Alabama to give him the good news in case he hadn’t heard. He had and he was ecstatic. He had a deal going with a gambling consortium backed with Venezuelan money.

Naturally they'd been a tad concerned over the past several days but no more. With luck, this deal would make him independent for life. So delighted were Halperin and Cobbler that they decided to call their mutual friend, Leroy Fanning D-Minnesota. Mrs. Fanning answered the phone, weeping. At six o'clock, Leroy, depressed by everything happening around him, tried to get some sleep. He took some new sleeping pills prescribed by his doctor but without his glasses on, misread the instructions. The EMT gentlemen were in the bedroom going through the motions, but there really was no hope. No hope at all.

In his plush hotel room in Yakima, Harvey Cantrell was awakened by an insistent ringing in his ears which turned out instead to be the telephone by his bed. He had left instructions to hold all calls. Annoyed, he lifted the receiver to hear the voice of Donald Federer, the network news chief.

"You dumb son of a bitch, what are you doing in bed? The biggest news story of the year breaks and you're under the covers pulling your pud, you asshole, while every other station is going fucking full throttle and you, you dense moron, haven't got a clue about what your job is and how to do it—" Harvey put the phone down on the table and half listened as he frantically raced to his closet to grab his clothes. Federer was still going strong as he slipped into his trousers.

Sitting in the plush den of his faux-French Chateau Beverly Hills mansion, prolific Hollywod movie producer Freddie Feldman watched the news interruption with fascination, no longer pissed that the network had broken in on Dave. Now this was a story. No, this was a FILM. Rasputin-like whack-job killing off Congress, suddenly trapped in his fortress- like house deep in the woods kills himself in despair and—No, no, scratch that. Brave FBI guy with balls of steel digs his way into the house. It's seven against one but our guy drops ‘em all. Great part for Stallone or maybe Steven Segal. He tried to remember if he still had a pay or play with that guy. Note to myself. Check business office in morning. Try to buy rights.

Elsewhere in the Great Pacific Northwest, hardware store owner Jeb Kramer, former Green Beret Lewis Dunlop and Brigadier General Terence McCarver Ret. were collectively dismayed by the turn of events in Yakima. Certainly this was no time to back off from their avowed intentions to reinvigorate the country. On the other hand, with Childers dead, the FBI's focus would be turning to others. Perhaps this would be an excellent opportunity to regroup and lay low, at least for a while.

And in the study of his home on Cape Ann, the man known as Galen watched the unfolding events with growing dismay. The networks, all of them, had written the obituary of Sic Semper Tyranis. It was done with, finished, over. Nothing to worry about. Tomorrow morning, all would be well. The daily papers like the NY Times and the Washington Post and the other liberal house organs for the Democratic Party would join in the celebration. The American people, relieved that the national nightmare was over, would go back to their patio barbecues, Pop Warner football, 'American Idol', Thursday night poker games, their Ipods and Blackberrys, Miley Cyrus concerts and everything else they'd been preoccupied with before the past several weeks. And why not? For the most part they didn't know any better. And why should they have to? They thought they'd elected people to take care of them, to watch out for the warped and venal people who would destroy the nation given half a chance. It was hard to blame them. Americans were a trusting people. It was difficult to rouse them to anger. Once they realized they were being deceived, their wrath could be awesome, but seldom was it sustainable. Too often, apathy and indifference returned and those who would harm them rose from the shadows. A little over sixteen hours remained and then he and the others would have to act. He dreaded the arrival of the six o'clock deadline.

Galen walked over to the bookcase and removed six volumes of the collected works of Edgar Allan Poe. Behind them was a laptop which he took down and carried to his desk. He opened the cover and turned it on, then clicked his way into his Mailbox. He sat for several minutes, then typed in the e-mail addresses for Dr. Hammond Chambers and Dr. Grayden Walsh. He began typing a message.

CHAPTER TWENTY

When he and Jennie had tumbled into bed together the night before the last thing they were thinking about was getting up in the morning. So when Paul roused himself at six-thirty it was totally instinctual. Disoriented momentarily and just a tad hungover, it took him a minute or so to remember what it was he had to do. He would be on a quest for a computer, a very special computer which just might contain all the proof he needed to tear apart the conspiracy.

He looked down at Jennie, sleeping soundly, scrunched up with a pillow under her head, her ash blonde hair carelessly arranged on the white percale cover. There was just the slightest trace of a smile on her lips. He had to laugh at the unromantic way he'd proposed to her the night before but she hadn't seemed to mind. That was one of the things he loved about her. She was right up front, no coyness, no silly girlie games. She knew who she was and what she wanted and in his heart Paul thanked God that Jennie wanted him.

He slipped out of the bed quietly, gathered up his clothes and exited the bedroom. He left an erotic note for her on the kitchen table and left. When he got out onto the street, he scratched his head, trying to remember where he'd put his car, then realized he'd left it parked outside of McNaughton's. He hailed a cab and when he got to the pub, his car was still parked where he left it, adorned with a

$150 parking ticket.

Shoving the ticket in his glove apartment, he drove to his apartment, catching what he could of last night's developments in Yakima. When he entered the apartment, he turned on CNN to make sure he wasn't missing anything. He glanced over at his phone. The red light on his answering machine was blinking. Murray or the Old Man, one or the other. He punched the play button. It was Schoenfeld.

"Hey, Paul, it's me. Look, things got a little out of hand last night and we both said some dumb things, especially me. So, look, I'm sorry. Let's just forget it and start from scratch. You want a little more money, not a problem. You deserve it. Give me a call and we'll get together, maybe split a pizza at Tonios for lunch. Ciao." The message ended.

Paul looked down at the machine for a few seconds, then pushed the erase button and walked into his bedroom. Twenty minutes later, he emerged, showered and shaved and neatly dressed in crisply ironed chinos, a pale yellow cotton shirt and a lightweight forest green windbreaker which he might or might not need depending on which way the weather broke. It was 50-50 for rain in the New York area by noon. He had no idea what the Connecticut forecast was.

His eye fell on the wall calendar over his desk and he frowned. He moved quickly back to his phone and dialed a number.

"Hey, Terry, it's me."

"What? Up already? ," his sister said. "It isn't even nine o'clock yet. Are you in jail?"

"Sis, please." he said defensively.

"I've got no bail money. I can barely pay the rent this month."

"I'm fine. Honest. What're the plans for Sunday?"

"Sunday?" Teresa sounded a little confused.

"Sunday. Mother's Day. Am I the only one who remembers holidays around here?"

"Oh, Christ, Mother's Day," she muttered. "I don't know. Maybe

Mom and Pop are going out."

"Look, I gotta run. You call Pop, you tell him Chang's on Sunday. It's on me. You bring that gym teacher you've been screwing around with. I'll bring Jennie."

"You getting serious with her, bro?"

"Come Sunday, you watch. Then you tell me. Love you." He hung up and glanced over at the television set where Nathan Halperin was holding a press conference back in his home district in New York. The audio was bad but Paul got the general idea. There were a lot of people there asking a lot of angry questions and whatever Halperin had to say his people weren't buying it. He clicked off the set and left the apartment.

For the third time in ten days he was heading north on Route 8 toward Waterbury. The sky above was dark and foreboding and he'd put the top up. The radio was tuned to a news-talk station and America's favorite right-wing pundit was in the middle of one of his forty minute rants after which he would take three or four calls from people who had been waiting for about an hour and a half to play stooge with their questions. The big fella always liked to boast that he had the smartest audience in the world but Paul wondered how smart they could be, hanging on a dead phone line for that long for no apparent good reason. Well, love him or hate him, he usually had his facts straight even if he did espouse them with a certainty usually associated with Papal encyclicals. At the moment, he was talking about an upcoming special election in California.

"I have to tell you, folks," he was saying, "the fight over Jerome Tolliver's Congressional seat has been downright weird. Three days ago they announced that Tolliver's adminstrative assistant was going to run and within hours, literally hours, dozens of people were milling around outside Democratic headquarters ready to throw bottles and rocks or ripe fruit. I mean, it was really bizarre. And so the chief honcho starts asking these people who they'd like to see and they all get together and compare notes and guess what, you're not going to believe this. They are putting up a 28 year old high school history teacher with absolutely no political experience. Oh, sure, he mans the polls on Election Day and goes to meetings, but face it, this guy is a total novice. Now here's the kicker. The Republicans are all set to nominate this old party hack who was once the school board chairman. No, no, say the Republicans. We want somebody with half a brain that'll work for us, not City Hall which apparently started getting very nasty threatening phone calls. So who are they putting up? A florist. That's right. A forty-year old flower lady named Pansy—I kid you not—Pansy Detweiler who also has never held any kind of public office. Now, folks, could someone please tell me what the hell is going on out there? Are the people in this district actually going to elect someone who is not a professional politician? Words fail me and you know, that doesn't happen very often."

Paul had to laugh. Political events didn't dumbfound the big fella very often though he had to admit it was kind of refreshing. You'd think maybe the country was getting the message, despite the heinous way it was being delivered. Now, if only there were some way to get around that 6:00 deadline and let things play out on their own. He checked his watch. 10:30. Seven and a half hours to go. He felt himself deflating. What the hell kind of a fool's errand was he running? He was chasing after a computer that might never have existed and if it did it might be at the bottom a landfill somewhere. And if he could find it, there was no guarantee that it would still contain any kind of useful information. This was lunacy. And yet, what else did he have? Out there somewhere was a deranged maniac posing as a patriot who was determined to murder another dozen men and women. When you break one of the most sacred of the Commandments in the name of liberty, what kind of a patriot can you be?

He was coming up on the turnoff for Route 63 when his phone rang. He wasn't sure about the law in the state of Connecticut but he didn't want to have time to pull over. He answered the phone, risking a ticket.

"Hello?"

"Castle, it's Fowler Briggs." The FBI agent was calling on his cell phone from his window seat on a 737 about fifty miles out of New York City.

"Congratulations. I see you got the guy in Yakima."

"I didn't get him, his wife did," Briggs said.

"Yeah, but I thought the TV report said—"

"You still believe everything you see on television? Shame, Mr. Castle, you're smarter than that."

Paul was taken aback. "The wife. Wow."

"One shot close in with a .44. The Lord told her to do it."

"I doubt he'll be missed," Paul said. "I'd plead her diminished capacity. Hell, they might not even charge her."

"Wouldn't break my heart. So where does that leave us with your gang of doctors, Mr. Castle?"

"In serious trouble. I'm on my way to Bergensberg, Connecticut. Rose Temple's hometown. The family doctor's a guy named Walsh. He told me her health was good when she was actually dying of Huntington's Disease and he knew it. Walsh is one of this gang and we're guessing that these guys communicate with each other via second computers, not the ones they use on a daily basis. We have reason to believe Walsh's second computer quit on him and he had to replace it, the question being, what did he do with the original? If I can locate it and we can reconstruct its files we might have the evidence to put these guys out of business."

"Okay. Sounds reasonable," Briggs said. "What can I do?"

"For the moment, nothing. We need this computer to enable you to get wiretaps and warrants. Until then, we're hamstrung."

The New York City skyline was coming up on the left as Briggs looked out the window. It was a sight that never failed to stir him. "All right. You need anything, you yell," Briggs said.

"WIll do." He clicked off and made the turn onto Rt. 63, heading northeast toward Bergensberg.

It was just past eleven when Paul crept into town, sneaking a quick peek back at the abandoned vegetable stand where the town's police car, ever vigilant, was once again on the lookout for evildoers. As he reached the main shopping area, he kept his eyes open for any sign of an electronics store. His only hope was that the replacement computer was bought locally. If something like a WalMart were involved, he'd have no chance and if Walsh had bought it in Waterbury, population 100,000+, he'd be looking for a toothpick in a woodpile. He drove slowly enough to barely outrace an oldster on crutches, but finally he spotted it, three blocks down from Margies in a little stand-alone house on an otherwise vacant lot. The sign over the front facade read : "Earl's Radio and TV" and under that in smaller lettering: "Electronics." The windows were decorated here and there with decals, some for long forgotten brands like Philco and Sylvania.

He pulled to a stop, got out of the car and went inside. The place was dimly lit and musty. A couple of big screen TVs were mounted on one of the walls. Another wall was mostly shelving with smaller model televisions, clock radios, and a very small selection of cell phones and personal electronic devices. There wasn't a computer in sight nor was there, for that matter, an Earl.

"Hello. Anybody here?" Paul called out.

After a moment, a shriveled up little man emerged from a back room. His hair was white and wispy and his body was slightly stooped. On the bridge of his nose were a pair of thick-lensed glasses which he peered over with an expression that was hard to fathom. Either he was surprised to see a stranger in his store or he was surprised to see ANYONE in his store.

"Mornin'" he said.

"Mornin'" Paul replied. "You must be Earl."

"Junior."

"What?"

"Earl Junior. My Daddy's the one on the sign. Earl Senior. Opened this place in 1948. Been here ever since. Sixty two years."

Paul nodded appeciatively for want of anything to say.

"What can I do for you?" Earl asked.

"Well, I'm looking to buy a computer," Paul said.

"Can't help you there, mister. Don't sell 'em."

"Oh," Paul grunted, disappointed.

"Don't use 'em, don't understand 'em, don't sell 'em," Earl said.

"I guess I was misinformed, "Paul said. "Somebody said you sold one to Doc Walsh."

Earl grinned, showing yellowing teeth. "Oh, that. No. Doc came in here lookin', same as you. I told him what I just told you. He asked me if I could order one for him. I said, no, I didn't order but I was going into Waterbury that afternoon and if he knew what he wanted, I'd be happy to pick one up for him. So Doc goes out to his car and brings in this thing with a half-eaten apple on its cover and he says 'Just like this one'. He gives me a thousand bucks cash which he thinks might be enough and he says 'Take the old one. Maybe they'll take a trade in.'"

"Did they?" Paul asked apprehensively.

"Nope, but the cash was enough so I brought it back along with the new one. Doc gives me forty bucks for my trouble and says to keep the old one. I tell him, 'What am I going to do with an old busted computer?' And then it comes to me. Buddy Jenkins. Nice young colored boy. Takes care of my lawn once a week, me and a lot of other folks. Only eleven years old but he works like a horse and smart as a whip. Don't have much money though. Just him and his Mom and they're poor as dirt. Anyway I gave Buddy the thing. Told him it didn't work too well. He said he didn't care. He'd get it going. Sure enough, he came by yesterday. Says he's got her hummin' like brand new."

Paul nodded appreciatively. "Sounds like quite a kid."

Earl nodded. "That he is."

"Could you tell me where he lives?" Paul asked.

Earl cocked his head regarding him suspiciously for a moment. Paul continued quickly.

"Me and the wife just moved into the area a couple of weeks ago," He pointed vaguely. "A couple of miles up the road. Place we bought needs a lot of work, especially the lawn and the garden."

Earl nodded slowly. "You keep going along the street that way, maybe eight or nine blocks, you'll see Jefferson Road. Take a left, it's maybe four or five houses in on the right hand side. Red house, white trim. Names on the mailbox. Jenkins. You can't miss it."

"Thanks, Earl. Appreciate your help."

Paul walked out of the store, got in his car and did a U turn, driving back to the town's bank. He used his ATM card to withdraw $500 from his checking account, then got back in his car and went house hunting. It was right where Earl said it would be. Paul parked at the curb, walked up to the front door and rang the bell. An attractive looking black woman appeared in the doorway. She didn't quite smile because she wasn't used to having white strangers ringing her doorbell, but neither was she unfriendly. "Can I help you?"

"Mrs. Jenkins?"

"That's Miss."

"Miss Jenkins, I'm sorry to bother you but, uh, is your son

around?"

Her eyes narrowed. "Why? Has he done something wrong?"

"Oh, no, ma'am. Not at all." He told her the tale about trying to buy a computer from Earl. "I just moved in up the road and, uh, I work at home and my computer just quit on me and I have to get a report in to the home office by four o'clock and when Earl told me about Buddy and his computer, well, I'd like to buy it if he'd like to sell it. I'm uh, kind of running out of time."

"And how much would you be trying to buy this computer for?" Miss Jenkins asked suspiciously.

"I was thinking maybe $500," Paul said.

She nodded thoughtfully. "Well, since Buddy and I were talking about it and a new one costs maybe $900, that seems fair enough. But you must need it awful bad," she said.

"You have no idea," Paul smiled.

"Well, sir, if you want to buy it, that'll be up to Buddy. He's out mowing the Campbell's lawn right now. I expect he'll be back in maybe a half hour or so."

Paul registered disappointment. "Like I said, time's a problem. If you could tell me where these Campbells live—"

She pointed. "Back to the main road, turn right, back through town, turn right at the Mobil station—that's Hatcher Street—go down a few blocks. Big white house on a big lawn. She looked up at the darkening sky. "Unless it starts pouring, Buddy'll be out there mowing."

He smiled and thanked her. Back to the car. A quick glance at his watch. Past 11:30. A little over six hours to go. He drove back through town, remembered to slow down just in time and crept past the foreboding town cruiser at a sedate 19 miles per hour. Ahead was the Mobil station. He turned right and headed down Hatcher Street, then realized he was very close to where Dr. Walsh's home and office were. And just then, as if by the hand of fate, he looked down a cross street and saw Walsh emerging hurriedly from his home/office carrying an overnight bag. Something in his body language told Paul that the man was highly agitated, almost frantic. Paul pulled up out of sight and looked back as Walsh backed out of his driveway and sped to the cross street and turned right toward the main road. Paul was torn. Which way? Ahead to the kid and the computer or turn around and follow Walsh. He made up his mind quickly. The computer would always be there. He did a quick u-turn and sped after the doctor. At the intersection with Main Street, Walsh turned right, heading away from town. Paul stayed with him as he headed southeast on Route 47 headed for God knows where.

At seven minutes past noon at the offices of Representative Alberto Sanchez, D-Texas, three men arrived unannounced to see the Congressman. His receptionist, not recognizing their faces, told the men that Congressman was in an important meeting and that his calendar for the day was solidly booked. When the men gave their names, she immediately buzzed into Sanchez' private office. Within seconds he emerged, apologizing profusely and inviting the men to join him. As they sat down in plush leather chairs around an antique coffee table, Sanchez offered them drinks, Cuban cigars, coffee, anything they wished. He was at their service.

Lloyd G. Humphrey, owner of the second largest cattle spread between San Antonio and Corpus Christi, spoke for the group which included Jaime Morales, president of the second largest bank in Floresville, and Oliver Nording, owner of the second largest oil refinery on the Gulf Coast. The message they had come to deliver was short and to the point. Sanchez had become a liability. After fifteen years in Congress, he had become arrogant and unresponsive and worst of all, he was supporting most of the harebrained schemes being dreamed up by those Commie idiots in the White House. There was to be a primary in mid June. Humphrey suggested that Sanchez not enter his name. If he did he would not be nominated. If by some fluke he were nominated, he would not be reelected. The three of them, along with others, would see to it.

Sanchez, totally at sea, pleaded with them. What have I done wrong? Haven't I always cooperated? Yes, Humphrey said. You know it and we know it and now with what's going on, everybody in the district knows it. We can't afford you any more and we damn sure can't afford to become a banana republic like Venezuela. But who are you going to put up that will be better than me, Sanchez demanded to know. Maybe somebody honest, Humphrey replied. Morales and Nording looked at each other and then at Humphrey, not sure they'd heard him right. The heated discussion was so noisy that it could be heard clearly in the anteroom, specifically by a newspaper reporter who was waiting patiently to interview Sanchez for a puff piece in their Sunday edition. He wondered which of the cable news networks might give him a much better paying job for a scoop of this magnitude.

In New Jersey nominations for the Special Election to fill the vacant seat of David Johansson were opened. Four Democrats immediately filed. A real estate broker, a veterinarian, a retired Naval Officer and a priest. With vigilantes apparently running amok, the local Democratic machine turned its back on the whole process, preferring to stand clear of the fray. Let be done what will be done. The Republicans were putting up a successful woman novelist who had run and lost in the two previous elections. The third might turn out to be the charm.

And in Florida, Hector Villanueva, having narrowly escaped death once at the hands of Elsa Galesko, decided that the prudent career move would be to withdraw gracefully and leave the field open to others. The problem was, the Democratic movers and shakers who had a short time ago agreed to ship Elsa Galesko into limbo now couldn't agree on anything and there was an outside chance that the Republican candidate would run unopposed in the November election.

By three o'clock these stories and several others would dominate the afternoon news cycles, in many ways confounding the pundits. Conventional wisdom dictated that with the death of Emanuel Childers, public anger would have subsided, but if anything, the people seemed to be madder than ever. Charles Krauthammer, the sagest of the sage, may have put his finger on it when he suggested that the accumulated frustration of the public, once permitted to boil to the surface, had now taken on a life of its own. Like a hurricane bearing down on the Florida Keys, it wasn't about to stop any time soon.

It was several minutes past one o'clock and the burgundy Lexus driven by Grayden Walsh was heading north on I84 toward Massachusetts. Paul was following at a respectful distance. If Walsh was at all afraid he was being followed it would be pretty difficult to disguise a vintage red Mustang convertible. But no, it seemed to Paul that Walsh was oblivious. If he stayed back far enough there was little chance he'd be seen.

Paul had been listening to news stations wall to wall ever since he'd left Bergensberg. Parading their ignorance along with their biases were the usual suspects. For the most part administration supporters hailed the end of the reign of terror while those on the right were not quite so sure that the voices from the Great Northwest had been totally silenced. The vast majority who lay in the middle were celebrating nothing. Never again did they want to see this country go through this sort of upheaval. They had roared angrily in 2009 when the Administration very nearly rammed through the House-inspired universal health care bill. But when the crisis had subsided and the socialists had backed off their single-payer power grab, the country once again slipped into a can't-be-bothered lethargy. Emboldened, the House Socialists were determined to try again, but again they miscalculated. Having been awakened once again, it appeared that America was determined not to make that mistake a second time.

The President's plans for a prime time speech were thwarted by the networks who were now in the middle of May sweeps and had better things to air that evening, such as part three of Big Brother, the "Mad About You" Reunion show, and the season finale of "House M.D." in which, the network promos promised, one of the regulars would be brutally killed by a psychotic patient. (Presumably the agent for the actor involved had made outrageous salary demands on his behalf). The President settled for a 10 minute slot from the Rose Garden where he lauded FBI chief Zwick for his brilliant handling of the crisis. The Presidential Medal of Freedom was nowhere in sight.

Just as Paul was passing through West Willington heading for the Masschusetts border, the little red light on his dash started to blink. He'd been so preoccupied with his thoughts that he'd failed to notice the needle riding on empty. He looked ahead. The Lexus was just sweeping around a bend in the road some 600 yards ahead. An off-ramp loomed up on his right and a roadside sign promised a service station close at hand. Worst case scenario: running out of gas. He pulled onto the ramp. At the stop sign, a helpful arrow indicated gas to the right. He turned and sped down the two lane country road. (Close at hand was a misnomer). Three minutes later the station came into sight. He pulled up to a pump, jogged into the mini-mart and grabbed a black coffee and an apple while the tank was filling and inside of two minutes was circling back toward the interstate. He figured he was now about ten minutes behind. It would be hard to make up without risking a ticket.

As he accelerated onto the interstate, he moved into the fast lane to pass a lumbering semi and then as he passed it, saw ahead a Connecticut State Police cruiser holding to the speed limit in the right hand lane. God, why hast thou forsaken me, he muttered to himself as he slipped into the right lane a respectful distance behind keeping pace with the trooper who showed no inclination to speed up. It went like that for several miles as Paul kept looking anxiously at his watch. And then God, who had not actually forsaken him, lent a hand. A couple of huge supermarket semis had wedged themselves between Paul and the police car. Suddenly in his rear view mirror he spotted a BMW roaring toward him in the fast lane. The Beamer whooshed by, overtook the two trucks and then a few seconds later, his brake lights lit up. Too late. A half mile up the road Paul passed by the driver and the state policeman who were having an animated conversation at the side of the road.

After a suitable interval had elapsed, Paul put his foot to the floor and prayed mightly that the officer's twin brother wasn't lurking half hidden behind a billboard a few miles up the road. He estimated he was now about 20-25 minutes behind with absolutely no clue as to where Walsh was headed. He could only hope that Walsh, too, would have to stop for gas.

He crossed the state line at Marshapaug Pond and within a few minutes found himself approaching the Massachusetts Turnpike. He had a choice. Left or right. Straight was not an option. Right made more sense. It lead to Worcester and Boston. Left led to Springfield, but he remembered as he'd gone through Hartford he'd seen signs for I91 North to Springfield. If that were his destination Walsh would have turned onto it back then. Paul took the ramp heading east. The posted speed limit was 70. He was doing 83 and keeping his eyes shifting in every direction.

He scanned ahead looking for some sign of the doctor's Lexus knowing there was no way he could have closed the gap this soon.

His phone rang. He was tempted not to answer it. He certainly wasn't about to pull over to the side of the road. No, it might be something important. He took the phone from his pocket and flipped it on.

"Yo," he said.

"Yo yourself," the voice said. "Where are you?" It was Kovacs.

"On the Massachusetts Turnpike running a fool's errand ," Paul said. He filled him in on the computer which he had tracked down and then Dr. Walsh's strange behavior. "I could be wrong. He could be taking a vacation for all I know."

"Don't count on it," Kovacs said. "That tail we put on Dr. Chambers may have paid off. My boys followed him to LaGuardia where he caught a commuter flight to Boston about two hours ago."

"The plot thickens ," Paul said.

"It sure does, young fella, and I don't like the idea of you chasing after this doctor without some kind of backup."

"I'll be all right. I know this man. He's not dangerous."

"Balls!" Kovacs snapped. "These men kill people. I'm going to call Boston PD and see if I can get you some help."

"No. If Walsh is on his way to some kind of meeting we don't want to break it up before we find out who's involved. The cops will just bull their way in, arrest Walsh and Chambers and we'll be nowhere again."

"I'll take the chance. I don't want you getting hurt."

"Thanks but—"

"What car are you driving? That beat up old red Mustang? How far out of Boston are you?"

Instead of replying, Paul flipped the phone closed and turned off the power. He knew all he needed to know. Boston was the destination and something was definitely up. He pressed down on the gas. The needle moved slowly past 86.

Paul caught up with the Lexus just as they were bypassing the town of Newton, about 15 miles west of Boston. Walsh was maintaining a steady 70 except when forced to slow by the ever increasing traffic flow. As before Walsh seemed totally unaware of Paul's presence. It was nearing three o'clock when Walsh turned onto Route 1 and headed north. Just before Quincy Market, he took a right turn toward Boston Harbor. Paul could tell from the roadsigns that if Walsh were meeting Chambers it wouldn't be at the airport. Sure enough, Walsh turned into the entrance to the Boston Harbor Hotel and pulled up to the valet stand. Paul parked at the curb across the street as Walsh got out and approached the parking attendant in animated conversation. The doctor slipped him a bill from his wallet and the attendant went to his stand, picked up the phone and placed a call. Five minutes later, Dr. Hammond Chambers emerged. He, too, was carrying a lightweight overnight bag. The two men embraced quickly, then got into the car. It darted into traffic and headed north. Paul, who was parked facing the wrong way, checked traffic and made a quick u-turn to follow. He prayed they hadn't noticed him.

If he had been paying a little more attention to his rear view mirror instead of the Lexus, he might have noticed the non-descript black sedan parked in the next block which also made a dangerous u-turn. A black man was driving. He carried a gun. So did the white man in the passenger seat. They had been following Paul ever since he left his apartment in New York. They had remained undetected because that was their business. In tandem, the three cars left the city and headed north on Route 1A, destination known only to the lead car.

CHAPTER TWENTY-ONE

Just past Revere, the Lexus stopped for gas. Paul stopped to pee. He was learning that you can either follow someone nonstop for several hundred miles or you can drink a lot of coffee to stay awake but you can't do both. According to his watch the time was 3:55. Two hours left. Galen had been adamant about resuming SST's agenda if the Congressional resignations had not been forthcoming. According to news reports airing all day, the magic number was down to 12, an even dozen of the targeted few who refused, for whatever reason, to give up their seats. Did Galen mean what he said? Did he speak for everyone involved? Was there dissension in the ranks, perhaps even revolt. Is that why Walsh and Chambers were on the road, to meet with Galen and perhaps others? Whatever the reason time was growing perilously short.

Onward Walsh drove, past Lynn and Salem and Beverly. At Route 128, the Lexus turned east and drove north toward Gloucester which was situated at the tip of Cape Ann. The weather, which had been in a threatening mode all day suddenly turned ugly. The skies morphed into a charcoal grey and the clouds above, heavy with moisture began to relieve themselves. At first it was a gentle mist, then a pitter patter of raindrops and finally an onslaught of water. The Mustang' wipers, unused to such conditions, were overwhelmed. Visibility became a major problem.

Up ahead, Paul could see the taillights of the Lexus They would disappear momentarily, then reappear. Paul speeded up, fearful of losing sight and not particularly worried about being spotted in the downpour. Huge puddles of water began to appear on the road's surface. The Mustang hit several of them with full force sending bucketfuls of water splashing across the hood and onto the windshield, turning it momentarily opaque. And through it all, the Lexus kept pressing forward..

And then suddenly it was gone. Paul peered ahead. Lightning shattered the darkness and for a moment he could see far ahead. The Lexus had disappeared. Then he remembered. A short way back, he'd seen it out of the corner of his eye. A road to the right. A small directional sign. Manchester-by- the-Sea. Furious he braked, fishtailing on the water soaked road, spinning toward the shoulder. He yanked at the wheel and managed to come out of the spin. A lumbering black sedan came at him through the rain, narrowly missing his rear end. He straightened out the car and raced back down the road, eyes searching for the turnoff. It came up suddenly and he lurched to the left. This time the Mustang took it well and straightened itself speeding down the small country road. No sign of taillights. The road was in need of repair but Paul couldn't slow down. He was in the middle of a horrendous thunderstorm, heading God only knew where and without the Lexus to guide him, he was totally lost. Potholes and ruts, the Mustang slammed into them without discrimination. He was discovering rattles and creaks in the old heap he never knew existed. And then suddenly, there they were, up ahead. Taillights. But whose taillights? The Lexus? By God, they'd better be.

As he entered the small town of Manchester-by-the-Sea, the lights from some of the buildings and another flash of lightning illuminated his quarry. He sagged in relief. No problem, Houston. We have reacquired the target.

In the middle of town the Lexus turned left and headed east, following the barely visible shoreline. Paul could see the surf roiling angrily, white caps abounding. Up ahead, the Lexus slowed severely, almost stopping. Paul did likewise. He was now about three hundred yards away with no cover. To stop now would be a total giveaway.

The Lexus slowly turned left into a driveway and stopped at a set of iron gates. A small security shack was posted by the gates. Paul kept going, driving slowly past the site as a man in a yellow slicker emerged from the shack and went to Walsh's window. The security man was holding a clipboard.

Paul continued on, slowly. The property on his left appeared to be fenced with wrought iron, Beyond the fence the grounds rose slowly toward a well-lit house that appeared to sit on a level site overlooking the bay below. Lightning flashed and he got a quick look at the place. Two story, white frame, at least 6000 square feet.

Well out of sight of the security shack, Paul pulled to the side of the road and stared up at the mansion, outlined against the storm clouds. He knew who lived here. Galen. It had to be. A black sedan drove by him, not speeding, not crawling, at a pace usually reserved for sightseeing. He flipped on the mirror light and checked his watch. It was twenty past five. He sat for several minutes contemplating his next move. If he was smart he'd call Fowler Briggs, but just then Paul didn't feel very smart. He didn't even feel much like a journalist, even though he probably had his hands around the biggest story of the decade. What he felt was scared. He was in over his head and he knew it. A group of men who would assassinate Congressmen in cold blood wouldn't hesitate for a moment to eliminate him if they thought he were dangerous.

He flipped open his phone and tapped in Briggs' number. Nothing happened. The storm had wiped out service. Aw, what the hell, he thought. He did a U-ey and headed back toward the gates. He remembered a line from "Body and Soul." John Garfield had looked at the bookie he'd double -crossed and said "What are you going to do? Kill me? Everybody dies." Music up. The end. The end, indeed. He turned into the driveway and stopped in front of the gates. A moment later the security guy in the yellow slicker emerged from the shack and came to the car. Paul rolled down the window halfway.

"May I help you, sir?" the guard asked.

"My name is Paul Castle. It's not on the list and I'm here to see Galen."

"I'm sorry, sir, you must have the wrong house. There's no Galen here."

"No, I have the right house. A couple of minutes ago you let Dr. Grayden Walsh and Dr. Hammond Chambers through the gate. I'd appreciate the same courtesy."

The guard fixed him with a hard stare. Paul stared back.

"Sir, I told you, there's no Galen here."

Paul looked a lot braver than he felt but he persevered.

"Fine. You tell whoever owns this house that Paul Castle is parked outside the gate and that he wants to speak to Galen, And moreover, if he doesn't get to speak to him, he is going to camp across the street and take down car models and license plates of every car that leaves the premises. Oh, yes, and as soon as the weather clears, Mr. Castle is going to notify the FBI to get its collective rosy red asses up here to help him dismantle SST. Got it?"

The guard paused, then turned and moved quickly back into the shack. Paul watched as the man picked up the phone and placed a call. He started to shiver, a chill seizing his body. His hands began to shake uncontrollably and he put them down between his legs and clamped them with his thighs to keep them warm and still. After a minute the guard came out again just as the gates started to slowly open. The guard pointed toward the house on the hill. "Park anywhere in front of house." Paul thanked him and drove through the gates and slowly began to wend his way up the smoothly finished asphalt drive.

The other five cars in front of the house had taken the closest parking spots so the dash to the portico had soaked him. He rang the door bell and stamped his feet, feeling a subtle squishing sensation in his shoes. His windbreaker had shed a lot of water but the chinos had been a magnet. His hair was wet and he ran his hands over it, hoping to make himself presentable as the front door was opened by a tall dark man in a dark suit. He was pleasantly swarthy, perhaps of Italian or Black Irish heritage. Probably in his mid to late 50's, he weighed well over 200 pounds but carried it well. He also carried firepower, Paul noted, from the bulge inside his jacket near his left shoulder.

"Come in," the man said, stepping out of the way. Paul entered, looking around at a foyer designed and furnished in tasteful opulence. To the left were double doors possibly leading to a dining room or a library. To the right, what appeared to be the living room. Paul heard angry voices, a man's and a woman's, neither of which he recognized.

"May I take your jacket, Mr. Castle?," the man in black asked.

"Sure," Paul said. "I'd give you my pants, too, but I don't want to cause a scene, not on my first visit." The man in black smiled as Paul slipped out of the windbreaker and handed it over. "Nice weather you have around here," Paul said.

"I'll announce your arrival," the man said, moving to the double doors and stepping inside. Having not been ordered by the man with the gun to stay put, Paul wandered over to the living room and stepped inside. Congregated at the far end of the room were six people, only two of whom Paul recognized. The two arguing were a short stocky man with black hair and a discreet chin beard. The woman was at least four inches taller, matronly but not unattractive, streaked blonde hair done in up in a bun, wearing silver rimmed glasses. The little man seemed out of sorts. The woman was suggesting politely that he find himself a set of balls. Hammond Chambers was standing by a window looking out over the rear of the property. Grayden Walsh was sitting on a sofa, arms folded across his chest, staring straight ahead as if not hearing the contentious argument only a few feet away.

For whatever reason, at that moment, Walsh chose to look up and his gaze met Paul's. It took a moment to register and then Walsh loudly blurted out, "Oh, my God!" Conversation ceased as they all looked at Walsh and then turned to look at what Walsh was looking at. The stocky little man's jaw dropped. The woman said, "Jesus Christ!." Chambers turned from the window. He seemed puzzled. One of the other men glared at Paul and then looked around at the others. "Who the hell invited him?" he said angrily.

Walsh got up from the sofa and walked over to Paul. If he was fearful, he gave no sign of it. "You shouldn't be here, Paul," he said quietly.

Paul nodded. "I know. It's pretty inconvenient."

"How did you get here?"

"Brilliant detective work. Dazzling deductions. Actually, I followed you from Bergensberg."

"And now that you're here?" Walsh asked.

"I intend to put an end to the party." Paul said.

Walsh shrugged. "In my opinion the party's pretty much over already," he said.

"Mr. Castle?" He turned. The man in black was standing in the open archway. He gestured. "This way."

With a final look at the group and then at Walsh, Paul turned and followed the man to the double doors. The man opened them and ushered Paul in, then stepped back into the foyer, closing the doors behind him.

It was a library. Two walls were totally shelved, top to bottom, each shelf filled to near capacity with volumes of every size and description. The shelving was walnut, deeply and richly stained. Another wall displayed all sorts of memorabilia. Photos, awards, trophies, a couple of autographed baseballs. One looked old enough to carry Lou Gehrig's signature. The far wall was completely glass, featuring sliding doors that opened onto a covered patio that in turn looked out at the neighboring hillside and the bay beyond and below. The curtains were fully opened and Paul could see the lightning still dancing though now farther off. The rain seemed to have subsided. A small wet bar was tucked into the corner. A man was standing there fixing a drink, his back to Paul. Without turning, he spoke.

"I'm fixing myself a Manhattan, Mr. Castle. May I offer you something?"

"No, thanks."

"How about some hot coffee and a dry pair of socks?" the man said as he turned .

Paul's head jerked slightly in surprise as he recognized him. "No. I mean, yes. I mean, if it wouldn't be too much trouble, Mr. Vice President."

Thaddeus Wayne smiled. "No trouble at all." He took a small electronic pager from his pocket and pressed the button. A few seconds later, the double doors reopened and the man in black stepped inside.

"Yes, sir?" he said.

"Tim, would you get Mr. Castle a pair of warm wooly socks from my bedroom and have Mandy bring us in a coffee service."

"Yes, sir," Tim said, leaving the room.

Paul had been carefully studying the former Vice President. His was a face known to almost everyone in the country. The hair, once greying, was now white, the lines in his face were more pronounced, but his skin carried a healthy tan. He was a man much beloved by his fellow citizens, even more so than the President he served under. Although a lifelong Democrat, hundreds of influential Republicans were proud to call him a friend. During the four years he served, his President managed to bungle himself into some sorry messes, but Wayne was always able to bring people of opposite persuasions together to solve the problem for the betterment of the country. It was inconceivable that this man could be Galen. And yet, he was.

"I've known Tim for more than twenty-five years," Wayne was saying. "He was assigned to me by the Service and we became good friends immediately. When his hip went out, they tried to transfer him to a desk job. I made him a better offer."

The details of Wayne's life started to bubble up in Paul's brain. Long before Paul was born, Wayne enlisted in the army the day after the Japanese attacked Pearl Harbor. He rose from lowly private to a battlefield commission to the rank of Lt. Colonel at the close of the war. He used the G.I. bill to get an education, a state school Paul seemed to recall, and then with superlative grades, was accepted into Johns Hopkins Medical School. After serving his internship and residency at Mount Sinai in New York, he went into private practice in a small community in the Upper Midwest. He prospered for many years but eventually got tired of dealing with the state's onerous and archaic medical regulations. He led an insurrection and got himself appointed Chairman of the State Medical Board where he turned everything inside out. He established scholarships for bright but impoverished young men and women to attend medical school. He set up clinics in depressed areas, supported by state funds but run without interference by volunteer doctors from every medical specialty. His personal popularity was so great that the Democrats ran him for Governor. He won with 55% of the vote. Two years later he was picked by the Presidential nominee to be his running mate and in November they won the election by a narrow margin. Pundits believe had it not been for Wayne's charisma and his optimistic can-do personality, the ticket would have been severely trounced. Four years later there was another election. Nothing could save the President this time around. Thereafter Wayne devoted himself to public service, primarily in the health care field, and then with the passing of his wife Edna, he retired from the limelight to spend his final years reading and occasionally writing and generally enjoying the slow pace of life on Cape Ann.

"You have always instilled love and loyalty, Mr. Vice President," Paul said.

Wayne smiled. "How about just plain Thad," he said.

"How about Galen?" Paul said.

The older man smiled and gestured to a chair by the nearby coffee table. "I think we're beyond that now, Mr. Castle. Paul. May I call you Paul?"

"Absolutely," Paul said. He smiled. "You're sure those socks are coming?"

"Positive," Wayne replied.

"I'll take your word." He removed his shoes and started to peel off his wet socks.

"So, tell me, sir—and 'Sir' is about as chummy as I can really handle—tell me, how did Galen and all of this come about?"

"Well, Galen is a simple enough alias if you know your Greek history, which I presume you do."

"I'm an expert," Paul replied straight-faced.

"As for the rest—"

He looked up as Tim, the man in black, entered carrying a pair of woolen socks. He was followed through the doorway by a servant carrying a sterling silver coffee service. In the few moments that the double doors were open, Paul could hear heated and acromonius conversation emanating from the living room.

"Thank you, Mandy," Wayne said as the servant placed the tray on the table. "It's all right. I'll pour."

Paul took the socks from Tim. "Thanks," he said, then realized he had an unsightly pair of wet socks in his other hand.

Wayne, seeing his embarrassment, said, "Mandy, would you take those wet socks from Mr. Castle and run them through the dryer for a few minutes?"

"Of course, sir," she said, taking them between the tips of two fingers at the very edge of the toe and walking out, holding them like a dead fish that had been out in the sun too long.

"Will there be anything else, sir?," Tim asked.

"Not right now, thank you, Tim. Just see that we're not disturbed."

"Yes, sir," Tim said and went out.

Wayne poured the coffee. Paul slipped on the warm and wooly socks. He sipped the coffee and then it was obvious, it was time to get down to the business of the day.

"We were about to discuss how and why you got into this situation." Paul said.

"Are you wired, Mr. Castle?" Wayne asked pleasantly.

"No."

"Because if you're not, I have a tape recorder you can use to make sure you get all of this right."

"I've got a good memory," Paul said.

"I'm sure you do. I also thought you might like to have a taped record of what we say here."

Paul nodded. “Possibly. I think that’s going to depend a lot on what we have to say. You do realize you’ve murdered sixteen human beings.”

“Yes,” Wayne said.

“I’m going way out on a limb and assuming you and the others did this in order to save the country.”

“That is correct.”

“And in whose opinion did you feel the country needed saving?”

“Mine. And many others.”

“And you could come up with no solution other than wholesale murder?”

“No, we could not.”

Paul leaned back in his chair and fixed Wayne with a disbelieving stare. “I find that hard to believe.”

“So did I, at first. Paul, I’m trying to answer your questions as bluntly and as honestly I can. I am not making excuses. I am not apologizing. I can elaborate, if you wish, on the thought processes that went into this, but that would seem like mitigating my responsibility. Sixteen human beings are dead and all of us will have to live with the guilt and the shame and the horror of that for the rest of our lives, however long that might be. If you would like to hear the ‘why’ I will tell it to you. If not, then let’s move on.”

“I’m listening,” Paul said.

Wayne nodded, took a small sip of his drink and set it down on a coaster. “First, you must accept the premise that we are at war. At war for the very heart and soul of America. For many years now an overwhelming number of people with a single agenda have been worming their way into the political process in just about every state in the union. They start out at the local level, mask their true beliefs and because they are willing to work harder and persevere longer, they prosper. In many ways the people of this country, as blessed as they are, have fallen into a 'Let Joe do it' frame of mind. I have a family to raise, better things to do. Complacency is the fodder on which this other faction feeds. It started in the permissive sixties which spawned a host of radical thinkers, young anti-establishment rebels who saw little to love about this country. Lyndon Johnson and Mayor Daley did nothing to dispel their feelings. You weren't around in '68 were you, Paul?"

"Just missed it," Paul said, "but I've seen the newsreels."

"They were accurate. No computer editing, no exaggerating. It was a dreadful time and led to a Presidency which was unprecedented in its arrogance and moral corruption, further cementing the belief that this country had lost its morality. Professors everywhere preached it and young minds with no sense of what this country really was accepted it. They had no appreciation of the liberties and personal freedoms that this nation guaranteed them. They thought Viet Nam was an evil blunder and in retrospect perhaps it was. The young men of this country paid dearly for this national tragedy. And anti-government, anti-American sentiment continued to grow and fester as the champions of socialism continued to expand their influence." Wayne noticed Paul's cup was empty. "You need a refill."

"I'm fine," Paul said.

"Nonsense. Apparently you've been driving for over eight hours. You must also be hungry. Can we fix you something?"

Paul shook his head. "Really, I'm okay. You were saying, about the champions of socialism."

"Yes. Well, you're a smart young man. You can fill in the blanks that have led us to this point. Last year this country nearly destroyed itself over the issue of universal health care. If the people had not pushed back as violently as they did that original socialistic monstrosity perpetrated by Speaker Bomford would be the law of the land right now and most of your personal freedoms, if they had not been already taken away, would soon have disappeared."

"So that's what this is all about. Health care."

"That's a big part of it, "Wayne said, "because that is the broadsword that affects everything else. I love my profession, Paul. I truly believe we do God's work and no other nation on earth can equal the quality of our hospitals, the competence of our doctors, the intensity and determination involved in our medical research. And yet these people in Washington would tear it all down and reduce it to bureaucratic rubble. Rationed health care, procedures approved or denied at the whim of some government flunky, old people refused care because they no longer mattered, citizens who can afford it denied the opportunity to personally pay for care outside the system, every doctor and nurse a slave to a cumbersome, unresponsive government department. And what doctors, Paul? What nurses? Who is going to be foolish enough to go through four years of college, medical school, internship, and then residency to finally go to work on a pay scale determined by some medical czar? How many of our best and our brightest are going to stand for that?" He stopped. "I'm sorry. I can't discuss it without become very emotional."

Paul nodded. "Look, Mr. Vice—Look, sir, I'm sorry I have to be here. I'm sorry I have to ask you these things, but there must be answers and this—" He waved his hand. "—all of this cannot be ignored." He glanced up at a clock on the wall. "Besides which it's past six o'clock."

Wayne also looked at he clock. "So it is." He finished the rest of his Manhattan and then poured himself some coffee which by now was lukewarm. "I'm sure you realize, Paul, that it's not just the health care initiative that terrifies us. It's the outrageous carbon bill they passed last year that's resulted in a doubling of prices for just about everything. And the hundreds of billions in so-called stimulus that has weakened our dollar almost beyond repair. The Chinese understand. They're not going to buy any more our T-bills and who could blame them. How the President is going to overcome that I haven't the slightest idea. I used to be a proud Democrat, Paul, but these radicals have hijacked my party."

"We always have the ballot box, sir," Paul said. "The vote has always been the backbone of our democracy."

"Yes, it was, Paul. But no more. At the end of last year, a few of my colleagues and I analyzed what was happening and tried to formulate a peaceful way of reversing the country's slide into a socialistic state and we discovered, after a lot of research, that the overriding problem was the House of Representatives. It was the key to our demise but it could also be the key to a return to normalcy. In the House there were 36 egregious members, professional politicians who were entrenched in their seats because they were elected from very safe districts. By that I mean, at least a 60-40 edge in registration. These people were by and large radicals and I'm ashamed to say most were Democrats. Because of longevity, they had taken over the power structure of the House. The Speakership, the Majority Leader, the Majority Whip, the Chairmanships of all the powerful and most important committees. They set the agenda, they called the tune, to buck them was to beg for ostracism. 36 men out of a total of 435 were ruling the country but—and listen to me very carefully here—not elected by the country. They were elected by a tiny fraction of the populace to represent their districts. That's all. Their districts. But since they did not have to answer to the voters, they were able to put a socialist stranglehold on the workings of the House at large. There was no way the ballot box was going to remove these people from their dictatorial positions of power and yet they had to be removed."

"And so you persuaded a dozen or so terminally ill patients to carry out the dirty deeds for you."

"No one needed persuasion. They were all volunteers and for the record, it wasn't a dozen, it was well over a hundred scattered throughout the country," Wayne said. "So why, you're probably wondering, did we ask these people, these poor doomed souls, to participate. Because, Paul, we wanted to persuade America that this assault on the worst of Congress was coming from ordinary Americans just like themselves. Not right wing radicals sniping with rifles from hiding or cowards blowing up vehicles from a position of safety. Nor was the attack coming from jihadists. In either case the Administration would have been able to rally people in opposition. The big bugaboos they always loved to trot out: right wing fascists and Muslim extremists. We were determined not to let them hide behind that lie."

"It's still murder, sir, no matter who pulls the trigger." Paul reminded him.

"It is not if you are waging a war. When I plunged off the LST on June 6 in 1944, I was one of the fortunate few to reach the beach and survive that bloody slaughter. Within five minutes seventy five percent of the men on that LST were dead in the water. The dead from that one small craft alone numbered five times the casualties that have been inflicted in the past ten days. Tell me, would you prefer armed insurrection?"

"Of course not."

"Well, that's what you'll be getting if these radicals win out. You can mock the Emanuel Childers of the world but in their own minds, they are the last line of defense against this Socialist takeover. The situation will grow worse and then intolerable and then one day, the fighting will begin. They can't win, of course, but a lot of people will die in the process, not only the outnumbered, outgunned rebels, but hundreds, perhaps thousands of law enforcement officers, National Guardsmen, even the military. Young men and women with spouses and children, dying and maimed for a cause they couldn't possibly believe in. If that comes to pass, we surely will have failed at everything we've tried to do."

Wayne looked past Paul toward the windows. "It's clearing," he said. Paul turned his head. Indeed it was. The rain had stopped, the dark clouds had passed them by and the sun, low on the western horizon was casting a golden hue on the neighboring hillside. Wayne got up from his chair. "I could use some fresh air."

Paul followed him over to the sliding doors and they stepped out onto the patio. Wayne breathed deeply. "Did you ever notice, Paul, that singular smell, the clean aroma in the air, when a thunderstorm has just passed through? God, it's invigorating."

Paul said nothing. He walked to the edge of the patio and stared down at the inky blue waters of the Bay, calm now, white caps only a memory. A thousand thoughts were tumbling about in his mind as he tried to sort it out. The Vice President made total sense. What they had done had to be done and to do nothing, faced with the alternatives, would have been tantamount to treason. And yet he couldn't get past the inhumanity of it. Maybe that was because all wars were inhumane. Paul turned toward the Vice President. "You know that I have to report this."

Wayne nodded. "If you must."

"Obviously, you can stop me. Tim can stop me. That bulge in his jacket is not a bologna sandwich," Paul said.

"You're free to go whenever you like, Paul. We're not at war with you," Wayne said.

"The killing has got to stop," Paul said.

"It stopped three days ago. It won't resume."

Paul nodded in the direction of the house. "Do they know that?"

"They will. I wish those twelve Congressmen would step down but now I doubt they will. By the way, have you been listening to the news broadcasts today?"

"Some."

"It may be too early to tell, but it seems to me that some sort of peaceful revolution may be taking place. I pray it's true. Maybe this time America has become angry enough and frightened enough that they won't sit back in their easy chairs and let the other guy handle it."

"Oh, I think you've seen to that," Paul said wryly.

"I can only hope that your revelations about our activities don't undermine what's happening out there."

"If that's a suggestion that I keep silent, it won't work."

"Nor should it," Wayne said. "But let me point out a couple of things you should consider before you act. You may, of course, name me as the ringleader of this cabal. That won't do much for my legacy but that's hardly important right now. I won't admit to anything nor will I deny being involved. Like the others I will stand mute. If the government can dig up any proof against me and succeeds in getting an indictment, it will be moot because within two or three months, I will be dead." Wayne noted Paul's startled reaction. "That's right, Paul. Liver cancer. Too old for a transplant, even if I wanted one. I don't."

"I'm sorry, sir. I—"

"Thank you, Paul, but right now I just want to hurry along and join Edna, if I am able. I miss her a great deal. As a Catholic I know I have great deal to answer for. I knew that when I became involved. I am ready to accept what comes. As for the others I doubt you'll be able to uncover much in the way of proof. Their patients won't give them up. They won't give each other up. Yes, you can create a lot of turmoil but in the end it won't result in much aside from savaging their reputations."

"You can't expect me to remain quiet."

"I don't expect anything, Paul. You're free to go and say whatever you have to say, do whatever you have to do." Wayne moved to Paul and put out his hand. Paul shook it. "I only ask that before you act, get your priorities in order."

With that Wayne took him by the arm and led him back into the house, through the library and out into the foyer. Paul's windbreaker, now dry, was folded neatly on a chair. Resting on the windbreaker were his socks. Tim handed them to him.

"Keep my woolies as a gift, Paul," Wayne said.

Paul thanked him and stuffed his socks into his pants pocket, then slipped into his windbreaker. Wayne escorted him to the front door, then shook his hand again.

"Whatever you decide, Paul, it's been a pleasure to get to know you. You're a credit to your profession and we both know there are not too many of those around any more. Good luck."

And then Paul was out the door, heading for his car. Wayne watched him go from the open doorway, then he slowly went inside and shut the door behind him. Paul got in his car and drove down toward the gates at the bottom of the hill. He checked his rear view mirror, half expecting to see Tim following him, but no, he was alone. The gates opened, the security guard, now without slicker, nodded a farewell and Paul was on the road, headed back toward Manchester-by-the-Sea. Fifty yards up the road, two cars were parked. Three men were standing by the cars, the two agents who had followed him from the city and Special Agent Fowler Briggs of the FBI.

Briggs waved his arm, signaling Paul to pull over. Paul did so and got out of the car. Although Paul didn't recognize them, he assumed the other two men were his tail from DeWitt Clinton park.

"Hail, hail, the gang's all here," Paul said.

Briggs nodded. "When my cohorts told me where you were and what you were up to, I hopped the first plane to Boston." Briggs' eyes shifted to the large white house on the hill. "So what's going on?"

Paul look up at the house. "You know who lives there." It was more a statement than a question.

"I do now," Briggs said. "Tell me."

Paul looked at the FBI man thoughtfully.

"It's over," he said.

"What do you mean, over?" Briggs wanted to know.

"I mean, over. The killing has stopped for good."

Briggs looked back up at the house. "What's he got to do with it?"

Paul shook his head. "Look, Briggs, this is a nest of wasps you don't want to shove a stick into. The people you have in custody are all terminally ill. They'll never come to trial. They'll go to their graves silently and if there were others involved—I say, if—you haven't a prayer in hell of building a case against any of them."

"But—"

"No buts. You can get a warrant. You can go busting in there and throw your weight around. It won't do you any good and considering who you'll be dealing with it could get very bad for you very fast. Right now you're the hero of Yakima, the guy who put an end to all the killings. Why not just leave it that way?"

Briggs hesitated, looked up at the house, then back to Paul. "No more killings?"

"None. Word of honor."

"Yours?"

Paul looked back over his shoulder at the house.

"His," he said.

Briggs nodded, taking a long thoughtful pause. "I suppose we could wait for a day or two, to see what happens," he said.

"We could do that," Paul agreed. "And if it stays quiet?"

Briggs shrugged. "Then I guess we could wait for a few days more."

Paul agreed. "Yes, that sounds like a plan."

Briggs shoved his hands into his pockets, taking one last look at the big house on the hill. "When we went through that little town back a ways I noticed a nice little steak house. You hungry, Mr. Castle?"

"Matter of fact I am, Agent Briggs," Paul said.

"Then let's eat."

They piled into their cars and headed back toward Manchester-by-the-Sea, leaving behind a coterie of self-styled patriots. Perhaps they were, although history would never judge them. Their judgement, when it came, would be delivered by a much higher power.

EPILOGUE

Four years have passed since the terrifying Spring of 2010. The Democrats have retained control of Congress but by the narrowest of margins. The Senate is wildly divided with 48 Democrats, 48 Republicans and three men and one woman who ran as third party Independents. Whenever an important piece of legislation starts to emerge they become the most popular personalities in Washington. Happily for America none of the four are ideologues. None wants to stay in the Capitol for one more minute than they have to. Unlike many of their colleagues within the Beltway, they have lives which extend beyond the halls of Congress.

In 2012, the country elected a moderate Republican with a substantial majority, repudiating in toto the agenda fostered by the previous administration. While the national debt remains dangerously high, due to the unfettered spending spree of 2009, the budget for the past two years has been balanced.

Twelve states, with the help of government subsidies, have been able to decimate the huge bureaucracies that had been overwhelming the states' educational programs. Money was now being funneled directly to individual school districts bypassing layer upon layer of pencil-pushing do-nothings. The savings have run into the hundreds of billions. Directors of Education for the remaining 38 states are carefully studying the results of these programs.

The dreaded single-payer health reform so beloved by the former President is dead, replaced by a system of semi-compulsory private insurance plans. The cost of these individual policies have been reasonably low, due in part to bi-partisan legislation that allowed any and all insurance carriers to do business in every state of the Union. Federal hospitals and clinics have been constructed throughout the country to treat those unable to pay for private policies, primarily those on public assistance, the temporarily unemployed, those with pre-exisiting conditions, and the chronically unemployable. The cost of this program has been estimated by the CBO at about 5% of what the socialized national program touted by the Democrats in 2009 and 2010 would have cost. In addition tort reform legislation was enacted, despite the pained squeals from the nation's trial lawyers. Compensation for so-called pain and suffering was capped at fair and reasonable amounts. Young people. no longer afraid of instant bankruptcy, were starting to once again look to medicine as a viable career.

In 2013, with little opposition, the National Carbon Emissions Act of 2009 was repealed. Within four months the consumer price index fell 9% and the unemployment rate dropped from 5.1% to 4.8%.

The Universal Identification System, floated several times in 2010 and 2011 finally ran out of steam and made its way into the Congressional trash basket, never to be heard from again.

Also in 2011 Time Magazine ceased publication. The cover story for this final issue was 'How Fascist Republicans are Destroying America'. Five months later Newsweek joined them. In early 2012, the New York Times, saddled with still plummeting readership and shrinking ad sales, finally tossed in the towel and converted to a Sunday-only periodical. This was good news to many subscribers who felt that the Sunday crossword puzzle was really the only valid reason for buying the paper in the first place.

Sadly, in the summer of 2010, at his home on Cape Ann in Massachusetts, former Vice President Thaddeus Wayne passed way. Much beloved by citizens of all political persuasions, his death due to liver cancer was mourned throughout the country. Letters of condolence poured in. Tens of thousands of candles were lit in Catholic churches from Portland, Maine, to San Diego, California. World leaders, past and present, eulogized him. A funeral mass was celebrated at Wayne's parish church, internment to follow. The principal speaker was the President of the United States who lauded him for the great contributions he had made for the protection and the well-being of the country he so dearly loved. The President had no idea just how true his words really were.

Aaron Kovacs retired from the police force in 2013 with his full 30-year pension. He and his wife Alma retired to a small home near Green Bay, Wisconsin, where the fishing and hunting were first rate. Their only daughter, Rebecca, lived with her husband and their three kids about forty minutes away, close enough to participate, far enough away so that they didn't become pests.

Fowler Briggs, who made his reputation in the triumph at Yakima, was promoted to Special Agent in Charge of the Miami office. Still single but still looking, he found the weather much to his liking.

Louis Marchetti, after months of wrangling and appeals, finally pleaded guilty to racketeering charges and went off for a long stay in Leavenworth. As a result Vittorio and Herb got their cab company back. A dozen times Vic contemplated retirement and each time changed his mind. What would he do with himself? Play golf? The only thing he hated more than fresh air was salt water so Florida was definitely out. No, he'd stay put, live where he'd always lived with people he'd known for decades. Besides he and Dee had already put money down on the cemetery plot.

Paul Castelli (no longer 'Castle') and his wife Jennie packed up their personal possessions in their new SUV and headed west to Monterey, California. The beloved red Mustang, the symbol of his bachelorhood, was used for the down payment. With money saved from his stint at 'Playback' and a generous loan from a local bank, Paul bought a small weekly newspaper which he turned into a money maker within a year. Jennie hooked up with a local lawyer who needed help in his growing practice. A partnership was in the offing. Politically, Paul aimed his editorIal blowtorch at politicians of all persuasions. The incumbent Congressman, a Democrat who had replaced a Bomford lackey in the 2010 election was doing a good job but Paul made sure he kept after him. In early 2014, the opposition party approached Paul about running for the Congressional seat. He politely declined. He was not needed. He also felt that six years was long enough for anyone to hold a House seat and if the incumbent didn't see it that way, well, come see me again in 2016.

In mid-2014, with five months left to go before the off-year elections, Grayden Walsh was reasonably happy with the way the country had rebounded. More and more it felt like the country he had grown up in. Not entirely. Those years could never be recaptured. Times changed. New generations brought new ideas to the table. But happily America had remained a nation where liberty and personal freedom trumped all else. Oh, yes, there were a couple of Congressmen and one Senator who apparently had short memories or no brain cells (take your pick) but by and large, all was well. Walsh was watching a Sunday afternoon broadcast on CNN featuring the first term Senator from South Dakota.

"I firmly believe," the Senator said to the host, "that a federally mandated program of daycare centers for children three years old and up would do wonders for improving our educational system. If we get these kids young enough, we can sort them out by intelligence, by aptitude for math or science or whatever, and steer the right course for them, perhaps putting them into special schools at age five instead of shoving them into an unproductive year in kindergarten. Parents are great, God love 'em, but you know, so many of them don't have the time to do the right kind of job shaping these kids and I believe in the long run, that'll result in a great loss to the country."

Walsh watched all of this with growing dismay and then, when he'd heard quite enough, he picked up the phone and dialed his good friend Hammond Chambers.

THE END

ABOUT THE AUTHOR

Peter S. Fischer is a former television writer-producer who currently lives with his wife Lucille in the Monterey Bay area of Central California. He is a co-creator of "Murder, She Wrote" for which he wrote over forty scripts. Among his other credits are a dozen "Columbo" episodes, several made for TV movies and mini-series. In 1985 he was awarded an Edgar by The Mystery Writers of America. This is his first novel.

TO ORDER ADDITIONAL COPIES

If your local bookseller is out of stock, you may order additional copies of this book through The Grove Point Press, P.O. Box 873, Pacific Grove, CA 93950. Enclose check or money order for $8.95. We pay shipping, handling and any taxes required. Order 3 or more copies, take a 10% discount. 10 or more a 20% discount.